LOVE'S DESPERATE DECEIT

Kay McMahon

ZEBRA BOOKS
KENSINGTON PUBLISHING CORP.

ZEBRA BOOKS

are published by

Kensington Publishing Corp.
475 Park Avenue South
New York, NY 10016

First printing: October, 1988

Printed in the United States of America

Prologue

The velvety black sky cushioned an array of tiny sparkling lights and reflected the bright glow of the full moon. A stillness enveloped the earth. Winter cast a blanket of cold, crisp air across the countryside, disturbed only by the thin, spiraling shafts of smoke as fires were stoked and stirred to ward off the chill. Against the silver and ebony backdrop, a huge mansion, its diamond-shaped paned windows filled with the soft shade of candlelight, challenged the darkness and marked the destination of the men on horseback. The threat of evil accompanied them, and without a word, they spurred their animals onward through the dense growth of trees masking their arrival.

Alone in his bedchambers, a man stood solemnly before the hearth, his gray eyes sad and moist with unshed tears as he stared up at the huge painting of his beautiful wife hanging over the mantel. Six months had passed since her death, and his grief was still just as strong as the day he saw her buried. He sorely missed her, and many worried that his sorrow would bring about his own end. Neighbors and friends had become his companions, and even though their visits cheered him greatly, it never seemed to be enough. Business matters filled his days, but he spent his nights alone, in this room, remembering.

The shattering of glass from somewhere below interrupted his thoughts, and he frowned, turning an ear to listen. Silence followed, and although the house had many servants, he knew they had long since retired. Curious, he decided to investigate. Lifting his red velvet robe from the foot of his bed, he slid his arms into the sleeves as he crossed to the night stand and the hurricane lamp sitting on top.

The soft glow from his candle cast an eerie flickering pattern along the hallway as he walked to the top of the staircase. There he paused, listening. Platinum streams of moonlight flooded the foyer below him in an ashen light, and he instantly noticed the shards of glass scattered across the marble floor. A quick survey of the area revealed the absence of the beautiful crystal vase from its usual place on the buffet a few feet away, and his frown deepened as he wondered how the piece had managed to get broken, since it seemed everyone in the house was abed.

An uncomfortable feeling came over him then, and he raised the lamp high above his head where the bright flame could no longer shine in his eyes. If one of the servants had accidentally knocked over the vase and sent it crashing to the floor, he wouldn't have just left it there. He would have picked up the broken remains and swept the floor for slivers. Something about this bode ill. He couldn't put a name to it, but he sensed that perhaps there was an intruder in the manor.

Unnerved, he glanced back toward his bedchambers, considering whether or not he should return there for his

6

pistol or call out for his trusted manservant, Thomas. Perspiration dotted his wrinkled brow. He knew that Thomas probably wouldn't hear him, since the man's room was in another part of the house. In fact, all of the servants' quarters were in another part of the house, too far away to hear him if he called. Wracked by indecision, he nervously looked down at the foyer again, silently praying that Jessie, the housekeeper, would suddenly appear with her broom and dustpan in hand, ready to clean up the mess she had made. To his dismay, the silence seemed to intensify, and without much thought, he moved off the landing and started down the stairs, his slippered feet treading noiselessly against the wooden steps while he balanced himself by sliding one hand along the wall beside him.

At the bottom, he cautiously peered around the corner toward the front door, gasping when he saw that it stood ajar and that the cold night air, not unlike an uninvited guest, boldly swept into the room. Frightened, for surely it could only mean one thing, he turned and fled back up the stairs, the tails of his robe flying out behind him. Rushing into his bedchambers, he dashed across the room to his desk and roughly set the lamp on the corner, its glass chimney rattling loudly from the abuse as he yanked open a top drawer. Withdrawing a minutely carved wooden box, he lifted the lid and seized one of the two dueling pistols from inside. His trembling hands clumsily loaded it, and once he had cocked the hammer, he turned back for the door. Highwaymen had been reported in the area of late, and although they usually only robbed unsuspecting travelers, there was always the chance they had grown reckless enough to want to try an easier prey—such as an old man living alone with a handful of servants as inept as he. Well, he'd show them that this was one old man who'd put up a fight before ever allowing bandits to take something of his.

He neither saw nor heard the man standing to the right of his bedroom doorway in the hall until it was too late and his pistol had been snatched from his fingers. Even before he could scream and sound an alarm to the others in the house, he felt the muscular arm of his assailant being clamped around his neck in a viselike grip that nearly choked the breath from him. Not physically strong enough to overpower the attacker, and fearing the man would snap his neck for trying, the old man reluctantly abandoned his gallant thoughts of challenging the thieves and instead concentrated on the difficult feat of merely sucking air into his lungs. Let them take what they wanted. He just didn't want to die.

A second bandit emerged from the shadows behind him, a man he didn't recognize, but one he swore he'd always remember. Who could ever forget a face like that? Or the cold-blooded look in his eye? Suddenly, he realized these men weren't here to rob him. They were after something else. He wanted to believe different, but in his heart he knew why they were there, and unless one of the servants came to investigate the same noise he had heard, he would be murdered while everyone slept. A tremor of fear slithered down his spine, and in a panic he tried to wrench the arm from around his throat only to have it tighten all the more.

Horror darkened the old man's gray eyes when a huge hand came up, caught his jaw in a grip of iron, and squeezed, forcing him involuntarily to open his mouth wide enough to accept the rag that was thrust into it. Another strip of cloth was tied around his face to hold the gag in place and thus prevent him from spitting it out while the two men feverishly worked to bind his hands and feet. Together, they lifted his thin, struggling shape in their arms and easily carried him back into the bedchambers where they brutally dropped him on the floor. Pain shot through every inch of him, but it seemed only secondary as he watched the strangers hurry about their work. The first closed the doors to ensure their privacy, while the other crossed to the desk to retrieve the chair sitting behind it. As he dragged it to the middle of the room, his companion withdrew a knife and went to the bed where he swiftly cut down the bell pull, a satiny length of rope that obviously satisfied his needs. He held it out for his friend to see; the second man nodded approval and stepped up onto the chair, his hand extended toward his partner and the piece of rope he held. A few moments later he had secured one end around the post of the chandelier hanging from the ceiling and was proceeding to loop the other into a noose.

A whimper shook the old man's body as he lay there watching. How could anyone be so callous? And why had they chosen him? What had he ever done? Tears filled his eyes when the two men—their work completed—advanced toward him. No! he screamed, but the sound was nothing more than a muffled sob. Drawing on all the strength he had left, he fought furiously against the hands that grabbed his arms and legs, wiggling and squirming in an effort to break their hold. If only he could make enough noise to rouse one of the servants. . . . Suddenly, he was lifted off the floor and roughly deposited on the chair, his thighs imprisoned within the unyielding grip of strong arms that forced him to stand erect while the rope was slipped around his neck,

9

and he knew his battle had neared the end. If he struggled in the slightest, he would undoubtedly knock over the chair. All that was left him now was prayer, and he closed his eyes, begging God to intervene. A strange peace came over him then, compelling him to look at the painting of his wife, and the last vision he saw in this life was that of his beloved Anna.

The old man's death came slowly and painfully once the chair on which he stood was kicked out from under him. Several minutes passed while his body twisted and jerked on the end of the rope, and those responsible for his horrible demise merely stood to one side, watching. The expression on their faces showed no remorse or sympathy, only impatience that it took so long. Finally, once their victim's lifeless shape hung still and motionless, they hurriedly untied the strips of cloth from around his feet and hands and removed the gag from his mouth. No one must ever suspect that the old man had had late-night visitors. With one last quick examination of the room to make sure they hadn't left anything behind that didn't belong there, the intruders crossed to the door, opened it, and disappeared into the darkness.

Chapter One

"Shauna," Tyler Radborne shouted at his sister through the closed bedroom door. "Aren't you ready yet? We'll be late if we have to wait on you."

"I'll be down in a minute," came the equally heated reply. "And since when have you ever worried about being on time?"

A roguish smile lit up Tyler's youthful face as he thought of the young woman who planned to attend Sir Blakely's party. Her name was Elizabeth Anderson, and she had the most beautiful blue eyes he had ever seen. She was shy, reserved, and soft-spoken, and she blushed whenever someone paid her a compliment; a distinct difference from the woman he claimed as kin. Shauna was ten months his junior, but many said they could pass for twins. They both had the fair skin and blond hair of their mother, Roanna, and green eyes the shade of Pierce's, their father. They were both tall and willowy, and on Shauna it looked good, but Tyler always thought he was too thin. Their dispositions were nearly the same, and he blamed that for the fact that they always seemed at odds with each other. He loved his sister dearly, but at times like these, when her tardiness interfered with his plans, he wondered just how much he loved her.

"Don't tell me big brother's more interested in the guests attending the party than he is the gaming tables."

Shauna's playful remark snapped Tyler out of his thoughts, and he straightened his lanky frame, a bit embarrassed, and cast her a scornful look as she stood in the open doorway to her bedchambers. "At least one of us is attempting to give Father the grandchildren he so greatly desires to have," he jeered, once Shauna's maid politely disappeared into the adjacent waiting room.

"Ha!" Shauna hotly rebuked. "You're *supposed* to get married first."

The sting of her accusation cut deep and spoiled his mood. "And what's that supposed to mean?" he rallied, following the swish of pink satin and lace as his sister spun around and went back into her room.

"It means, dear brother," she scoffed, plopping down on the bench before her dressing table, "that I pity the poor woman who's caught your eye. Underneath all your charm and good looks lies the soul of a scoundrel." Her pale green eyes glared back at him in the reflection of the mirror. "Or are you claiming sainthood?"

Such an idea made him laugh. "Nay, never that. The mere sight of a lovely young thing sets my blood on fire." The subject of marriage was one Shauna always tried to avoid, and one he never let pass. "But what of yours, sweet sister? Has not a single man stumbled upon a way to melt that rock of ice you call a heart?" Ignoring her sharp intake of breath, he grinned back at her in the silvered glass, then let his gaze fall to the full swell of her bosom straining against the décolleté ballgown she wore. "You certainly dress invitingly enough."

"'Tis fashion, Tyler," she hissed. "I wouldn't be

12

wearing it if it wasn't."

"Ahh, let me guess," he mocked, a fingertip tapping his chin, his brows drawn together as if he were deep in thought. "You'd wear the garb of a nun."

His taunt failed to incite her temper. "If it would keep other scoundrels like you at bay . . . aye."

Masking a smile, Tyler turned for the door. "Well, I don't think you really have to worry about that, Sis. You're doing a very nice job of keeping men in their place without high collars and dark cloth. I have yet to see one gentleman walk away from you who hasn't looked a little frostbitten."

"As well they should," she snapped, jumping to her feet, her pink satin skirts rustling about her slim ankles as she spun to face him. "None have seen me for what I am. They're blinded by our father's wealth. *If* I choose to marry—though the possibility as I see it is very remote—my husband will have to prove himself first."

Genuinely puzzled by her comment, Tyler paused at the doorway to glance back at her. "Prove himself? Whatever do you mean?"

"That his feelings for me are true and honest." She took a step closer. "That he doesn't look at me and measure my worth by how much my father owns. I want him to love *me*, not the social standing our marriage would bring him. Is that so much to ask?"

A sadness reflected itself in Tyler's green eyes as he studied the puzzling young woman standing before him. Shauna Radborne had a temper like no other woman he had ever met—including their mother—and a wit and sharp tongue to match. She never wasted time on idle chatter, nor did she flirt unnecessarily. She knew more about politics than any one of their father's associates.

13

She was well read and could put her thoughts down on paper faster and more astutely than the most learned of scholars. Her beauty far surpassed that of the comeliest wench in all of London . . . or the whole of England, so far as Tyler was concerned, and despite the chilling look she could give a man for his folly in thinking she was nothing more than a piece of fluff, Tyler knew better than anyone else what a rare treasure his sister was. But this . . . to hear her openly decree her demand for unequivocal love, took him totally by surprise.

"No, Shauna," he answered softly, "it's not too much to ask. 'Tis what we all expect . . . or long for. But it's not what we always get. For hundreds of years marriages have been arranged, and I can't see where that will ever change. If you marry a man of class or one who is poor, you'll never be assured that he loves you . . . not at first. Perhaps, after—"

"Then I shan't marry."

Her declaration cut him short and sparked his temper. She had done it again. She had set her trap, and he had fallen blindly into it. She hadn't asked because she wanted reassurance. She had done it to prove a point. If given the choice, Shauna would remain unwed and be all the happier for it. Managing household affairs, acting as hostess, and bearing a man's children was not her idea of excitement. Like Tyler, Shauna thrived on the fervor one could only experience at the gaming tables. In truth, it was her only weakness that Tyler could see. Someday it would be her ruin, and he hoped he wasn't around to witness it.

"Then I suggest, little sister," he scoffed as he backed into the hallway, his hand catching the doorknob and pulling it slowly toward him, "that you pack a few things

14

while you have the chance and make good your escape. Nelson Thorndyke is downstairs right now talking to Father, and I think I heard him say something about it being time you settled down."

Tyler missed the horrified look that came over his sister's lovely face just then, for he had already closed the door. Not that it mattered. He was reasonably sure what her reaction would be, since she had made it quite clear time and time again just how much she disliked her father's business associate. What she wasn't aware of, however, was that Tyler hadn't honestly heard a word the two men said to each other. She had tricked him into letting down his guard, and he was simply paying her back. Chuckling out loud, he headed for the stairs, wondering how long it would take her to figure out she had been duped.

A mixture of anger and worry crimped Shauna's smooth brow as she stood there staring at the sealed portal. Nelson Thorndyke had told her only the night before that he intended to speak with her father sometime today about a matter that would greatly concern her future. She really hadn't been able to imagine what it could possibly be, but now, after what Tyler had told her, it wasn't hard to figure out. Nelson had hinted several times about his desire to wed and start a family, but she had never dreamed he had her in mind when he said it. What frightened her more than anything was her father's growing displeasure with her failure to find a suitable beau. Yes, he wanted grandchildren as Tyler had said, but more than that, Pierce Radborne wanted to see his daughter wed.

An unflattering snarl curled Shauna's mouth as she whirled back to sit down at her dressing table again. Tyler understood her feelings about marriage, since he had no more interest in being tied down than she did. And *that* was all right with their father. Tyler could wait as long as he liked. But not Shauna. Not Pierce's little girl. Women her age were already married and had several children by now. How many times had he told her that? And Lord forbid Papa's friends should start talking about her! How would he ever live down the shame? Was it his honor that drove him to choose a husband for her? Pierce Radborne had threatened on several occasions to do just that if she didn't take it upon herself to find a proper mate. But Nelson Thorndyke?

It's just not fair! she silently raged, glaring at the green-eyed reflection in the mirror. She might have been partly playing with Tyler earlier when she'd said those things about wanting her husband to love her for herself and not her father's money, but it wasn't altogether a falsehood. She didn't relish the thought of living with a man, having him—she cringed at the word—touch her, just because it was his husbandly right, without there being some sort of feeling between them. A vision of Nelson Thorndyke popped to mind, and she groaned aloud, her eyes closed and her chin raised in the air, the long golden strands of her hair cascading down her back. *Papa, how could you even consider him? He's twice my age, and older than you! He should be looking for a gray-haired widow to marry, not me.*

Irritated with herself for letting it spoil her evening, she jerked herself upright on the bench, called out for Moira, her longtime confidante, maid and friend, and reached for her hairbrush. Working the long silken strands into a cord, she twisted the golden mane into a knot on top of her head and secured it there with several

16

hairpins, while she forced herself not to think about that horrible subject. But only a few minutes passed before an angry frown formed a line between her tawny brows, and she was muttering to herself all over again, only half aware that Moira had joined her.

"Nelson Thorndyke! Even Tyler dislikes him, which is saying something in itself. Tyler hasn't met anyone yet whom he doesn't like . . . except *him!*"

"Aye, mum," Moira agreed with a puzzled frown. It wasn't the first time her mistress had rambled on about something as if she expected Moira to understand, and as always Moira pretended she did as she reached for the gauzy cap lying on the dressing table.

Shauna sat erect and held very still while the petite Irish maid covered her hair with the cap and then settled the elegantly coiffured wig into place. She truly detested wearing the thing, but fashion demanded it . . . just as it did the low-cut ballgown. A sarcastic half-smile wrinkled her cheek as she thought of the black dress and headgear she had seen the nuns at Worcester Cathedral wear, and she found herself wishing the ladies of London would see the practicality of its style. A woman could hide a great number of faults in its many folds, and someone like Shauna would be freed of the lecherous stares she often received. The image in her mirror changed suddenly, and Shauna found herself staring back at the fair-complected, somber face of a nun.

"I could always join a convent," she blurted out.

Moira paused in her work. "A convent, mum? And why would ya be wantin' ta join one of them?"

The devious smile on Shauna's lips disappeared with Moira's question. She hadn't realized she had spoken aloud, and rather than have to explain to her inquisitive

17

maid, she waved off Moira's inquiry with a flip of her hand. Moira thought a lot like Tyler, and if Shauna told her what was on her mind, Moira wouldn't approve, either. The one big difference between her brother and the sassy little Irishwoman was that Moira would do whatever Shauna asked of her, even if it went against her own principles.

While Moira worked to secure the perfumed wig in place, Shauna's mind raced for another solution and came up with only one alternative. If her father was determined that she wed, and that she marry Thorndyke—her lovely mouth puckered as if she had just tasted something bitter—then her only recourse would be if she were already married . . . to someone else. The image of a dark-haired stranger with broad shoulders and exquisitely tailored clothes came to her mind, his identity blurred in the indistinct vision she had of him. But it was enough to spark her interest and set her imagination to work. That was it! She'd find a man who had the same dislike of wedlock and offer him a proposition. Her brow furrowed. But what? What could she offer to a man to change his desire to remain single? Wealth? Then she'd be doing exactly what she had told Tyler she would never do! She thought of Nelson Thorndyke again, the fifty-year-old man with lifeless brown eyes, thinning gray hair, tall, barrel-chested physique and sour disposition, and she decided going against her principles was totally understandable in this case. She would have made her father happy, saved herself from having to endure Nelson's romantic advances—if one could call them that—and continue her life the way she wanted it. Leaning in to study her reflection once Moira was done, Shauna dabbed rice

18

powder over her face, rouged her lips, smoothed out the line of her eyebrows with a moist fingertip, and pinched her cheeks, thinking that she should invest some serious time to her idea. A soft smile parted her lips. And she'd start tonight . . . at Sir Blakely's party. There were always single men at such functions, and with the sole purpose of bettering their status by finding a wealthy bride. She'd have her pick of them! Gracefully rising to her feet, she studied her image in the mirror, her smooth brow wrinkling as she debated having Moira help her change into her emerald-green gown, the one with the silver fox trim. It was her most provocative and would certainly catch the interested stares of the men.

"Tyler, go up and get your sister," Roanna Radborne snapped as the two of them waited in the foyer. "I've never liked being late. It draws too much attention, and I'd prefer that as few as possible realize your father hasn't accompanied us this evening." Her dark brown eyes glared at the closed study door. "Honestly, you'd think he could put aside business for one evening."

A sympathetic smile lightened Tyler's eyes as he leaned down a mite to kiss his mother's temple. "He would if he could," he assured her. "Think of it this way. If he had no business to attend to, we'd *all* be staying home tonight."

A slight frown appeared on Roanna's face, then vanished once she understood his meaning. "Yes, I suppose you're right." Her gaze fell on the sealed door again, and she lowered her voice. "But to tell the truth, it would almost be worth it, if it meant your father wouldn't have any further dealings with Nelson Thorndyke. I truly don't like the man."

Tyler patted her clasped hands. "You're not alone, Mother. No one in this family does." He thought of Shauna and the lie he'd told her and smiled devilishly. "Most of all, my little sister."

The mention of her youngest child reminded Roanna of her earlier instructions, and she gave Tyler a gentle nudge. "Go and get her and drag her down the stairs if you have to. Otherwise, we'll leave without her, and she'll have to stay home." Her attention shifted back to the study a third time. "Unless she can talk her father into changing his mind."

Or she could ask Thorndyke to accompany her, Tyler thought, struggling with the laughter burning his throat. In a way, he wished the man would attend Sir Blakely's party. It would add a little zest to an otherwise quiet evening—watching Shauna trying to avoid the pompous reprobate. Yet on the other hand, Tyler doubted he'd have the time for such entertainment. If Beth was there, as he prayed she would be, he'd be too busy to bother with his sister. Another shove toward the stairs made him blink, and he came to attention, bowed playfully to his mother, and turned around, ready to ascend the steps and carry out his task in the way his mother had suggested when a movement at the top of the staircase caught his eye. Lifting his head, a puzzled frown wrinkled his face as his gaze fell on Shauna and the dark green dress she wore.

"I'm sorry to keep you waiting," she warmly apologized, her satin-slippered feet gliding from one tred to the next. "I hope we won't be too terribly late."

Roanna said something in return, but Tyler wasn't listening. He was too preoccupied with his inability to figure out his sister's need to change. "Something wrong with the pink satin?" he whispered, taking her hand and guiding her down the remainder of the steps.

Shauna ignored him to check her appearance in the gold-framed mirror hanging over the buffet in the hall. Tyler tried again.

"This is even more suggestive, Sis," he warned, low enough for her ears alone, his gaze absently resting on their mother as she readjusted her shawl and called out to Walter, their butler.

"Is it?" Shauna purred, pleased with what she saw. "I'm glad you think so."

Tyler's confused frown deepened, and he shook his head, tapping his palm against his ear as if he feared his hearing had failed him. "Correct me if I'm wrong," he offered, "but didn't you tell me a few minutes ago how you disliked being on display like that?"

Shauna turned bright green eyes on him. "Did I?" she asked, feigning bewilderment and fluttering her lashes coquettishly at him.

Tyler's own eyes narrowed in return, wondering if his sister ever spoke the truth, and if she did, whether he would recognize it. Hearing his mother call for them to hurry and seeing that Walter had already opened the front door, Tyler held out an arm for his sister. "All right," he said, escorting her across the hall and out the door of their townhouse, "I misunderstood you. And should I glance up sometime this evening and see a pleading look on your face for my help in disengaging the arms of some overzealous admirer from around your—" He glanced at the creamy white mounds of flesh threatening to spill from their restraints, then to her face. "Well, I'll just assume I misunderstood again, and let you fend for yourself."

Shauna knew better, but she didn't say anything. Tyler was more protective of her than her own father. They might carry on as though they truly abhorred each other, but under all that crust they would each do just about anything for the other. Realizing that, Shauna stole a glance at her brother as they walked the stone pathway toward the wrought iron gate and the carriage that awaited them. If he knew what she had planned for herself this evening, would he try to stop her? If she failed and their father set about making the arrangements for her marriage to Nelson Thorndyke, would Tyler step in? He loathed Thorndyke and never tried to hide it—from the man himself or from the eldest Radborne.

The sweet smell of roses growing on either side of the walkway wafted up to fill Shauna's senses with their honeyed fragrance, ironically darkening her mood. Even if Tyler voiced his disapproval to a marriage between his sister and Thorndyke, that would be the extent of his interference. If Pierce Radborne wanted his daughter to marry the man, then that was how it would be. All that would stop it was for her to announce her engagement to someone else. She sneaked another sideways look at Tyler just as they reached the gate and he let go of her arm to step forward and assist their mother into the carriage. And yes, Tyler *would* try to stop her from fulfilling her plan to find a man willing to marry her in name only. That was why she must keep it a secret, and something the man she chose had to pledge never to reveal.

A new thought disturbed her as she climbed into the carriage and took the seat opposite her mother. How— after this fallacious wedding took place—would she be guaranteed her new husband wouldn't change his mind about the conditions under which they had agreed, and try to claim his rights . . . in the bedchambers? The vision of a scrawny little man flared up in her mind's eye, and she quickly cast her gaze out the carriage window, praying her mother and Tyler wouldn't see the smile that dimpled her cheek. She'd simply choose a man who hardly weighed more than thistledown and had the courage of a mouse. That way if he ever thought to go back on his promise, she could send him racing from her bedroom with the threat of a broom landing a well-placed smack to his bony rump. Another vision came to mind then, one of a knock-kneed, pasty-white-complected man, with round, frightened eyes and trembling hands standing before her without a stitch of clothing on, and this time laughter spilled from her before she could stop it.

"Pray, what do you find so amusing, daughter?" Roanna asked, still a little miffed over the reason they were late. "Do share it, please. I fear I need something to brighten my state."

"Now Mother," Tyler soothed, reaching over to pat her hand. "In a few minutes you'll be laughing and flirting with every man there at Sir Blakely's, and you'll have forgotten all about Father and his business meeting."

Glad Tyler had turned the conversation away from what she had been thinking, Shauna quickly asked, "Did I miss something?"

"Not really," Tyler replied, shaking his head. "Mother's upset because she must attend the party alone."

For a moment, Shauna wondered why. Roanna Radborne loved to flirt, just as Tyler had said, and with

23

Papa there, her dalliances would be limited. Settling back in the rich leather seat of the carriage, Shauna secretively studied her mother. As a child, Roanna Hargrove had never enjoyed the luxuries wealth could bring. Her father had been a blacksmith, and her mother had taken in laundry to help feed their seven children. Grandmother Hargrove had died before Shauna was born, and although Roanna didn't talk much about her mother, Shauna sensed the woman's early death had come about simply as a release from all those years of hard work. Roanna had never really voiced her thoughts on the way her mother had lived, but Shauna guessed Roanna had made up her mind at a young age never to end up like that, and when Pierce Radborne came along, she had found a way to live up to that pledge.

There hadn't been any love between them at first— Roanna had let that slip one time, and the marriage document Shauna had seen, dated six months before Tyler's birth, rather confirmed it—but as the years passed, Roanna had grown to care a great deal for him, even if it wasn't in a way Shauna would have liked. Pierce had taken her out of poverty and dressed her in fine silks and furs, and Roanna expressed her gratitude by bearing his children and managing the household. Yet Shauna was sure Roanna would leave him if some disaster befell the Radborne family and they found themselves in the streets. Maybe her father knew this. Perhaps that was why he worked night and day. Heaving a breathless sigh, Shauna turned her head to stare out the window again, wondering if her father also knew about his wife's numerous affairs.

Sir Charles Blakely's mansion sat atop a knoll in the richest part of London. A widower, he liked to entertain as often as possible and fill his house with scores of merrymakers. Every window sparkled with the warm glow of candlelight, and the drive already teemed with elegant coaches by the time the Radborne carriage pulled onto the cobblestone lane leading to the canopied front entrance. Several groomsmen scurried about, aiding the guests from their rigs and then hurriedly directing the drivers where to take the coaches and open up the way for the next group of partygoers. The soft strains of the minuet drifted out to greet them, and the excitement in the air set everyone in a festive mood. All save Shauna.

Ordinarily she would have been as eager as Tyler and their mother to descend the carriage and go inside. Sir Blakely's dining room always displayed a huge buffet of foods and drinks in a wide variety that would appease even the finickiest of tastes. The ballroom buzzed with dancers, and waiters roamed about the place with large silver trays filled with an assortment of wines, brandy, and even champagne. Across the hall and behind closed doors, those who enjoyed a game of chance could play undisturbed by the noise of those who preferred a livelier sort of recreation, and it was there Shauna and her brother always headed once they had paid their respects to Sir Blakely, chatted awhile, and possibly even danced a time or two. But the social gathering this night meant something else to Shauna. She wasn't here to enjoy herself. She was here to find a husband, and the thought of it made her stomach churn, unsure of whether or not she could actually go through with it. She thought of the man who at this moment was talking to her father in his study, and she silently told herself *anything* was better than being married to Nelson Thorndyke.

"Shauna, are you all right?" Tyler asked once the

three of them had left the carriage and were waiting their turn to speak with Sir Blakely at the door. "You seem distracted tonight." He grinned mockingly. "Or should I say more so than usual?" He remembered his parting comment to her before he closed the door to her bedchambers and decided to add fuel to the fire just in case there was a slight chance she had believed him. "I wouldn't worry too much about Thorndyke. He's a gambler at heart—he'd have to be to want you for his wife—so I'm sure once you're married he'll still allow you to come to Sir Blakely's parties. That is what's bothering you, isn't it?"

"Would you believe me if I said no?" she rallied in a whisper. She didn't want their mother to overhear their discussion.

"I might," he relented, his attention momentarily drawn away from the woman at his side when he thought he saw Beth among the crowd ahead of him, "providing you tell me what is."

Shauna looked at him askance. "Then I guess you'll have to be content in knowing *something* bothers me, for I have no intention of trusting you with my secrets."

He gave her his full consideration. "Secrets, is it? Since when do you and I keep secrets from each other?" They were always bantering words back and forth, trying to outwit the other, but Tyler had never found it necessary to hide the truth. And he had always assumed she felt the same way. Shauna might be his sister, and a younger one at that, but he looked upon her as his best and only true friend. It worried him to think she had a problem she wasn't willing to share.

Shauna heard the concern in his voice and recognized his sincerity in asking. She would have liked telling him of the decision she had made, but she knew he'd be angry with her for even entertaining such a notion. His help in convincing their father that he had made a bad decision regarding her and Thorndyke would have been greatly appreciated, but help was all he could give her. She needed a solution. Reaffirming her choice not to tell him, she cast him an impish look.

"Come now, big brother. Surely you don't think I tell you everything?"

"You do when you're upset," he argued, his green eyes shaded by his frown.

Wishing to change the subject lest he press too hard and discover the truth by the look on her face, she laughed and turned her head away, as if to say he had been fooled by her trickery again. "'Tis nice to know you care, brother dear, and better still who has the keener wit."

While they talked, the guests ahead of them had taken their turns chatting with Sir Blakely and moved on, leaving the Radbornes next in line and spoiling Tyler's chance to comment on which of the two of them was indeed the smarter. It was a fact they were always trying to prove, but this time Tyler honestly believed Shauna wasn't playing. Watching her closely as she curtsied prettily for Sir Blakely and thanked him for inviting her, Tyler decided he'd pay special attention to her tonight. He just might learn the root of her strange mood by a word or a movement, though he rather doubted it. If Shauna didn't want him to know what was troubling her, then the chances were he'd never find out.

As expected, the dining room bustled with guests, their plates full of delicious pastries, warm meats, breads, candied sweet potatoes, and various other tasty delicacies. Traditionally, the Radbornes stopped here first to eat a light meal and then ventured to the ballroom, but Shauna hadn't any appetite this night. All she really wanted at the moment was a glass of wine . . . or two. And from the looks of the men in the room, none of them even came close to what she had in mind for a husband.

"I'm really not hungry," she replied when her mother asked why she hadn't picked up one of the Haviland china plates stacked at the end of the table.

A frown deepened the faint lines at the corners of Roanna's eyes. "Aren't you feeling well? Maybe your brother should take you home."

"She's all right, Mother," Tyler cut in as he reached for a plate and began to fill it. "Her mind is somewhere else, that's all."

"Oh?" their mother questioned. "And where might that be?"

Tyler cast Shauna a devilish look as he popped a sugared date in his mouth. "Why don't you ask her?" He laughed off the angry glare he received in return and concentrated on the steaming platter of roasted boar smothered in a thick, rich gravy.

"My mind is where it should be, Mother," Shauna remarked, her green eyes snapping fire at the man who ignored her. "I'm just not hungry, that's all. I had a late lunch today."

Apparently satisfied with the answer, Roanna spooned a small helping of white potatoes on her plate. "Well, you really should take something anyway. You wouldn't want to insult Sir Blakely."

Shauna's bare shoulders dropped downward in disgust. "Yes, Mama," she replied, reaching for one of the smaller plates and plopping a cloverleaf biscuit on it. Napkin and plate in hand, she moved away from the table to nibble on the bun in peace.

"I'm telling you, Margaret, he's the most handsome man I've ever seen," she heard one of the two women standing behind her say. "You really must ask Richard to dance with you."

"And what good will that do?" Margaret challenged. "I'm married, and chances are, so is your gentleman."

"Oh, but he's not," came the hurried response.

Her interest aroused, Shauna turned her head slightly so as not to miss a single word.

"Well, if he's as handsome as you say, then why wouldn't he be married?" Margaret asked, a bit skeptical. "Is there something wrong with him?"

"Not that I can tell," her friend giggled. "I'd say he just prefers single life. Fewer complications, if you know what I mean."

Shauna rolled her eyes. She knew what the woman meant. Her gaze shifted to her mother as Roanna conveniently maneuvered her way into a conversation with the group of men standing off to one side of the table. Whoever this gentleman was that the women were talking about, he preferred his liaisons with someone in her mother's position. A married woman wouldn't make demands.

"So who is he, Irene?"

Margaret's question brought Shauna's attention around, and she smiled to herself as she finished off the biscuit. Give my mother a few minutes, and she'll tell you his name, she thought with a mental sigh. Roanna Radborne knew everyone . . . especially the men.

"I haven't heard his name," Irene replied. "But I did hear someone say he's a Colonial. Or he was. Now that the war's over he's returned to London to live. I guess this is where he grew up."

"Listening to idle gossip, dear sister?"

The sound of Tyler's voice made Shauna jump. "It's better than listening to you rattle on about something that doesn't concern you," she rallied, moving away from him to set down her plate. "And more entertaining." She cast him a meaningful look over her shoulder, saw that he had missed it since he was busy discarding his own plate, and started for the door, saying, "If you'll excuse me, I'd like to go to the ballroom now."

"Certainly," Tyler answered, not the least put off by her iciness. "I'll come with you."

Shauna stopped dead in her tracks and spun around to glare at her brother. "On one condition," she snapped, arms akimbo.

Tyler drew up short. He'd seen that look in Shauna's eyes before. She was angry. And when his sister was angry, Tyler knew it was time he slowed up a bit. The two of them might be adults, and they might be in the midst of company, but Tyler knew that if he pushed too far and Shauna lost her temper, she wouldn't care who watched her throw a tantrum. He nodded his blond head and waited for her answer.

"That you don't say another word to me for the rest of the night."

Tyler's smooth brown wrinkled. "Well, that could get a little tricky, Shauna. If I'm not allowed to say anything to you, how will I be able to introduce you to someone?"

Shauna's spine stiffened. "You know what I mean, Tyler Radborne! Not another word about Papa or Nelson Thorndyke or . . . the predicament I've gotten myself into. You might think it's funny, but I don't." With that parting comment, she turned on her heel and hurried out

30

the door.

"Shauna, wait!" Tyler called after her. Surely she had figured out he had only been teasing when he said he had overheard Thorndyke and their father in the study. She was too smart to take him seriously. Or so he'd thought. Could that be the reason why she had been so distracted all evening? Well, he'd have to set her straight. A mischievous smile curled his mouth as he left the dining room and nudged his way through the crowded foyer toward the ballroom and his sister. But why should he correct her misassumption? Since when had he ever been one up on her? And what harm was there in it? So her evening was spoiled. How many times had he endured the same sort of torture because of her?

Clearing the open entryway into the ballroom, Tyler paused at the trio of steps leading down to the dance floor and craned his neck to see past the heads of the numerous couples enjoying the minuet. He had seen a flash of dark green enter through the doors and knew she was here, but he was having a difficult time spotting her. And in that low-cut, immodest gown, he didn't want her getting out of reach. She was asking for trouble wearing such a bewitching dress, and he wanted to be close by just in case she needed his assistance. She might be angry with him, and maybe she thought she'd prefer he keep his distance, but she'd soon change her mind if someone got a little too bold for her to handle. Thinking that perhaps she might be inclined to go outside for some fresh air, Tyler glanced to the right of the dance floor where the double set of french doors opened up to the gardens in back of the Blakely mansion and caught just a glimpse of her as she stepped through them. Excusing himself as he cut between the couple who stood in his way, he

31

hurriedly set off after her.

Something about the fragrant night air always soothed Shauna whenever she was upset. Maybe it was the solitude she experienced during her late-evening walks that brought her peace, but whatever the reason, it was working. She hadn't meant to snap at Tyler. It wasn't his fault their father had decided it was time she settled down. It just made her angry that he could take it so lightly. She doubted Tyler would find it even remotely amusing if he were in her place, and it hurt her to hear him make a game of it. She wanted his sympathy, his support, not mockery. It was hardly a laughing matter.

The sound of men talking up ahead on the gravel footpath convinced Shauna that it was time she went back inside and found her brother. A woman walking alone invited problems, and she already had enough of them with which to deal without asking for more. Besides, she wanted to make her appearances, have a glass of wine, and then move on to the gaming tables, since it was the second-most-important reason she had come here tonight. As she neared the open doorway again, the scent of a fine cheroot drifted over to her, and she paused, a vision of her father filling her senses. He liked to smoke a good cigar but seldom did, since Roanna always seemed to choke and gag whenever he lit one. Shauna, on the other hand, liked their smell. Or maybe it was only because the scent reminded her of her father. Without realizing it, she turned her head as if she expected to find Pierce Radborne standing somewhere close by. Instead, she saw the dark silhouette of a man standing in front of a wrought iron settee, his foot resting on its seat, the weight of his upper torso braced against his elbow, which rested on his bent knee as he talked with

32

the young woman sitting beside him. They were too far away for Shauna to hear their conversation, but the gay laughter of the girl in response to something he said struck an envious cord in her. It had been a long time since a man made her laugh—honest, heartfelt laughter—and for a moment she silently reviewed her life up to this point. She lived in an elegant house, dressed in fine clothes, went to all the important social gatherings, had numerous male suitors, and was never in want of anything. Yet, through it all, she had never really been happy. Something was missing, and she didn't know what it was.

"There you are," a somewhat irritated voice accused, and she glanced over to find Tyler standing in the doorway. "I wish you wouldn't go running off like that, Sis."

She started to tell him it was his fault she had, changed her mind, and stole a second look at the couple in the gardens. Obviously Tyler's reprimand had drawn their attention, for the man now stood erect, and through the darkness that hid their identity, Shauna could see that both the man and his companion were staring at her. Embarrassed, for some strange reason, she turned away from them, caught her brother's arm, and hurriedly ushered them back inside, telling him that she'd appreciate a glass of Sir Blakely's exquisite white wine and his silence on how she behaved. Tyler gave her a scolding look, but didn't say anything before he turned from her to fulfill her request.

Alone at the edge of the dance floor, the sweet strains of the violins filling her ears, Shauna lost herself in the moment, a dreamy expression softening the shade of her eyes as she watched the smooth, synchronous movement

33

of the couples before her. She liked to dance. There was something about being caught up in the magic of it that settled her nerves. And Lord knew she could use a little of that right now. Distracted by the sound of a woman's light laughter, she turned her eyes to the source, but never really focused on the lady, rather on the man who accompanied her as the couple entered the ballroom through the french doors. In all her young life Shauna had never seen a more stunning-looking gentleman than this one, nor had she ever been so totally surprised by a man's handsomeness that she forgot her manners to stare, openmouthed and wide-eyed.

He was tall, taller than Pierce Radborne's six-foot frame. Thick raven-black hair darkened his already darkly tanned complexion. His rich clothes hugged his muscular build in a soft shade of plum, and when he turned his head slightly her way as he scanned the crowd for someone, she had an unrestricted, unnoticed view of his face. Magnificent black brows gave him a rugged, sensuous look. His lean jaw was square and showed a quiet strength beneath the muscle that flexed in it. His nose was thin and straight, and the only imperfection she could see was the narrow scar that ran high on his left cheekbone. But even that added an unquestionable manliness to his appearance, and Shauna found herself imagining all sorts of gallant, heroic ways in which he might have acquired such a mark, for surely a man of his stature and prowess must have been caught off guard. He didn't seem the type to lose a fight, unless tricked by a cowardly foe. Suddenly, warm dark brown eyes were staring into hers, and her heart leaped in her chest. She stood transfixed, unable to blink or draw a breath, much less pull her gaze away from him. He was recklessly

34

handsome, and a flash of white teeth showed with his devilish smile as he nodded politely at her. Shauna had never before been so captivated by the appearance of a man, and she had trouble understanding why. She had played host to an assortment of gentlemen callers, but none of them had ever affected her in this manner. Her gaze dipped to his full parted lips and the seductive half-smile he gave her, and she suddenly wondered what it would be like to have him kiss her. That thought startled her out of her trance, and she snapped her mouth shut, stiffened her spine, and averted her eyes, wishing Tyler would come back with her drink. She needed that sip of wine now more than ever. But only seconds passed before she gave way to her uncontrollable temptation to look at the stranger again.

A puzzled frown curled her brow, the mood of a moment ago shattered, when her gaze fell upon a different man, a short pudgy, older gentleman standing in the very spot where *he* had been. Unaware of her actions, Shauna stretched up on tiptoes to see over the heads of the other guests in search of the mysterious stranger. He couldn't have been the makings of her imagination. She could never conjure up the likes of him in her wildest dreams! Yet, the longer she scanned the crowded room without seeing him, the more she doubted her sanity.

"Are you looking for someone in particular or just me?" Tyler asked with a frown. He had approached his sister a short while before and seen the urgent, almost frantic way she was studying the guests as if looking for someone special. He couldn't imagine who that might be, since she never seemed interested in anything other than playing a game of cards.

Shauna could feel her face redden. "I . . . I was looking for Mother," she replied without lifting her eyes to him. She centered her gaze on the glasses he held. "Is one of those for me?"

Tyler started to say that he didn't ordinarily drink two at a time, noticed the flushed look on her face, and merely offered her the wine instead. She had been acting strangely all night, and he would have given just about anything to know why. But short of hazarding a guess, he'd have to go on wondering. Shauna wouldn't explain unless she wanted him to know.

"After you've finished your drink, would you care to dance?" he asked. "You'd have a better view from the middle of the floor."

"Better view?" she questioned. "Of what?"

Tyler shrugged and took a sip of his wine. "Of the room. You might spot *Mother* from there." He stressed the name, but wouldn't look at her. Their games had suddenly become a bit tedious. "Except, I doubt you'll see her. She usually spends the evening chatting in the library." His green eyes looked askance at his sister. "But then you already know that, don't you?"

Shauna's slender shape drooped. "All right, Tyler, if you must know, I was looking for—" Her confession was cut short when she glanced over at him and found that he wasn't paying the slightest attention to her. Something on the opposite side of the room had caught *his* eye, and pleasantly so, for he had a big smile on his face, and she could see the excitement sparkling in his eyes. It had to be a woman, she deduced. He never looked so enthusiastic at the gaming tables, and nothing else in Tyler's existence ever sparked this kind of emotion in him. Turning her head in the direction he stared, she quickly

36

glanced over the selection of ladies presented to her and immediately settled on the pretty young woman staring back at him, a smile on her lips and a light blush in her cheeks.

"Very nice, Tyler," Shauna complimented. "Do you know her, or is that your goal for tonight?"

"Oh, I know her," Tyler sighed, his eyes still locked on the young lady. "I was introduced to her a few days ago. Her name is Elizabeth Anderson."

"Anderson, Anderson," Shauna murmured, trying to place it. "I don't believe I know anyone by that name. Is her family from London?"

"No, well, sort of," Tyler corrected. "She and her parents live just outside the city. But you wouldn't know them. They're . . ." He paused, trying to choose the proper word. "Well, they're not the sort of people Sir Blakely would invite to his parties."

"You mean they're poor?" Shauna knew Tyler had no restrictions when it came to the women in his life. And a person's wealth or lack of it really was never that important to her, either. What surprised her was how Miss Anderson had come to be in attendance at the very party Tyler said her station wouldn't offer. Surely she hadn't come here alone. She looked at the girl again. And if her father was without means, then where did she get that beautiful dress? The diamond necklace? That superb wig? A chilling thought struck her, and she faced Tyler again.

"She's not married, is she?" Shauna blurted out. She truly detested women who were unfaithful to their husbands. And that included Roanna Radborne, as well as this . . . this woman who had her brother all starry-eyed!

37

"Any day now," Tyler wistfully replied, failing to hear the disapproval in Shauna's voice.

"Dear Lord, Tyler," she exploded, "what can you be thinking?" If her brother planned to woo a girl who was engaged to someone else, then he wasn't any better than the *ladies* who deceived their husbands! "Tyler!"

The sharpness of her tone jarred Tyler out of his daydreams, and he turned a frown her way. "What?"

Shauna narrowed her eyes. "Don't play dumb with me, Tyler Jacob Radborne. You're to stay away from Miss Anderson."

The expression on his face changed to surprise. "Why? Because she's poor? Really, Shauna. I never thought you were a snob."

"A snob? Being one or not has nothing to do with it. The fact that she's engaged does!"

"Engaged?" he echoed. "Who said Beth was engaged?"

"You did!"

"I did not," he rallied. "You asked if she was married and I said—"

"And you said, 'Any day now.' If that's not engaged, I—" Tyler's outburst of laughter stilled her further reprimand. Her brows knitted angrily, she glared back at him and waited for his humor to fade. "Do you really find it so amusing?"

"Yes!" he chirped. "It's what I said, but not what I meant. Beth isn't engaged to anyone. I'm just hoping to change her mind." He chuckled again as he watched the color in Shauna's cheeks darken. "You little fool. What kind of a man do you think I am?" Tyler quickly changed his mind. "No. Don't answer that."

An awkward moment of silence followed for Shauna.

She wanted to apologize, but wasn't sure exactly how to do it. She really didn't think her brother would overstep his boundaries when it came to the matter of women, but the impression he had given her certainly hinted that he might. She took another sip of wine and studied something on the floor. "So where did you meet her?"

"Through a mutual friend," Tyler easily admitted. "His name is Brad Remington, and she's a childhood friend of his half-brother."

"Brad Remington?" Shauna repeated, lifting her eyes to look at him. "I've never heard you mention his name before."

A silly smile kinked Tyler's mouth. "Well, he's sort of a new friend, too. I only met him last week. He's been trying to arrange a meeting with Father."

"Oh?" Shauna cocked a pale brow, suspicious of her brother's 'new friend.' "And now he's hoping you'll help him out." She glanced back at the young woman, who hadn't moved since the moment Tyler had spotted her. "Amazing, don't you think, how a person conveniently acquires new friends?"

"I know what you're thinking, Sis, but you're wrong. It didn't happen that way."

"Really?" She didn't try to hide her skepticism. Tyler had fallen victim to the shrew manipulations of one Elliot Winston a few months ago and hadn't realized the man only pretended to be Tyler's friend to get to their father's money.

"Yes, really. I saw Brad and Beth having dinner together at The Golden Lion Tap, fell in love with her the instant I saw her, and decided to find out if the man she was with was her husband. Since the place was horribly busy and there weren't any empty tables, I asked if I

39

might join them."

"You didn't!" Shauna gasped. "How could you be so bold?"

Tyler sighed wistfully and pressed his hand over his heart. "A man will do just about anything in the name of love."

A soft smile teased the corners of Shauna's mouth as she shook her head. "Oh, Tyler. How many times have you been in love?"

"Hundreds," he readily admitted.

"And what makes this any different? By the end of the evening, you'll have found three others you would die for."

"Perhaps." He grinned wickedly. "But for now, I only have eyes for Beth." He pulled his gaze away from the young woman and settled it on his sister. "Would you care to meet her?"

"Of course," Shauna quickly agreed. "I'd like to say I talked with her before you announce your engagement." Playfully, she slipped her hand into the crook of his arm. "Do you think there'll be time to introduce her to Mother? The family really shouldn't be the last to make her acquaintance, you know."

Tyler was quick to join her revelry. "I think something can be arranged." Setting his empty glass on the tray of one of the nearby waiters, he started them across the dance floor toward Beth.

"Something still bothers me, Tyler," Shauna whispered before they had traveled very far. "She isn't here alone, is she?"

Tyler shook his head. "Brad's father was a longtime friend of Sir Blakely. I'm sure Beth came here with Brad at Sir Blakely's invitation."

"Then where is he? 'Tis rather rude to leave her alone," Shauna observed, her opinion of the man she had yet to meet dropping considerably.

"Maybe he just went to get her a glass of wine. The way I left you to do the same," Tyler pointed out, a slight frown drawing his brows together. He hadn't missed the implication in her tone, and since he truly liked Brad Remington, he was sure his sister would too once she got to know him. He didn't want them to start off on the wrong foot, for it seemed once Shauna made up her mind about someone, nothing would change it.

A pleasant smile graced Shauna's lips once Tyler had presented her to Elizabeth Anderson. Her brother was a bit of a rogue when it came to women, but his taste was always the same. She shook off that evaluation, however, at the moment Beth dipped her head and swept out her skirts in a polite curtsy. This young lady was different. She far exceeded Tyler's usual preference, and what convinced Shauna of it was the blush she saw on the young girl's face once she had risen. There was an innocence in her blue eyes, something seldom associated with the ladies of society, and regardless of the white wig, diamond necklace, and rich gown she wore, her beauty came from within, not helped along by a touch of rice powder or rouge. Tyler had outdone himself, and Shauna was proud of him. Perhaps he only teased when he said he wanted to marry her, but Shauna felt no one in the family would object if he suddenly announced his decision to settle down . . . with Beth. Father would approve . . . wholeheartedly. Of course, he'd then expect the same of her.

Well, brother dear, she mused, if you're truly serious about this young lady, you'll have to hurry if you intend to stand before the altar ahead of me. I'm not leaving Sir Blakely's until I've found a suitable substitute for Nelson Thorndyke.

"It's an honor to meet you, Miss Radborne," Beth was saying, and Shauna blinked away her thoughts on matrimony.

"Please, call me Shauna. And may I call you Beth?"

The young girl's blush seemed to darken as she nodded her consent. Shauna liked that. It made her feel . . . well, the women to whom Shauna usually talked always appeared stilted and insensitive. Beth certainly wasn't that.

"So tell me, Beth," she said, "what is it about my brother that you don't find repulsive? I've been looking for years and still haven't found one redeeming attribute."

"Shauna!" Tyler exploded.

An impish smile lit up his sister's green eyes. "Well, don't you think she should be warned? We women have to stick together when it comes to associating with scoundrels."

"Don't listen to her, Beth," Tyler cut in. "She thoroughly enjoys embarrassing me."

Shauna waited for Beth's confused look to fall on her while Tyler's was focused on Beth before she secretively resolved the girl's puzzlement with a wink of her eye. "Oh really, Tyler. You make it sound as if you don't manage that all on your own." She turned to Beth. "He thinks he's such a lady's man." The devilish twinkle in her eye sparkled all the more as she cast her gaze back on her brother. "If you were really a gentleman, Tyler Radborne, you'd have already excused yourself to get Beth a glass of wine."

That remark obviously made Tyler uncomfortable, and Shauna had to bite her lip to keep from laughing out loud. He shifted his weight from one foot to the other, nervously glanced at Beth's empty hands, then furtively looked about the room for one of the waiters. To his chagrin, it seemed every one of the uniformly dressed men had disappeared.

"Oh, don't bother, Tyler," Beth spoke up, her blue eyes dancing with suppressed laughter. "Brad's already getting me one."

Tyler's tall frame relaxed, and Shauna had to avert her eyes when he reached up to wipe the perspiration from his brow. Apparently Tyler liked Beth more than he wanted to seriously admit, and his failure to make a good impression on her troubled him deeply. If Shauna laughed, he'd never forgive her.

"Are you enjoying the party?" Shauna asked, changing the subject. Her brother had had enough.

"Oh, yes," Beth replied. "I've never been to anything like it in my life. It was really very nice of Brad to ask me."

"Tyler says you're a friend of Mr. Remington's half-brother."

"Yes." A hint of sadness had crept into her voice, and neither Shauna or Tyler missed it. "Alec—that's Brad's half-brother—Alec and I grew up together. After his mother died, Alec left London for the Colonies. While he was there, he met a woman, fell in love, and married her. I haven't seen Alec since the day of his mother's funeral."

"Then how did you learn—"

"Brad told me," Beth quickly finished. "He's a wonderful man. I think the world of him. As soon as the treaty of peace was signed between England and the Colonies, he decided to come back home. He'd hardly been here a day before he paid me a visit. He knew from talking with Alec how much Alec and I meant to each other, and he said such news should be told in person and not in a letter. I really appreciated that. Now we're good friends. He takes me everywhere." Her cheeks began to pinken again, and she lowered her eyes. "And he's too generous with the money he has left."

Shauna's first impression of Brad Remington was beginning to surface again. By Beth's own naive admission, she had rather confirmed Shauna's previous suspicion that the man wished to speak with her father concerning money . . . the loan of it, probably, since Pierce Radborne was one of the wealthiest men in London. She'd have to keep her distance from this knave, lest he think to use her as a means to get to her father. He wouldn't be the first to have tried it, but he'd most definitely be added to the list of those who had failed. And it would be interesting to hear his story.

"Money he has left?" Shauna cunningly asked. "You make it sound as if he's fallen on hard times."

"Well, he has, Sis," Tyler broke in. "That's why he wants to talk with Father."

Shauna turned her attention to Tyler, hoping the expression on her face didn't mirror her true feelings on the matter. "Oh? May I ask what about?"

Tyler started to respond, then changed his mind when something he saw in back of her distracted him. A broad, friendly smile parted his lips, and he nodded past her. "Why not let him explain?"

Tyler's comment announced the arrival of the man about whom they talked, and before Shauna turned around to face him, a mental picture of Elliot Winston flashed before her eyes. Short, plump, and well-dressed, with a hollow smile on his pockmarked face and a devious look in the depth of his eyes. Shauna assumed Brad Remington would look much the same. Like Elliot, he was probably a smooth talker, since he had won Tyler's friendship without much trouble and had Beth singing his praises. Well, he was just about to meet his match. Shauna wasn't easily fooled by anyone, and she had already guessed what lay beneath his honorable facade. With one tawny brow cocked in warning, she raised her chin in the air and turned around.

Any words Shauna might have wanted to say to him never reached her lips. A buzzing droned in her head, and everything from that point on seemed to transpire in slow motion. Her mouth went suddenly dry. Her heart pounded in her chest. Her knees trembled, and although those warm brown eyes never left her face, every inch of her body was aflame as if that sensuous gaze had undressed her and exposed her flesh to his touch.

She was vaguely aware of her response once her brother had introduced her to Brad Remington, but she wasn't at all sure if she smiled and bobbed her head or just stood there. She hadn't had the chance to put him in his place, and he already had the advantage. He had caught her staring at him earlier with her mouth hanging open and more than apparent approval for what she saw shining in her eyes. No wonder Beth thought the world of him. He was indeed the most handsome man Shauna had ever seen, and if his generosity with Beth was truly virtuous and not a ploy to hide his true nature, then a woman would have to be insane not to be attracted to him. That thought triggered an alarm in Shauna's brain and brought her to her senses. But of course! He used his deceptive good looks to wile his way into a woman's confidence. And, dear Lord, it had nearly worked on her. With trembling hand, she raised her wine glass to her lips and took a long swallow.

"I hope you'll forgive us when you find out we were talking about you," Tyler quipped, his manner at ease and provoking a disapproving scowl from his disquieted sibling.

"Well, it wouldn't be the first time I've been discussed without my knowledge," Brad admitted with a smile, pulling his gaze away from the most desirable woman he had ever had the good fortune to meet. "I trust it was favorable."

"For the most part," Tyler teased. "Beth would make you King of England if she had her way. My sister, on the other hand, believes all men are scoundrels, including me, and she wouldn't hesitate in the least in telling you so. Would you, Shauna?"

Those captivating brown eyes found hers again. "All men, Miss Radborne?"

"With one exception, perhaps." She smiled warmly back at him before taking another sip of her wine, but it wasn't enough to hide the sarcasm in her tone. She wanted him to assume she meant him. "My father."

A hint of laughter tugged at the corners of Brad's mouth, and he masked the urge to display his mirth when he reached up and ran one fingertip along his lower lip. "Since I have yet to meet the gentleman, I must conclude you are correct, Miss Radborne. As for the rest of us—" He smiled at Tyler, then set his gaze back on Shauna. "I, for one, can be named as such, as many a fine lady would attest to."

"Oh, Brad. That's not true," Beth cut in. "You

shouldn't tease. You'll have Shauna thinking the worst of you."

Brad leaned down to place a light kiss on Beth's cheek before murmuring, "'Tis too late, I fear. My reputation has obviously preceded me."

"Then send all who doubt you to me," the young woman continued, a slight frown on her lovely face, "and I will set the record straight. You are more of a gentleman than any I have known."

"And you, dear lady," Brad grinned, "have had too much wine."

Fearing she had somehow embarrassed him, Beth glanced at the glass she held. "Perhaps." A moment passed before a playful smile parted her lips. "Or not enough." Her bright blue eyes lifted to look at Brad. "'Tis the best I've ever had."

Shauna watched their exchange in silence, and while the others in her group laughed at Beth's comment, she sensed Tyler would have a difficult time winning the young woman's affections away from Brad Remington. Beth obviously cared a great deal for the man, though Shauna honestly couldn't understand why. She didn't like him.

The soft strains of a new song tempted Tyler to ask Beth for a dance, and before Shauna realized what that meant, she found herself alone with the very man of whom she had warned herself to stay clear. She had yet to be in the company of someone who unnerved her, and the discovery that that was exactly how she felt at the moment made her frown. She hurriedly raised the wine glass to her lips, swallowed every drop, and then focused her full attention on the couples twirling about the floor.

"Would you care for another?" the deep, beguiling voice beside her asked.

Shauna merely shook her head, too afraid to open her mouth. She was sure nothing would come out, and that he'd sense what bothered her.

"Then perhaps you'd care to dance?"

Her white powdered curls shook with her polite, but silent refusal.

"A walk in the gardens?"

That was the last place she wanted to go, and certainly not with him. "Nay. Nothing, thank you," she managed to reply.

The song ended and another began, and Shauna inwardly cursed her brother for not leaving the dance floor.

"They're a handsome couple, wouldn't you say?"

Failing to understand whom he meant, she frowned up at him.

"Tyler and Beth," he answered.

She shifted her gaze back to the dance floor and shrugged one delicate shoulder in response.

"Even if he is a bit of a scoundrel."

Shauna heard the mocking edge to his words, and her nervousness suddenly disappeared. *No one* made light of her opinion and got away with it. Extending her empty goblet to him, she smiled audaciously at him and said, "Perhaps I would enjoy another glass of wine. Would you be so kind?"

With a deep nod of his dark head, Brad replied, "'Twould be an honor, Miss Radborne."

Her pale green eyes turned the icy color of emerald stones as they glared at the broad back of the man walking away. Brad Remington would come to curse the day he ridiculed Shauna Radborne.

Chapter Two

A quiet serenity had come over the city by the time the Radborne carriage rolled to a stop before the canopied entrance to Sir Blakely's mansion and the three Radbornes ascended into it. It was well past midnight, and as always they were very nearly the last to leave. Not that Sir Blakely minded. In truth, he would have preferred the party to continue until dawn. From the doorway he waved his farewell to the family and lingered until their coach had pulled out of sight, knowing his house would be full of guests before the summer was out, since he was already planning one of the biggest masquerade balls London had ever seen.

"I swear I shall never walk again," Roanna moaned, falling back against the leather seat. "I don't believe I sat down all night."

"Does that mean you had an enjoyable evening, Mother?" Tyler asked, stifling a yawn.

"The best I ever recall." She smiled happily and laid her head back, her eyes closed. "I must have danced a hundred times."

I wasn't sure there were a hundred different men at the party, Shauna thought, too tired to evoke any kind of emotion to match her words.

"And I must say, Tyler," her mother continued, "that new friend of yours is enough to take a woman's breath away."

"New friend?" Shauna repeated, her interest aroused and drawn away from the scenery she had been studying through the carriage window. "What new friend?"

Roanna opened one eye to peer at her daughter. "Didn't Tyler introduce you? He should have. Even you would have found him attractive." She lowered her lashes again.

Shauna didn't miss her mother's subtle criticism. She simply chose not to comment. Both Shauna's parents had been trying for years to match her up with someone. Roanna had all but given up. Pierce was more determined than ever.

"She's talking about Brad," Tyler supplied. "And yes, Mother, they were introduced. Shauna simply didn't like him."

"Didn't like him?" Roanna sat upright with a jerk. "What's not to like? He's handsome, charming, an excellent dancer—"

"There's more to a man's character than his looks and how he moves around a dance floor, Mother," Shauna scoffed. She stared out the window again. "At least to me there is."

"And that attitude is the reason you're still unwed," her mother snapped. "Honestly. I'm beginning to agree with your father. It's time you settled down, and if you won't choose a husband on your own, then maybe your father should do it for you."

"And I suppose you'd have Father pick a man my age with no other interest in life than hoarding his money,"

Shauna dryly remarked. "Of course, that does have its advantages. For one, I'd still be relatively young when he died."

"Age isn't important, Shauna," her mother rallied. "Only money. You wouldn't enjoy living the kind of life I had to endure before I met your father. I can assure you of that."

"Oh, I don't know, Mother. I think if a person's happy, the kind of food one eats or the clothes one wears or the parties one attends are of little matter." She cast her mother a challenging look. "Are you truly happy, or do you just think you are, because of the diamonds on your fingers, the silk gowns you wear, and the social functions you're invited to?" She answered her own question before Roanna had the chance. "I think not, Mother, for I have yet to see you smile, the kind of smile that comes from your heart."

"Shauna!" Tyler rebuked her. He knew where this conversation was headed, and he hoped to put a stop to it before either of them said something they'd regret. "You're not being fair. Mother only has your best interest in mind."

"Does she? Then why not allow me to live the way I choose?"

Tyler started to answer, but Roanna raised a hand to silence him. "Don't waste your breath, Tyler. Both your father and I have tried to explain our position to her time and time again. It would serve her right to marry someone like Brad Remington."

The mention of that one jerked Shauna's head around. "Brad Remington? I thought you liked him."

"I do," Roanna nodded before closing her eyes again. "But the man is practically destitute."

51

The image of Brad's plum-colored coat and breeches, the gold brocade waistcoat, the silk shirt, and the diamond stickpin and ring he wore flashed into her mind. "I think you're mistaken," she quietly replied and turned back to stare out the window again.

"No, Mother's right," Tyler spoke up. "If you hadn't run off the way you did, he might have told you why he wanted to meet with Father."

"I didn't run off," she mumbled. "I merely went to play a game of cards."

"While you sent him after a glass of wine."

Shauna wasn't aware of the smile that wrinkled one corner of her mouth, or that Tyler noticed it. She had used that ploy on many a man who thought an evening with her was his, but Brad Remington was the only one who hadn't made a second attempt. In fact, after their short conversation there in the ballroom, she never saw him again.

"He isn't the kind of man you're used to, little sister," Tyler added, as if reading her thoughts. "So be warned."

Her tawny brows dipped downward as she cast him a disbelieving look. "Of what?"

"He won't play games."

Her slim nose raised a notch. "I wasn't aware that that's what I was doing."

"Not with Brad, possibly. But I saw the way you were flirting with every other available man there tonight."

Shauna stiffened in her seat. "I was not! I was merely enjoying myself." She gave him a scalding look and turned her head away. She hadn't honestly thought anyone would notice, most of all Tyler. She'd figured he'd be too preoccupied with Beth. All she could hope for was that he hadn't guessed why. A breathless sigh

52

escaped her as she thought of how unsuccessful her evening had been. She had come away from Sir Blakely's party without finding even one hopeful prospect for a husband, and she feared time was running out . . . more so now that her mother had stated her feelings on the matter.

"Now that I think about it, Shauna should marry someone like Sir Blakely," Roanna proposed, more to herself than to either of her children.

"Sir Blakely!" Shauna moaned. "Whatever for? He's a sweet man, but I doubt he'd live long enough to reach the altar."

"He's not that old," Roanna replied. "And he has the same interests as you. And the money to pay for them."

"There you go again. Money. That's all that really matters." Shauna heaved an irritable sigh. "If I didn't dislike him so, I'd suggest to Father that he consider Brad Remington as a choice for my husband, just to prove a point."

"What? That you can be just as unhappy without money?" Tyler asked, chuckling at the absurdity of her statement. "Well, you're out of luck, Sis. Even if Father agreed, Brad wouldn't." Feeling the effects of the long evening, Tyler rolled his head from left to right and back again to stretch the tired muscles in his neck, unaware of the pained expression that had come over his sister's face.

Although Shauna doubted her brother had meant it as an insult, it felt like one just the same. "And why not, may I ask? Did he tell you he found me undesirable?"

Tyler glanced over at her from out of the corner of his eye, one pale eyebrow lifted. "No. In fact, he never mentioned your name all evening. You made it quite clear that you weren't interested, and even if you had been, I doubt it would have extended to more than one glass of wine and one dance." He closed his eyes and rested his head back against the carriage wall, the light of the coach lanterns casting odd shadows on his lean face.

Shauna straightened and twisted around on the seat to look him squarely in the eye. She couldn't accept the idea that a man like Brad Remington, with all his supposed charms, wouldn't be inclined to flirt with the daughter of a very wealthy man. Had she been wrong about him? "And why not? Am I that horrible to be with?"

A playful smirk kinked Tyler's mouth. "Careful, little sister. You sound as if your feelings have been hurt."

"I could care less whether or not he finds me attractive," she fumed. "I merely want to know why you think he'd turn down a marriage proposal that would afford him great wealth."

"Because he's not interested in marriage. All he wants is to buy back his father's estate."

A frown creased her smooth brow. "What has that to do with it?"

Settling himself more comfortably in the seat, he crossed his arms over his chest, eyes closed, and exhaled a long sigh. At the moment all he really cared about was going to bed. As always, he had had a little too much wine, and his overindulgence made him sleepy. "According to Beth, Brad and his brother, Dane, decided to sell their father's property after the old man died so that they could buy a ship and travel for a time. They wound up in Boston, liked it, and stayed. After Dane got married and moved to Philadelphia, Brad more or less settled in Williamsburg, Virginia. From what Beth has gathered from talking with Brad, he was—up until that point—a bit of a scoundrel, just as you had guessed. Or he was until he met Penelope Dawson. He'd had trouble with other women in his life before then and was a little leery of giving in to his feelings. Once he was able to, it was too late. She was killed during the Revolution."

"The poor man," Roanna murmured. "I was wondering why he never took a bride, a good-looking man like him. Is that what made him decide to return to England?"

Tyler nodded. "At least Beth thinks so. The Colonies never really were his home, and after that, there was no reason for him to stay. But that's not even the worst of it."

Sitting erect, her interest aroused, Roanna asked, "There's more?"

"Yes. Brad figured to sell his ship once he returned to London, and use the money to buy his father's estate. But they encountered a storm just off the coast and it sank. Along with most of his crew."

"Good Lord, that's awful!" Roanna gasped.

"To most men it would have meant the end of everything," Tyler admitted. "But not Brad. He's still determined to raise the money he needs to buy Wrenhaven. And that's the reason he wants a meeting with Father."

Shauna couldn't stop the smirk from curling her mouth. "Father will never loan him the money he needs."

"Nor does Brad intend to ask it of him," Tyler corrected her, annoyed by his sister's insensitivity.

"Then—"

"You really haven't figured it out yet, have you?" Tyler interrupted. "Since the day Brad and his brother sold Wrenhaven, it hasn't been lived in. And you know why? Because the new owner already had a place to live." His attention was drawn away momentarily when their carriage rolled to a stop outside their home and a groomsman hurriedly opened the door for the passengers. He glanced first at the stone face of the townhouse, then back at his sister. "This place," he said, his hand extended toward the front entrance.

Alone in her room, Shauna paced the floor, her brow furrowed thoughtfully. Everyone else in the house had gone to bed long ago, and she had considered doing the same. Moira had helped her remove the wig, change out of her ballgown and into her silk nightshift, undo her long cord of hair and brush it until it shone, and then waited until after Shauna had washed her face and slipped under the covers before retiring to her own quarters. But the silver streams of moonlight coming in through the window fell across Shauna's bed and kept her awake. Before long, her mind raced with the events of the evening and the conversation she had had with Tyler, and she left the warm haven she had found to aimlessly trek back and forth across the floor. He might not know it, but Tyler very well might have given her a solution to her problem. All she had to do was convince Brad Remington into agreeing.

Brad Remington. Just the mention of his name made her doubt her success. Tyler had said he wasn't interested in marriage. But then, neither was she. Not in the biblical sense. She needed a husband in name only, and he wanted to regain ownership of Wrenhaven. He had something she wanted, and she could get him what he craved most—his father's estate. It was a very astute business deal. Even Pierce Radborne would have to agree.

A worried look wrinkled up her face. Getting Brad to consent to her wild scheme was one thing. Talking her father into giving her Wrenhaven as her dowry was quite another. The eldest Radborne prided himself on the amount of land he owned, and unless the Remington estate was small, he might not be willing to give it up. Another thought troubled her, and she crossed to the bed, plopped down on the feather mattress, and pulled her crossed ankles beneath her. She mustn't allow Brad to talk to her father before she had the chance to make her offer. If Pierce Radborne already knew how much Brad Remington wanted Wrenhaven, then he'd never agree to their marriage. He'd think Brad was doing it only as a means of obtaining the property. A half-smile kinked her mouth. Of course, that would be the absolute truth, but her father mustn't ever suspect. He'd never allow the marriage to take place under those conditions. He'd consider Brad Remington to be no different from Elliot Winston.

A feeling of total failure washed over her, and she fell back on the bed, her golden hair fanned wide against the rumpled coverlet beneath her. Her pale green eyes stared pensively up at the canopy overhead as she considered the way in which she would have to trick her father into believing she loved this Colonial and that marrying him was her sole purpose in life. A shudder trembled her thinly veiled body, and she rolled up on her knees, grabbed the heavy quilt, and slid beneath it, her head resting back on the large pillow. It meant she'd have to smile affectionately at him, hold his hand, maybe even

57

let him kiss her when Papa was around to see it. *But only when Papa could see it!* she silently vowed, squeezing her eyes shut. That rogue wasn't to touch her otherwise. Scooting down further under the covers, she set her gaze on the bright glow of moonlight playing in the gracious folds of the lace curtains. Now, how was she going to be able to guarantee herself that their obligatory attentions wouldn't go any further than public view? Maybe she could get him to sign some sort of contract: that if he violated that agreement, he'd lose Wrenhaven. Her upper lip curled. Brad Remington would never agree to that! Then what else could she do? Once they were married, he'd have the right to share her bed, and no one would argue with it. Not even Tyler. Especially Tyler! He liked Brad Remington.

A shroud of doom wrapped its mystic arms around her, and she moaned aloud, flipping the covers up over her head as if it would do some good. Within the darkness of her refuge, she thought of Nelson Thorndyke and realized that if given the single choice of *that* one or Brad Remington, she'd rather surrender to the Colonial.

"I prefer to surrender to *no* man," came the muffled, defiant response from beneath the mound of blankets. "*No* man!" A moment of silence followed. Then, in a fit of temper, she flung the covers away and bounded out of bed. "Maybe I should do as Tyler suggested and run away." Her lower lip jutted out in a pretty pout. "And where would I go? Who would take me in? I'd be forced to live in the streets." She began her aimless trek across the room again. "Joining a convent is out of the question. Oh, damn!" she wailed, throwing her head back. Her eyes closed and her hands knotted into fists. "I'm trapped. I'll have to seek out Brad Remington whether I like it or not!"

Returning to her bed, she threw herself into it and angrily jerked the covers up under her chin. She'd forget about it for now and go to sleep. She'd think on it again in the morning when her mind was clear. But a few seconds later, her worried green eyes studied the gentle movement of the lace curtains as they swayed in the soft breeze coming in through the open window.

Intrusive bright sunshine fell against Shauna's closed lids and roused her from a restless sleep. Groaning, she rolled on to her side, hoping to block out the light, only to have it grow even more intense. Wondering if there were, perchance, *two* fiery golden orbs this morning, one in the east, the other in the south, she carefully opened an eye and hurriedly squeezed it shut again once she discovered the persistent orange menace had found a devious way to reflect itself in her dressing table's mirror. Muttering beneath her breath, she buried her head beneath her pillow, intent on sleeping until noon the way everyone else in the Radborne household probably would. To her dismay, however, the loud chirping of song birds just outside her room permeated the quiet. The sound drove her from her bed in a rage.

Racing to the window, she threw open the sash and leaned out, waving her arms and shouting at the noisemakers to find some other tree in which to perch. But they, like the sun, blatantly ignored her demands. Was this, perchance, how the rest of the day would unfold for her? Would every aspect of it defy her? Moaning, she withdrew from the window and returned to her bed, falling back against it with legs and arms outstretched, her eyes shut. And until the matter of her marriage was settled, would she ever enjoy a full night's rest? Realizing the senselessness in trying to delay the start of her morning, Shauna sat up and caught the image of a blond-haired woman staring back at her in the mirror. The angry expression faded from her face, and Shauna tilted her head as she studied the reflection. Long, thick strands of golden hair fell wildly about her shoulders. Clear green eyes framed in dark lashes contrasted with her pale, smooth skin, and even without the aid of rouge, her lips and cheeks had a pinkish glow. A high forehead accented her finely arched tawny brows, and a thin, straight nose added a subtle prettiness to her appearance, like that of a porcelain doll. A puzzled frown knotted the flawless brow as she wondered what had to be improved to make Brad Remington notice her. Pursing her lips, she sucked in her cheeks, straightened her spine, and thrust out her bosom. Perhaps her chin was too pointed or her mouth too full. Maybe he liked women with dark hair and brown eyes, instead of the fairness her features offered. She relaxed her posture and snarled at the mirror. Maybe he didn't truly like women. Oh, wouldn't *that* be the answer to her prayers? Yielding to the scant possibility of that being true, she briskly pushed herself up from the bed and reached for the bell pull.

"Good mornin', Miss Shauna," Moira beamed cheerfully as she entered her mistress's bedchambers a moment or two later. "Ya be up early today." Her dark brown eyes sparkled with the same reddish tint that gleamed in her black hair. "Didn't ya sleep well?"

Shauna chose not to comment. She wasn't in the frame of mind to bandy words with her maid, even though she considered her more of a friend than a servant. Moira had a way of always hitting upon the truth, and right now

Shauna didn't want to be told how foolish her scheme was.

"I'd like to take a bath, please," she said, sitting down at the dressing table to brush out the tangles in her hair. "Would you ask Harold to bring the water?"

"Aye, mum," Moira replied, one dark brow raised curiously. Her mistress never could hide anything from her. "Would ya be carin' ta talk about it first?"

Her green eyes glanced back at Moira through the reflection in the mirror. "It?"

Moira nodded and quietly closed the door. "Aye. Whatever it is that's botherin' ya. I've never known ya to get up before noon on the day after a big party. Might it have somethin' ta do with the argument ya had with your brother?"

"My brother?" Shauna repeated coolly. "What argument, Moira?"

"The one ya two were havin' before ya left for Sir Blakely's last night."

Shauna spun around on the bench to stare heatedly at her maid. "Were you listening at the door again?"

Moira's chin came up. "I wasn't listenin' on purpose, Miss Shauna. Had I known your conversation was meant to be private, I would have waited downstairs. But since I didn't, and I couldn't help overhearin', maybe ya'd like a few comfortin' words."

"Such as?" Shauna cocked a brow.

"That I don't think your father would force ya ta marry Mr. Thorndyke if he knew how ya detested him so. Your father loves ya, Miss Shauna, and he'd see ya happy first. Besides, Mr. Radborne doesn't like the man. Why would he want him as kin?"

Shauna wanted to agree, but she couldn't. Twisting

61

back around on the bench, she picked up her brush and worked the knots out of her hair again. "Because Father wants me wed. He wants grandchildren, and he's tired of waiting for me to decide." Unknowingly, a half-smile wrinkled her cheek, and the maid was quick to notice it.

"Saints preserve us," Moira sighed. "Ya got somethin' in mind, don't ya? 'Tis why ya changed out of your pink satin and wore the emerald gown last night." Although Moira was close to five years older than her mistress, her cherubic face with its sprinkling of freckles masked her age and made her appear much younger. She had worked in the Radborne household for nearly fifteen years, the last ten as personal maid to Shauna, and she had learned to recognize her mistress's every mood. This one hinted at trouble. And if Shauna intended to see it through, it meant Moira could be just as guilty as she, for whatever Shauna did, Moira was there to help . . . whether she agreed or not. "So are ya goin' ta tell me what ya got planned or am I ta guess?"

Shauna would have liked to postpone telling Moira about it. She was simply too drained of energy to argue with her. And that was exactly what Moira would do . . . argue. She'd tell Shauna that she had been talking to too many leprechauns to believe she could succeed with such a plan, and deep down inside, Shauna couldn't really disagree. It was awfully farfetched. But she hadn't any other choice, and she had no one else she could trust with her secret except Moira. Squaring her shoulders, she turned sideways on the bench and paused a moment to gather her thoughts.

"Sit down, Moira," she instructed with a nod toward the straight-backed chair beside her. "I think you'll be glad you did." She waited until Moira had done as she requested and had focused her attention on her before she took a deep breath to explain. "Now, I want you to just sit there and listen to everything I have to say before you start telling me how wrong I am. You promise?"

Moira's dark brows slanted downward, and several moments passed before she reluctantly agreed. It had always been difficult for her to keep her opinion to herself for any length of time.

"Whether you believe Father won't force me into marriage or not, I do. He's warned me of it often enough. Now Mother has decided she's through waiting as well, which means there's a strong possibility I'll be dressed in white much sooner than I wanted. Only I don't intend to become Nelson Thorndyke's bride."

Moira started to say something, remembered her pledge, and snapped her mouth shut again.

Unable to sit still, Shauna left the bench to stroll aimlessly around the room. She seemed to do her best thinking while she walked. "So I came up with a solution. Or I should say, Tyler did. He introduced me to someone last night, a man who isn't interested in marriage, and more specifically, he isn't interested in me. He's not too terribly old; he's charming and rather pleasant looking, according to my mother. A far cry from any compliment I could give Nelson. Anyway, Tyler told me that this gentleman has fallen on hard times and is therefore unable to buy back his father's estate, which he sold several years ago." She glanced over at Moira to find her scratching her head, totally confused. "What? What, Moira?"

"Ya not be meanin' ta marry this man—this one who has no interest in ya—just to fool your father, are ya? 'Tis the only solution I can be thinkin' of, and a stupid one at that. If the man's poor, how will he be puttin' food in your belly and clothes on your back?"

"Well, he's not poor, actually. He just doesn't have enough to buy Wrenhaven."

"Oh, Moira murmured, trying to understand. "Then where will ya live? Here? Under your father's own roof?"

"No," Shauna laughed. "That's the beauty of it. You see, Tyler told me last night that Papa owns the estate this gentleman wants to buy . . . Wrenhaven," she added at Moira's questioning look.

Suddenly, the expression on the young woman's face changed from bewilderment to shock. "Ya aren't . . . ya can't be thinkin' . . . oh, Miss Shauna, that's blackmail."

"No it isn't!" Shauna rebuked. "It's a business deal. I'll give him Wrenhaven, and he'll give me his name."

"For how long?"

"What?" Now it was Shauna's turn to be confused.

"Ya said it was a business deal. But are ya aware it's one that will be lastin' the rest of your life?" Shauna started to object, but Moira cut her off when she came to her feet, her fists knotted on her hips. "What will ya do if in a year or so ya meet the man ya should have married? What will ya do then? Ya won't be able ta do anythin'."

"Moira . . ." Shauna warned, but the girl wasn't listening.

"Don't be tellin' me it won't happen, Shauna Radborne. A lass like yourself was meant ta be happy, ta know the love of a man, ta bear his children—"

"Enough!" Shauna raged, her hands clamped over her ears as she twirled away. "In a year or so it won't matter whose wife I'll be. I'll be married . . . period. And unless that special someone you claim is out there looking for me right now—unless he walks through the front door of

64

this house . . . today . . . this very morning, he'll be too late. I've made up my mind, and I'll see it finished without delay. Tonight, in fact, just as soon as I learn where he's staying."

Moira realized the truth in that statement and that any further argument on her part was useless. But there was still the matter of her opinion. "This gentleman, the one ya plan ta—" She paused, tempted to use her earlier term of observation, and decided against it. "The one ya'll be offerin' a deal, what does he look like?"

Shauna glanced back over her shoulder at Moira. "What has that to do with it?"

"Well, is he old, fat, simple-minded?"

"No," Shauna frowned, failing to understand the point behind the question. "I already told you that he's charming and handsome—"

"And young. He's never been married and obviously his heritage means somethin' ta him or he wouldn't be tryin' ta buy back his father's property . . . Wrenhaven."

"So?"

"So ya think a young man, a handsome, virile young man is goin' ta agree to the conditions of your offer? I assume you're plannin' on havin' separate bedchambers."

Shauna's face flamed instantly, and rather than respond, she hurried back to the dressing table where she sat down and began brushing her hair again.

"Ah, lass," Moira moaned, coming to stand behind her where she could study Shauna's reflection in the mirror. "Can't ya see the dangers in what you're doin'? The man might agree at first, if it's the only way he can be gettin' back his father's property, but what about later? You're a

65

beautiful woman, Shauna Kathleen Radborne. How long will your husband pretend he doesn't notice? How long do ya think he'll be able to ignore the woman he calls his wife? A man would have ta be blind not ta want ya. And bein' your husband gives him the right, lass, no matter what ya say or what ya agreed on before ya said, 'I do.'"

The angry, frantic brushing of her long, golden hair stopped abruptly, and the ivory-handled brush thumped loudly on the tabletop where it was thrown. "If we were talking about Nelson Thorndyke, I'd have to agree. But we're not. We're talking about Brad Remington, a man who has already shown his disinterest in me and one who'd probably do anything to regain Wrenhaven. It will work, Moira, and there's nothing you can say to make me think different. If he wants the property, he'll give me his word, and everyone knows a gentleman never goes back on his word." Rising, she skirted past her maid and went to the armoire, flinging the doors open wide as she ordered, "Now see to my bath, please, while I decide what to wear."

Heaving a sigh, her slim shoulders sagging, Moira turned to do as bade. Trouble lay ahead for her mistress. She could feel it coming.

The hall clock had chimed eight musical notes by the time Shauna had finished her bath, donned a pretty pink cotton gown with Moira's help, brushed her hair back off her face and tied it there with a satin ribbon, and was descending the stairs on her way to the dining hall. Moira had informed her that the eldest Radborne had already eaten his breakfast, had closeted himself off behind the closed doors of his study, and had done so with the instructions that he wasn't to be disturbed under any circumstance. Although she would have enjoyed her father's company at the breakfast table, Shauna knew better than to go against his wishes when it came to interfering with business. Thus, she dismissed the temptation to knock on the door and ask if he'd care to join her out on the terrace overlooking the spacious back lawn. She'd simply have Doreen bring a tray out to her and sit there alone, since neither Tyler nor their mother had made an appearance yet this morning.

Halfway down the long circular staircase, a rather demanding knock on the front door penetrated her thoughts, and she paused to watch Walter hurry across the foyer to answer the summons. They seldom had visitors this early in the morning, and since Moira hadn't said anything about her father expecting to meet with someone, her curiosity as to the guest's identity and his reason for being here drew her full attention. However, once Walter had pulled the door open and the bright sunshine spilled into the hall and clearly revealed her presence as well, Shauna was wishing she had minded her own business, for there, haloed in the framework, stood the very man who had plagued her every thought since the moment Tyler had first mentioned his name.

Warm brown eyes, reflecting the rakish smile on Brad Remington's handsome face, locked onto hers the instant he noticed her standing there, and Shauna could feel the hot blush rising in her cheeks as she watched him doff his tricorn and present her with a slight bow. What was he doing here? Had he come to see Tyler? She glanced nervously back up the stairs toward her brother's room and mentally shook off that idea. Whatever had to be said to Tyler could wait until a more respectable hour.

Then? Suddenly, the answer exploded in her brain. He was here to discuss Wrenhaven with her father! She jerked her head around, breath drawn and ready to say the first thing that came into her mind, only to have it catch in her throat when she found both men staring back at her. The color in her cheeks heightened and she forced a weak smile while she gathered her composure.

"That will be all, Walter," she managed to instruct, waiting until after the butler had nodded in response and turned to leave them before she decided to see if her feet would move. Her knees trembling, she clasped the handrail and slowly finished her descent.

"If you've come to speak with Tyler, Mr. Remington, I'm afraid it's a bit early," she said, crossing the hall to stand near the door and cunningly pull it shut a ways to hide Brad's tall frame from anyone who might happen to walk into the foyer. "He's seldom up before noon." The smile on her lips hardly agreed with what she truly felt. She hadn't time for polite conversation. She had to make him leave before someone else saw him—someone like her father or Tyler or God forbid, Roanna.

"And I apologize for my boldness in coming here unannounced."

The deep timber of his voice seemed to rumble in his chest, and Shauna was able to catch herself before she allowed her gaze to lower to that wide expanse.

"But I was told your father could usually be found working here at home at this hour, and it's imperative I speak with him."

Those dark eyes never left her face, but Shauna felt as if she stood before him in a state of complete undress. If she didn't send him on his way and quickly, she was sure she would swoon.

"Ordinarily, he is," she replied, adding just a hint of empathy to spice her tone. "But not today, I'm afraid. He's at the courthouse seeing to some documents, I believe." She smiled lopsidedly and shrugged delicate shoulders. "After that, who knows? I think I heard him say something about meeting an associate for tea later." Her bright golden curls bobbed with a shake of her head. "I don't know where."

Brad's obvious disappointment showed clearly on his face. His brow furrowed and he heaved an irritable sigh while glancing off down the street in the direction of the courthouse.

"And I'm sure he's terribly busy all afternoon and well into the evening," Shauna hurriedly added. "But might I suggest something?" She didn't wait for his response. "Why don't you tell me where he can send a message to arrange a meeting, and I'll be sure he learns you were here." When he looked back at her, she smiled. "It's really the best I can do. Papa's always so busy you might never catch him here if you don't arrange something first."

Brad thought about it for a minute, then nodded. "I'd appreciate your help, Miss Radborne, and that you tell him it's very important for us to meet. I'm staying at The White Horse. I have a room there."

"Which one?" Shauna asked, a bit too enthusiastically. "So his messenger will find you without any trouble. You said it was important," she added with a sweet smile. She didn't want him to suspect who really needed to know. If she was to visit him later, she didn't want to announce their rendezvous by asking the innkeeper which room Brad Remington occupied.

"Second floor, end of the hall on the right. I have some

matters to attend to this morning, and once I've seen to them, I'll return to my room, in case your father happens to have time to see me yet today."

"He won't," Shauna blurted out. "I . . . I mean I don't think there's much of a chance." She shrugged her shoulders again as if to apologize and held her breath until he had nodded his farewell and had turned to descend the stairs. Once his back was to her where he wouldn't see, she exhaled in a rush and straightened her shoulders, mentally cursing herself for letting his handsomeness affect her so. If she was to keep the upper hand in this forthcoming arrangement, she'd have to steel her emotions against him. He was the first man ever to make a tongue-tied, dull-witted fool out of her, and she hated him for it.

Shauna could hardly believe her good fortune that night when Moira begrudgingly told her that Tyler had left shortly after dinner to meet a friend, that her father and several business partners were working in the study and weren't expected to show themselves for hours, and that Roanna had retired early to her room with a headache, leaving Shauna free to come and go as she pleased. Yet, while she bathed, washed her hair, and scented her body with lavender soap and rose water, her stomach knotted horribly. It wasn't so much out of fear of being caught by a member of her family, but rather the dread of meeting Brad Remington face to face . . . on his own ground, alone, in his room. Moira was going with her, but the girl's presence didn't offer the confidence she needed. Granted her proposition would back Brad Remington into a corner, and if he was foolish enough to turn her down, she'd still have other men she could consider. But that wasn't what bothered her. Tyler's pledge that Brad Remington didn't play games kept coming to mind, and with the exception of Elliot Winston, Tyler was never wrong. Even Moira had warned her, and the young woman didn't even know Brad Remington. And then there was the fact that she had no effect on the man whatsoever. They had been together twice and both times he had acted as if she were of no more importance to him than the selection of what color hose he should wear. Her brow kinked with the thought, and she hurriedly left the tub.

"Which of my dresses do you think is the prettiest, Moira?" she asked while the maid wrapped her in a large linen towel.

Moira glanced at her, but didn't answer.

"Well?" Shauna tried again.

"And what difference would that be makin'?" Moira asked, her temper and her disapproval apparent in her tone. "The blue taffeta is me favorite, but if you're thinkin' to impress Mr. Remington, the emerald green one will catch more than just his eye."

"I can't wear that one," Shauna complained. "He's already seen it."

"Then don't be askin' me," Moira snapped, her movements rough and angry as she helped her mistress dry herself and drape another towel around her hair. "You'll pick whatever one ya think will do the most damage with or without me approval." Turning her back on Shauna, Moira went to the dresser for fresh undergarments, muttering, "And if ya ask me, all the perfume in the world won't make a man do somethin' he doesn't want to do."

Shauna started to voice her own feelings on the kind of entrapments she thought would or wouldn't work on someone like Mr. Remington and changed her mind. It would simply invite further comment from Moira, and Shauna didn't feel like defending her actions just now. She had more important matters to consider than whether or not Moira agreed with her method. Bending at the waist, she tossed her head forward to allow her damp hair to hang free and began vigorously rubbing the moisture from it.

"Have ya given any thought ta what ya'll be doin' if Mr. Remington turns down your proposition? Or worse, if your father learns of what you're plannin'?" Moira asked, her words laced with sarcasm.

Shauna ignored her.

"He won't like it, I can tell ya that," her maid continued. "And what will guarantee ya that this *gentleman* won't use your idea against ya?"

Moira struck a raw nerve in Shauna, and she slowly stood erect to stare at her, pale green eyes reflecting her horror.

"Aye, ya didn't think of that, did ya?" Moira scolded with a nod of her head before she turned to lay the lacy underthings on the bed. "You're assumin' the best of a man your brother has known only a week. Not a suitable length of time, I'd say, to know a man's character. If he wants Wrenhaven badly enough, but on his terms, he might seek out your father with a deal of his own."

"What kind of deal?" Shauna's voice sounded weak and fearful.

"The property for his silence."

Shauna felt as if the icy winds of winter had just swept into the room. "His . . . his silence?"

72

"Aye. What father on the face of this earth would want it known that his daughter was willin' ta sell herself for the price of a plot of land?"

To hear it stated in such words chilled Shauna to the bone. She wanted to deny it, but couldn't. Moira was right. Vaguely aware that her maid had taken the linen wrap from around her slender body and was helping her into the chemise, Shauna's mind raced for a positive alternative. She wanted to believe Moira was wrong about Brad Remington, that Tyler hadn't been duped again by Elliot Winston's protege, and that Elizabeth Anderson truly meant all the kind things she had said about her friend. Yet, a trickle of worry seeped its way into Shauna's expectations and formed a knot of panic on her smooth brow. She'd have to come up with a method of insuring her father never learned of her outrageous scheme . . . even if it worked.

Chapter Three

A dark frown settled over Brad's brow as he stood by the window in his room staring out at the lengthening shadows of dusk. He had spent the better part of the day here . . . confined to the small cubicle these four walls made, and he was growing restless. He was used to the open seas and the freedom of moving on anytime he chose. When he had finally made up his mind to return to England once the war had ended and he felt the British townsfolk would accept him as one of theirs again, he was ready to give up his life at sea, with its constantly changing scenery, for a place he could call home. Now he wasn't so sure he had made the right decision. The only family he had left lived in the Colonies—or the United States as they called it now—and he had chosen to leave them behind in exchange for the way things used to be when he and his brother lived at Wrenhaven. At the time he had felt roaming the land of his father's estate and reacquainting himself with the large rooms of the mansion would help him forget the painful memories of his life in Williamsburg. And maybe it would have. But nearly three weeks had passed since he'd arrived in London, and he wasn't any closer to fulfilling his dream than when he started out two months before. What ate away at his conscience was that in the process he had lost his ship, the only immediate means he had had to buy back Wrenhaven. He had considered asking his cousin Beau's help in obtaining the money he needed, but his pride always stood in the way. This was something he wanted to do on his own.

A soft breeze wafted in through the opened window, carrying with it the smell of jasmine. Breathing in the scent, he was surprised to discover that it wasn't the little redhead he thought of in that moment, but rather an intriguingly beautiful socialite by the name of Shauna Radborne, the first woman he had ever met who he could honestly say had ice in her veins instead of blood.

Crossing his arms over his chest, he leaned his shoulder against the window frame while he studied the vivid oranges and golds of the sunset, its bright colors painted against a canvas of dark blue. He was again reminded of Williamsburg. There had been a lot of women in his life, some whose memory lasted longer than others, some whose names he couldn't even remember. But only one came to mind time and time again; Penelope Dawson. The odd part about his relationship with Penny was that in all the years they had known each other, he had never once made love to her. Maybe that was what made her special, and why her unexpected death was so hard for him to accept. He had cared a great deal for the young woman, and if the war hadn't interfered, he might have married her. He had come close to asking her several times, but something always got in the way, and he was wondering now if there was some hidden reason for it. A half-smile creased his cheek and deepened the lines at the corners of his dark eyes. Perhaps it was God's way of telling him that he wasn't meant to get married. After all, what woman would want him? He had been a scoundrel and a rogue.

The sudden image of a golden-haired beauty dressed in pink cotton flared up in his mind's eye, and he couldn't contain the laughter that restricted the muscles in his throat. Shauna Radborne would agree with his analysis, even if no one else did. And from a woman's point of view, she was probably right. Although he never took advantage of a situation, he wasn't one to pass up a moment's flirtation and anything that followed. He enjoyed a woman's company, and whatever she was willing to give he accepted. His dark eyes got a faraway look in them as he wondered how many men had tried to reach beyond that cold aloofness of Shauna Radborne and failed, for obviously she had yet to experience love and anything connected with it. If he hadn't had more important matters to attend to, he thought he might almost be willing to make an attempt.

The rattling of a carriage on the cobblestone street below him drew his attention, and he absently watched the expensively built landau roll to a stop outside the front entrance to The White Horse. This wasn't the part of town or the kind of establishment frequented by men of wealth, and the carriage's arrival piqued his curiosity. Straightening to get a better view, he quietly observed the coachmen jump to the ground and hurriedly open the door for its passenger. For a brief second, he wondered if it might be Pierce Radborne inside and quickly shook off the idea. Someone of Mr. Radborne's social standing would send a message if he had the time to meet with a potential business partner. And he certainly wouldn't come in person to a place like this.

Another thought struck him, and he smiled. Perhaps it was a beautiful woman waiting to make her descent, her identity masked in the deep folds of her cape; a married woman on her way to meet her lover. It was quite a common practice, but he had trouble justifying The White Horse as a love nest. Although the inn was clean, it lacked the atmosphere associated with such romantic trysts. Yet, when the coachman held out his hand toward the dark recess of the carriage as if to assist its passenger from inside, Brad's rugged brow crimped in both curiosity and surprise. His jaw sagged when he saw the slender gloved fingers reach out to accept the help, and he straightened sharply to learn his second theory was correct. A trim ankle showed beneath the uplifted hem of her skirts as she placed a tiny foot upon the carriage tread, and yards of flowing cloth from her cape hid both her identity and any further evaluation of her womanly form from his view. An odd smile played upon his lips as he watched who he thought was probably the woman's maid hurriedly climb down from the carriage after her, and in that moment he wished he was the one this woman was coming to see. Other than a few flirtatious moments at Sir Blakely's party, his love affairs had dwindled to nothing. He might not be meant for marriage, but he was still a man.

He watched the mysterious woman draped in dark cloth, the hood of her cape pulled forward to shadow her face and the color of her hair, until she and her maid had stepped through the front door of the inn and out of sight. What this woman did and who she planned to meet was none of his business, and he shouldn't spy. Turning away from the window, he crossed the room to the small writing desk and sat down in the chair as he grabbed the quill from its well. He owed his brother an explanation for the mess he'd made of his life, and there was no time like the present to put it down on paper. After all, what else did he have to do?

But only a few moments passed before a pleasant smile parted Brad's lips and the quill found its place back in the well. Whenever he thought of Dane, he thought of his brother's wife, Brittany, and their three sons; and that same old feeling of loneliness would surface every time. Even Alec, his half-brother, was married, and he and his wife were expecting their first child. Ten years ago Brad never would have guessed he would envy a married man with children, but he did. He had done the traveling, lived the adventure, and seen the sights of faraway countries. He was ready to settle down . . . just as soon as he had a place to raise his family—Wrenhaven.

A soft knock on the door of his room jolted him out of his thoughts and he quickly came to his feet, his brow furrowed and his gaze darting to the pistol lying on the night stand. He hated having to live this way, never sure who stood on the other side of the door, friend or foe. Hopefully, that would end once he was settled in Wrenhaven again. With cautious deliberation, he approached the sealed aperture and called out for his visitor to identify himself. The soft feminine voice he heard in response made him doubt his own ears.

"Me name is Moira Flanagan, sir. Might I have a moment of your time?"

A quick mental accounting of the other guests staying at The White Horse told Brad that this lady was not one of its patrons, and he wondered if she had come to his room accidentally, since her name wasn't familiar to him. Or might she be a front for some overconfident hulk planning to rob him?

"State your business," he answered in return, cocking his dark head toward the door.

A moment of silence passed, then, "Wrenhaven, sir."

As far as Brad was concerned, only two people other than himself knew of his interest in the estate; Beth, and his new friend, Tyler Radborne, and he had asked them both not to mention it to anyone. He didn't want Pierce Radborne learning about his desire to buy back the property beforehand. Apparently one of them had let it slip. Reaching for the knob, he slowly swung the door open to reveal a pretty little brunette with deep brown eyes and a befreckled, anxious-looking face staring back at him.

Moira was wishing her mistress had forewarned her of just how truly handsome Brad Remington really was. If she had, Moira wouldn't be standing here with her mouth hanging open and her pulse beating wildly in her ears. She never liked surprises, and this was almost more than she could handle. Forcing down the lump in her throat, she drew in a breath and gave him a short, polite curtsy.

"Me mistress would like ta speak with ya, sir, regardin' your future. Would ya be kind enough ta allow her a moment to explain?"

"Your mistress?" Brad repeated, one dark brow lifted questioningly as he stared at the top of Moira's head, since the young woman refused to look at him again.

"Aye, sir," she answered, then lowered her voice to a whisper. "Miss Radborne."

The shock of her announcement left Brad speechless, and he unconsiously glanced back at the window in his room. His early assumption about the occupants in the carriage had been partially right. The coach did belong to

Pierce Radborne, but it was his daughter who had come to speak with him. Masking his surprise, he turned back.

"Tell her I'll be down in a moment. We can talk in the commons."

"Oh no, sir," Moira quickly objected, round dark eyes glancing up at him. "She asks your discretion in the matter, sir. No one is ta know she was here. Will ya give me your word on it?"

Brad decided he would agree to almost anything if it meant finding out what had brought Shauna Radborne to him. "You have it, Miss Flanagan. If you'll give me a minute to don my coat, I'll meet her outside. I assume she'd like the privacy of her coach."

"No, sir," Moira mumbled, the color in her cheeks pinkening.

Brad tilted his head to one side. "Then where?"

Moira released a shuddering sigh. "Here, sir. In your room where no one will hear what she has ta say. 'Tis why I asked for your word on the matter. Her reputation would be spoiled if—"

"No one will learn about it, Miss Flanagan, I assure you. At least, not from me. But if she's standing at the end of the corridor right now or on the steps hiding, you'd better go and fetch her before someone sees her. Not every man living here can be trusted with her secret."

"Aye, sir," Moira hurriedly agreed as she bobbed her tiny frame in a halfhearted curtsy and turned to dash back down the hallway.

So Shauna Radborne knows about Wrenhaven, Brad mused as he went to the armoire and took his jacket from inside. Tyler must have told her. But how much? And why? Better yet, what interest did she have in his wanting to regain ownership? Slipping the coat up over his shoulders, he stole a quick glance at himself in the mirror hanging above the dresser, smoothed back his hair, and then returned to stand next to the door. Well, whatever prompted her to take such a bold chance in coming to his room, he'd find out soon enough. Leaning a broad shoulder against the edge of the open door, he waited. A few seconds later he could hear the sound of someone's hurried footsteps heading in his direction, and he forced back a smile. Miss Radborne wasn't the type who tolerated being laughed at, and he didn't want to send her running off in a rage. His curiosity wouldn't allow it.

In all of her young life, Shauna Radborne had never executed something as daring as what she was about to do, and the closer she came to the end of the hallway, the more she doubted her nerve. Think of Nelson Thorndyke, she told herself, squaring her shoulders and hurrying her steps. Every time you start to change your mind, imagine what it would be like to have his hands on you, to share his bed, bear his children. With this man you'll be free to do whatever you want. All he wants is Wrenhaven, not a wife, a woman to give him sons. Moira was wrong about that. Tyler said so.

Her heart thumped loudly in her chest by the time she reached the open doorway. It nearly lurched to her throat once she saw him standing there, acting so casual and at ease, as if inviting a woman into his room was something he did every day. Her upper lip started to curl in disdain. But, of course, he did. He was a scoundrel. All men were. Halting only long enough for him to silently ask her in with a sweep of his hand, Shauna suddenly knew what it must feel like for a moth caught in a spider's web. The moment she stepped through that door, she was

81

trapped. Then trapped she'd have to be, for this was the only solution she had managed to find for her problem. Biting the inside of her lip, she crossed the threshold and moved to the center of the room, the edges of her cape clasped tightly in her hands to hide their trembling and her gaze quickly taking in the appearance of the place.

The scent of lavender assailed Brad's senses the moment Shauna swept by him, and he was again reminded of how long it had been since he had found himself alone with a woman . . . yet in a more disturbing manner. His blood warmed the second he thought of the way in which most women came to have such a fragrance, and he quickly pulled his gaze away from the lithe form draped in dark cloth to close the door and shut out the image of willowy limbs glistening in the waters of her bath. He had given his word to Shauna's maid that no one would learn of this meeting, and he was sure Miss Flanagan had asked because she thought he was a gentleman. He was, to some degree—when it came to a man's honor. But this temptation was quickly pushing his restraints to the limit.

"Miss Flanagan said you wished to discuss Wrenhaven," he said, surprised at how calm he sounded when in truth he was struggling just to speak.

The deep resonance of his voice tingled the flesh along Shauna's arms and she unknowingly hugged them to her to chase away the chill. "Yes," she replied, reaching up to brush the hood of her cape back off her head. It fell in deep folds over her shoulders and revealed a stark contrast between her gold hair and its dark fabric, something Brad quickly but silently appraised.

"I hope you'll forgive me when I say I fail to see all this need for secrecy. Discussing Wrenhaven—and I assume

Tyler told you about it—is something that could and should have been done in more respectable quarters, Miss Radborne. My desire to own the property hardly calls for a midnight rendezvous."

"It's not midnight, Mr. Remington," Shauna snapped, "and this can hardly be labeled a rendezvous." His tone left her angry and feeling as though she had just been reprimanded by her father. "And once I explain, you'll have to agree that I made a wise choice in coming here unannounced and inconspicuously."

"Then, please," he urged, nodding his head, "do explain, for I fear I cannot determine your purpose in seeking me out under any circumstance. The purchase of Wrenhaven is a matter for your father and me to discuss, not you."

The underlying insult in what he had said pricked Shauna's ego. He implied she hadn't the intelligence to understand anything more involved than choosing what necklace to wear with what gown. Fighting back her temper, she unhooked the velvet frog at her throat and whirled the cape off her shoulders, unaware of the effect it had on Brad.

Shauna had chosen to wear a simple gown in peach satin, void of ruffled trim. Its high stand-up collar disappeared beneath the thick mass of ringlets cascading down the back of her head and accented the square décolletage of the bodice. The white eyelet inlay peeked through the tightly laced front and strained to hide the full swell of her bosom, a tempting treasure that made Brad clench his fists against the desire to caress the silken flesh with his fingertips. Sucking in a deep breath, he exhaled slowly, fighting to pull his gaze away from the forbidden fruit, and failing. Wide hooped panniers drew special, deserved attention to her narrow waist and billowed her skirts full around her trim ankles. Puffy sleeves, gathered below the elbows by the same white eyelet, fell in thick, tiny pleats to her wrists, and while her attention was away from him, Brad continued to stare. He had yet to see a more stunning vision of beauty in his life. Yet underneath all the satin and petticoats, he recognized a woman made of stone, and despite his criticism, his blood ran warm. If only he had the opportunity to take her down a notch or two. . . .

"Perhaps you feel I'm not worthy of discussing business matters, Mr. Remington, but I assure you, I am," she was saying, and Brad forced his eyes to meet hers when she turned to look at him. "I'm here to offer you a proposition you'll find impossible to turn down."

"Concerning Wrenhaven," he finished.

"Yes." Her bright curls shimmered in the dying glow of the sunset streaming in through the window as she inclined her head slightly. "It's my understanding that you haven't the sum necessary to buy Wrenhaven at this time. Is that true?"

Brad didn't appreciate the condescending manner in which she asked. There had been a time when the Remington name carried as much importance as Pierce Radborne's, and had Aric Remington's sons stayed in England, there was a good chance they would have been wealthier than this arrogant wench's family.

"My financial status, Miss Radborne, is not something I wish to discuss . . . with anyone." His expression turned stony, and before he gave in to the desire to hand her her cape and escort her out of his room, he dropped his gaze away from her and went to the dresser where he poured himself a glass of wine from the decanter the innkeeper had brought to his quarters.

Shauna released a breathless sigh and shook her head. Men were so vain. They'd never admit monetary ruin to a woman. They'd cut out their tongue first. Or lie. And denying the fact was a waste of time in Brad Remington's case. She already knew about it. Otherwise, she wouldn't be there. Her gaze scanned the room a second time, but it didn't change its appearance any. The rug was still threadbare. The paint on the walls and ceiling was still cracked, and the furniture left a lot to be desired. There was no hiding the obvious. He couldn't afford anything better. Glancing back at him, she watched him take a long swallow of his wine and noticed how the muscle in his cheek flexed once he had lowered the glass from his lips and stood staring off toward the single window in the room. She had embarrassed him, and ordinarily she would have apologized for it. But not today. It was important he realize how hopeless it was for him to even *think* he stood a chance of convincing her father to sell when he had nothing to use to accomplish such a transaction. Crossing to the window, she too stared outside for a moment before she faced him again, deliberately standing in his line of vision.

"Whether or not you care to discuss it is not the issue, Mr. Remington. The reality is you'd do just about anything to own Wrenhaven. You know it and so do I. Luckily for us, my father doesn't."

Brad's gaze slipped to the long white column of her slender throat, and he fought down the urge to wrap his fingers around her neck and squeeze. She was the most haughty, self-righteous, contemptuous female he had ever encountered. What made him even angrier was that she was right. He'd do just about anything to own

Wrenhaven. But he wasn't sure how much longer he'd stand here and listen to her insults. Glass in hand, he moved to the writing desk and perched one hip on the corner, his wrists crossed and resting over his thigh, his dark eyes locked on hers.

"I assume there's some point to all this."

Shauna didn't miss the razor-sharp edge to his words, but she wasn't intimidated by it, either. Nor did she allow the chilling look in his dark eyes to set her back a step. "You have something I want, Mr. Remington, and if you'll give it to me, I'll give you Wrenhaven in exchange."

When Brad looked back on this confrontation later, he would wonder how he had ever managed not to show any reaction whatsoever, but he didn't. He merely stared at her a moment or two, then slowly lifted his glass to his lips and finished off the wine. Twisting slightly, he set the goblet on the desk, then folded his arms over his chest and set his gaze on her again, one dark brow cocked skeptically.

"And what do I have worth the price of Wrenhaven? You've already made it quite clear that I'd be wasting my breath speaking to your father without the necessary coin to back me up. Are you asking for my soul, Miss Radborne?"

Shauna's willowy frame stiffened indignantly. How dare he insinuate she worked for the devil! "I rather doubt it's yours to give, Mr. Remington," she hissed through clenched teeth.

Her sharp wit amused him and he smiled. "Then what, if not my soul, and my pockets are empty? All I have left in this world is my name."

Shauna's chin raised loftily. "Precisely."

In that moment, Brad felt as if the very earth he had just mentioned had fallen on him. His jaw slackened, the humor faded from his lips, and his dark brown eyes lost their sparkle. "Surely you jest!" he exclaimed. "You're proposing marriage?" Overcome by the absurdity of it, he threw back his head and laughed . . . loud and long.

Shauna's temper began to boil. "I see no humor in it, Mr. Remington," she snarled.

"Oh, please. Call me Brad," he roared merrily. "After all, we're practically engaged."

Her nostrils flaring and her brow knotted in a fierce frown, Shauna gnashed her teeth and waited while he had his fun. If she didn't need his help so badly, she'd don her cape and march out of the room, out of his life. Then how long would he laugh? Once he realized what he had passed up and tried on his own to regain Wrenhaven's title, he'd have a surprise waiting for him. She'd see to it he *never* set foot on that property again for as long as he lived! She'd marry Thorndyke and demand the estate as her dowry. With her arms folded in front of her, one tiny foot tapping irritably against the floor, she glared at him until he had managed to bring his mirth under control.

"Are you finished?" she spat, watching him wipe a joyful tear from the corner of his eye. "We have a lot to discuss and little time to do it." Suddenly his head came up and his mood turned mysteriously ominous, an observation that frightened her. She took a tentative step backwards. Was he perhaps a madman, subject to rapid, unexpected changes in his personality? Was that the true reason he had yet to marry? Then his gaze dipped downward to her flat, lean belly, and his unspoken question rang in her ears. "How *dare* you!" she raged.

"How dare I what?" he countered, his own wrath

crackling each word. "How dare I question the reason why the daughter of a very wealthy, very influential man sneaks around at all hours of the night and finds herself here in my room, unchaperoned, and offering something as preposterous as marriage to a man she doesn't even know? A man, I might add, who, at your own admission, hasn't the coin it takes to pay for something better than this?" His outstretched hand indicated his lodgings. "Have I no right to be suspicious?" He bolted from his place on the corner of the desk and stormed across the room to the window. "Is this a trap, dear lady?" he proposed, glancing outside. "Is there, by chance, a paid witness lurking somewhere near who will name me as your lover?" Dark eyes glared back at her. "Or shall the title be rapist? What better way to hide the babe's true father's identity?"

Shauna went livid. "You . . . you bastard!"

"Tsk, tsk," he mocked. "That, good woman, is what your child shall be called, for I will not succumb to the whims of a spoiled brat. I am not a hero, madam, no knight in shining armor ready to defend the honor of a foolish chit bent on revenge against her lover—married, I assume, that he would not make right the wrong he had done her, and therefore press her into acts of blackmail; a name for her unborn child in exchange for my father's land!"

His tirade, growing louder with each word, made her chin tremble and brought stinging tears of rage to her eyes. Her slender body rigid, her chest heaving with indignation, she discovered, much to her chagrin, that no utterance passed her lips in retaliation and defense. She merely stood there motionless, her bright green eyes wide and her jaw sagging.

"What?" Brad ruthlessly continued. "Have you no reply? No flood of tears to melt my heart?" His dark eyes boldly swept the length of her. "Surely it would not be the first time you plied your womanly wiles to get what you wanted. But I, madam, am no fool."

The stinging slap of her open palm against his cheek rocked his head to one side and surprised Brad more than hurt him. But a slow rage darkened his eyes as he lifted them to look at her again, and it that same instant he shot out his hands, brutally seized her arms just above the elbows and yanked her forward into his embrace, his open mouth swooping down to entrap hers.

The shock of his reaction to his hands bruising her velvety skin and to his ardent kiss left her paralyzed, her mind whirling. She wanted to scream, to rake her nails against his arrogant face, to curse his boldness and name him the lecher that he was. She had never been so humiliated in her life, and now he sought to shame her. *Who did he think he was?* In a rage, she began to struggle, her eyes flying open when his mouth twisted against hers and his tongue pushed inside. Yet the more she fought him, the stronger his hold became. His iron-thewed arms encircled her trim form and crushed her to his massive, rock-hard chest. The warmth of his body penetrated the thin cloth of her gown, burning her flesh, branding her soul and awakening in her a chilling desire for more. She had to make him stop. It mustn't go any further! Wedging her hands between them, she pushed with all her might, tearing her lips from his and wrenching her body free of him. She staggered back several steps, breathless and panting, her cheeks hot with unbridled passion and her green eyes snapping with fury.

"A bigger fool I have yet to meet!" she raved, tossing

her head aristocratically and sending her luscious gold mane shimmering down her back in a torrent. "I did *not* propose we wed as a means to hide the results of some sordid liaison, as you so indelicately put it, but to save myself from a marriage to a man I detest!" A stray lock of hair fell defiantly against her brow, and she angrily brushed it back as she said, "'Twas all I wanted, and in return, you would have had your precious Wrenhaven."

Brad wasn't buying it. "You'd marry me to escape another? That's absurd!"

"Under certain conditions," she snapped back at him.

"Such as?" His dark eyes narrowed, leery of her provisions. Shauna Radborne could marry any man she chose, and without rules.

"That it's a marriage in name only."

This was too much! Shaking his head disbelievingly and with a somewhat pained smile on his face, Brad turned away from her to pace the floor. "If what you say is true," he finally responded, "then I ask your forgiveness in assuming the worst of you. But you must, at least, yield to my confusion in the matter, and see the situation as I saw it." He stopped his pacing and faced her. "Cloaked in the shadows of dusk, her identity hidden, a beautiful woman arrives at my doorstep with an offer of marriage. Not only is she a virtual stranger, but the daughter of one of the wealthiest men in London, an attribute that would lay anything she desired at her feet, if she so wished it. Her suitors, I imagine, would number every available man in the country, as well as a few who would abandon their wives and children. Yet she seeks me out, a poor wretch with nothing more than a dream in his pocket of owning the land where he once played as a youth. 'Tis a hard knot to swallow. But that is only the beginning. By agreeing to her insane proposition, that dream will become fact. And at what price? That I marry her and have myself gelded. For that, dear lady, would be the only way I could live with a wife such as you and not find myself tempted to consummate the union."

A mocking smile kinked one corner of her mouth. "That, sir, can be arranged."

His chin lowered, and a dark frown shadowing his eyes, Brad countered, "In my sleep, no doubt, and probably by your own hand, for I'm sure the Ice Maiden takes special pleasure in seeing that no man is capable of proving just how cold she really is."

"Ice Maiden!" she stormed, highly insulted. "Me?"

Brad's gaze quickly swept the room and settled on her again. "I see no other here, do you?"

The lace ties in the bodice of her gown strained against her rapid intake of breath as Shauna gritted her teeth, stiffened her spine, and jutted out her chin. "Perhaps it is your pride speaking rather than any evidence you can claim. As you already admitted, we are strangers . . . except for two brief moments when we hardly said ten words to each other. Yet in that short span of time, your manly charms were bruised when I shunned you openly and with good cause."

Realizing the uselessness in arguing that point, he chose not to correct her assumption, but instead replied, "Then why, pray tell, have you ignored your dislike of me and ventured here to my room—alone—and offered something as binding as marriage? I would think the opposite side of the globe is where you'd rather be."

"It is," she assured him, her upper lip curling. "And had I the means, 'tis where I'd see you sent. But alas, I am caught in a trap of my own doing and see no way out of it but that of what I offered."

Brad stared curiously at her a moment, before he shook his head and went to the desk to retrieve his glass and refill it with wine. "I won't pretend I'm interested in what kind of a trap you've made for yourself, but I would like to know why you've chosen me to help you out of it. After all, I'm sure you could have your pick of any man."

"'Tis simple," she replied, unaffected by his indifference. "Tyler said you're not interested in marriage, only in obtaining Wrenhaven. I, too, am not interested in marriage and all that goes with it, but since my father is determined to see me wed, I wish to do so under my conditions. The man I select must be one who will not look upon me as a wife, but merely a woman who happens to live in the same house as he."

A soft chuckle parted his lips and he raised the glass of wine to take a swallow before turning to face her. "So what you're saying is that you're doing this to please your father."

"In a way."

"And when no children are forthcoming, you'll simply shrug your shoulders and tell him that you're barren."

His remark brought a sudden warmth to her cheeks. "Nay," she slowly replied. "I had planned to tell him that you're incapable of siring children."

Struck by the absurdity of such a statement, he couldn't stop the laughter that erupted within him, and it took him a second to choke off his glee by clearing his throat. Although Brad couldn't honestly claim any offspring as his, he had never considered the possibility that what Shauna suggested might be true. There was nothing wrong with him when it came to women. He had merely counted himself lucky in that respect. Yet what

Shauna proposed would never allow him the chance to find out one way or the other. It also gave him an idea. He finished off his wine, set the glass aside, and clasped one wrist, letting his arms relax in front of him.

"That much of your wild scheme will bear some truth to it," he announced with a sigh, his expression solemn, "for in your desire to wound me, you have hit upon my secret. I cannot name one son or daughter as my own, and it's the true reason I never wed." He let the rest go unsaid. He wanted her to draw her own conclusions . . . the wrong ones. *If* he agreed to this idiotic plan of hers, he knew he'd be hard pressed to abide by the conditions. After all, she was still very alluring, despite her selfish nature, and he wasn't about to suppress his male needs just because she demanded it. Therefore, if she thought him less than a man, she might take pity on him in the future months, and he would have all he ever wanted; Wrenhaven, a wife, *and* children. He struggled with the grin that pulled at the corners of his mouth.

Shauna couldn't explain the sensation that came over her then. It was a mixture of surprise, empathy, doubt, and even suspicion. Her gaze quickly took in the appearance of the man standing before her. He was broad-shouldered, thickly muscled, and totally masculine. There wasn't a single flaw . . . at least not in what she was able to see. How devastating it must be for someone like him to learn he wasn't able to father a child. For the first time in a long, long while, she regretted letting her temper rule her words, and she debated apologizing to him. Especially after he turned away from her to stare out the window again. With a frown marring her smooth brow, she considered the results and quickly changed her mind. After all, she had been provoked and he had said very much the same thing to her without knowing if he'd strike upon the truth. No, if she told him she was sorry, she'd lose everything she had gained thus far, and her goal was too important to allow someone's feelings to stand in the way.

"Perhaps you'd like some time to think this out," she said instead, turning to lift her cape off the chair where she had tossed it.

"Yes, perhaps I should think of my alternatives before I agree to such a permanent arrangement," he sighed heavily, his back to her. "I might not be the sort of man most women look for in a husband, but I'm not sure I'm prepared to live the life of a monk, either."

"Oh, that's no problem," she quickly assured him, and Brad couldn't stop the victorious smile that came over his face. "As long as you're discreet, you may have any woman you want. And all the better since there will be no proof of your . . . unfaithfulness." She smiled softly as she slid the cape up over her shoulders, thinking that this scenario was turning out better than she had ever hoped it would. "In fact," she continued, moving toward the door and lifting the hood of her cloak up over her blond curls, "I wouldn't object—nay, I'd understand if you took Miss Anderson as your mistress." Reaching for the doorknob, Shauna failed to see Brad's tall, muscular frame stiffen. "All I ask is that you don't take too long in deciding. Father is through waiting, I fear, and if he isn't made aware that I'm interested in someone, I could be walking down the aisle within the week. And not with you there to take my hand, but Mr. Thorndyke." She started to pull the door open and paused. "Oh, and one more thing, Mr. Remington. If you should happen to decide against my little proposition and think to obtain the title to

Wrenhaven in some other way, you should be warned that I'll insist on the property as my dowry no matter whom I marry." She gave him one last look, saw that he hadn't moved or turned around, and concluded that what she had said had proven to him that she wasn't some brainless twit. She was a woman who had outsmarted him. "Good evening, Mr. Remington," she smiled triumphantly. Then in a whirl of peach satin and petticoats, she opened the door and gracefully left his room.

"Well? What did he say?" Moira pressed once the two of them were safely in the carriage and on their way home again. "Did he agree or tell ya what a fool ya are?"

Shauna gritted her teeth, exhaled slowly, and cast her maid a warning look. "I'm sorry to disappoint you, Moira, but Mr. Remington is giving my proposal his full consideration. I should have his answer in a day or two, and I'm confident in what his decision will be."

"Are ya now?" Moira challenged. "I'm supposin' ya think he'll say aye."

A devious, satisfied smile parted Shauna's lips as she turned her head to stare out the window. "If Wrenhaven means anything to him, he'll agree."

"I don't see where that matters any," Moira rallied. "There's more than one way to kiss the Blarney stone, ya know."

"And what does that mean?" Shauna lazily asked.

"It means, me good woman, that if Mr. Remington is determined ta own his father's property again, but not by marryin' you, he'll find some other means of doin' it. In fact, I'm willin' ta bet tomorrow mornin' will find him in

95

your father's study makin' a deal of his own." Settling herself more comfortably on the seat opposite her mistress, Moira flipped the edges of her cape up over her thighs for added warmth against the cool night air, dismissing what she said as fact.

"He's welcome to try," Shauna grinned devilishly. "But it won't do him any good, and he knows it."

The straight line of Moira's brows wrinkled as she jerked her head around to look at Shauna. "And why not?"

Shauna continued to stare out the window. "Because I made it perfectly clear to him that no matter whom I marry, Wrenhaven will be my gift to my new husband."

Moira straightened sharply, her chin sagging and her brown eyes wide. "And ya were able ta walk away on your own two feet? Me God, Miss Shauna, a threat like that could have gotten ya the beatin' ya so rightly deserve."

"Moira!" Shauna gasped, bright green turned suddenly her way. "What a horrible thing to say. I don't deserve to be beaten. I'm merely using my wit and the advantages afforded me to get what I want."

"Aye," Moira agreed. "As ya have been doin' since ya was a wee lass. And it worked on your father, but let me warn ya, me little darlin', ya aren't triflin' with your father's affections now. You're toyin' with a man who isn't interested in pleasin' ya. He wants his father's land and could care less about your predicament. If ya tweak his nose and laugh while your doin' it, ya very well may be askin' for more than ya can handle."

"I didn't tweak his nose," Shauna denied, irritated.

"No. Ya simply gave the man no choice." Shaking her head, she leaned back in the seat and stared off into space, muttering, "I can see it now. After the vows are spoken, he'll take his new bride to Wrenhaven and wring her pretty little neck."

"Oh, Moira, he will not," Shauna snapped, her temper wearing thin. "Mr. Remington is a businessman, and he sees this as nothing more than a way to obtain what he wants. It's good, practical, logical sense."

"Is it now?" Moira raised a brow at her companion. "Maybe from his point of view it is, but have ya given it much thought from your side? Sure, ya'll be rid of Mr. Thorndyke. But what are ya gettin' in return? What do ya really know about this man—I mean other than his foolish desire ta own Wrenhaven?"

"Foolish?" Shauna barked.

"Aye. It has ta be foolish if he's willin' ta give up his freedom for it. But aside from that, what else do ya know about him?" She hurried on without giving Shauna a chance to draw her breath. "Nothin'. Ya know nothin' about him. Did ya see the scar on his face? How do ya suppose he got it? Everyone assumes he was injured in the war, I reckon. But supposin' he wasn't. Suppose it's the only evidence of his deep, dark, secretive past? Maybe some other young, rash female thought ta trap him into marriage the way you're doin', and he only agreed so he could have something he really wanted, and then once he had it, he killed her, and the scar is from the struggle she put up. Or maybe some outraged father tried to beat him to death when he refused to marry his pregnant daughter?"

"Or maybe he slipped and fell down the stairs," Shauna added wearily, knowing Moira's last scenario couldn't even be considered.

"Or maybe he was tortured by his father as a young lad, and the memory of it has driven him crazy. On the outside he appears calm, sensible, and as normal as your father. But once he's got you alone in that house—the place where—"

"Oh, Moira, shut up!" Shauna demanded. "You're letting your imagination run wild. There's nothing wrong with Mr. Remington." Shaking her head, she stared out at the scenery passing by.

"Aye. On that we agree," Moira replied with a nod. "And you'll be findin' that out on your weddin' night."

Shauna closed her eyes and let her head fall back on the edge of the carriage seat, her mind awhirl with Moira's accusations. "First you claim he's a murderer, then a rapist, a madman, and finally that he's absolutely harmless."

"Nay," Moira quickly spoke up. "I did not say he was harmless. I said there was nothin' wrong with the man, except for bein' a little dimwitted, and that *man,* your *husband,* will prove it to ya once he has ya alone."

Shauna peered over at her maid through half-opened eyes. "Then I guess I'll have to sleep with a loaded pistol under my pillow. Now . . . may we change the subject? Or better still, not talk at all?"

"Whatever ya wish," Moira replied, readjusting her cape over her lap. A moment passed, then, "But don't come running to me when ya find out the truth about him. By then it will be too late. You'll be husband and wife."

"Moira!"

Shauna's glance dared Moira to say one more word before both women stubbornly turned their attention on whatever happened to be just outside the carriage window. Moira wanted to say more. She wanted to convince her mistress that what she had planned for herself was dangerous, and that it wasn't too late to back out. And until the very second Shauna started down the aisle on her father's arm, Moira intended to keep reminding her of the fact. Shauna, on the other hand, was already considering it. Brad Remington wasn't what she expected. While other men stuttered and stammered and made complete fools of themselves in her presence, he was poised, self-assured, and every bit a man. He was no dandy or milksop eager to do her bidding. If he were, he would have agreed to her offer without a moment's hesitation. Suddenly, her cheeks burned hotly and she could almost feel his lips pressed against hers, his hands boldly roaming her spine, and the sensation of his steely frame molded against her, the masculine scent of him, his mastery in winning that kiss, and she squirmed in the seat. If he had wanted more, he would have taken it, and she knew it. Maybe she should sleep with a pistol under her pillow. A worried frown drew her tawny brows together and she unknowingly hugged her arms over her bosom, trying unsuccessfully to erase the burning illusion of his hands gently caressing her breasts and the stimulating image of his open mouth slowly lowering to claim one rosy peak.

Chapter Four

Bright sunshine intruded rudely upon Shauna's sleep when Moira flung open the drapes the next morning with little care to her mistress's preference to stay in bed a while longer. Groaning her disapproval, Shauna rolled onto her stomach and buried her head beneath the pillow, closing out the light and muffling her maid's cheery greeting that it was indeed a beautiful sunrise and that Shauna shouldn't miss it. Little did Moira know that Shauna had already seen the early markings of dawn and had just now managed to fall asleep. She had spent the entire night pacing the floor, rocking in the rocker, staring down at the warm yellow flames of the fire in the hearth, or tossing and turning in bed, all of which had failed to distract her thoughts away from her meeting with Brad Remington. *And this was all Moira's fault!* If her maid hadn't put doubts in her head, she could easily have lain the incident to rest, as well as her mind, and slept comfortably all night. But that wasn't the way it turned out. She kept going over the accusations Moira had made and then unwillingly compared them to the things Brad Remington had said.

Wait until he gets you alone—as husband and wife—

he'll beat you—there's nothing wrong with the man—I'm not sure I'm ready to live the life of a monk.

Each time Shauna thought about that last declaration, an image came to her mind, one she fought desperately to avoid. Darkness encased her bedchambers, save for the bright glow coming from the fireplace. Everyone in the house had retired, and she was about to do the same. Moonlight fell softly on the balcony just outside her room, a place she didn't recognize, and even though she was only dressed in a thin, silky nightgown, she was drawn to the serenity beyond the closed french doors. Barefoot, she trod noiselessly across the floor in a trance and freed the latch. Surprisingly, warm, fragrant air rushed in and billowed the white shimmering fabric of her gown, luring her to step out past the threshold. The full moon shone overhead, and bright silver stars sparkled in the velvety black sky. She could hear the distant hooting of an owl and crickets chirping their rhythmical song below her in the gardens. Closing her eyes, she lifted her chin to breathe in the sweet smell of lilacs, her long strands of golden hair tumbling down her back in a thick mass of soft curls. Contentment flowed through her, a sense of victory that her life was as it should be. Then a noise from in back of her spun her around, and she could barely make out the tall silhouette of a man standing in the open doorway to her room, his face shadowed by the light behind him in the hall. At first she couldn't imagine who he was, until the faint voice of her maid whispered in her ear: "Husband and wife. There's nothing wrong with him. He's all man. And you're a woman, his wife."

Suddenly he was standing before her, bathed in the alluring glimmer of silver light, and he held out his hand to her invitingly. Unable to resist, she rested her fingers against his open palm, and a shiver tickled her spine when he gently covered them with his own, their warmth melting away any doubt she might have had. Drawing her back into the bedchambers with him, he guided her toward the hearth, and there she was able to see the firm set of his jaw, his rugged brow, the intense brown color of his eyes, and his sensuous mouth, lips parted slightly and drawn upward in a seductive smile. Her heart beat faster and her blood pulsed through her veins. A mere look, the come-hither gleam in his eye, had ignited a flame of passion, a stirring desire in her to give herself freely to him without question or denial. After all, they were husband and wife.

Warm, moist lips caressed the smoothness of her throat and a delicious moan escaped her. He nibbled on her ear, trailed the tip of his tongue along the delicate line of her jaw, kissed the tip of her nose, her chin, each closed eyelid, and finally claimed her sweet mouth. His fingertips traced the contour of her long, slender neck and across her shoulder, skillfully entrapping the lacy strap of her gown to push it aside. The other followed, and the shimmering white silk glided to the floor. Standing naked before him, every inch of her flesh burned with desire for his touch, yet he hesitated.

"Husband and wife," she murmured, her gaze lowering to the wide expanse of his muscled, bare chest, and her heart fluttered at the sight. A dark, crisp matting of hair covered the width and trailed to a fine line, disappearing beneath the waistband of his breeches. His bronzed skin glowed in the soft yellow light of the fire, and she lifted her hand to run her open palm against the sinewy breadth, only to have him catch her wrist and deny her the pleasure. A puzzled frown marred her fair brow, and she lifted her pale green eyes to him questioningly.

"Monk," he replied.

Suddenly and mysteriously, he was gone and the sounds of laughter floated up from the gardens. Racing to the balcony, she saw him there, his incredibly perfect physique stripped of his clothing and his muscular arms enveloping the tiny figure of a woman. She too was naked, and at first Shauna wondered how she could be locked in his embrace and watching from the balcony at the same time. Then in the next startling, heart-rending moment, the couple turned to look up at her, and she painfully recognized Beth.

The vision had always been the same, but each time she imagined it, her reaction changed. The first was tears, coming from her feeling sorely injured by his blatant rejection of her. Then came indifference. It was how she had wanted it, nay, proposed it to be. Next was anger. He was her husband, and no matter what the terms, he should be faithful. And finally, an overpowering feeling of loneliness would assail her. Perhaps they lived under the same roof, shared the same dinner table, attended parties together, claimed to be man and wife, but underneath it all, they were strangers, and she was destined to live out her life never knowing the joy or the sorrow of a man's love. Damn! If only she could have the best of both!

"Did you hear me, Shauna Kathleen?"

The sound of Moira's heated question jolted Shauna out from under her pillow and the mound of blankets that had tangled themselves around her scantily clad body. Sprawled on her stomach, golden hair falling wildly about her face and shoulders, eyes wide, she pushed herself up on her hands and asked, "Hear what?"

Standing at the side of the huge four-poster bed, Moira cocked her head, settled her fists on her hips, and gave her mistress a rather disgusted look. "Now why is it I guessed ya'd be sayin' somethin' like that ta me? And where do ya suppose your mind has been? Thinkin' of him, no doubt."

"I was not!" Shauna retorted hotly, flipping over on her back and angrily straightening the covers up under her chin.

"Ya was not what?" Moira baited.

"Thinking of Brad Remington," Shauna snapped, closing her eyes and hoping Moira would get the hint that she wanted to be left alone.

"And what makes ya assume I was referrin' to Brad Remington? I could have meant most anyone else."

Although that was a distinct possibility, Shauna knew better. If he was on *her* mind, more than likely Moira couldn't focus her attention on anyone or any*thing* else, as well. She opened one eye to glare at her maid, closed it again, and rolled over on her side.

"But since ya brought him up—"

"Moira, I don't want to talk about him," Shauna warned. "All I want to do is sleep. You know what that is, don't you?"

"Aye. It's what ya obviously didn't get last night," Moira rallied, crossing around the end of the bed to the armoire and opening the doors. "But I forgot. Ya weren't thinkin' of him."

Shauna rolled onto her stomach again and growled into the feathery depth of her pillow.

"And if that be the case, ya won't care if he's in your

father's study at this very moment, the way I told ya he would be this mornin'.''

Shauna bolted upright in bed. "What?" she shrieked. "He's here?" Her round, worried eyes shot a glance at her closed bedroom door, as if she thought she could see right through it to the room downstairs. "He's with Papa?"

"Well, he didn't come here to speak with you," Moira scoffed, selecting a pretty aqua-colored gown from the wardrobe and turning around with it draped over her arm.

A thousand reasons why he wanted to talk with her father clouded her mind, none of them good. The trickster had figured a way to buy Wrenhaven. And he had acted on it before she had the chance to tell her father that she wanted the property as her dowry. Damn him! Damn his soul to hell! Flipping the covers off her, Shauna frantically scooted out of bed and raced to the dresser, yanking open the top drawer in a frenzied rush to find something to wear.

"Well, don't just stand there, Moira," she ordered, her back to the woman. "Help me dress!" When the maid didn't answer or appear at her side, Shauna straightened and glared back at her in the mirror's reflection, the angry frown on her face lessening once she saw Moira holding up a fresh dress and lacy underthings.

"I don't suppose ya'd be wantin' ta take a bath first?" Moira foolishly questioned as she laid the garments on the foot of the bed, then helped Shauna out of her nightgown.

"You're right. I wouldn't," Shauna briskly replied, stepping into her underthings, securing them at the waist, then slipping the chemise down over her head. "Unless you'd like to go down to Papa's study and ask them to wait for me before they discuss business."

"Business?" the pert Irishwoman mocked. "Is that what ya think they're doin'? Discussin' business?"

Hurrying to her dressing table, Shauna sat down on the bench and handed Moira her hairbrush. "Well, what else would they be talking about?"

Moira shrugged and began stroking the mass of tangled curls into some semblance of order. "I'm thinkin' they're discussin' some way of turnin' a foolhardy girl into a respectable woman."

"Very funny, Moira," Shauna hissed. "Just finish up with what you're doing and keep your comments to yourself. I have enough to worry about without having to deal with one of the servants who can't seem to remember her place."

Moira's Irish temper flared. "Me place, is it now? And what place is that, Miss Radborne? Are ya sayin' I should draw your bath, comb your hair, see that your clothes are always fresh and clean, help ya dress, and not give ya a piece of advice? Have I suddenly gone from friend to strictly maid? Has the last ten years of me life spent carin' for ya, soothin' your bumps and bruises, lyin' to your father when ya lost more money at the gamin' tables than ya should have—has all that been for nothin' if it doesn't give me the right ta say I love ya and I'm worried for ya?"

Moira's scolding cut deep and quick, and Shauna was instantly sorry for saying what she had. Turning, she reached for the hairbrush, took it from Moira's hand, and then pulled the woman down on the narrow bench beside her. "Of course, it hasn't been for nothing, Moira," she pledged softly. "I know how much you care, and I hope you realize how much you mean to me. It's just that everything you've said is true, and I'm not willing to hear it, much less agree. I really don't want to marry anyone . . . not quite yet. I don't want the responsibility. I want the freedom . . . to come and go as I please, flirt with whomever I want, if I so choose . . . sleep late, get up before sunrise, decide what parties to attend or those I prefer to avoid, wear my hair loose or in a braid or stuffed beneath a wig. I *don't* want someone deciding for me, and I don't want to be told when to stay home or where to go. I don't want a man to think he has the right to . . . to . . ." She lowered her gaze. "Well, I'm not ready to have children. I'm not really sure I ever will be. And I most definitely don't want to give that all up by marrying that pompous ass, Nelson Thorndyke!" Her body shook with the repulsive shudder his name evoked. "Would you?"

Tears had gathered in Moira's brown eyes, and she quickly blinked them away. "No, lass. He isn't good enough for ya. But I don't want ya ta marry just anyone to escape him. I want ya to know the joy of lovin' a man." A strange look came over Moira's face, and she quickly left Shauna's side to go to the bed and pick up the dress she had laid there.

"Moira? What is it?" Shauna asked, for she had seen the pain registered in the woman's eyes. "Something's troubling you. I could see it in your face." Leaving the bench, she hurried over to her and gently touched her arm. "I hate to resort to this, Moira, but since I told you how I felt, you owe it to me to return the favor."

Moira's narrow shoulder jutted upward in response. "Not much ta tell, lass. I was just thinkin' of Keelan."

"Keelan?" Shauna repeated. "I've never heard you mention him before. Who is he?"

"Was," Moira corrected, forcing a smile. "He was

me husband."

Shauna couldn't have been more surprised if Moira had said she had committed murder earlier this morning and would have come here sooner had she not had trouble wiping the blood from her hands. "You never told me you were married."

"It happened a long time ago, and it was over in a month."

"Over?" Shauna questioned, afraid of Moira's answer.

"Aye. Keelan was twenty, I was sixteen when we met. We loved each other very much, but his father didn't care. He was a wealthy man and wanted Keelan to marry for money. My family didn't have any. When his father arranged a marriage to a lass who fit the requirements, Keelan rebelled, especially when he found out his intended bride was much older than he. So we ran off together and got married. Ta say the least, his father was outraged. He hired men ta track us down—we had left Dublin so he couldn't interfere, but it didn't do any good. They found us anyway, and—" Moira's voice cracked and she moved away from Shauna, wiping the corner of her eye with her fingertip and drawing in a long, trembling sigh. "Keelan refused ta go. He told the men he would die before he'd do as his father wished."

"What happened, Moira?" Shauna tenderly asked when Moira seemed reluctant to continue.

"There was a struggle—a pistol was drawn. It was an accident, but . . ." she paused to swallow the knot in her throat, "Keelan was killed."

"Oh, Moira, I'm so sorry," Shauna whispered, coming to wrap her arms around the woman and give her a squeeze. "You must think I'm horrible to be complaining so about my own problems."

108

"Nay, I do not," Moira corrected her. "I understand. 'Tis only that you've not thought it through. I'm sure there's a Keelan out there for you, if you'd only just wait."

"But I can't, Moira. Papa won't let me. He says I've waited long enough already."

Brushing away her tears and her memories, Moira's spirit returned, as strong as always. "So ya'll marry the first man who comes along."

"The first man of my choice," Shauna interjected stubbornly. "It's not too unlike your decision to wed Keelan. Not really." She could see the contradictory look in Moira's eyes and elected to avoid further discussion on the issue. "But if I don't hurry, even that will be taken from me." Returning to the dressing table, she sat down on the bench and proceeded to brush her hair back off her face and tie the lush gold strands with a ribbon. "I know you don't agree, Moira, but things are done differently in a family such as mine," she added, leaving the bench to gather up her hose and garters. "What Papa says is law, and *no one* argues. However, he will relent a little if I show any interest at all in someone other than the man he's chosen." Sitting on the edge of the bed, she hurriedly donned the stockings and lacy straps, rose and went to the armoire for her petticoats. With Moira's help, she finished dressing and made one last examination of herself in the mirror. She would have liked having a little more time to select the right clothes to wear, but time wasn't something she had a lot of to waste. And besides, she wasn't planning on making an impression on her father's guest. She merely wanted to intervene before he ruined her chances of getting what she wanted . . . her freedom.

"Miss Shauna," Moira called out when her mistress reached for the doorknob on her way out of the room. "If what ya say about your father is true—that he'd relent if ya showed an interest in some other man—then why not use Mr. Remington for that purpose?"

"But I am," she laughed, failing to understand Moira's real meaning.

"Not by marryin' him, ya aren't." She hurried on when she saw Shauna frown. "Ya could pretend ta be interested in Mr. Remington while ya look around for the man ya really want ta marry. If ya go through with your idea, ya'll be giving up any chance ya might have had at happiness."

A soft smile graced Shauna's fair features. "There's only two things wrong with what you're proposing, Moira. Two very important facts. First of all, if I had my way, I'd never get married. The thought of it turns my stomach. But more than that, Brad Remington would never agree."

"How do ya know unless ya ask him?" Moira quickly argued.

"Because he's only after one thing: Wrenhaven. If he isnt' assured of getting it, why would he help me out? What would be in it for him? I know that if I were in his place, I'd tell me to take a very long walk into the ocean." She turned the knob, freed the latch, and pulled the door open. "And if I don't get down there right now, it might be too late already."

"I think you're misjudgin' the man."

Moira comment stopped Shauna before she had stepped into the hall. "Misjudging him? What do you mean?" she asked, turning back around.

"I mean, he strikes me as the type ta want ta help a

110

woman in your sort of trouble . . . with or without a reward."

Flashes of the argument the two of them had had came into her mind and Shauna quickly shook her head. "I don't think so, Moira. Not after what was said between us. If anything, the man despises me." A cocky grin parted her lips. "And now that I think about it, that's all the better. If he dislikes me, he'll be more than willing to sleep in separate bedchambers."

"For a while anyway," Moira added, her dark brow raised sarcastically.

The vision of that titillating scene before the fire rekindled itself in Shauna's head and brought a hot blush to her cheeks. Not wanting Moira to comment on it, Shauna quickly turned around and stepped into the hall. Nor did she wish to continue the debate of a topic on which they would never agree. All that was important right now was getting to her father's study and interrupting the conversation the two men were having before Brad Remington had a chance to make his offer, whatever that might be.

At the top of the stairs, Shauna paused to fluff out her hair and straighten her bodice—not for Brad's sake, but for her father's. She had to look her best, and she needed a moment to collect her wits and force that haunting image of the two of them from her mind. If a simple daydream could set her back on her heels, seeing him face to face would certainly take its toll if she wasn't ready for him. Inhaling quickly and letting it out in a rush, she squared her shoulders and started down the staircase, her eyes riveted to the closed study door. She was in full control now. All she had to do was—

Suddenly and unexpectedly, that aperture glided

111

noiselessly open, and a second later—before Shauna had time to prepare—Brad's tall, well-muscled, richly clothed physique filled the frame, and she nearly missed the last step. A quick hand on the banister steadied her balance and kept her from falling, but the tremor that shook her body and weakened her knees didn't come from her near mishap, rather from the electrifying sensation that charged through her when her eyes met his.

The subtle shade of emerald velvet he wore enhanced his dark hair and coppery complexion. The sleek texture of the cloth seemed to hug every well-defined inch of him and accent the wideness of his shoulders, the muscular firmness of his chest, and the lean length of his hip and thighs. But none of that set her heart aflutter as much as the handsomeness of his face; the square jaw, wide cheekbones, full, sensuous lips, and the dark brows that shadowed those unreadable eyes. Had she had her wits about her, she would have noticed the hard look he gave her and taken warning from its message. She didn't. She was too busy just trying to draw breath and pretend she hadn't really noticed anything more than that her father had company. Then he smiled, slow and lazy, and once his lips parted and she could see a flash of white teeth, her gaze was drawn to his mouth, his sensuous, alluring, beguiling mouth, and she was sure she was about to faint. She could feel that hot, demanding kiss of the night before, his hands caressing her spine, the hard length of him pressed against her, and the wild fury that arose within her . . . much as was threatening to do this very instant. For some unknown reason that discovery snapped her out of the dreamlike state she was in, and a flood of color heightened her already pinkened cheeks.

112

"Welcome back, daughter," her father's deep voice teased, once he was honored with her attention.

He had followed his guest from the study and had been about to direct Brad to the terrace where they planned to have a light breakfast and a cup of tea, when he noticed that Brad seemed interested in something he saw on the staircase. He, too, was surprised to find his daughter standing there, spotlighted in the bright glow of sunshine streaming in through the stained-glass window at the top of the stairs. She looked radiant this morning, as she always seemed to be no matter what time of the day it was, and it pleased him to find that Brad thought so, too. But then, very few men ever showed disinterest in his daughter. Some saw her beauty. Others saw the wealth to be gained by offering her marriage. The majority recognized both, and only a select few were able to look beyond those points and see her for what she really was. They could be numbered as true friends, and they were, he hated to admit, not many. Shauna knew this as well, and it pained him to realize it was her reason for shunning any and all romantic overtures. He glanced briefly at the handsome gentleman standing next to him and then back at his daughter. Perhaps this time it would be different.

The young man obviously approved of what he saw, and Shauna appeared to be struck mute, an alteration in her character that both surprised and pleased him. Shauna was quick to judge a man's intent and never tried to hide her findings . . . from the man or her father. That had been the topic of many heated discussions between father and daughter, often resulting in a chilly silence between the two and in his decision that perhaps his youngest offspring was too critical of the men who

113

showed specific interest in her. For her own good he had come to the conclusion that it was best *he* choose her future husband, lest she remain unwed the rest of her life. And Shauna wasn't meant to be alone.

However, once he set about his task, he too found that the pickings were slim, and he soon realized *his* standards were too high, as well. The only man to whom he had even given second thought was Nelson Thorndyke. He was an excellent businessman, but there was something about his personality that grated on Pierce's nerves. This man, however, this Brad Remington, was a different story altogether. He had charm, social manners, good looks, and youth, attributes Thorndyke didn't have. His only flaw as far as Pierce could tell was his—hopefully—short-term lack of funds. Marrying for love was one thing. But a man had to be able to give his wife the luxuries she was accustomed to if they were to build a solid, lasting relationship. He thought of his own wife, frowned, and then hurriedly dismissed the conflicting aspects of that situation. He focused his attention on something he was sure he could control.

"Shauna," he said, walking to the bottom of the staircase and holding out his hand to her, "I believe you know Brad Remington."

"Yes, Papa," she replied, surprised by how weak her voice sounded. "We've met." Taking her father's proffered assistance, she smiled back at him as he protectively tucked her hand into the crook of his arm and guided her toward their guest. With great effort, she forced herself to look at Brad. "Mr. Remington."

"Miss Radborne, I trust you're well," he replied, the deep resonance of his voice, the masculine scent of him, the warmth of his hardened frame attacking her from all directions.

"Yes, thank you. And you?" She hated being polite. Especially with him.

"I was until a moment ago," he returned, his serious expression suddenly turning warm. "Until I saw you on the stairs just now. Your beauty makes a man weak." But not me, he added to himself. It reminds me of what a devious little chit I'm up against.

Shauna smiled and nodded her head in response to the compliment, while in her thoughts she recognized the vagueness of his statement. She truly doubted he included himself among those who were left faint in her presence. "So, what brings you to our home, Mr. Remington? Business with my father?" Though her tone was sweet, it had an icy edge to it.

"In a manner of speaking, I suppose," he admitted, smiling at the man standing beside her. It was then he noticed the striking resemblance between father and daughter. Although Pierce Radborne was four or five inches taller than Shauna, they had similar builds: tall and willowy, with an air of refinement and presence of mind. Where Shauna had a fair complexion and light blond hair, Pierce was olive-skinned and dark-haired, with gray at the temples. But their eyes, a remarkable shade of green, seemed to look right through a man to his soul, and Brad wondered how long it would take the eldest Radborne to recognize the game his daughter played. The two men had only talked a short while before stepping into the hall, but it was long enough for Brad to measure Radborne's worth as a man. Keen-witted, both in humor and in a business sense, he also conveyed the message that he wasn't easily fooled . . . by anyone. His daughter might have the advantage—Brad could see the love for her radiating in the man's smile, his words, and the way he looked at her—but Brad also guessed that even she would pay the price should she truly anger him. And what she had planned for herself would most assuredly fail in that category.

"And as I told Mr. Remington," Pierce cut in, "business should always be discussed on a full stomach. We were about to go out on the terrace. Will you join us, Shauna?"

Join you? she mused. Threat of death wouldn't stop me. "If I'm not intruding," she said aloud.

"Excellent," her father beamed, obviously pleased. "Then why don't you show our guest outside while I find Walter and tell him to set the table for three." A frown flitted across his brow and disappeared as he glanced over his shoulder toward the stairs. "I don't suppose your mother would be up this early." He answered his own query with a shake of his head. "No, I think not," he replied, turning back. "If you two will excuse me, I'll meet you on the terrace in a moment." Leaning in, he kissed his daughter's brow, nodded approvingly at Brad—something Shauna missed—and walked away, leaving the two of them alone in the hall.

Shauna silently watched her father's tall, proud, lanky frame until he had turned at the end of the hall in the direction of the servants' quarters and kitchen, before she settled her full attention on Brad. He had been closely studying her, and to find those dark eyes resting on her when she turned her head made her pulse quicken a mite. If only he had a wart on the tip of his nose or missing front teeth, *anything.* . . . Lifting her chin and presenting him with an air of confidence, she held out a directive hand. "Shall we go to the terrace?"

Brad answered her invitation with a slight bow, his gaze never leaving her face. But once she had dropped her own away from him and moved to lead the way, a devilish smile broke the serious line of his mouth. He wasn't sure, but he suspected his presence made her extremely nervous, and he planned to use that possibility to its full advantage.

"I hadn't imagined you'd be up at this early an hour, Miss Radborne," he observed as they stepped through the double set of doors and onto the terrace. "I hope it isn't because you couldn't sleep." With her back to him, he grinned openly to see how rigid her spine became. He would have loved to have watched the reaction on her face.

"How I sleep is none of your concern," came her icy rebuttal as she crossed the colored flagstones to the wrought iron glass-topped table with its matching chairs.

"You misunderstand," he gently corrected, pulling out a chair for her and noticing how exquisitely the blue-green shade of her gown accented her lucious curves and complimented the hue of her eyes. "I'm not in the habit of trying to learn *what* a lady wears to bed. Although I'd guess with you it isn't much . . . if anything." He ignored the shocked expression on her face to draw out the chair next to her and sit down. "But if you'd like to tell me. . . ."

"I most certainly would not!" she shrieked. "And you are a rogue to even suggest I might!"

"A rogue," he repeated, settling back in the chair, one elbow resting on its arm, his thumb braced against his jawline while his fingers gently rubbed his chin and his dark eyes seemed to devour every inch of her. "I believe that fact has already been established, Miss Radborne."

117

"Reaffirmed," she snapped, a faint line showing between her brows as she glared back at him. "Why are you here?"

He stared at her a moment longer, then casually indicated the table with a slow sweep of his hand. "To have breakfast. Unless you have something else in mind." He forced himself to suppress the laughter that burned his throat at the rush of color he saw darken her cheeks.

"I have many thoughts about you, Mr. Remington, none of which, I'm sure, you'd find attractive," she hissed, her eyes narrowed dangerously.

"And shall I tell you about mine? Concerning you?" he challenged, his playful mood ebbing.

Shauna arrogantly tossed her head, the thick mass of curls shimmering in the early-morning sunlight. "I don't think I'd care to hear them, sir," she replied acidly. "I've never had the desire to listen to a man's lecherous thoughts."

"They're far from that, *Miss* Radborne. Uncomplimentary, yes. But don't flatter yourself by assuming I would think of you and the pleasures to be had in bed at the same moment."

His admission had a double-edged impact on Shauna. It pleased her to hear that he wasn't intimately interested in her and hurt her ego at the same time. She wasn't inexperienced with a man's groping and pawing of her, and had, in fact, usually had to fight them off whenever she had unwittingly allowed her pursuer to get her alone somewhere. Since she had already grouped all men together as the same type, she had trouble separating Brad from the others. *Especially* Brad. And what about that kiss? When he'd had her alone in his room last night? That certainly wasn't the kind of behavior one would expect from a man who claimed he wasn't interested in her.

"I'd like to believe that was true, Mr. Remington, but your actions of last night rather contest that statement," she argued hotly. Then, remembering where they were, she quickly glanced back toward the house to make sure no one had stepped out onto the terrace where they might have heard what she had to say. Satisfied that her secret was safe, she looked at him again. "Why are you here?" When he opened his mouth to respond, she hurriedly added, "Other than to have breakfast. If you're thinking to make some sort of deal with my father for Wrenhaven, let me assure you that you're already too late. Papa and I had a long talk last night . . . about my future *and* my choice of a dowry."

"Did you?" he questioned, the tone of his voice clearly hinting at his doubt. "Then why has my presence here this morning made you so nervous?"

"Nervous?" she countered with a sarcastic laugh.

"Yes, nervous. If your future is as secure as you imply, you wouldn't be sitting here with me now demanding answers." He smiled crookedly at her, his gaze dipping down to the low neckline of her gown, on to her narrow waist, then back to her face. "And as to my behavior of last night. I don't know of any man alive who wouldn't have taken the opportunity to kiss a beautiful woman." He deliberately paused a moment to allow her the false sense of being complimented. "However, that was not the case in that instance. I merely sought to teach you a lesson, Miss Radborne."

"A-a lesson?" she gasped, failing to see where one needed to be taught. "What kind of lesson? That you more than any man shouldn't be trusted? I knew that before I ever came to your room. You simply confirmed it."

His dark brows gathered in an angry frown. "And had you also considered then what might have resulted had I been inclined to take more than just a kiss?" He cocked his head and lifted one brow at the crimson stain he saw appear suddenly in her cheeks. "No. I'm sure you didn't. Not *before* you entered my room. Chances are, however, you've thought of nothing else since, and it's more than likely the reason you're sitting at this table right now. You're honestly worried I'll tell your father about your little escapade, *and* your scheme to blackmail me. Not to mention your fear that I've figured out some other way of having Wrenhaven without marrying you. Because if you truly were assured of your future, you'd be sound asleep in your bed."

Green eyes wide and turning a dark shade of emerald, she stared back at him. "You wouldn't dare," she breathed venomously.

"Wouldn't I?" he challenged. "Are you willing to find out?"

"Then you're a bigger fool than I gave you credit for. How would you ever hope to obtain Wrenhaven by embarrassing my father? Providing, of course, that he believed you."

"Maybe I'll resort to the same methods you employed. The property for my silence."

Shauna's whole body shook with rage. "I'd see you dead first."

"Tsk, tsk," he mocked, pulling back as if he were offended. "I never would have guessed you'd stoop to murder."

"To protect my father I'd do just about anything," she railed through clenched teeth.

"To protect your father?" he countered with a vague smile. "Wouldn't it be better said that you'd do just about anything to have your own way? I doubt you even considered your father's feelings in the matter before you came to see me. As I've said already, Miss Radborne, you're a spoiled brat."

Shauna bolted to her feet. "I think you should leave, Mr. Remington."

"Do you?" he lazily replied, ignoring social custom to remain in his seat. "Well, I don't. And since I came here to speak with your father and not you, *he'll* have to be the one to ask me to leave. Now, I suggest you sit down and be quiet. Otherwise, I'll be compelled to tell him why you won't be having breakfast with us." He gave her a moment to understand his threat, then added, "And yes, that's blackmail. The same strategy you used on me."

It pained Shauna to do as he instructed, but he had left her no choice. Slowly sinking back down into the chair, she glared her hatred of him. "Moira was right about you," she spat in little more than a whisper. "You *are* an unprincipled cad."

"Manners I learned from my late-afternoon visitor, Miss Radborne," he casually offered in self-defense as he reached inside his coat for his tin of cheroots. "But somehow I get the feeling your maid didn't truly say such a thing. In the short time we spoke, I got the distinct impression she was against your coming to my room." Having lit the cigar, he took a long drag on it and exhaled a white puff of smoke, which he watched curl upward and disappear. "Perhaps she is even against your proposal that we wed, and 'tis her fear of its outcome that

121

plays havoc with your conscience." He settled his brown eyes on her again. "And she's right, you know. Once I have my father's land in my possession, legal and binding, who's to say I'll stick to our agreement?" He studied the tip of the cheroot he rolled between his fingers and thumb. "Who's to say I won't find fault with my wife in the first month and send her out into the streets to fend for herself? Aye, 'tis true she may and most assuredly would return to her father's house. But what then?" He looked at her askance. "Would a proud father not find her a new husband? Perchance one Nelson Thorndyke?"

Shauna fought hard not to reach over and dig her nails in his eyes. The arrogant, overconfident, calculating miscreant! He had thought of everything. However, his mistake was in presuming he had outwitted her. Lifting her chin to a lofty height, she looked down her nose at him. "And what say you if I told you the conditions of my dowry?"

"Conditions? To a dowry?" he repeated dubiously. "I would say you jest to assume such a thing."

"And that, dear sir, is where you show your ignorance. My father has had training as a solicitor and therefore will know how to add a clause to the deed." She grinned triumphantly at him. "If the marriage lasts a day or one hundred years, the property I brought into the union will remain mine. What I bring, I take back."

Brad eyed her closely as he took a second puff on the cheroot and exhaled slowly. "And in the event of your death? What happens then? Shall Wrenhaven be legally mine? Or will the grieving father come to claim it?" He grinned openly at the horrified look on her face. "Mine, if death comes naturally. His, should you meet with a questionable accident." He frowned, as if considering something else. "But what if there's no body?" He scratched his chin thoughtfully and stared out across the gardens. "Who will rightfully own Wrenhaven if I return home one day to find a message from my wife saying she has decided to visit America, and months pass with no word from her? Must we assume then that she has met someone else and will never come home to me? Or that perhaps her ship encountered a terrible storm at sea and sank." His angry eyes glared at her again. "Do not threaten me, Shauna Radborne," he warned, his voice low. "I promise you will not like the results."

A terrifying fear gripped its icy fingers around Shauna's heart, and she struggled to draw air into her lungs. Why—with the wide variety of men from which to choose—had she picked this one? He was cold, unfeeling, shrewd, devious, and obviously willing to commit murder! Unable to move, she sat very still while she waited for the paralysis to lessen its hold on her. The deal was off. She wanted no part of him. She'd find someone else to marry. And it wouldn't be Nelson Thorndyke. And she'd make sure this viper never lived at Wrenhaven again. Swallowing the knot in her throat, she took a deep breath and pulled her sagging frame erect, chin high, shoulders back.

"If you'll excuse me, Mr. Remington," she managed to say, "I'll see what's keeping Father." On trembling legs, she started to rise just as her brother made an unexpected appearance before them.

"Brad," he called, a bright smile on his face as he hurried forward, his hand extended. "What a pleasure it is to see you."

"And I, you," Brad grinned, rising to accept the warm handshake.

Tyler's green eyes darted from Brad to his sister and

back. "Surely you're not here to see Shauna? It's too early in the day to deliberately ruin the rest of it," he teased, motioning for his friend to sit down again as he turned his attention back on Shauna. "Imagine what it would be like to have to live with her the way I do."

"Actually, that's just what I was doing," Brad replied, his lips parted in a soft smile and the anger in his eyes gone.

Tyler missed the subtle meaning in Brad's comment. "Oh, I can assure you, there's never a dull moment," he laughed, leaning down to kiss Shauna's brow. "Good morning, Sis. Sleep well?" Without waiting for her reply, he moved around to take the chair opposite Brad. "You're up early. Any special reason?"

"I had hoped to have a quiet breakfast," she mumbled without looking at either man. "But I see there's no chance of that anymore."

Her sarcasm brought good-natured laughter from Tyler. "See there, Brad," he said. "Never a dull moment." The smile disappeared instantly when Shauna made to rise. "You're not leaving because of me, are you, Sis? I promise to behave."

"Actually I was on my way to the kitchen to find Father," she replied solemnly, starting to push herself up from the chair and flashing Tyler a dangerous look when he caught her arm and held her down.

"Don't bother," he said, nodding toward the house.

Glancing in that direction, she spotted Pierce's tall figure step out onto the terrace on his way to join them, and she gave a mental groan at having lost her excuse for leaving.

"Sorry I took so long," he apologized as he pulled out the chair next to his son and sat down. "But I took a moment to jot down some notes on a deal I'm working on with Thorndyke." He smiled at the blond-haired youth beside him. "Good morning, Tyler. I can't remember the last time we ate breakfast together."

"And if you don't wish to spoil my appetite, you won't mention that man's name again."

"Tyler doesn't like him," Pierce chuckled as he looked at Brad. "Neither does my daughter. And although I've never heard her say it, I imagine my wife doesn't, either."

The arrival of several servants carrying trays of covered dishes interrupted the conversation for the time being, and all three men seemed perfectly comfortable with filling their stomachs. Shauna, on the other hand, wanted nothing to do with food or the company her family had so easily invited to sit down at the table with them. If she had some way of knowing that her father wouldn't be furious enough to send her off to a convent once she admitted to everything, she thought, she'd tell both Radborne men just exactly what kind of a man Brad Remington really was. Her father might believe her, since he had only just met him. But Tyler wouldn't. He'd already made it very clear how much he liked Brad Remington, and if she tried to convince her father that the scoundrel was in every sense a scounrel, she'd have Tyler to contend with. And that would only lead to disaster. Men never gave credit to a woman's say in a matter. Accepting the cup of tea Doreen had poured for her, Shauna sat sullenly quiet while the others ate. Her life was a shambles, and she had only herself to thank for it.

"So, Brad," Tyler spoke up a few minutes later as he shoved his empty plate away, "is there anything important happening in your life that I should know about?"

In a fog, and not really interested in anything Brad Remington had to say, Shauna motioned for Doreen to refill her cup with hot tea.

"Allow me to answer that, Brad," Pierce cut in. "It's a piece of news I've waited a long time to announce." He smiled first at Tyler, then across the table at his daughter, waiting until the maid had set down the teapot and stepped back. "Brad has asked my permission to court Shauna."

The shattering of a china cup and saucer against cold, hard flagstones echoed in the quiet morning air.

Chapter Five

"For heaven's sake, lass," Moira snapped, "will ya stop that infernal pacin' and tell me what's wrong? And quit bitin' your nails. Ya know a lady shouldn't do such things."

"He's going to murder me, Moira," Shauna pledged as she continued her trek across the room. "It's only a matter of time. And he'll make it look like an accident. No. No, he'll do just as he said. He'll hide the body and tell everyone I went away." She threw her hands in the air and moaned, "Oh, Moira, how could I be so stupid? I'm doomed!"

"Ya're crazy, that's what ya are," the Irishwoman argued. "Who's gonna kill ya? And why? What have ya done now?"

Shauna stopped halfway across the room and turned frightened eyes on her maid. "Brad Remington, that's who!"

Moira shook her brown curls, wondering if she understood correctly. "Mr. Remington is planning ta murder ya? How do ya know?"

"He told me! Just now." She rushed to her bedroom window and pointed down at the terrace below. "Out there. Before Papa and Tyler came. He didn't want witnesses. Oh God, Moira, what will I do?"

"Ya'll tell your father, that's what ya'll do."

"Papa?" Shauna laughed a bit hysterically, bright tears shining in her eyes. "Papa wouldn't believe me."

"And why not? You're his daughter. Why would he be thinkin' ya'd make up such a story?"

"Because Brad Remington just asked Papa's permission to court me, that's why." She practically screamed the declaration back at the woman. "If a man asks permission to court a woman, it would mean he's interested in marriage, not that he's planning to kill her! If I told Papa that, he'd laugh in my face."

Even though Moira had never seen her mistress in this state of mind before, she also knew Shauna had a tendency to exaggerate when something wasn't going her way. Gently but firmly, she took Shauna by the arms and pushed her toward the bed. "Sit," she said, shoving her down on the mattress, "and start at the beginnin'. I want ya to tell me everythin', and then I'll tell ya what I think ya should do." Bending, her nose close to Shauna's, she warned, "And don't be leavin' anythin' out to suit your purpose. I'll be knowin' if ya lie to me."

A few moments later Moira was pacing the floor, a frown on her pretty face and a thoughtful look in her eyes as she absently chewed on the thumbnail of her left hand.

"Well?" Shauna finally asked when she thought the woman's endless trek back and forth across the room would never stop. "What should I do?"

"Nothin'," Moira replied, glancing over her shoulder at her.

"Nothing?" Shauna repeated, jumping to her feet. "The man tells me he's going to murder me and you expect me to do nothing?"

128

"And what else can ya do?" Moira challenged. "Ya can't tell your father. Not yet, anyway. Ya'll have to have proof." Turning sharply to face her mistress, Moira asked, "Is he still in the house?"

"Who? Papa?"

"Mr. Remington!" Moira grated out.

Shauna shook her head. "I don't think so. But I'm not sure. Why?"

"Never mind," Moira replied, heading for the door. Once she reached it, she paused with her hand resting on the knob and looked back at the young woman. "Ya stay in your room until I come back."

"Come back? Where are you going?" Shauna demanded, taking several steps forward, then hesitating once she realized that her room was the only place she really wanted to be right now.

"It's best ya don't know," Moira admitted. "Now promise me ya won't go anywhere and that ya won't say a word of this to anyone. Especially your brother. Ya promise?"

Shauna lamely nodded her head, green eyes glistening with unshed tears, her hands clapsed together and clutched to her bosom. The sound of the latch clicking shut behind her maid as Moira left the room seemed to bounce off each vertebra in Shauna's spine. Weak-kneed, she staggered back to the bed and sat down. She had done some pretty foolish things in her life, but never anything so stupid as threatening a man like Brad Remington. With a look of hoplessness on her face, Shauna stared at the closed bedroom door, her mind frantically searching for the right words to say. If she apologized, would he change his feelings toward her?

*   *   *

The distance to Beth Anderson's farm just outside of town could be covered in only a twenty-minute ride on horseback. Trees and dense shrubs lined both sides of the winding dirt road, and only an occasional glimpse of blue sky peeked through the leafy canopy of branches overhead. Brad had traveled this road countless times before, both as a youth on his way home to Wrenhaven with his family, and recently, on the many visits he had paid Beth and her parents since returning to England a few weeks ago. But the trip had never warranted his full attention as it did today. He was being followed, and he had no way of knowing if the man planned to rob him or just spy on him.

After leaving the Radborne house, Brad had decided to look up an old friend and ask a favor of him. Shauna had claimed her father was bent on forcing her to marry Nelson Thorndyke, yet when his name was mentioned at the breakfast table, Pierce Radborne had openly admitted his family didn't like the man. Radborne himself had been noncommittal about his feelings toward Thorndyke, saying only that he had business dealings with him. Brad had learned long ago that a man didn't have to like someone in order to do business with him, but there was something about the situation that sparked his curiosity. And since he planned to marry Shauna, knowing a potential foe's history just might give him the advantage. What really puzzled Brad, however, was Radborne's obvious delight over Brad's request to court his daughter. If he wanted Shauna to marry Thorndyke, why had he been so eager to give his permission to Brad? It didn't make sense for Shauna to lie about it. There was nothing for her to gain by blackmailing a stranger into marrying her. In fact, all she'd be getting out of the arrangement was a husband. He wondered again if she might be in a family way, and it was that thought that prompted him to look for Harrison Roxbury, a childhood friend and now member of London's social elite. Harrison would know more about the Radbornes and Nelson Thorndyke than what Brad could learn about them in a week.

His visit with Harrison proved both satisfying and disappointing. After saying how good it was to see Harrison again and that he hoped they could renew their friendship, Brad had carefully chosen his words when asking his friend's opinion of the Radbornes by telling Harrison that he was interested in Shauna Radborne, but that he knew very little about her romantic involvements. Harrison admitted he couldn't be absolutely sure about the beautiful young woman, but as far as he knew, her name had never been romantically linked to anyone. And her brother, Tyler, seldom let her out of his sight, thus leading Brad to believe that it was highly unlikely that Shauna wanted a husband for any other reason than to please her father. Harrison went on to say that Pierce Radborne was one of the wealthiest businessmen in all of London and one of the most respected—which meant his family was, too. Other than his business friendship with Nelson Thorndyke, Radborne was considered a very intelligent man. When asked why the man's association with Thorndyke would raise a few brows, Harrison revealed his own skepticism about Thorndyke. No one really knew much about the man's past, other than that he had been relatively unknown until about five or six years ago, and that of a sudden he seemed to be a very wealthy landowner. It was rumored that he had lived in the Colonies before and during part of the war, but no one could prove it. And as far as Harrison's family was concerned, however Thorndyke had obtained his wealth, it had to be questionable. But if that were true, then why would Radborne have anything to do with him? Brad had asked him. Harrison had shrugged in response to Brad's observation, saying that if Brad really wanted to know, he'd have to ask Radborne. However, Harrison did admit that Radborne conducted business much the same way as his stepfather had . . . shrewdly. Money was money, no matter whose hand passed it around.

It was well past noon before Brad left Roxbury's house, with the guarantee of having dinner with Harrison very soon. Mounting the stallion he had tied to the hitching rail out front, Brad rode off toward the edge of town on his way to Beth's. He had promised Beth's father that he would help him do some repairs on the barn, then stay for supper as payment and enjoy a few leisurely hours of conversation before returning home. But his purpose had suddenly become something else entirely. He must tell them of his future plans to wed, and reluctantly advise Beth that polite decorum forbid them from seeing each other on a personal level. He hated the thought, but it had to be done, and he hoped Beth would understand once he explained why. Wrenhaven, his very heritage, meant everything to him, and since this was the only way he could see to regain it, he'd take it. A faint smile had parted his lips when he thought of what else he'd be getting in the bargain; a fiery, hot-tempered, manipulative female as his wife. A *spoiled*, fiery, hot-tempered, manipulative female, and he truly liked the package. Underneath all that hostility and ice he was sure he'd find a sensitive, loving woman who would someday let down her guard, and when she did, he'd be there to reap the harvest. The vision of her golden strands of hair, lush curves, creamy white skin and well-rounded bosom flashed into his mind. And God, what a harvest *that* would be! Shauna Radborne had her faults. She was the only woman in his life ever to have so fully trapped him into doing something against his will and to smile victoriously while doing it, but he took up the task as a challenge. She'd soon learn what kind of man she had chosen to snare, and that her well-contrived plan would have some serious penalties for which only she could answer.

Because of the busy streets in town, Brad hadn't noticed the giant of a man following him until a small child darted out into his path, forcing him to haul back sharply on the reins and nearly spin his horse around to avoid trampling the youngster. The result had placed him in clear view of the stranger behind him, and Brad probably wouldn't have given him a second look if it hadn't been for the man's size. He nearly dwarfed the buckskin he rode, and in addition to that, he wore a black eye patch. He was dressed cleanly, his garb that of a peasant. Times were hard for the people of London, and many had resorted to stealing. Brad might only have a few coins in his pocket, but this man didn't know that. If he was determined to rob him, Brad decided his only chance of surviving an attack from a man that size would be if he struck first . . . or lost him. That idea proved impossible almost immediately. The crowded streets never thinned out enough for Brad to maneuver his stallion around a corner, into an alley, and out of sight ahead of the giant, or even to gain distance. If he was to trick the would-be robber, he would have to do it on the open road leading out of town.

Once the way opened up, Brad nudged the stallion into a canter, thinking he could use the same strategy on the road that he had planned back in town. He'd use the cover of trees once he rounded the bend, then hide within the thick denseness until the stranger rode on by. Behind him, Brad would then be able to approach from the rear and club the man over the head before he knew what was happening. All he had to do now was find a broken tree branch large enough to do the job. For a fleeting second he wondered if he'd have the strength to lift one that size.

Up ahead a few yards, Brad could see his first opportunity approaching. The road took a severe turn to the left, around which, he remembered, was a huge rock nestled among the trees. He'd tether his horse deeper in where the man wouldn't see it, then crouch behind the boulder until after his opponent rode past the spot. Once he was clear, Brad planned to spring up on top of the huge piece of granite, plant his feet, and then bounce something off the giant's skull. Enough force behind the blow should render the man unconscious. At least Brad was praying it would. If not, he figured he'd have to contend with the likes of a grizzly whose winter's sleep had been disturbed.

The temptation to look back as he guided his steed around the bend almost took away Brad's advantage. The success of his scheme depended on the stranger's thinking that he wasn't aware of him, and it was that recognition that forced him to keep his eyes trained on the road ahead of him as he listened to the echoing hoofbeats of the second horse closing in on him.

"Moira."

Looking up from the rose bush where she had knelt to cut several of the blossoms, Moira spotted Walter on the terrace waving what she thought was a piece of paper at her.

"A message just came for you," he shouted.

"For me?" she frowned, pushing herself up and laying the long-stemmed flowers in her basket. "Are ya sure?"

"Do we have another Moira Flanagan working here?" he asked a bit sarcastically.

"No," she whispered under her breath as she dusted the soil off her skirts and started toward him. "But your hearin' isn't what it used ta be."

"What? What did you say?" the gray-haired butler called back.

"I said, thank you," she returned, hurrying her step. "Who brought it?"

"A young boy. He said a man paid him to deliver it. A stranger."

Taking the proffered note he handed her, Moira moved away from him to open it. She liked Walter. He was a nice man. But he was also a bit of a snoop.

"What is it, Moira? Trouble?" Walter asked with a frown once he saw the concerned look on Moira's face.

"I hope not," she mumbled, folding the parchment and tucking it in the bodice of her dress as she headed across the terrace toward the side entrance into the house. "I have to run an errand, Walter," she called over her shoulder. "Will ya tell Miss Shauna for me? I shouldn't be long."

"I'll tell her, Moira. But shouldn't you have someone go with you?" he warned, following her inside and pausing at the door to her room while she retrieved her shawl from the armoire. "It's not safe for a pretty woman like yourself to walk the streets these days."

"I'll be all right, Walter. I'm not goin' far, and I won't be gone long," Moira promised, gently touching his cheek with her fingertips as she passed by him on her way to the front hall. "'Tis sweet of ya ta care enough about me welfare ta say so."

"Well, caring won't be enough," he said, draping the shawl over her shoulders and then opening the door for her. "Not if you run into trouble along the way."

"I won't," she assured him, stepping outside and hurrying down the stairs toward the wrought iron gate. Moving through it and out onto the sidewalk, she turned back to wave at him before setting off on her mission.

John Byron lived in a small room above the bakery about five and a half blocks away from the Radborne townhouse. She had made friends with him years ago when he had come to her defense in the alleyway behind the bakery. Ordinarily she wouldn't have taken that shortcut home, but she had been in a hurry and hadn't honestly thought anyone would bother her. She had been wrong. With an armload of pastries and freshly baked breads needed for the last-minute dinner guests who had arrived unexpectedly, it was her misfortune to come across a group of hungry youths in the deserted street. Head down, she had started past them when an arm shot out and caught a handful of her skirts, abruptly delaying her passage and spilling her packages to the ground. Her Irish temper had gotten the better of her then and she had rattled off some not-so-nice metaphors on the way the boys were raised. She had regretted it almost instantly once she saw how angry she had made them and that they had fanned out around her in a wide circle and were about to attack. It was at that moment that John

Byron had stepped out of the back door of the bakery and saw what was about to happen. His appearance more than his angry shouts had scared them off, and Moira knew the second she saw him that they would be friends for a long, long time. And now he had sent word that he needed to speak with her. Had something happened to him? Was John in trouble?

Entering the alleyway, Moira paused long enough to see that it was empty before she hurried toward the back door of the bakery. Upon reaching it, she rushed inside and scampered up the long flight to the door at the top, not hesitating in the slightest to knock loudly on the oak panels.

"John!" she called out. "'Tis me, Moira. May I come in?"

A puzzled frown kinked her brow as the door swung slowly open and she saw her friend sitting at the table across the room from her. Then his sullen expression shifted from her questioning look to something behind the door, and a chill darted up her spine. Her feet frozen to the floor, Moira didn't know if she should concede defeat or turn around and force herself back down the stairs.

"He knows, Moira," John mumbled as he dropped his gaze to his huge hands folded and resting on the tabletop in front of him. "I'm sorry, but he figured it out without my saying anything. You might as well come in."

Before she had the chance to decide for herself, the tall, dark figure standing behind the door moved out where Moira could see him, and her breath caught in her throat. Yet instead of the angry look she expected to see on his handsome face, a half-smile lightened his dark eyes, and his manner was almost playful as he presented her with a low, mocking bow and gestured for her to enter.

"Please join us, Miss Flanagan," Brad instructed lightheartedly. "We have a lot to talk over, and I'd prefer no one else hear about it."

One dark eyebrow raised, Moira challenged bravely and a bit foolishly, "Are ya plannin' ta kill us all in order to keep your secret?"

Brad had expected her to say something like that. "I'm not planning to kill anyone, Miss Flanagan. And if you'll allow me a moment to explain, I'm sure you'll understand how this all got started." He motioned her into the room again.

"All right," she yielded, moving past him to pull out one of the other chairs encircling the table next to John. "Explain." She plopped down on the seat, crossed her knees, folded her arms over her bosom, and glared back at Brad. "But I think I should warm ya. If what ya have to say doesn't convince me, I'll be goin' to Mr. Radborne with the whole truth. I'll see ya lose Wrenhaven for good."

"Fair enough," Brad agreed, "but don't you think it should be discussed privately?" He nodded toward John. "If you're frightened of being alone with me, your friend can wait at the bottom of the stairs."

Moira knew John well enough to be assured he'd lay down his life before he told something Moira had asked him to keep secret, but the fewer who knew about Shauna's impetuous behavior, the better. She jerked her auburn head toward the exit. "Give us a couple of minutes, John." She glared at Brad again. "But be listenin' real close for me ta scream. I'm willin' to admit I don't trust this Colonial."

138

If Moira meant for the title to be an insult, it wasn't. Brad was proud of the years he'd lived in America and that he had fought for her independence. Smiling, he dropped his gaze away from her, the thumb of his right hand idly tracing the scar on his cheekbone while he listened to the sounds of the giant's chair being pushed away from the table and his footsteps bringing him to where Brad stood.

"*Mrs.* Flanagan means a lot to me, Mr. Remington," he warned quietly as he squinted his one good eye at Brad. "You might have tricked me once, but I assure you it will *never* happen again. Harm one hair on her head and I'll kill you for it."

Brad had been threatened before, none of which he ever took too seriously. But of those who challenged him, none of them had even been three-fourths this man's height and build, and Brad suddenly learned a new meaning for the word respect. "She'll not be harmed, Mr. Byron," he pledged in all seriousness. "In fact, if you'll give me a few minutes, you'll hear her laughing, not screaming."

John glared at him a moment longer. "For your sake, you better be right." Then, after glancing at Moira, he stepped into the hall and pulled the door shut behind him.

"How did ya know I was the one who sent him after ya?" Moira asked, curious. "I don't think ya could have beaten it out of him."

"Simple deduction," Brad admitted as he came to sit down in the chair John had vacated. "His message was that I was to forget about any plans I had for disposing of my wife, that there were people who knew about my intentions and who weren't afraid to talk." Leaning forward, he braced his arms against the table and toyed with the ring he wore on his right hand. "Now, since I'm not married, but because I have been considering it, I immediately thought of dear Shauna, my soon-to-be betrothed. Even though we have yet to announce our engagement, I have already fought the urge to strangle her. She is a very trying individual. With that came the recollection of the conversation we had this morning." The faint sparkle in his dark brown eyes disappeared as he stared directly at the woman across from him. "Did she bother to tell you that she's blackmailing me into this, *Mrs.* Flanagan?" he asked, his temper short. "Well, whether she did or not, I'm telling you that I don't like being forced into doing something against my will. And it's bad enough when a *man* does it, but to be trapped in that kind of situation by a conniving woman is far worse! Not only is it humiliating, but it takes away any chance a man might have had in doing something about it. I'm not in the habit of dueling with women." Realizing that he had let his anger get the better of him, he laughed halfheartedly and took a deep breath as he fell back in the chair. "After her visit last night, I'll admit I was furious. What man wouldn't be when a wench dangles his father's property and marriage as a means to have it in front of his nose? I spent the whole night thinking about it—about *her,* and I finally realized how damn dangerous her scheme was." His frustration over the matter renewing itself, Brad left his chair and went to the window to stare outside. "She had no idea what kind of man I was, yet she took the chance anyway. I have to respect her for that. It took a lot of courage. But then she started making threats this morning, and I decided she needed to be taught a lesson, a serious lesson. She needed to know that she can't control people's lives to suit her own. She even got you involved. And now Mr. Byron. That's when I suggested she might have gotten herself in too deep, that once we were married, I'd be the one in control. I didn't mean it. I only said it to prove a point." Grinning, he faced Moira and lazily leaned his shoulder against the window frame. "I guess it worked. A bit too well."

"So ya've changed your mind. Ya won't marry her," Moira guessed, oddly disappointed. She might not know this man all that well, but instinct assured her she could trust him. Besides, she liked his way of thinking.

"No," he said, smiling. "I haven't changed my mind. I want Wrenhaven at any cost." His grin widened. "But after being with her, I don't think it's I who will pay."

The sounds of Moira's laughter echoed down the narrow flight of stairs and brought a surprised look to John Byron's face.

For as long as Shauna could remember, she had always hated thunderstorms. The bright flashes of light and ear-piercing cracks of thunder that rattled the window-panes and shook the whole house would awaken her from a sound sleep as a child. In the dark, she'd call out to her mother for comfort and more times than not Roanna would never answer her. On the rare occasions when she would come to Shauna's room, it wasn't with soothing words, but a reprimand for disturbing her mother's rest. Shauna was a big girl, Roanna would tell her, and five-year-olds shouldn't let loud noises and silly storms frighten them. They didn't frighten anyone else in the house. Fearing more her mother's anger, little Shauna would apologize and then hide beneath the covers until

141

the tempest had passed and she could fall asleep again. But there was one storm Shauna never forgot. It happened on the night after her father had traveled to northern England on business, leaving his wife and young children alone in their townhouse. Shauna and Tyler had been put to bed, and although she was too young to tell time, she knew it was very late when the loud crashes of thunder woke her up. In tears, and thinking her mother couldn't hear her over the turbulence, Shauna had left her bed and scurried down the hall to her parents' bedchambers, delighted by the sounds of a man's laughter mingling with her mother's. Too innocent to understand what was happening, she opened the door without knocking and called out to her mother. The laughter stopped. The man in bed with Roanna hid his face. And her mother's rage sent Shauna fleeing back to her own room.

Years had passed before Shauna was old enough to realize what had been going on that night in her father's bed, but she never spoke of it to anyone, not Tyler, not her mother, and most of all, not Pierce Radborne. It had been her deepest secret, and the reason she had never truly loved her mother. She had learned from that one incident what money really meant to some people, and she had vowed it would never mean that much to her. She would use it to have her way, to unmask those men who pretended they loved *her* and not her father's wealth, and to enjoy her life as she saw fit, but she would never believe a man who pledged undying devotion, even if he did so on bended knee. No one would play her for a fool the way Roanna had done Shauna's father. *If* she married, it would be on her terms, and her husband would *never* have control over her *or* her money.

142

As Shauna stood by the window in her room staring out at the dark shapes of the trees being tossed back and forth in the strong wind, she wondered if that would be the case once she was married to Brad Remington. He seemed more the type to be caught in a married woman's bed rather than the sort to be intimidated by his wealthy wife's demands. And now there was his threat of killing her. A bright flash of light and the ensuing crack of thunder made her jump, and she hugged her arms tighter to her. Moira wouldn't tell her how she planned to insure Shauna's long life, and her offhanded remark about not worrying over it did very little to ease Shauna's fears. She had to have a guarantee, not an empty promise, and she had to be assured Brad Remington understood it *before* her father announced their engagement. And she was sure her father intended to do just that, and very soon. She had seen his reaction to the man. He liked Brad Remington. *Tyler* liked Brad Remington. *Roanna liked him!*

Her stubborn, defiant spirit returned, and she glanced over at the mantel clock sitting above her fireplace. It was well past midnight, and she felt reasonably sure everyone in the household had long since retired—including, and more specifically, Moira. She needed to pay the rogue a visit, alone, without her maid's interference. She was tired of Moira's constant debates and the warning looks the woman always gave her. Besides, this was Shauna's problem. She had gotten herself into it and she'd get herself out. Turning for the armoire, she shimmied out of her nightgown and kicked it aside. She'd show Moira *and* Mr. Remington that *no one* frightened her—not for long, anyway.

By the time Shauna had dressed, sneaked down the

stairs and through the darkened kitchen to the side door, she thought the worst of her journey was over. But once she turned the knob and opened the portal a crack, cold, wet wind came rushing in, and she quickly pushed the door shut again, her heart pounding in her chest. There was no reason for her to be frightened of the storm. It was only a lot of noise and rain, something her mother had always tried to tell her. But maybe it wasn't just the howling wind and icy raindrops that bothered her. Maybe it was her reason for needing to be out in it that truly set her nerves on edge. Shaking off that idea and ignoring the possible forewarning of the thought, she pulled the hood of her cape down over her brow, seized the knob, and yanked the door open.

A few minutes later, Shauna relaxed back in the thickly cushioned seat of the carriage, listening to the steady rhythm of the rain against the roof and the hum of the wheels as they clattered over the cobblestones. She had deliberately roused young Otis from a sound sleep and asked that *he* harness up the carriage. She knew Otis would do just about anything for her, and if she wished it, he'd keep it a secret. Otis liked her and never tried to hide it, and although his attention flattered her, she felt guilty using him. She'd feel even more guilty if her latest scheme didn't work and he had gotten himself soaked to the skin for nothing. In the shadows of the carriage, for she hadn't wanted the lanterns lit, she frowned worriedly as she absently watched the strips of white light periodically seeping in around the edges of the leather window flaps.

The only excuse Brad could give himself for his having

been awakened by the rumbling of thunder was simply that he hadn't been that soundly asleep in the first place. Why he hadn't fallen into deep slumber the second he fell into bed was something he'd never understand, since he had just put in one of the longest, most tiring days of his life. After his visit with Shauna's maid and the woman's henchman, he had taken up his trip to the Andersons' farm, spent an exhausting afternoon tearing down a section of the barn and rebuilding it, relaxed for a while over dinner, and then ridden back to his room at The White Horse again after dark. Every muscle in his body ached, and he had had to pay a handsome price to the innkeeper for the tub of hot water brought to his room. The bath helped ease the soreness from his tired limbs, and once the porcelain tub had been cleared away, he had slipped naked beneath the covers on his bed, intending to doze right off. It hadn't worked out that way. While every inch of his body begged for rest, his mind refused to shut out the events of his day, and the vision of Shauna repeatedly flashed before his eyes.

His talk with Moira wasn't one he ever cared to have to repeat, but now that they had had the opportunity to voice their opinions about Shauna's foolishness, he was glad they had. Moira loved her mistress very much. Brad knew that just by the way she spoke of her. She also wanted Shauna to be happy. Moira didn't know what it was exactly that had set the young socialite against marriage, or more precisely, men, but Moira was sure that once Shauna met the right one, she'd change her mind. A smile parted Brad's lips as he recalled the subtle way Moira had hinted that she felt Shauna had already met him, and how she had looked right at him without batting an eye. Shauna needed a man who wasn't afraid of her, Moira had said, of her wealth or of her father's power. So far the only one who met that requirement was Nelson Thorndyke, and Moira easily admitted she'd rather see Shauna waste away in a convent than marry that man. When he asked Moira why she disliked Mr. Thorndyke, the woman told him that she couldn't honestly explain it—other than the fact that Thorndyke never looked at Shauna with love in his eyes but with lust—the way he did *any* woman who happened to be in his presence. Besides, he was too old! Shauna needed a young, vibrant man, one who could keep up with her.

A blinding flash of light filled his room and vanished, hurting Brad's eyes and bringing him fully awake. Thinking that perhaps the taste of a good cheroot might be enough to make him sleepy again, he flipped off the covers and stood, shivering when his bare feet touched the cold floor. He was surprised by how chilly it had gotten, and instead of reaching for his tin of cigars, he grabbed his breeches off the chair, hurriedly donned them, and then went to the hearth to start a fire. Moments later, a pleasant warmth invaded the room and the amber light from the flames chased away the darkness, and for some odd reason he thought of his brother, Dane. As boys they had shared the same room, the same bed, until Dane had decided he was too old to share *anything* with Brad. He remembered that first night without his big brother there, and that it had rained that night, too. The fire had gone out in the hearth, and rather than summon one of the houseboys to rekindle it, Brad had done it himself. He recalled thinking how grown up he felt at the time, but he also remembered the loneliness of having that big room all to himself—much the same kind of loneliness he was feeling right now. It wasn't that

146

he longed for those days when he and his brother did things together. He was just wishing he had *someone* with whom to share his quiet times. He thought of Shauna again, but no smile graced his lips. She had made her conditions very clear. They would never share the bedchambers with each other.

A knock on the door startled him out of his musings and he jerked his head around. Who would be foolish enough to be out on a night like this, and what was so important that it couldn't wait until morning? He took a tentative step toward the door, intending to answer the summons, and called out for his visitor to identify himself instead.

"A business partner, Mr. Remington," the soft, hypnotic voice replied. "Please. I must speak with you right away."

Brad had assumed Shauna Radborne had pulled just about all the surprises she could manage by now, but this one took him completely off guard. Mindless of his attire, he hurried to the door, turned the key in the lock, and pulled the portal wide, his pulse quickening the instant the firelight enshrouded her. Golden curls spilled from beneath the hood of her cape and fell against a cushion of black cloth. Ivory skin, sensuous pink lips, and the tip of a slim nose peeked out from within the shadows of the enveloping cloak, allowing no further hint of her identity. But Brad knew who she was. Shauna Radborne, the Ice Maiden, the vixen of deceit, his soon-to-be betrothed.

Gathering his wits about him, Brad quickly glanced past her for Moira, surprised and a bit leery to discover that she was alone. He stepped to one side and motioned her in. The sweet fragrance of her loomed out to attack

147

his senses as she passed by, and Brad sucked in a silent breath to calm his quickening heartbeat. Then, with one last look into the hallway to make certain John Byron wasn't lurking in the darkness somewhere ready to rip out Brad's heart for the thoughts racing through his head, he quickly closed the door and faced the woman who had plagued his every waking hour of late.

Beneath the thick folds of her cape, Shauna's entire body trembled. She had expected to disturb his sleep, but she hadn't imagined he'd receive her dressed only in his breeches. Unable to look at him, she went to the window to stare outside at the white flashes of lightning dancing behind the clouds.

"I'd like to say I'm surprised by your visit," she heard him say, the deep, seductive tone of his voice tickling her flesh, "but nothing about you really surprises me anymore."

Biting her lower lip, Shauna took in a long breath to steady her nerves. "We have matters to settle, and since ours is a private affair, I saw no other way to discuss them but here . . . at a time when everyone else is abed." The soft glow of candlelight suddenly filled the dark corners of the room and Shauna found herself wishing he hadn't bothered. She preferred the shadows right now.

"And what matters are those, Miss Radborne? I thought the conditions of our arrangement were settled. Are you saying now that they are not? 'Tis a little late, I féar, since I have already spoken to your father and he's given his consent. If our meeting tonight nullifies our original plans, how will you convince your father that it would be unwise for us to see each other?" He paused a moment waiting for her reply. When she remained silent and continued to stare out the window, he added, "For I, dear lady, have my mind set. I want Wrenhaven, and if marrying you is the only way I can have it, then—"

"I am here, sir, about your threat," she cut in, turning her head to glare at him, the hood of her cape masking most of her face. Noticing that he hadn't elected to don his shirt, stockings, and shoes, she quickly looked outside again.

"My threat, madam?" he asked, puzzled. "What threat is that?"

Mocking laughter trickled from the darkly cloaked figure he watched, and Brad soon realized that the haughty Shauna Radborne had returned. Wondering if the chill he felt radiated from the air or from the woman who shared the room with him, he turned for the armoire and withdrew a shirt from inside, tugging the sleeves up over his shoulders but not bothering to button it. Her attitude provoked him, and rather than yield to social graces—a lady wouldn't come unchaperoned to a man's room, anyway—he donned the garment only for warmth and for no other reason.

"As I recall, you stated your plans to dispose of me once the vows were spoken, thus giving you what you truly wanted from the start: Wrenhaven, free and clear. Free of a wife and clear ownership of the property." To convince him that what she was about to announce was the truth, as well as wanting to see his reaction, she faced him. Yet, her own knees began to shake once her gaze fell upon him. He had moved to the hearth and stood with his arms folded over his wide, half-naked chest, one shoulder pressed against the mantel and his dark eyes locked on hers. Firelight glimmered in his raven-black hair and caressed the strong line of his jaw. His mouth was set in a hard line, and the muscle in his cheek flexed as he gritted his teeth in obvious anticipation of what she planned to say. Certain her voice would crack if she spoke, she averted her eyes and decided to sit down in the rocker next to her. It would give her a moment to collect her courage and cool the strange warmth that had attacked her.

"I am here, Mr. Remington," she said with surprising calm, "to tell you that I have taken precautions to insure my health." She courageously lifted her eyes to his, mentally forcing herself not to look any lower; not at his sensuous mouth; his lean throat; the muscular expanse of his darkly tanned chest; flat belly; snug-fitting breeches that left little to the imagination, or the firm, straight, bare legs and masculine feet. If she failed, she'd be lost. She knew that. "I have written down—at length—the discussion we had this morning at the breakfast table, every detail, every word you spoke. I recorded your desire to have Wrenhaven at *any* cost, and that once you had it, you would do away with the one thing you didn't want—a wife." At his continued silence, and because of the strange look in his dark brown eyes, Shauna decided that she had gained ground. She had his attention, and the knowledge spurred her on. "Most of what I wrote is true. I had planned it that way in the beginning. Then I realized what a devious mind you have, and I decided to add a little twist." Feeling confident now, she smiled back at him as she unhooked the fastenings of her cape, pushed back the hood and dropped the damp garment from her shoulders. "In the event of my death, whoever reads the document will learn that marrying me for Wrenhaven was solely your idea, that *you* approached *me*, and that you threatened to kill my father if I didn't go along with it."

"And you have given this . . . document to a solicitor," Brad finished. "It's not to be opened until your death. Am I right?"

Since there really was no document or the need for a solicitor, Shauna could agree to most anything. And since his observation seemed to bury his chances of changing the future in quicksand, she nodded her blond head and smiled victoriously. "Very astute, Mr. Remington."

"And a bit farfetched, Miss Radborne," he added, pushing away from the mantel and going to the dresser where he picked up his tin of cheroots.

"Farfetched?" Shauna echoed, feeling insulted that he hadn't believed such a . . . a . . . believable story.

"Yes, farfetched," he repeated, striking flint against steel and turning back around to stare at her as he took a long drag on the cigar and exhaled slowly. "And quite unnecessary."

The angry look in his eyes sent a tremor of worry through her. "Why is it unnecessary? You told me—"

"What *did* I tell you, Shauna? Was it fact or fantasy? Was I reciting the future or merely rambling on about the way I wished things could be? I told you then and I'll tell you now, I don't like being threatened."

"Well, neither do I!" she raged, jumping to her feet.

He took another puff on the cheroot and watched her through the gray-white haze of curling smoke. A long silence hung in the air while he twisted around to flick the ash in a glass dish. Then, "If I wanted you dead, Shauna, I certainly wouldn't tell you about it. I'm not that big a fool. I would have married you, murdered you, seen you buried, mourned your death, and then carried on with my life as if you had never existed." His dark eyes

151

raked over her and settled on her face again. "And the last of that, I truly wish was fact."

Her green eyes widened in surprise as she spat, "I beg your pardon?"

"You heard me," he retorted callously. "If it weren't for my turn of bad luck, I would have spoken with your father weeks ago about Wrenhaven—with money in hand. I would have purchased the property and moved in without ever having met his impudent, scheming daughter. I'd be making plans to refurbish the mansion rather than deciding on what friends I should invite to my wedding. And if that isn't bad enough, I'm being blackmailed into it. A business deal is one thing, Shauna Radborne, but what you're doing is very underhanded."

Her pride injured, Shauna raised her nose in the air. "What I'm doing . . . ? It's not blackmail, Mr. Remington, not really. The choice is and always has been yours to make."

"Ah, yes," he chuckled derisively. "And what a choice." Raising the cigar in front of him, he studied it a moment, then turned and snuffed it out in the ashtray. "So tell me, Miss Radborne, what would you do if I suddenly decided all of this wasn't worth it?" he asked, leaning back against the dresser, his arms folded over his chest and his dark eyes locked on hers.

Shauna knew what the answer to that one would be. She'd either be running away or planning her wedding to Nelson. "I'd find someone else," she answered instead, her voice a little shaky and lacking her earlier confidence.

"Some other unsuspecting, poor soul to blackmail," he added with a half smile. "What would you tempt him with this time? Money? A promise of power?" His deep brown eyes slowly traveled the length of her, lingered on her heaving bosom, then moved back to her face. "I'm sure you'd never promise a night of passion. The Ice Maiden isn't capable of such an emotion."

Shauna sucked in a sharp, outraged breath, ready to hurl her denial, and changed her mind. Lowering her chin, she glared back at him. "I know what you're up to, Mr. Remington. You want me to claim that isn't true so you can ask me to prove it. Isn't that right?"

Brad raised one dark brow. "Now quite, Miss Radborne. I hate to shatter your illusions, but I don't find you the least bit attractive. I've already lost a great deal of blood due to the war, and I'm not interested in doing so again." When she opened her mouth to retaliate, he hurried on. "I prefer that the women I bed be loving and gentle, not some sort of sharp-tongued minx."

"Which I'm sure number many," she barked, thinking to insult him and all his past lecherous affairs.

He stared at her a moment, then smiled. "Yes. There have been many. And it's the reason I hesitate to marry you. I rather dislike the idea of giving that up."

She started to tell him that he didn't have to, that that was already a part of their agreement, but he cut her off.

"Tell me, Miss Radborne, have you ever made love?"

Shauna's cheeks flamed a scarlet hue. "Of course not! What do you think I am? One of your harlots?"

Brad decided to let that taunt go unchallenged. "Then perhaps you won't mind a piece of advice. Once you're in bed with your lover, don't tell him what to do and how to do it. If you can, try to relax, and let *him* be the aggressor . . . the way it's supposed to be between a man and woman."

"You're disgusting!" she raged, grabbing for her cape.

"Why? Because I'm not afraid to tell you what's wrong with you? What's the matter, Shauna, does the truth hurt?"

"How would you know what the truth is? You don't know me. You don't know anything about me," she hissed, clutching her cape against her trembling body.

"I know more than you think," he calmly replied.

"Oh?" she snapped. "Like what?"

Unfolding his arms, he pressed the palm of each hand back on the edge of the dresser behind him, and as he did, the silky white shirt he wore fell open, exposing the rock-hard muscles across his chest and lean belly, a sight Shauna had trouble not noticing.

"I know that under all that cool aloofness is the soul of a woman waiting to be tested."

Shauna's upper lip curled. "And you'd like to be the one to try," she dared.

Brad shook his head. "Not really. I don't think I have the energy or the patience."

"Oh, yes," she sneered. "I forgot. You're not attracted to me."

"That's not what I said," he corrected. "If you recall, what I actually said was that I don't find you attractive. But I am, for some odd reason, attracted to you. There's a big difference."

"Would you care to explain it to me?" she mocked, her head tilted to one side. "I'm having a bit of trouble grasping your meaning."

Pushing off from the dresser, he walked by her and went to kneel before the fireplace where he added another log and rekindled the flames. "To be attractive, one must have charm." Rising, he dusted off his hands and turned around. "You don't."

Shauna's spine stiffened. "Thank you very much," she jeered.

"Not that I've seen, anyway," he added with a vague smile. "You haven't exactly been gracious the few times we've been together."

"I've had no reason to be," she countered. "But please, go on with your explanation. You've truly raised my curiosity, and I fear I shan't sleep tonight without knowing how you feel about me."

Any anger he might have felt before vanished with her comment. If anything, Shauna Radborne had a quick wit, and he liked that in a woman. "To attract someone, one must have a certain quality that is appealing. You don't necessarily have to be attractive to attract someone's attention. Do you understand now?"

"I think so," Shauna replied sarcastically. "If I may, I'll use you to demonstrate." She draped her cloak over her arms, folded them against her stomach, and rested her weight on one foot. "In your case, you're handsome, or as you put it, you're attractive. But there's nothing else about you that's appealing. So therefore, I'm not attracted to you." She cocked a tawny brow at him. "Am I right?"

A broad grin stretched his lips, and Brad couldn't stop the laughter that spilled forth. "Pretty close," he relented.

"So what is it about me that attracts you?" she went on, not at all amused the way he was. "My money? Future opportunities you think you might have being married to me? Or the fact that I'm probably the first woman who isn't panting for a chance to lie in bed with you? Although I must admit I'm curious as to what it is exactly that would interest a woman in you."

"*How* curious?" he grinned devilishly.

Shauna released a long sigh, very aware of his offer. "Not *that* curious, thank you." Dropping her gaze away from him, she fanned out her cape and twirled it around her shoulders, preparing to leave "About all I am right now is sorry I came here in the first place."

"Why?" he asked, stepping forward to straighten out the wrinkle of cloth folded back over her shoulder. "Are you afraid of what you might learn?"

His closeness and the warmth his body radiated seemed to touch Shauna everywhere. Not daring to look at him, she concentrated on hooking the silk frog at her neck. "Don't flatter yourself, Mr. Remington. Remember, I'm not attracted to you."

"That's what you say," he murmured, his hands covering hers when she had trouble with the catch. "But I'm having a difficult time believing you. Especially after the last time you were here."

Shauna could feel a strange knot forming in her stomach. Ignoring it *and* him, she stepped past him toward the door. "I think your conceit is nearly as big as your imagination, Mr. Remington. Nothing happened between us the last time I was foolish enough to speak with you alone." She paused near the door and looked back. "You forgot your manners and got fresh with me, but that was the extent of it."

"You slapped my face. I merely retaliated."

"You deserved it."

"You asked for it."

"I did not!"

"You wanted me to kiss you."

"You're mad!"

156

"Then why didn't you fight me?"

"I . . . I did!"

"Not at first. You were enjoying it until you realized you were." A lazy grin spread across his face. "And that wasn't proper. Not for Shauna Radborne, the daughter of a wealthy, respected man of society, a young socialite, the Ice Maiden."

"Stop calling me that!"

"Have you a better name for the way you react to men?"

Shauna straightened her back, raised her chin, and cocked a brow at him. "Well, I certainly can't be called stupid. Men have only one thing on their mind, and I'm smart enough to recognize it."

"Really?" he chuckled. "And what's that?"

Shauna gave him a sarcastic look. "Are you pretending you don't know?"

"I know what's on *my* mind," he grinned roguishly. "But I'd like to hear you say it." The smile disappeared from his lips but it still sparkled in his deep brown eyes. "Just to make sure you're right."

Shauna foolishly saw this as her chance to tell him exactly what she thought of him. "You *want* me to tell you what's going through your mind right now?"

"Yes, I do. Is there a problem with that? I mean, are you afraid to tell me? Or afraid you'll be wrong?"

"Oh, I won't be wrong. I'm just reasonably sure that whatever I say, you'll deny." She shrugged one shoulder. "Therefore, there's really no point in it, is there? Except that you'd know I'm on to you."

The smile returned as Brad crossed his arms over his chest. "Then there will be some benefit. I'll know what you think of me."

157

"Which isn't much," she spat, taking up the challenge. "First of all, you're conceited. You think because of your handsomeness that any and all women should fall madly in love with you. *That* was your first mistake with me. I'll admit I might have taken a second look had Tyler not inadvertently warned me about you there at Sir Blakely's. Yet even so, it wouldn't have taken me long to figure you out. What puzzles me is why you've hesitated in accepting my *business* deal. Your kind is after wealth first. Any extras you might get in the process are appreciated, but not necessary. In our case, *I'm* the something extra. You see me as something to be conquered. Because of your ego and my resistance to you, you've taken up the quest to win my . . . affections, shall we say? I sincerely doubt it would mean anything to you *if* you were to succeed, other than having another name added to your list. So you've started by insulting me, calling me the Ice Maiden, thinking I'll become outraged enough to prove you wrong." She narrowed her green eyes at him and jutted out her chin. "But don't hold your breath waiting," she warned. "I don't have to prove it to you or to myself. I know what I am. Or I should say, what I'm not." She squared her shoulders and continued. "As for what's going through your mind right now, that's simple." She moved closer to him, almost saunteringly. "You'd like to kiss me. You'd like to wrap your strong, firm arms around me and pull me against your bare chest. You'd like to entwine your fingers in my hair, feel its texture, smell my perfume. You'd like to brush your warm lips along my throat and nibble on my earlobe. You'd like to drive me wild with passion." She stood only inches from him now, positive that she had guessed correctly and that each added illustration had struck home, that she had stirred his blood, his desire, and that out of pride, he couldn't— *wouldn't* yield to them. With a seductive smile curling her lips, she lifted soft green eyes to gaze into his. "You'd like to strip my clothes from me and carry me to that bed." She jerked her head in its direction but kept her gaze securely fixed on his face. "But what you'd really like is for me to do all those things to you." Reckless, she raised one hand and lightly traced the steely ripples of flesh over his ribs where the shirt fell open. "It would be a true victory for you if that happened." She raised up on tiptoes, her lips close to his. "Wouldn't it, Brad? Admit it. Tell me the truth. Tell me you find me attractive *and* you're attracted to me," she whispered, feeling the warmth of his breath against her face. A bit cocky and absolutely sure he'd rather die than surrender, she ran her hands up over his chest and slid the white, silky garment off his shoulders. "Should I start here?" she teased, lightly kissing his chin. "Or here?" Her lips moved to his throat. "Why don't you tell me to stop, Brad? Tell me I'm wrong."

Suddenly and shockingly, his arms encircled her, crushing her to his massive, naked chest and taking her breath away.

"You're not," he replied huskily, his open mouth swooping down to capture hers.

Shauna instantly knew her stupidity in tempting fate, in tempting *him!* This was what he had planned all along! He had tricked her! Struggling furiously to break his hold on her, she managed only to tear free the fastening on her cape. The garment slid from around her and Brad quickly flung it away, then trapped the back of her head in his wide hand, while he slanted his mouth across hers and thrust his tongue inside, his other hand pressed firmly to the small of her back and pulling her hips against his hardened frame. His desire was quite evident, and Shauna's entire being rebelled. She tore her lips from that burning kiss.

"Stop! Stop right now!" she panted breathlessly, startled and even a little fearful of the strange sensation coursing through her. No man had ever stirred more than her disdain, and this man more than any other deserved all she could give. Yet when his moist lips found the sweet, fragrant spot of flesh beneath her ear, her demand that he cease, her desire that he cease disappeared, and she closed her eyes, moaning softly. His mystical power engulfed her, left her weak and craving his touch. Even the storm outside the room, which hadn't eased its assault against glass and stone, lost its talent for frightening her, indeed, it took no place in her thoughts at all, for she had been lured above all earthly happenings to a world unknown to her. She forgot her dislike of men, their lies, her distrust. Her body turned against her vow of chastity, and without the will to bring an end to her wanton desires, Shauna turned her head to eagerly accept his kiss.

Brad sensed the change in her almost at once. What had started out a game suddenly became reality, and while his conscience warned him to take heed, that there would be a greater price to pay, his desires raged uncontrollably within him. The smell of her, her silken skin, the feel of her slender frame molded against him were too much for him to pretend they didn't affect him. He wanted her as he never wanted any other woman in his life, and if he regretted it on the morrow, then so be it, for tonight she was his, wholly and without guilt. He would teach her passion and tenderness, and that the titillating rapture of her secret dreams was as it should be, that she had nothing to fear. He would guide her, instruct her, and lead her to a heavenly sphere she would long remember and desire again. His hands slipped to the button up the front of her dress. But more important, when she thought of this night and the passion she had experienced, she would also think of him.

Her mind reeling with confusion, Shauna only slightly felt his long, lean fingers unfastening the bodice of her dress or the warmth of his touch as he slipped the garment off her shoulders. Yet once the yards of cloth and white petticoats pooled at her feet and cool air brushed against her flesh, she broke loose of his searing kiss and pressed her open hands against his thickly muscled chest, the crisp dark curls tickling her palms as she looked into his face.

"Brad . . ." she whispered. "I . . ."

"Hush," he murmured against her lips. "I won't hurt you." His pledge seemed to ease her troubled thoughts, yet he knew he must be gentle with her, for he doubted a few stolen kisses could compare with or have readied her for what was to come. Cupping her face in his large hands, he sweetly brushed his lips against hers while he fought the urgent cravings of his body.

Shauna eagerly, passionately welcomed his kiss as their hunger for each other turned hot and demanding. Her pulse raced. Every inch of her flesh burned. Her heart thundered in her ears, and beneath her fingertips she could feel the frantic beating of his own. They no longer played games. He wanted her, and more surprisingly, she wanted him. Slipping her arms around him, a delicious moan escaped her when his mouth followed the long, slender column of her throat to a creamy white shoulder where he nibbled on her flesh. His lean brown fingers worked loose the satin laces of her chemise and freed the ivory breasts from their restraints, and Shauna let her head fall back, the thick mane of golden hair cascading earthward in a brilliant torrent as his kisses trailed a hot path to a rose-colored peak, his tongue teasing, his teeth nibbling softly and her passion mounting rapidly. His wide hands caught her around the waist and held her steady as he sampled the second treasure he had found, claiming it with his open mouth to suck greedily, while her fingers entwined themselves in the thick mass of his dark hair as if to guide him and hold him close.

Impatient now to have her, Brad raised up and swept her delicate form into his powerful arms, carrying her to the bed where he bent his knee upon the mattress and gently fell with her upon its feathery softness. He rolled her beneath him, his mouth covering hers, and their kisses became savage and fierce, his hand caressing her naked breast, her nails raking the wide, hard expanse of his back. Their breathing quickened, their passion ran high, and for a brief moment, Brad left her to shed his breeches and strip away her lacy camisole. A long, sensuous while passed as he hungrily feasted upon the beauty of her nakedness: her full, ripe breasts; the perfect curves of her hips and waist; the long length of her willowy legs; the gleaming white skin; and the lust burning in her eyes. Towering over her, he parted her trembling thighs with his knee and slowly lowered himself down, his hands braced on either side of her head, his lips parted and expectant of the kiss.

The flickering light of the candle on the bedside table

danced alluringly over Brad's handsome face, enhancing his bronze complexion and vividly accentuating the gleaming muscles of his shoulders, chest, and arms. The masculine scent of him, his rugged good looks, and the dark, lustful gleam in his brown eyes turned Shauna's blood to fire. Her body thrilled at the expectation of him pressed against her, of his manhood, hot and hard, thrusting deep within her, and of the sense that they would be as one. Innocent of the pleasures to be had, yet eager to learn, her womanly instincts took over, and while she studied his face, his parted lips, the passion burning brightly in his dark eyes, she ran her hands over the sinewy breadth of his shoulders and chest, across the flat belly to his muscular sides and lean hips, digging her nails in the hard flesh of his buttocks as she pulled him down against her. Their lips met in a searing kiss, tongues clashed, pulses raced. His hands roamed the full length of her, then cupped one breast, his thumb stroking its peak while Shauna explored the rigid muscles in his back and across his shoulders, her legs coming up to encircle him. The manly boldness of him touched the soft flesh of her womanhood, teasing, tempting, throbbing urgently, and Shauna arched her hips. A fiery wave of pain shot through her once his probing staff hit its mark, and she gasped, her body stiffening.

"It will pass," he whispered tenderly, his kisses trailing to her throat as he held her close, and before her denial had formed in her mind, a warmth began to spread deep within her, reigniting the fires of passion and spurring her on. Their bodies met in the wild frenzy of love, moving, arching, soaring to new heights as he thrust his manhood deep inside her. His open mouth sought hers, and he responded to her urgent need to be as

163

one, almost savagely. Shauna lost all sense of existence as the raging fire within consumed her, lifting her ever higher to greater, hotter plateaus, scorching her mind, her thoughts, her very being, until an explosion of chilling rapture turned her world upside down, and she was left to float earthward on the wings of fulfillment and breathless ecstasy.

Slowly, delightfully, the heavenly bliss she had experienced began to fade, its enveloping arms settling her upon a cushion of feathery softness, and the warm glow she was feeling ebbed. Drunk with pleasure, she closed her eyes, murmuring inaudible words and snuggling close within the protective circle of her lover's embrace. She could hear the steady beating of his heart, and felt his body tremble with his contented sigh, sounds that pleased her and brought a smile to her lips. Warm firelight bathed their naked bodies in its golden aftermath and glistened against their moist flesh, and Shauna silently marveled at the rapturous peace she had found locked in a man's arms. A devilish grin parted her lips.

"'Twould seem my scheming rogue, that you have won," she breathed, pushing herself up to roll on top of him. "As I'm sure was your plan from the start."

Laughter rumbled deep in his chest. "Ah yes, so I have," he beamed, lifting a stray curl from her brow. "And no greater victory can any man claim. I have changed the Ice Maiden to a fiery little vixen who clawed and scratched my back and begged for more."

"I did not," Shauna giggled. "Perhaps your imagination has gotten the better of you."

His dark eyes looked long and hard into hers, and a soft smile played upon his lips. "If this was only a dream, I hope I never wake up," he murmured, kissing the tip of her nose, then hungrily claiming her mouth again.

A distant crack of thunder and bright flash of light reminded Shauna of the time and that young Otis was still waiting for her outside in the rain. Reluctantly, she broke away from Brad's sensuous kiss and reached for her underthings.

"I must go," she sighed. "My driver's waiting, and I fear I've been too long already for him to think pure thoughts of me."

Bracing himself up on one elbow, his head cradled in his hand and the comforter draped over his bare hips, Brad watched her dress and fought with the desire to pull her back in bed with him. She was, indeed, the most beautiful woman he had ever seen, and the thought of her being his wife truly pleased him. What they had shared this night was only the beginning. Once they were married, there would be no walls separating them. They would be husband and wife in every sense of the word. A thought struck him and he chuckled.

"Please, sir," she teased, turning a playful frown his way. "Do not make my situation any worse than it is by laughing at me. If you were in my place, I'm sure you'd find little to amuse you. And I am cursed twofold. If God smiles on me, I might be able to hide this from my father, but Moira is a different matter entirely. She will know the instant she looks at me."

"You misunderstand," he grinned, his eyes drinking in the last sight of long, willowy legs before she stepped into the circle of petticoats and raised them to her waist to fasten them. "I was thinking of our bargain."

The pleasing warmth that had enveloped her and the smile that graced her lips slowly waned. She stared at him a moment, then reached for her dress and quickly donned it, hooking the buttons up the front in record time. "What about it?" she asked quietly, eyes averted. She sensed she wasn't going to like his answer.

"Only that your conditions have changed somewhat. There won't be a need for separate bedrooms anymore."

The color of Shauna's eyes turned an icy emerald. The thought had crossed her mind, but the decision was hers to make, not his. "Oh really?" she baited, nostrils flaring slightly. "And why do you say that?"

"Surely you jest?" he exclaimed with a half-smile and a frown wrinkling his brow. "You wanted a marriage in name only, and although we have yet to speak the vows, you must admit we've rather altered that part of the deal."

"Because you say we have?"

Brad's puzzlement increased. Grabbing the comforter, he wrapped it around his lanky frame and left the bed. "I'm not ashamed to admit I haven't the vaguest inkling of what you mean. Are you saying this changes nothing?"

When he moved to stand close to her, Shauna whirled away to retrieve her cape from the floor and toss it over her shoulders. "What I'm saying is that it's *my* choice to make. If I want a marriage in name only, then that is how it shall be," she snapped, hooking the catch at her throat and flipping the hood up over her head.

"Oh, for God's sake, Shauna," he groaned irritably. "You're not serious?"

"Quite," she answered with a haughty toss of her head. "One of the main reasons I never wanted to get married in the first place was because I resent the idea of being told what to do. Another was that I refuse to allow a man to think that he could snap his fingers and expect me to jump in bed anytime the urge struck him. *I'd* be the one to deal with the consequences, not him."

"You mean children," Brad guessed, his temper sorely tested.

"Yes, children." She gave him a long, hard look, her scalding gaze raking him from the top of his tousled head to his bare feet and back. "At least I won't have to worry about that part of it with you." She turned to leave.

"Think again, Shauna," he snarled, his stinging words stopping her cold just as she reached out a hand for the doorknob.

The color drained from her face, she spun back around. "What?" she breathed, her horror etched clearly in her expression.

"I believe I made myself perfectly clear," he rallied as he went to the dresser to relight the cheroot he had laid in the ashtray.

"But you said—"

"I said I had no sons or daughters I could claim as my own. I never said there wasn't a possibility." He took a long drag on the cigar, exhaled a puff of white smoke, and then focused his angry gaze on her. "But for both our sakes, I hope this union hasn't produced any offspring. I certainly wouldn't want to force you to do something against your will."

Too numb even to think much less reply, she simply stood there, her chin sagging, her breathing shallow and tears threatening to spill down her cheeks. What had she done? *What had he done?* This couldn't be. Everything she had worked so hard to achieve, her plans, her scheming all for naught. And now this . . . this awful chance that she might be carrying his child! A sob choked her, and she lifted glistening eyes to look at him. The cold, unfeeling expression on his handsome face tore at her heart and clearly told her that she would find no sympathy in him. Shauna's willful spirit surged anew. Yea, perchance she was with child. But then again, perhaps not. And since when did she look upon the dark side of life? She was, after all, a gambler at heart. She had played her hand, raised the stakes, and had nothing more to do but sit back and wait. Besides, the odds were in her favor. If he had lied once, he could be lying now. With chin held high, she cast him an arrogant look and proudly left his room.

The anger crimping Brad's brow deepened as he stared at the empty doorway. The little minx deserved everything she got—and if it weren't for Wrenhaven, he'd speak with her father first thing in the morning and tell him that he'd changed his mind about courting her. No man with any brains would deliberately walk into a marriage with her, and certainly not with his eyes wide open. Living with her promised to be pure hell! In a rage, he jammed the cheroot into the ashtray, went to the door, slammed it shut, and locked it, and then threw himself into bed, growling when the comforter seemed purposely to tangle itself around his legs.

"Damn!" he howled, ripping it from him and hurling it to the floor. "And damn Shauna Radborne!"

Suddenly drained of his energy, he fell back against the pillow and stared idly up at the ceiling overhead, the lingering fragrance of her perfume invading his senses. A moment passed before his mood softened and a slow smile parted his lips.

Chapter Six

"I think you should know, Marcus," Lucas Billingsly admitted over the rim of his teacup, "that I heard a bit of news today I don't think you're going to like."

Dark brows came together sharply over Marcus's brown eyes. Billingsly had a knack for annoying him, and the little scarecrow of a man was doing it now. "Then why not tell me and get it over with?" he grated out, his warning very clear in the tone of his voice.

"All right," Lucas consented, not at all bothered by his companion's obvious irritation. "It seems Miss Radborne has a suitor interested enough in her to ask Pierce's permission to court her. I'd say ol' Nelson took too long to make his move, wouldn't you?"

Motioning for the servant to clear away his breakfast dishes, Marcus waited until he and Billingsly were alone again before he leaned forward against the table with his hands wrapped around his teacup and his dark eyes locked on his companion. "And why is it *I* haven't heard about this?"

Lucas chuckled and set aside his cup to dab at the corner of his mouth with his napkin. "Simple, my good man. You and I travel in different circles."

Marcus's eyes narrowed. "Not for long, I guarantee you. If all goes as planned—"

"Well, it isn't," Billingsly cut in. "*Nelson* was to marry Miss Radborne. Now that's rather impossible."

Marcus's huge frame stiffened. He didn't like Lucas Billingsly. He was cocky and offered a constant threat. "And I say you've been listening to gossip." Lifting his teacup, he added, "It seems to be the only thing you're really good at—listening to and spreading gossip."

Lucas shrugged off the barb. "I'd hardly call it gossip when I heard it from Miss Radborne's own brother." Knowing that would change his friend's attitude, Lucas deliberately averted his eyes and reached for the snuff box he carried in his waistcoat pocket. He popped open the lid, dotted a pinch of tobacco on the back of his hand, and held it close first to one nostril then the other, inhaling sharply. He always preferred snuff to a smelly old cigar, and detested men who chose the latter . . . including Marcus Deerfield. He settled pale blue eyes on his companion.

"Who's the man?" Marcus asked, his voice low and crackling with rage.

Lucas purposely took his time touching the tip of his lacy white handkerchief to his nose. "His name is Brad Remington."

"Remington," Marcus repeated thoughtfully. "There used to be some Remingtons living near London years ago, but I don't—"

"Same one," Lucas interrupted. "In fact—and you'll love this—Brad Remington's family used to own Wrenhaven. After the old man died, his sons sold the property to Radborne through a proxy and left England for the Colonies. From what I gather, Remington has returned here with the sole purpose of regaining ownership."

"By marrying Shauna," Marcus finished, the muscle in his cheek flexing and his brown eyes snapping fire.

"Well, Tyler didn't say that. He seems to think Remington is truly interested in his sister and not for the property her father owns." Enjoying how angry his announcement had made Marcus, Billingsly added, "But it certainly is cause to raise a brow, don't you think?"

A huge fist smashed against the tabletop, rattling the silver teapot, sugar, and creamer, and nearly toppling Lucas's teacup. "Damn!" Marcus raged. "One isn't good enough without the other!"

Thinking that perhaps he'd step too far if he continued to goad Marcus, Billingsly remained quiet for a spell until some of Deerfield's anger had ebbed. "So what will you do, Marcus?" he asked quietly. "You can't have Remington killed. It will draw too much attention, and it wouldn't insure that Miss Radborne would then marry Nelson." He reached for his teacup. "She hates Nelson Thorndyke, you know."

A wide, powerful hand shot out and caught Billingsly's thin wrist. "Then she'll have to get over it, won't she?" Deerfield snarled.

Tears of pain springing to his eyes, Lucas held perfectly still, fearing Marcus would break the tiny bones he crushed between his fingers. "But how, Marcus? How will you get Miss Radborne to change her mind? She's very headstrong, you know. She gets it from her mother."

"That bitch!" Marcus growled, releasing his cohort's arm with a healthy shove that knocked over Billingsly's cup and spilled hot tea across the white tablecloth and into Lucas's lap. "I should have disposed of her the way I did your uncle."

Frantically blotting the scalding liquid from his ivory-colored silk breeches with a napkin and biting back the desire to cry out, Lucas felt his temper flare. "Shhh!" he demanded, his gaze darting to the doorway of the room. "Do you want someone to hear? You know the servants have their doubts about me as it is."

"They don't like you, Lucas," Marcus sneered. "Their loyalty was, is, and always will be with Edgar."

"Well, your presence here doesn't help any," Lucas snapped. "They like you even less. *I* don't like you."

An evil, sinister smile parted Marcus's lips. "Are you thinking to hurt my feelings by telling me that, Lucas, ol' boy?" Deerfield challenged. "Well, you're not. I don't care who likes me, least of all you. I needed you, and that's the *only* reason you are where you are today." He leaned closer, his arm resting on the edge of the table as he glared back at Billingsly's frightened blue eyes. "You had better be a little more careful with your thoughts, Lucas. Remember, I'm still holding several of your notes, and if I wanted to, I'd see you blamed for your uncle's death."

"You . . . you wouldn't dare," Billingsly countered nervously. "You still need my help. I'm—I'm the only one who can get to Radborne."

Smiling broadly, Marcus crumpled up his napkin and threw it on the table as he rose. "Yes, that's true, *friend*. But don't let it go to your head. I created this position for you, and I could easily do it for someone else—someone who *likes* me." Deep laughter rumbled in his massive chest at the horrified look on Lucas's face. "And in the process, my new partner would see you share a prison cell

172

with Radborne. Wouldn't that be fitting? Two thieves sitting side by side and chasing off the rats nibbling on their toes." Amused by the vision he'd conjured up, Marcus threw back his head and laughed loudly as he turned to leave. "Good day, Lord Billingsly. I hope it's pleasant."

"And I pray you've met your match in Brad Remington," Lucas mumbled low enough that Deerfield wouldn't hear. "And I wish I had the courage to warn him about you, to warn Radborne. And I pray Miss Radborne marries the man before you can do anything about it."

"Pierce, I thought you knew how I felt about Shauna," Nelson Thorndyke rasped, the deep lines in his brow furrowed in an indignant frown.

"Yes, I did, Nelson," Radborne nodded as he closed the study door and sealed in their privacy. He motioned for the man to sit down in one of the wing chairs before the hearth, then crossed to the wine decanter sitting on his desk and poured too glasses full of the rich red liquid. Goblets in hand, he came to stand beside Thorndyke and held out a glass for him to take. "And I have nothing against that, Nelson," he assured him as he sat down in the chair next to Thorndyke's. "But Shauna has never shown any interest in you."

"And she has in this Remington fellow?" Nelson jeered. "Pardon me for saying so, Pierce, but until this morning, I'd never heard of Brad Remington. How can you say she's interested in him when they've probably not even met?"

"That's not altogether true. They met at Sir Blakely's

party the other night."

"Once? They met once?" Nelson's thick shoulders slumped. "Really, Pierce, I thought you took as much care with your daughter as you do your business affairs."

Pierce couldn't stop the smile that parted his lips. "I do," he argued softly. "A lot of my dealings are done on instinct, and I have to admit that's why I gave Brad my permission to court Shauna."

"On instinct?" Nelson exclaimed. "You're trusting your daughter with a man you don't even know?"

Taking a sip of his wine, Radborne relaxed back in his chair. "That's true to some degree, but not entirely. You see, Tyler met a young woman a few weeks ago, and because my son is somewhat impulsive, I decided to check up on her. It turns out she is a friend of Brad's, and in doing a little research on her, I also found out a few things about Brad."

"Enough to feel comfortable with his seeing Shauna?" Nelson challenged angrily. "Please excuse me for butting into your affairs, but what has this Remington character got to offer Shauna? Who is he? Where did he come from? There's no Remingtons around London."

"Not now, but there used to be," Radborne declared. "The name was familiar to me the moment I heard it, but for some reason I didn't make the connection. I suppose it's because I had never met Brad or his brother, Dane." He smiled openly at the confused look on his companion's face. "Fifteen, maybe even twenty years ago, my solicitor approached me with the chance to buy a very large estate. The gentleman who had owned it had died and his heirs wished to sell it. The property had a good-sized stream running through it, an exceptionally fine manor house, lots of trees, nice grazing land, and several acres of good

174

crop land. I bought it without a second thought. It belonged to a man named Aric Remington."

"Brad Remington's father," Nelson guessed.

"Yes."

"And now he's back hoping to regain ownership?" Nelson added, a dark brow cocked suspiciously.

"He hasn't said anything about it to me."

Nelson took a drink of his wine and stared into the dark fireplace, silent for several minutes. "Well, Pierce, I'll admit I did some investigating myself once I heard the news. The property you mentioned is Wrenhaven. And Brad Remington, a traitor to England these past several years, has returned here to London for one purpose, and it isn't to find a wife. He's here to buy back Wrenhaven." His dark brown eyes settled on Radborne. "But he's obviously got you thinking he's interested in Shauna." Nelson sat erect in the chair and twisted around to face his companion. "Did you also learn that Brad Remington hasn't a single coin in his pocket? Everything he owned sank in the Atlantic off the coast of Torquay; his ship, most of his crew, and all of the goods he had planned to sell along with the frigate. From what I understand, all he saved was what washed up on shore the next day. You're an exceptionally intelligent man, Pierce Radborne, but when it comes to your daughter, you're as blind as a sightless old man. He's not interested in Shauna. Not in the way you'd like to believe. He wants Wrenhaven, and to have it, he'll marry Shauna."

A faint smile parted Pierce's lips, and he took a sip of his wine. He was well aware of Brad's true reason for returning to London. He'd have had to be a fool not to have figured it out. Maybe Brad really only wanted Wrenhaven and saw Shauna as a way to have it, but

175

Pierce liked Brad. Tyler did, too, and that was more than he could say about Nelson Thorndyke. Nelson called him blind. Pierce felt a better word would be shrewd. The Remingtons had a fine reputation around London, and as for Nelson's claim that Brad was a traitor, that wasn't wholly correct. He might have fought against England in the war, but the results of the conflict had brought a few changes here, as well. King George was already losing a little of his power to William Pitt, the prime minister, and the wealthy landowners of London were beginning to share their influence in Parliament with a new class of society, the wealth of which lay primarily in industry, rather than in land. Pierce had seen it coming and was already making plans. Wrenhaven was an ideal place to build a factory, and Brad Remington was the man to do it. His lack of funds would make him hungry, and Pierce would finance his new son-in-law. They'd be partners, and Shauna would be wed.

"Perhaps you're right, Nelson," he finally said aloud. "Maybe Brad is only after Wrenhaven, but he'll have to marry Shauna to have it." He quickly raised a hand to silence Nelson when the man started to reply. "At one time the Remingtons were quite wealthy, and I'm sure if Aric's sons had stayed in London, they'd be richer than you and I put together. I'm sure Brad will be again. He had a bit of bad luck, but I doubt it'll keep him down. In fact, I'm sure of it. If he sees marrying Shauna as a way to have Wrenhaven, then he's smart enough to rebuild his empire." Finishing off his wine, he stood. "And I intend to help him."

The color in Nelson's face and neck had darkened. "But what about me, Pierce?" he objected angrily as he came to his feet and followed Radborne to the desk. "I care for Shauna. I have plenty of money. I have power and land. *I* don't *need* your help."

Pierce didn't want to hurt Nelson's feelings by telling him the truth, but he knew it had to be said. "The problem is, Nelson," he advised softly, "that Shauna doesn't like you. Now, you know her well enough to realize she'd do just about anything to have her own way, and if I told her she *had* to marry you, it wouldn't surprise me if she ran away." He rolled his eyes. "Or, God forbid, joined a convent." He shook his head and set down his glass. "I'd pity the poor nuns who had to deal with her rebelliousness," he added offhandedly.

"That's all well and fine, Pierce," Nelson cut in. "But I think you're forgetting something."

Radborne raised a brow questioningly.

"There's no guarantee she won't do the same thing, if you tell her she must marry this Remington character. Let's face it, Shauna is still unwed because she likes it that way. Her only real interest lies in the gaming tables, which, I might add, she's quite good at. *If* she marries Remington, that part of her life will have to stop, and you know it. *She'll* know it once she finds out he hasn't the money to buy—" A thought struck him and he straightened sharply. "Wait a minute. Are you telling me that you're planning to *give* him Wrenhaven—"

"As Shauna's dowry."

"But Pierce," Nelson strongly objected. "You know I've been wanting to buy that piece of property! Now you're willing to *give* it away?"

Radborne nodded. "To my daughter and her new husband."

Nelson's huge frame began to shake. His dark brown eyes snapped with fury. "Damn you, Radborne," he

177

exploded, seizing Pierce's shirt front in his hand and yanking him close. "You can't do this!"

Radborne's own temper boiled. "Take your hand off me, Nelson, before you regret this outburst," he snarled through clenched teeth, his nose inches from Nelson's.

The threat was enough to startle Nelson out of his rage. The fire disappeared from his eyes, the color in his face paled, and his fingers instantly let loose of Radborne's shirt. "I-I'm sorry, Pierce. I don't know what got into me. I-I've never done anything like this—please, forgive me." In a desperate attempt to make amends, he tried to straighten the ruffles at Radborne's throat, but Pierce brushed his hands aside and moved away before he could. "Please, Pierce," he begged. "I apologize. It's . . . it's just that I care about Shauna, and to hear that you've given permission for someone else to court her and that you intend to give her Wrenhaven as her dowry . . . well, it was just too much. I lost my head. Please. Say you understand."

"Oddly enough, I do understand," Radborne admitted with a heavy sigh as he crossed to the door and opened it. "And if you don't mention this again, neither will I." He jerked his head toward the hall. "I was about to have lunch. Care to join me on the terrace?"

Relief flooded Nelson's face and a smile lit up his brown eyes as he hurried across the room and stepped out into the corridor. "Will you at least allow me to try to persuade Shauna that I'd be a good choice for her?" he asked weakly as he watched Radborne pull the door shut behind them. "I promise not to hound her, and if she tells me outright that she'd prefer I leave her alone—"

"Yes, Nelson, you're welcome to try," Radborne laughed. "But don't be too disappointed in her answer."

Slapping the man on the back in a good-natured gesture of empathy, Pierce guided his companion toward the terrace. He could sympathize with the man's infatuation with his daughter. Shauna had a way of stealing a man's heart without really trying, and Nelson Thorndyke wouldn't be the first to walk away with a bruised ego. Besides, he always enjoyed watching two men battle wits, and Brad Remington was sure to give Thorndyke a contest he would never forget. Pleased with the prospect, he smiled to himself as he held out a hand for Nelson to go ahead of him through the double set of doors leading to the terrace, when another thought hit him. The smile disappeared and his steps slowed as he gave the idea consideration. Maybe, just maybe . . . he shook his head and mentally shrugged off the possibility. He was sure Brad wouldn't have any trouble whatsoever in winning Shauna over.

A new worry plagued Shauna's mind. Nearly a week had passed since her disastrous meeting with Brad, and he had yet to call on her. Her father didn't seem too upset about it, and Moira never mentioned it. But Shauna feared their last words to each other had changed Brad's mind and he was off somewhere right now working deals to obtain the money he needed to buy Wrenhaven rather than marry her for it. And then there was Nelson Thorndyke. It seemed, of late, that the man was always there whenever Shauna turned around: in the house, at dinner, in her father's study, at parties, in the shops, and on the street, always smiling at her, trying to draw her into conversation and sending gifts. He behaved more like the man who was supposed to be courting her than

Brad did, and she feared her father's attitude toward him would change. And now this. He had finagled himself an invitation to dinner at Sir Harold Winegar's home.

Sitting before her dressing table mirror, Shauna stared solemnly at her reflection while she listened to Moira hum a bright little tune as if the woman hadn't a care in the world and was totally unaware that her mistress did. Moira always was a happy person, but lately she seemed to be caught up in some sort of secret, one she wasn't willing to share. Yet whenever Shauna asked her why she was exceptionally cheery these days, Moira would deny that she was. Perhaps it only appeared that way because Shauna had nothing to smile about and to see someone else happy grated on her nerves. Shauna would object to her maid's evaluation, and they'd usually wind up arguing the point, but once tempers cooled, Shauna inwardly had to admit that Moira was probably right.

"Will Tyler be goin' with ya tonight?" Moira asked as she pulled Shauna's thick hair back off her face with a ribbon and styled it in long ringlets down her back.

"No," Shauna grumbled. "And I wish he was. He'd see to it that I didn't have to talk to Nelson."

Turning away, Moira hid her smile as she went to the bed to gather up Shauna's petticoats. "Is it fair to guess he's seein' Miss Anderson tonight instead?"

"Yes. And it's also fair to say Papa will probably have last-minute affairs to take care of and thus leave Mother and me alone to attend Sir Winegar's dinner party." She curled her lip at the image staring back at her in the mirror. "Which means I'll have to fend for myself. You know how Mother likes to flirt, and I'd be in her way. I like Harold and Cornelia, but with Nelson in attendance and me all by myself, it promises to be a horrible evening." She slid around on the bench to look at her maid. "I wish there was some way I could take you along."

"Me?" Moira laughed. "Now wouldn't that be proper?" She motioned for Shauna to stand and helped her step into the petticoats.

"Well, I don't think the Winegars would object, and you know how much I detest doing what's proper."

"Like askin' a man ta marry ya?" Moira chided with a lifted brow.

Being reminded of that little indiscretion also brought a vivid picture of Brad to her mind's eye—the way the firelight gleamed against his bronze skin, his ripply muscles, the comforter draped around his lean hips—and she could feel a blush rising in her cheeks. Her trip home that night had been uneventful, and neither she nor Otis had been missed. The next day, however, the young boy had been too sick to get out of bed, and his illness only added to Shauna's uneasiness. She was to blame for his ill health. She had made him wait outside in the rain while . . . The heat in her cheeks deepened. At least Moira hadn't guessed. And by the end of next week, she would know for certain whether or not she carried Brad's child. The idea made her cringe.

"What's troublin' ya, Shauna?"

Moira's question sharply penetrated Shauna's thoughts, and she turned startled eyes on her maid.

"Ya haven't been yourself these past few days," Moira went on, her brow furrowed. "Are ye havin' misgivings about your deal with Mr. Remington?"

Fearing Moira had somehow figured everything out in the last two seconds, Shauna turned away and went to the armoire to select a gown. "What makes you think *he* is

181

the cause of anything?" she asked, forcing her words to sound light and indifferent.

"Because ya haven't been the same since the first day ya laid eyes on him," Moira bluntly admitted. "Could it be ya find him attractive?"

The flesh across the back of Shauna's neck tingled, and her breath caught in her throat. How did Moira know what they had talked about? Had Moira seen her leave the house? Had she followed her? Had she stood outside the door of his room, eavesdropping? Sanity edged its way into her thoughts, and she exhaled a breathless sigh as she reached into the armoire and pulled out her favorite plum-colored gown. Of course Moira hadn't followed her. If she knew what happened in that room, she wouldn't waste a second telling Shauna that she did.

"I find him attractive, yes. What woman wouldn't? But—" She turned to look at her maid. "I'm *not* attracted to him. There's a big difference, you know."

A frown drew Moira's dark brows together and disappeared. "I suppose there is."

"What I mean is that Mr. Remington is very handsome to look at, but that's as far as it goes," Shauna continued as she handed the gown to Moira for help getting into it. "Underneath his good looks is a very cruel, coldhearted man. He thinks only of himself and no one else. He doesn't care about anyone's problems. He'll tell you so in no uncertain terms." Ducking under the hemline of the dress, she raised her arms and began to shimmy into the gown. "And you know what else?" she mumbled beneath the yards of cloth. "He expects me to do just as he says. Can you imagine? He actually thinks I'm going to listen to him. Well . . ." The gown slid down into place with only minimal damage to her coiffure. "He's got another

182

think coming if he expects me to act like his wife. I told him from the start that this would be a marriage in name only and that's just what it will be. I'll not jump in his bed just because he snaps his fingers. Not me! *I'll* not have his brats. Let him find someone else to satisfy his urges. Let him have Beth," she added, sucking in her breath while Moira finished buttoning up the gown. Then, without noticing the woman's puzzled expression, Shauna stepped into her slippers and went back to the mirror for one last look at herself. "But I doubt Beth would want him. Not if she knew what kind of a man he was."

"I think she already knows," Moira mumbled, her face wrinkled with confusion. Shauna had never rambled on like this before in all the years Moira had known her, and she couldn't understand what had set her off. It was almost as if the young woman wasn't even aware Moira was in the room.

"So, how do I look?" Shauna asked as she turned around. Smiling brightly, she clutched her skirts in both hands and swung them from side to side.

"Grand . . . as always. Mr. Remington should be pleased," Moira confessed, turning to gather up Shauna's robe and straighten the things on her dressing table.

"Mr.—" An uneasiness began to creep up Shauna's spine. "Why do you say that?"

"What?" Moira asked as she went to the armoire, draped Shauna's robe over a hook, and closed the doors.

"Why should the way I look please Mr. Remington?"

Soft laughter shook Moira's shoulders. "He'd have to be blind not to agree."

"But . . ." Shauna's pulse was beginning to throb in her temples and she pressed shaky fingertips to them. "You . . . you make it sound like . . ."

183

"Like what?" Moira frowned.

"Like . . . like he'll see me tonight." Her own fair brow wrinkled apprehensively.

Moira stared blankly at her mistress for a moment, unable to make any sense of what Shauna was saying, until it suddenly dawned on her that Shauna had missed lunch with her father and didn't know. Never one to pass up the opportunity to deliver a lecture, Moira faced her mistress, arms akimbo. "Well, if ya hadn't decided to spend your day in your room sulkin', ya'd know what I'm talkin' about." Shauna started to deny that her absence had been a chance to be alone and to feel sorry for herself, but Moira quickly interrupted. "Your father asked Mr. Remington over for lunch today to tell him that the Winegar dinner invitation included him. They'd heard about Mr. Remington's desire to court ya and they want to meet him. So, ya see, all your frettin' over Thorndyke was unnecessary."

"He . . . he was here? In the house? Today?" Shauna breathed. "Papa talked to him?"

"Aye. He was here." Noticing how pale Shauna's face had become, Moira frowned and came to stand next to her mistress, reaching out to touch Shauna's cheek. "Aren't ya feelin' well, Shauna? Ya look as if ya've seen a ghost."

"What did they talk about?"

"Who? Your father and Mr. Remington? I don't know. Doreen told me about your father askin' him to join ya at Sir Winegar's. Why, Shauna? What does it matter?"

Shauna shook her head and returned to the dressing table where she checked her appearance again. "It doesn't. I was just curious." Leaning forward a bit, she studied her reflection and pinched color in her cheeks. "Is he here now?"

184

"Aye. He and your father are in the parlor."

"What about Mother?"

Moira shrugged. "I don't know, but I doubt she's ready. Your mother likes to make a grand entrance and she can't do that until after you've gone down, now can she?"

A smile found its way to Shauna's lips. Moira never seemed to care who might hear what she had to say or what the repercussions might be. "Then I guess I shouldn't keep the men waiting . . . or Mother," she added with a smile, turning to face her friend. "Do you think Father will approve of what he sees?"

Wide panniers accented the narrowness of Shauna's waist, and the white ruffled inlay of eyelet lace at the low neckline flattered her full bosom, something Moira was sure Mr. Remington would notice right away. The plum-colored satin complemented her ivory skin, and the golden strands of soft curls added a sweet innocence to Shauna's appearance, an altogether deceptive touch. Shauna Radborne liked to make people think she was naive. It was one of her more cunning traits. Her father believed it. Even Roanna was a victim. But not Tyler or Moira. And now Moira was relatively certain Brad Remington knew the real Shauna Kathleen Radborne.

"Aye, your father will approve," Moire nodded. "And so will Mr. Remington." She motioned toward the door, ignoring Shauna's rapid intake of breath. The girl wanted to state that Brad's approval didn't matter, but Moira knew better. "Enjoy your evenin', Miss Shauna. But try not to embarrass your father." Before Shauna could demand an explanation, the pert little Irishwoman had left the room.

*　　*　　*

"I understand you've been living in the Colonies since your father died, Brad," Radborne commented as the two men shared a glass of wine in the parlor.

"Yes, that's right," Brad admitted. "Dane and I always were adventurous, and we used our inheritance to buy a ship. We wanted to travel a little, since we really had nothing holding us here in London."

"That's quite understandable," Radborne nodded after taking a puff on the cigar Brad had given him. "I've always been tempted to take some time off and go to the Colonies myself. I'd like to know what's so attractive about them." He glanced toward the open doorway and sighed disappointedly. "But I'm afraid if I did, I'd have to go alone. Roanna isn't much for travel, and Shauna has other interests. Tyler might have been willing if he hadn't met Miss Anderson." He smiled back at Brad. "I understand she's a very nice young woman."

"And a good friend," Brad finished. "Tyler couldn't do better than Beth if he tried. That is, of course, if money's not important."

Radborne laughed good-naturedly. "With Tyler it's hard to figure out just what *is* important to him. Being happy, I would say, comes first. I envy him that."

"Give him time, sir," Brad promised with a knowing smile. "He'll change. I did."

Radborne raised an interested brow. "Am I hearing a confession?" he teased.

"Sort of," Brad grinned. "I was a lot like Tyler when I was his age. Always looking for a way to have fun. I couldn't have cared less about what was expected of me. If it hadn't been for my brother's firm hand, I might have wound up dead in some alleyway years ago."

"And now you're ready to settle down," Radborne

observed before taking a sip of his wine.

Brad chuckled. "It's what I had planned. But so far it hasn't worked out that way."

"Meaning Wrenhaven," Radborne guessed.

In the few times they had talked, Brad had never mentioned his father's estate and had decided against doing so once Shauna had made it very clear what the results would be if he did. So he was more than a little surprised that Radborne already knew that there was some connection between him and Wrenhaven. Unless, of course, Tyler had mentioned it to him. Uneasy and not sure what he should say, he raised his glass to his lips and took a swallow of the amber wine.

"You don't have to pretend you don't know what I'm talking about, Brad," Radborne went on, his green eyes twinkling with humor. "I haven't gotten where I am by ignoring the obvious. And when a man shows an interest in my daughter, I'm inclined to do a little research on him. The ship you mentioned was to have been used to buy back Wrenhaven, but it sank off the coast of England . . . along with your plans. Now, either Shauna has truly caught your eye, or you're willing to endure her tantrums just to have Wrenhaven."

"Tantrums, sir?" Brad repeated hesitantly.

Radborne grinned openly. "Well, maybe that's not the right word for it, but I more than anyone know what kind of a woman she is. She'll do just about anything to have her way." He flicked off the ash from his cheroot and sat forward in his chair. "And I see you as a man who'll do the same. Makes for an interesting match. Two head-strong, determined people at odds with each other." He smiled again and retorted, "It's what she deserves. I'm not sure you do, but the choice is yours. And as a way of encouraging you, I'll tell you what I have planned." He finished off his wine, set the glass on the table next to him, and relaxed back in the chair, his ankles crossed and stretched out in front of him. With one elbow resting on the arm of the chair, he held up the cheroot and studied the thin white trail of smoke as it curled toward the ceiling. A moment passed before he looked at Brad again through the grayish haze he exhaled. "Marry Shauna and Wrenhaven is yours."

Brad could hardly believe his ears. First Shauna, now her father? Unable to answer, all he could do was laugh. The whole situation was outrageously funny.

"Now, don't think ill of me, Brad. Let me explain first," Radborne quickly added, sitting upright again. "I'm willing to give you an alternative, since what I've suggested is a little ignoble. I want you to get to know Shauna, dine with her, go for long walks, picnic in the woods, take her to a ball, that sort of thing. If you decide she'll make a good wife, then so be it. If not . . . well, I'll understand, and I'll be willing to work out some sort of deal for Wrenhaven."

"I thought you already had," Brad grinned lopsidedly.

A frown creased Radborne's brow and disappeared. "Yes, I suppose you could call it that. But I meant aside from marrying her to have it. Brad," he continued in all seriousness, "I love my daughter very much, but in doing so, I'm afraid I've spoiled her. She's long past the proper marrying age, and if I let it go on without stepping in, she'll remain unwed. She likes her life the way it is. She's told me so. *Many* times. Underneath all her aloofness is a very desirable woman. I'm sure of it. I'm just offering you the incentive to look for it. If Shauna doesn't like you, she'll run you off before you've had a chance to draw a single breath. And that would leave me with no choice but to announce her engagement to a man of my selection. I prefer you be that man, Brad. You're young, good-looking, with a sensible head for business, and the character to stand up to her. She needs someone like you." He frowned and looked away, mumbling, "I'm afraid to think what would happen if I allowed Nelson to marry her."

"Allowed him?" Brad questioned, puzzled. Shauna had said her father was considering it already. That was her reason for trapping Brad the way she had. Was she mistaken? Or was there some other reason she needed a husband? One she hadn't admitted to him?

Radborne shrugged and snuffed out the cheroot. "Yes. He's the only man Shauna's temperament hasn't turned away. Although I don't know why. She truly despises the man and isn't shy about letting him know it." He smiled crookedly. "Nelson is very sharp when it comes to money matters, but he's very slow in understanding Shauna's dislike of him. You'll see what I mean tonight." He shook his head as he rose to refill his wine glass. "He's managed to get himself invited to Winegar's dinner party." He held out the crystal decanter toward Brad, silently asking if his guest would like more. Brad declined with a raised hand. "So, what do you think, Brad?" Radborne went on. "Do we have a deal? Of course, it's best you never mention this to Shauna. She'd be furious if she ever heard I was selling her off."

"I imagine she would be, sir," Brad agreed, smiling. "And yes, we have a deal. But I'd rather call it an understanding, if you don't mind. As for keeping it our secret . . ." a devilish twinkle appeared in Brad's dark eyes, "I wouldn't dream of telling her."

189

A swish of plum satin cloth drew both men's attention to the doorway, and while Radborne went to greet his daughter, Brad politely came to his feet. He'd never seen her more radiant. Her golden hair shone in a thick mass of curls. Her gown complemented her shapely curves. Her skin glowed. But Brad was seeing her in a different vein. He was no longer obligated to marry her. If he wished, he could walk out of the Radborne townhouse right now and never look back. Wrenhaven was his no matter what Shauna wanted. He could . . . but he wasn't going to. He owed her, and he was going to pay her back . . . for every word, every insult, for the very fact she had tried to force him into doing something against his will. He'd make her life miserable.

"Shauna, my dear," her father was saying, "you've never looked more beautiful."

"Thank you, Papa," she murmured, forcing her attention away from Brad. Just knowing he was under the same roof unnerved her, but now that she had seen him, her heart beat faster and she could feel the warmth in her cheeks growing. Even though they were both fully dressed, she felt as if neither of them had on a stitch of clothing and that all her father had to do was look in her eyes to know what had happened between them.

"Is your mother ready?" Radborne asked, easing a little of her nervousness.

"I . . . I don't think so, Papa," she answered quietly, her gaze locked on him.

Pulling his gold watch from his waistcoat pocket, Radborne popped the lid and checked the time. "I'd better see what's keeping her. We don't want to be late." He returned the watch to its place and glanced at Brad. "Pour Shauna a glass of wine, will you, Brad, while I see

190

if I can't hurry my wife along?"

"Certainly," Brad replied with a courteous nod of his head.

Placing a kiss on his daughter's temple, Radborne turned and exited the room, leaving Shauna horribly alone with the man who had brought a very vivid change to her life. Drawing on all the courage she had left, she raised her chin and faced him.

"Where have you been?" she demanded coolly.

Setting his glass aside, he picked up the decanter and poured her a small sampling of wine, deliberately not answering her. Then, with both their glasses in hand, he turned and walked toward her, his dark eyes sparkling and resting on her face.

"I'm fine, Shauna. And how are you?" he mocked, holding out the offering of wine.

"I don't care how you are," she snapped, her voice low as she took the glass he gave her. "I asked where you've been."

Raising his drink to his lips, he took a swallow and watched her over the rim of the crystal goblet. "I don't see where it's any of your business, to be quite honest. We're not married yet, and even if we were, I wouldn't tell you. Not when you act like that."

Shauna's eyes narrowed, their icy hue turning dark. "And ours is not a conventional sort of arrangement," she hissed, glancing over her shoulder toward the open door. Fearing someone might hear, she moved further into the room, thinking he would follow. He didn't. "Need I remind you what will happen if you decide not to go through with this? Or if Father decides you've taken too long? He'll annouce my engagement to Nelson, and you'll have to find some other place to live."

191

"He's told you that?" Brad cunningly asked, his gaze briefly taking in the length of her before he chose to look away. It was difficult for him not to see her as she had been last time they had been together.

"Not exactly. We haven't really discussed it. But I know Nelson has talked about it with him."

"Oh?" Brad challenged, crossing to the hearth and resting an arm on the mantel as he stared down into the dancing orange flames. "How can you be so sure?"

Shauna's tawny brows gathered in a confused frown. "Tyler told me. He said he overheard them talking in the study. And Nelson himself told me on occasion that he was ready to settle down and start a family. Since we're not what you'd call close friends, I'm sure he wasn't confiding in me as he would in someone whose advice he wanted. Why do you ask?"

Brad shrugged one shoulder. "No reason. I'm just making conversation," he casually replied before taking a sip of his wine. So Tyler told her, he mused with a vague smile. And knowing Tyler, it was very possible he made up the whole thing just to get at his sister. He loved bantering with her. Brad had already witnessed that. But would he go to such an extreme? He took another drink. Of course he would. He just hadn't guessed what the results would be. Poor Shauna. She had stooped to blackmailing a stranger into marrying her when there really was no immediate need. Forcing back a smile, he turned around to set his empty glass on the table. "I understand I'll have the honor of meeting your Nelson Thorndyke this evening," he goaded her.

"He's not *my* Nelson Thorndyke, thank you," she rallied. "But yes, he'll be there. That's why it's important you act as if you're really interested in me," she instructed him. "For his sake and for my father's."

His dark brown eyes lifted to look at her. "The way I behave, Shauna, is my concern, not yours. I might have agreed to marry you, but we never discussed the method I'd use in winning your father's approval. Now, if there's any problem with that, we can call this whole thing off before it's too late."

"Don't tempt me," she sneered, roughly setting her wine glass down on the table next to his. "I'm sure I could find someone else eager to marry me for what I can offer him; namely your beloved Wrenhaven."

His gaze raked over her, touching her everywhere and burning her flesh. "Can you? Perhaps. But would it be in time? And think, if you will, what your new husband's reaction will be when he finds out his wife isn't a virgin?"

Shauna's face flamed, and she frantically glanced toward the door. "Keep your voice down!" she demanded, glaring at him again. "He won't *have* a reaction, you jackanapes. It's a marriage in name only. Remember?"

"I'm sure it will be. But that doesn't mean he won't find out," he threatened, his rugged brow creased, his dark eyes flashing, and his nose inches from hers. "Until now, you had the upper hand, Miss Radborne. You called all the plays. Everything was under your terms. Well, not anymore. If you want me to marry you, you'll have to do as *I* say." He pointed a finger at her. "And you'll keep your mouth shut."

"You . . . you lecher!" she shrieked. "You uncouth, vile barbarian! You'd actually *tell* someone? Why not just announce it to my father? Then no one would marry me and he'd probably send me to a convent!"

"Truthfully, my dear," Brad snarled, "it's what you deserve."

"Ohhhh," she howled, her tiny fists clenched at her sides, her trim form shaking with rage. "You're evil, Brad Remington."

"Am I?" he countered.

"Yes! You had this all planned from the start. You tricked me into . . . into . . ." She couldn't force the words from her lips. "You deliberately set out to entrap me so you could . . . could . . ."

"Blackmail you?" he finished.

"Yes!"

"Then explain how I lured you to my room that night. Tell me how I managed to get you to come alone. Show me the bruises, Shauna. If it was rape, why have you kept it a secret? If it was rape," he continued in a loud whisper, "why didn't you scream and try to claw out my eyes?" She started to whirl away from him but he caught her arm and jerked her back. "I'll tell you why. Because you loved it."

The resounding crack of her open palm against his cheek filled the room and brought an instant rage burning in his eyes, but it hardly matched the fire glowing in hers.

"You're loathsome," she spat.

"And you're a bitch," he rallied.

Her chest heaving, she strained to break his grip on her arm. Failing that, she brought up her hand to strike him again, but he captured it as well in a steely hold.

"And I'll tell you something else, Shauna Radborne. Once we're married, *I'll* decide whether it's a marriage in name only. If I want my husbandly rights, I'll take them, and you'll have no say in it whatsoever. I plan to win your father's respect, both as a man and as a son-in-law. He'll listen to *me* before he ever believes the rantings of his coddled, selfish daughter. In fact, if you get too out of hand, it'll probably be *his* suggestion that I give you the beating you should have had *years* ago."

"You—you wouldn't dare!" she breathed indignantly.

"Believe it, Shauna," he warned. "And know this, as well. If you try in any way to set him against me or think to run off or trick someone else into marrying you, what happened between us will become public knowledge. The *only* way you'll get out of our agreement is if *I* decide I don't want to spend the rest of my life living under the same roof with a shrew." He roughly shoved her away. "Now, I suggest you pick up your glass of wine, sit down, and pretend we've been discussing the weather. We don't want your father to even suspect what really went on here, now do we?"

Whether Shauna took his threat to heart he'd have to find out later, for in that same moment the sounds of someone coming down the stairs in the hall drifted in to still her answer. Yet the horrified look on her face rather convinced him that she had, and he was almost sure of it when she grabbed her wine glass and hurriedly sat down. However, the bright red stains in her cheeks warned him that she wouldn't be so easily subdued. There was still a lot of fight left in her, and he doubted she'd let it go to waste.

Chapter Seven

For the next two weeks, Shauna tried every ploy she could think of to avoid being with Brad. None of them worked, except when she pleaded a headache, and even that had its disadvantages. It meant confinement to her room, in bed, with Moira hovering suspiciously over her. The Winegars' dinner party had been a disaster as far as she was concerned. Although Brad had been her escort, he had blatantly ignored her to discuss business with her father, Sir Winegar, and several of the other guests, leaving her to fend off Nelson Thorndyke's constant, smothering attention. Repeatedly, he told her how much he cared for her and that if she'd give him the opportunity to prove it, he'd show her that he was a better choice for a husband. She had never seen him behave like that before, and at one point she was sure he was about to break down in tears.

Tyler didn't help matters, either. Once he had learned of Brad's interest in his sister, he did everything he possibly could to get them together—alone. He liked Brad and didn't try to hide it. In his opinion, they were meant for each other, and the sooner they got married, the better. Shauna continually tried telling him that there wasn't any hurry, and he'd retaliate by reminding her of Nelson. That thought always made her shudder, and for a brief moment, she'd grudgingly admit he was right. Then she'd have to face Brad, and doubt would creep in. She didn't like Nelson, and she had no way of controlling him when it came to the marriage bed, but after her conversation with Brad in the parlor that day, she knew she wouldn't be able to control him, either. That part of their bargain no longer existed. What made it all so terrible was the simple fact that she had un-knowingly trapped herself into the very kind of mar-riage she had hoped to avoid. *And there was nothing she could do to get out of it!*

"Damn!" she howled, spinning away from the window where she had been standing for the past twenty minutes idly watching the servants decorate the terrace for the party later that day, a job they had started some time shortly after dawn. If only she could think of something that would change Brad's mind. But what? he was determined to own Wrenhaven. Her upper lip curled as she flung herself backwards across her rumpled bed, her long golden hair fanning out across the coverlet, her bare toes kicking at the braided rub on the floor, and her arms crossed over her scantily clad bosom in stubborn resolution. This whole idea had come about because of his desire to have Wrenhaven, and now it was the reason she couldn't get rid of him. And then a slow dawning began to chase away the fire sparkling in her eyes and to soften the angry look on her face. It started as a fertile seed and exploded into full-blown color. But of course! she thought happily, springing upright with a snap of her fingers, her gossamer nightgown clinging to her shapely curves. Brad wanted Wrenhaven, not her! He had only agreed to marry her in order to have it, which meant their agreement would end if she couldn't produce the property.

"Ha *ha!*" she exclaimed, bouncing off the bed. "I've done it! I've figured out a way to get you out of my life, Brad Remington." A devious smile narrowed her eyes and wrinkled up her face. "Just you wait. That cocksure grin on your mouth is going to disappear faster than your hopes of ever living in your father's house again. I'll show you how stupid you were to even *think* about threatening me." She crossed to the window again to watch the activity going on outside on the terrace. "And I'll do it today . . . this afternoon . . . at my very own birthday party!" Whirling away from the window, she raced for the door and flung it wide. "Moira!" she yelled. "What about my bath?"

"Has he arrived yet, Moira?" Shauna asked as she doted her cheeks with rouge, then darkened her lips with it.

"I assume ya mean Mr. Remington?" her maid reflected, a slight frown darkening her eyes. "Aye. He's here. He's with your father in the study."

"Good," Shauna answered, tugging at the defiant curl that seemed to want to hang out of place. "I need to speak with him . . . alone."

"Well, ya best hurry if ya want privacy," Moira suggested. "Your guests are startin' to arrive as well, and it would be rude of ya not to greet them."

Coming to her feet, Shauna glanced briefly at her profile in the mirror, before turning to face Moira with a mischievous grin curling her lips. "What I have to say to him is more important than manners, Moira," she admitted. "I'm about to bring an end to this whole masquerade."

"An end?" Moira repeated, her mouth dropping open. "What masquerade? Ya can't be meanin'—"

"Yes. That's exactly what I mean. I have news for Mr. Remington that will send him on his way." She cocked her head triumphantly and waited for Moira's gleeful response. It didn't come.

"Oh, so you're planning ta wed Nelson Thorndyke after all," Moira answered coolly as she bent to scoop up the towel from the floor and collect the other remains of her mistress's bath.

Shauna's disappointment showed clearly on her face. "No. I don't intend to marry Nelson, either."

"And how will ya stop it from happenin'? Ya thought up this whole scheme because that's what your father had planned for ya. If ya don't go through with this—"

Shauna clamped her hands over her ears. "I don't want to hear it, Moira. All I know is that I can't go through with this marriage to Brad."

"And why not, may I ask?" Moira demanded, pausing in her work to stare at Shauna. "He's agreed to your proposition, hasn't he? Your freedom for his father's land. It is what ya wanted, isn't it?"

Shauna's delicate shoulders lifted in a slight shrug. "Yes."

"Then what's the problem?"

Shauna knew Moira would never give her any peace if she didn't say something to satisfy her. "He . . . well, he . . . ah . . . he's sort of gone back on the deal now that Papa's given him his permission to court me."

"How? What has he said?"

Shauna cast her maid a sheepish look and turned for the door. "I'd rather not discuss it. It's personal."

"Oh, now it's personal, is it? Ya've told me everythin' so far and now it's personal." Moira's Irish temper was up. "What could be so personal ya'd keep it from *me*, Moira Flanagan, the woman who practically raised ya like ya was me own little sis—" For a fleeting instant, the only thing she could think of that few women chose to talk about crossed her mind and widened her eyes into large circles. "There's only one part of the deal he can be goin' back on. Tell me he hasn't threatened ta consummate the weddin' vows."

Shauna's cheeks pinkened. But not at what Moira asked, rather the thought that it was already too late to stop that from happening, even if it was a bit early. The flash of a warm, glowing fire, the sounds of a thunderstorm, and the vision of Brad pressing her down in a cushion of soft feathers exploded in Shauna's head, and she clumsily reached for the doorknob. Without a backward glance, she left the room, unaware of the pleased smile that came over Moira's face or how difficult it was for the young Irishwoman to keep from laughing out loud.

The buzz of voices coming from the terrace floated up to greet Shauna as she hurried down the stairs on her way to her father's study. She had to speak with Brad before she lost her nerve, and more importantly, before he won her father's confidence . . . if it wasn't too late for that already. At the bottom of the staircase, Shauna paused long enough to see that the hall was empty and that the door to the study stood open. If she didn't talk with Brad now, the chances of their having a moment alone wouldn't come for some time. Roanna loved parties, and

Shauna was sure her mother had invited every person she could think of to ask. Swiftly and silently, she crossed the marble floor of the foyer and stepped into the room, her heart skipping a beat and her pulse quickening once her gaze found Brad.

He stood near the hearth, one foot resting on the stone slab, an arm laid along the mantel and a glass of wine dangling from his fingertips. His attention was on Shauna's father as Radborne searched his desk drawer for something, giving her an unexpected moment to appraise Brad's fine stature when her arrival failed to disturb his concentration. The rich cut of his clothes and their dark blue shade added to his handsomeness. The shiny cotton breeches hugged his thighs, the beige stockings molded his calves, and darkly polished black shoes adorned his feet. His coat, which he had unbuttoned, fell open and revealed the ivory-colored waistcoat and ruffled shirtfront. There was a stark difference between its opaque hue and his suntanned complexion. The strong line of his jaw and the slight frown on his brow gave him an air of rugged strength, and doubt chiseled at Shauna's confidence. Would he see right through her lie? Would he know in a second that she had never talked with her father about Wrenhaven? Would he play along? Would he become furious? Would he, God forbid, tell her father about their whole sordid affair, just to spite her? Shauna's knees began to tremble, and she glanced back over her shoulder, apprehensive, wondering if she shouldn't abandon her idea. Yet, what choice did she have? Either bring an end to their game or marry him and pay the consequences. Besides, her father wasn't a beast. If she explained to him that she didn't want to be Thorndyke's bride and that if he'd give her a little more time—

Suddenly, she had the distinct feeling someone was watching her. Certain she knew who it was, she slowly turned her head and found those dark brown, hypnotic eyes staring back at her. Her courage waned rapidly.

"Good morning, Shauna," Brad murmured with a soft, seductive smile. "And may I be the first to wish you a happy birthday?"

Each word he spoke tickled her flesh. She forced a weak smile and nodded her appreciation.

"And may I be the second?" Radborne joined in, rounding the desk and walking toward her with his arms extended.

Enveloped within her father's warm embrace, Shauna closed her eyes and wished that when she opened them again, she'd discover that none of this was really happening, that she was only twelve years old and her father was hugging her because he had just returned from a trip. It was what she longed for, but she knew it was impossible.

"So," her father smiled as he held her at arm's length, "do you feel any older?"

About a hundred years, she thought wearily.

"I do know you look more beautiful with every day that passes," Radborne went on. He turned to his companion. "Wouldn't you agree, Brad?"

Unwillingly, Shauna's attention rebelled and moved to the one who had silently witnessed the exchange.

"Without hesitation," he replied warmly, his gaze drinking in the lovely sight of her dressed in soft pastel pink before coming to rest on her face, her pale green eyes.

Radborne's laughter unknowingly broke the spell.

"Somehow I knew you'd say that." He turned to his daughter again and lightly kissed her cheek. "If you two will excuse me for a minute, I've left some papers on the night stand in my room that I'd like Brad to look over. You'll keep him company while I'm gone, won't you, my dear?"

"Of course, Papa," she mumbled with a bob of her head, her eyes lowered and forced on any object other than the one that made her heart thump noisily in her chest.

"I'll be right back. I promise," he added as he slipped past her and headed for the stairs.

Unable to look at Brad right away and wanting to be sure her father really was on his way upstairs, she watched his departure until all that was left was the sound of his footsteps fading in the upper hall. She also realized she hadn't much time before he returned. Taking a deep breath and quickly asking God's help, she faced Brad.

"Why is it," he asked, cutting her off before she had the chance to speak, "that I get the feeling your unexpected visit was preplanned?" He cocked a brow at her, then finished his wine and set the glass down. "Is it safe to say I'm beginning to know how your mind works? Or perhaps it's just obvious, since you prefer being where I'm not."

Shauna raised her chin a notch. "I think the latter is closer to the truth. But yes, I had planned to speak with you alone."

"Ah ha," he replied, clasping one wrist, his arms dangling in front of him. "So what is it that's so important you'd risk being alone with me? You've managed quite well these past weeks not to be."

"No thanks to Tyler," she scoffed, stepping further into the room.

Brad shrugged wide shoulders. "And your father," he added, grinning roguishly.

Shauna cast him a sarcastic look. "It's not the same. My father doesn't care for you all that much. I know it might seem that way to you, but your conceit has blinded you to a great many things in the past, as I'm sure it has done more recently." Feeling in control, she casually walked to one of the wing chairs and sat down prettily, spreading out her skirts around her and leaning back comfortably as she settled her gaze on him once more. "And it's because of that reason, I have bad news for you."

Brad raised questioning brows. "Bad news?" he repeated.

Shauna held out a trim hand to the chair opposite her. "Perhaps you should sit down. I don't think it's the kind of news you should take standing up."

Yielding to her suggestion, he presented her with a slight bow and did as bade, relaxing back against the green velvet cushion, his ankle crossed over one knee and his elbows resting on the arms of the chair.

"I spoke to Father a few days ago about my desire to have Wrenhaven as my dowry." She paused for effect, then, "He refused." She waited for some sort of reaction from him; a puzzled frown, a tic, an angry expression, even a word. Nothing. Had he heard? Did he understand? She tried again. "So you see, Brad, I'm afraid the deal is off. I can't give you Wrenhaven, after all. I'll have to find someone else to help me, since I'm sure you're no longer interested." Still he didn't move or blink an eye. Wondering if he was in shock, she leaned forward. "Did you hear me? I said I can't give you Wrenhaven. There's no need now to continue this farce. You're free. I won't hold you to our agreement."

"That's very gracious of you, Shauna," he finally replied, the expression on his face unchanged. "So how do you suggest we go about correcting our problem? You see, just before you came into the room, your father and I were discussing a date for the wedding."

Shauna felt as if she couldn't breathe. "What?" she gasped.

"I'm afraid so," he sighed, leaving his chair to collect his glass and refill it with wine. "Whether he likes me or not, he's agreed to my marriage proposal. In fact, I suggested we wait a month or more, but he insisted it be sooner." He glanced over his shoulder at her. "I'd say we have a bit of a problem, wouldn't you?"

A buzzing droned in her ears, and she felt light-headed. Suddenly, a glass of dark red wine was shoved in her hand and a much larger one directed the drink to her lips.

"Take a sip," Brad instructed, his brown eyes sparkling with suppressed mirth. "It will help."

The taste of it burned a little, but it quickly soothed her nerves. Visibly trembling, she pressed cool fingertips to her hot cheeks. She had to say something—*anything* to get him to agree with her. "Good heavens, Brad. What will we do? You certainly don't want to marry me now."

"I'm not sure we can do anything. Not without causing a scandal," he recited, turning away from her to fill his own glass with wine. Or so Shauna thought. She wasn't able to see the broad smile on his face. "Maybe he'd change his mind if you asked again."

"No!" she blurted out. She'd never had such a discussion with her father, but even if she had had, she wouldn't ask again. She didn't want to marry Brad, or anyone. Why would she try to change that? "I-I mean, it's useless to ask. Once Papa makes up his mind, nothing will change it." A frown crimped her brow as she frantically searched for a solution. "Maybe you should just disappear,' she proposed. "You liked the Colonies. Why not return there to live? You could leave me a letter saying that the thought of marriage scared you. I could act terribly hurt and even mourn your betrayal for a few years." She liked that idea. "Yes! That would work."

"No one would believe it," he argued. "Especially Tyler. He knows how much I wanted Wrenhaven. Besides," he added with a deep sigh, "I've decided to spend the rest of my life right here, and since I don't owe you anything, I'm not about to give that up just to suit your whim."

"My whim?" she echoed, outraged and bolting to her feet. "You make it sound like all of this was some sort of game. It wasn't! I never wanted to get married . . . to *anyone!*" She gnashed her teeth. "And least of all, to *you!*"

Glass in hand, he perched one hip on the corner of Radborne's desk. "Well. At least we've managed to agree on one thing. Being husband and wife—in any form of the word—is a fate worse than castration." He raised the glass to his lips and paused, adding, "Let me correct that a little. Being married to *you* is a fate worse than castration."

"How—" she exploded, lunging for him, long sharp nails posed and ready to claw his face.

Brad, seeing the impending harm, deftly slid off the desk and out of reach. "How dare I tell the truth?" he finished, skillfully putting the huge piece of furniture between them as he stepped around the end of it. "Have you been insulted, Shauna, to find out there's one man among us all who isn't afraid to admit you don't interest him?"

"Oh, really?" she sneered, shadowing his steps. "It didn't seem that way the other night in your room." She held her voice to a whisper. "Or are you saying it was all pretend?"

"Quite the contrary." He set aside his glass and backed toward the hearth where he artfully stepped behind one of the wing chairs. She still had that threatening look in her eye. "You stirred my male needs and I merely satisfied them. It had nothing to do with you. Not personally."

Shauna gritted her teeth. "Then any woman would have sufficed?"

A mocking grin wrinkled one corner of his mouth and danced in his dark eyes. "Yes. In fact . . ." He paused to rest one hand on the back of the chair while he rubbed his chin with the other as if considering something. "I do believe that at the time I was reminded of another pretty little blonde I had made love to." He looked at her again. "Of course, she was much younger than you, and much warmer. She knew how to please a man."

Shauna's chin lowered. Her nostrils flared and her hands knotted themselves into fists. "She was a whore, no doubt," she hissed, her entire body trembling with rage.

A brief frown showed on his face and disappeared. "I guess you could call her that. After all, we weren't married."

The implication was quite clear. "Are you calling *all* women who fall into your trap whores?" Her voice shook with fury.

The humor vanished from his eyes. "Only those who trifle with a man's emotions and then claim no harm done."

His admission surprised her. She straightened and stared silently at him for a moment. But before she could ask him to explain, a movement at the doorway interrupted.

"Well, well, well," Tyler grinned. "I should have known you two lovebirds would be off hiding somewhere. Am I disturbing something important?"

"If you were, we wouldn't tell you about it," Shauna scoffed.

"And why not?" Tyler whined playfully. "After all, I'm the one who introduced you two, remember?"

"Oh, I remember, Tyler," she guaranteed him. "I doubt I'll ever forget that I have my brother to thank for it."

He missed the subtle sarcasm. "Then maybe you'll name your first son after me."

"Tyler!" Her cheeks flamed a scarlet hue, and she refused to look at Brad. He, more than likely, was openly gloating.

"Well, what's wrong with that?" Tyler asked, not the least embarrassed by his boldness as his sister was. "Tyler Remington." He tested the name. "Not bad. And besides, it's not like you're not planning to get married." He grinned boyishly. "And I should know."

An uneasy feeling came over her. "What's that supposed to mean?"

Squinting his eyes at her, he smirked, "I just met Father in the hall and he said he had some very pleasing news to announce later. Now, since everyone in this

208

household has been living for the day you'd move out, I can only surmise he means he'll be announcing the forthcoming wedding bells."

Panic knotted her stomach. Glaring first at Brad, who quickly masked his smile, then at her brother, she started for the door. "Well, they won't be mine!" she promised, knocking Tyler aside when he didn't move fast enough.

"What the hell's the matter with her?" Tyler asked as he rubbed his bruised ribs where Shauna's elbow found its mark. He turned a questioning look on his companion. "Did you two have a quarrel?"

The corner of Brad's mouth twitched. "You could say that, I guess. She's upset because I accepted a dinner invitation from a friend of mine without consulting her first."

Tyler's face wrinkled disapprovingly. "Is that all?" he mumbled, crossing to the desk to pour himself a glass of wine. "She's acting more like she just found out you're marrying her for her money." He snickered and took a sip from his glass. "And in her case, it's probably the only reason a man would want to tangle with her." Turning, he leaned back against the desk behind him. "Are you sure you want to go through with this? It's not too late, you know. It won't be too late if you're standing next to her at the altar and the preacher's waiting for you to say 'I do.'" He took another drink and glanced at the door. "No one would blame you."

"That's a strange thing for her brother to be saying," Brad chuckled, rounding the chair and sitting down in it.

"Not really," Tyler confessed. "I've known her longer than you. I love her. Don't get me wrong. But she's a hellcat, and I doubt she'll ever change. She'll make your life miserable if you let her." Lifting his glass, he frowned into it, saying, "What she needs is a good spanking."

"She's a little old for that, don't you think?" Brad grinned, plucking at a piece of lint on the knee of his breeches.

Tyler laughed at the vision he conjured up. "Yes. I guess you're right. Whoever tried that with her would probably wind up with more bruises than her." He wiggled his tawny brows. "But it's a nice idea. And a good threat. You should use it on her. I'll bet she'd settle down."

Brad remembered having done just that and what her reaction had been. "It might for a minute or two. Just until she had time to think about it. Then she'd probably try to hit me with something."

"You're right about that, friend," Tyler howled. "I can't tell you how many times I had a lump on my head because of her." Chuckling, he silently reminisced about the squabbles they had had as children. "Of course, you have one advantage I never had."

Brad raised an eyebrow. "Oh? And what's that?"

"You're not her brother." He grinned suggestively. "Granted, I have no way of knowing if it would work— with her, I don't think any man does, so far—but a little romance usually turns the fieriest of vixens into soft, surrendering lambs."

Brad's eyes glowed with his laughter. "Speaking from experience, Tyler?" he teased.

The young man shrugged playfully. "I haven't been a monk, if that's what you're asking. And I've had a chance to soothe a few injured prides now and then. It's always worked for me." He glanced at the empty doorway again and sighed. "But in her case . . ."

In her case, Tyler, my friend, Brad mused, it works as

well. It's just the aftermath that needs improving. But give me time. I think the Ice Maiden is beginning to thaw.

"Nice party, isn't it, Marcus?" Lucas Billingsly goaded as he hid his smile behind his raised wine goblet and secretively studied the crowd gathered on the terrace. "Have you wished Miss Radborne a happy birthday? Or, for that matter, have you congratulated her on her upcoming wedding?"

"There's been no announcement," Deerfield hissed, his dark eyes locked on Shauna as she moved gracefully among her guests.

"Not yet. But I heard Mrs. Radborne telling a friend that her husband is planning a surprise later." He tipped his glass and savored the taste of the exquisite wine on his tongue. "What's Nelson going to do then?"

"What he's been doing all along," Marcus growled. "We won't have to change our plans until *after* they're married. *If* that ever happens."

"You sound as if you've figured something out." Billingsly's blue eyes brightened a little. "Have you?"

"If I have, I wouldn't tell you," Deerfield snarled, lifting his cheroot to his lips and taking a puff as he watched Pierce Radborne step out onto the terrace with his son and the man Marcus Deerfield had grown to hate. Brad Remington had become a threat, and if it hadn't been imperative for Marcus not to tip his hand, he would have liked to call the man out and meet him at dawn in a deserted field somewhere. Touching his glass of wine to his lips, he stared venomously over the rim at his dark-haired adversary. Something had to be done about Brad Remington, and soon. There wasn't time to turn

Radborne against him. And Shauna had no say in her choice of a husband. Sucking in another puff from the cigar, he squinted when smoke drifted into his eyes. An accident, perhaps? Or maybe he could see to it that Remington just disappeared. Marcus's gaze shifted to Roanna Radborne. Perhaps he could threaten blackmail. After all, Roanna's only love was money . . . and a romp in the feathers. Exposing her might work. He mentally shrugged off the probability. She was a stubborn bitch. She had already made him angry enough for him to threaten to tell Pierce about them, and she had laughed at him. She claimed Pierce would never believe him, that she had kept her affairs a secret, that no one in her family knew about her favorite pastime, and that even if Marcus succeeded in convincing Pierce, her husband loved her too much to cast her out. He inhaled a long drag on the cheroot. Maybe. And maybe not, he thought maliciously as he watched the bright red glowing tip. But sooner or later Pierce Radborne *would* learn of his wife's unfaithfulness, and that she had been unfaithful with the very man who had brought about his ruin. It was part of the plan. Before Marcus Deerfield was through, the bastard's whole family would be destroyed, and he'd have his revenge. But first things first. Shauna was his number one target, and this Colonial stood in the way. Suddenly, an idea came into his mind, and he straightened, an evil smile curling his lips. Setting down his glass, he turned to the man beside him and cruelly grabbed Billingsly's wrist.

"Pierce tells me you're from the Colonies, Mr. Remington," Eimile Clayton snipped, her disdain for the rebels obvious.

"I lived there for a few years," Brad replied politely. "After our father died, my brother and I decided to see a bit of the world, and we settled in Boston for a spell."

Her nose held loftily in the air, she asked, "And what made you decide to come here? I would think you'd have stayed in the Colonies now that you're no longer under British rule."

"Eimile!" her husband sharply scolded as he handed her a glass of wine. "It's none of your business. Besides, the war is over."

"It will never be for me, Russel. Our Daniel died over there."

"Well, I'm sure Brad had nothing to do with it." Soft brown eyes looked at him. "Did you, Brad?"

There was always the chance, Brad thought, since he had fought against many British soldiers, but he wasn't about to admit it. Not if he didn't want to upset Eimile Clayton. "We all lost someone in that war, Mrs. Clayton," he answered, thinking of Penny. "And it's only fair we feel a little bitter. But your husband's right. It's over, and we should put it behind us. That's part of the reason I came home."

"Home?" she echoed, surprised and a bit confused.

Brad smiled softly as he held out his hand toward the wrought iron chair someone had just vacated. He waited until she had sat down before continuing. "I was born and raised here in England. In fact, my father's property lies just outside of London."

"Really?" A slight blush rose in her cheeks. "I-I didn't know that."

"How could you, Mrs. Clayton? I've been away a long time, and my father died over twenty years ago," he told

213

her, setting down his glass on the table to pull his tin of cheroots from his pocket.

"Remington," Eimile murmured, trying to remember. "Aric Remington?" Her eyes grew wide, and she twisted to set her glass next to his before asking, "Was *he* your father?"

"Yes, madam," Brad grinned.

Eimile turned to her husband. "You remember Aric, don't you, Russel? He lived near your uncle."

"Yes, Eimile, I do. And I remember your mother, Brad. She was a fine lady."

Brad was about to thank Russel Clayton for the compliment when Nelson Thorndyke suddenly appeared in their circle.

"I hope I'm not intruding," he apologized, drawing everyone's attention.

"Of course not, Nelson," Russel quickly replied. "We were just getting acquainted with Brad. You've met, haven't you?"

"Yes, we have." Nelson nodded sheepishly, his gaze falling on Brad. "And I thought it was time I made peace with him."

His statement surprised Brad. He hadn't expected Thorndyke to give in so easily to the man who had all but stolen Shauna away from him. He held out one of the cheroots, which Nelson took, and then helped light it for him.

"Consider it done," Brad replied earnestly, unaware of the well-dressed man who had silently approached the group from the rear or that he had added a white powdery substance to one of the wine glasses sitting on the table. Nor did any of them see him quickly withdraw and disappear into the crowd milling about on the terrace.

"That's very generous of you, Brad," Nelson admitted, exhaling the smoke from his cigar. "I haven't been very cordial, I'm afraid, and I probably don't deserve your kindness." He smiled lopsidedly and looked down at his feet. "It's just that I've always had an eye for Shauna, and I thought some day she'd agree to be my wife." He sighed forlornly. "I guess that's impossible now." He seemed to collect himself then and smiled warmly at Brad. "I concede to you, Mr. Remington, and I congratulate you on your upcoming wedding."

Mrs. Clayton's chin dropped. "I didn't know it was official," she chirped, reaching for one of the wine glasses and coming to her feet. "I'd say that's cause for a toast."

Chuckling, Brad raised a hand. "Thank you for the thought, but it's a little premature, I'm afraid."

"Not from the rumors I've heard flying around here today," Nelson corrected.

"Rumors?" Russel asked. "What rumors are those, Nelson?"

"That Pierce has an announcement to make. What else would it be if not to publicly give his consent for Shauna to marry Brad?" He raised his own wine glass. "Premature, possibly. But only by a few minutes. And I'd like to be the first to toast your long life and happiness." He smiled softly. "And may we, at least, be friends in business, if not socially."

If anything, Brad had learned during the past few weeks how influential Nelson Thorndyke was beginning to become. It made good sense for Brad to accept the man's apology and win his friendship. Reaching for the only glass left sitting on the table, he noticed that someone had refilled it and turned back to salute Nelson with the crystal goblet raised high.

"To friendship," he said, his gaze passing from Nelson to Russel Clayton and finally to Eimile.

"To friendship," they all agreed, drinking to the toast.

"And lots of strong, fine sons," Russel added with a devilish chuckle.

"And daughters," Eimile corrected, wrinkling her nose at the somewhat bitter taste in her mouth. She never had liked wine and only drank it to be sociable.

Before any of the men in her party could respond, the tinkling of a silver bell drew everyone's attention and all heads turned to look at Pierce Radborne as he stood in the center of the terrace, his wife on one side of him, Shauna on the other. Bright afternoon sunlight glistened in her golden hair and her fair skin gleamed a creamy white. Her pink cotton gown added a healthy glow, and Brad found it rather difficult to pull his eyes away from her and concentrate on what Radborne was saying.

"First, I'd like to thank all of you on my daughter's behalf for helping us celebrate her birthday. It's friends like you that make our lives special." He laughed at someone's playful comment about the good food and fine wine being the main reason everyone had come, then settled his attention on the crowd again. "I hope that's not entirely true. But if it is, next time there won't be any." Several moans and heartfelt laughter followed, and Pierce waited for it to die down. "What I'd really like to share with you is this. As most of you know, my wife and I have been long awaiting our daughter's decision to settle down. It seems she's taken the first step."

"Here it comes, Brad," Russel whispered, failing to see how pale his wife had become and that she had sunk back down in her chair. "It's not too late to change your mind."

"And as our gift to Shauna, in the hopes it will soon become her new home, I'm turning over the ownership of Wrenhaven to her."

An applause went up, several of the guests crowded forward to congratulate her, and Tyler suddenly appeared before Brad.

"Well, ol' man," he beamed, shaking Brad's hand. "You've succeeded not only in getting back your father's property, but in getting a beautiful wife as well. I only hope you're up to it." He grinned mischievously. "She'll drain every ounce of strength you have."

"Of that, I'm sure," Brad agreed, his dark brown eyes staring back at the lovely, frightened face watching him. Lifting his wine glass, he gave Shauna a mocking salute and broad smile, his way of letting her know that he was ready for anything she might have in mind.

Suddenly, the happiness of the moment was shattered when Russel Clayton screamed for someone's help. Jerking around, Brad saw that Eimile was frantically clawing at her throat. Her eyes were wide, and she couldn't breathe. Roughly setting down his glass, Brad rushed to her side and pushed the hysterical Russel away. Before he could even think of what to do, the woman slid off her chair in a fit of convulsions and fell into Brad's arms. The faint smell of almonds wafted up to fill Brad's nostrils, and he painfully realized there was nothing anyone could do for her. Eimile Clayton had been poisoned.

"Brad?" Tyler called from the study doorway. "What's bothering you?"

217

Turning away from the window where he had stood watching the stream of guests leaving the Radborne townhouse, Brad leaned to snuff out the cheroot he had been smoking.

"If you're thinking there was more you could have done for Mrs. Clayton, you're wrong," Tyler assured him, coming further into the room. "She was getting on in years. I suppose her heart just gave out."

Brad nodded toward the open door. "Close that, will you? I'd like what I have to say to be private."

Frowning curiously, Tyler did as asked, then came to stand near his friend. "What is it?"

"Mrs. Clayton didn't have heart failure, Tyler. She was poisoned."

"What?" Tyler gasped, his tan complexion whitening. "How can you be sure?"

Turning back to stare absently out the window again, Brad remained quiet for a moment longer. "Several years ago, just before the war broke out, I used to run with a pretty rough group of men. Some of them were criminals, some were members of the Sons of Liberty. Leadership was important then—or I should say the power behind it. Those who weren't really fighting for the cause but the wealth they could get from it pretending they were, would kill off anyone who stood in their way by any means available to them: guns, knives . . . poison. I saw a man die pretty much the same way as Mrs. Clayton. He'd been poisoned with cowbane—water hemlock. His first mate had slipped some in his ale." He paused a moment to rub the tired muscles in his neck before he moved away from the window and went to sit down in one of the wing chairs before the hearth. "Dane was with me at the time, and once the man started acting like he couldn't breathe,

Dane figured he had something caught in his throat. He meant to pound on his back, but once Dane got close enough to him to know what had really happened, he backed away."

"Why? What tipped him off?"

"The smell of almonds."

"Almonds?" Tyler questioned.

"Hemlock leaves an odor of almonds on the person's breath. I smelled it on Mrs. Clayton's."

"My God, Brad," Tyler exclaimed, sinking down in the chair next to his. "Who would want to poison Eimile Clayton?"

Brad shook his head. "It wasn't meant for her."

"Then who?"

Brad's eyes, their brown depths revealing a mixture of anger, remorse, and sympathy, glanced over at Tyler. "It was meant for me."

Tyler was too stunned to answer. Silent, he fell back in the chair and stared into the cold fireplace.

"I didn't want to believe it at first, either, so I came in here to think it through and to be alone," Brad went on, staring at the same black void as his companion. "The more I thought about it, the more it made sense. That's when all the pieces started falling together."

"Like what? What pieces? Who'd want you dead?" Tyler rifled off the questions almost angrily.

"I'm not sure who. Or why," Brad said solemnly. "Only that someone tried."

"So tell me what happened. Maybe I can help."

Glancing at Tyler, Brad smiled softly, then stared at the dark hearth again. "I was standing alone having a glass of wine when Mrs. Clayton introduced herself. We talked a few minutes before her husband joined us. He gave her a full glass of wine, which I remember she set, untouched, on the table next to us. I had set mine down, as well, to light up a cheroot. Then Nelson Thorndyke came over."

"What did he want?" Tyler asked sharply.

"To aplogize."

"What?"

"He said he hadn't been fair to me because of Shauna, and that he hoped we'd be friends. That's when Eimile proposed a toast, which all of us drank to, including Eimile." His brow furrowed thoughtfully. "I remember thinking that someone must have refilled my glass, because when I turned back to pick it up, it was full. It wasn't when I set it down."

"Meaning?"

"That while our attention was drawn away, someone put the poison in my glass, but Eimile took it accidentally. *Hers* was full. Mine wasn't."

"Sweet Mother of God," Tyler moaned. "It could have been you." He sat upright and demanded, "Why? Why would someone want you dead?"

Brad grinned crookedly. "If we were in Boston, I could think of a few reasons." The smile faded and a frown drew his dark brows together. "But I really hadn't thought I had been in London long enough to win enemies. Guess I have."

"So what are you going to do?"

"I'm going to be very careful and I'm going to ask you not to say anything about this to anyone."

"All right. But may I ask why?"

"Well, there's no need to upset Russel Clayton any more than he already is. Knowing how Eimile died won't bring her back or ease the fact that she's dead."

"But she was murdered, and someone should pay for that."

"I agree. But since *I'm* the one they were after, they'll try again. If they think I'm not aware of that, they might get careless. It'll also give me the advantage."

"You keep saying 'they.' Is there a reason?"

Brad shook his head. "Just a figure of speech. At this point, it could be they, he *or* she. I don't know."

Both men fell quiet for a moment, each deep in thought.

"Sure ruins what should have been a happy time for you," Tyler murmured after a while. "I don't imagine Shauna is too joyful, either."

The mention of the golden-haired vixen brought a vague smile to Brad's lips. Shauna had a double reason not to be excited. Eimile Clayton's death was shattering enough to spoil anyone's day, but in Shauna's case, she had to deal with his knowledge that she owned Wrenhaven. The smile broadened as he settled back in the chair, his elbows resting on the arms, his hands clasped, the fingers held in a church steeple fashion and tapping his chin. He really didn't have to be with her to know she was probably pacing the floor in her room at this very moment.

Shauna had graciously thanked everyone who had come to her party, seen them off at the front door along with her father and mother, and then discreetly fled to her room to be alone. This had been one birthday she would never forget. Poor Russel Clayton had lost his wife of thirty-some years, and Shauna's father had publicly condemned her to a life with a man she detested. And what made it even worse was that because of her father's gift, Brad knew she had been lying when she'd said she had talked to him about Wrenhaven. As far as he was concerned, there was no reason why they couldn't get married now. He'd have his property and she'd be free of Nelson. She was trapped, and short of death, nothing would save her.

Then I'll have to talk to him, she mused as she continued her trek across the room. Maybe even tell him the truth . . . apologize . . . plead with him. She cringed at the thought. Chewing on a thumbnail, she glanced at the door, wondering if he would even listen to her, much less agree to anything she had to say.

"Well, there's only one way to find out," she mumbled, turning to give herself a quick once-over in the mirror.

As Shauna reached the bottom of the stairs, she noticed that the door to her father's study was shut, and she hesitated to interrupt whatever was going on inside. Her father probably wouldn't object if she did, but she respected his privacy as he did hers, and since she had seen Brad go into the study while she and her parents stood at the front door saying good-bye to their guests, she could only assume the two men were there now discussing something meant for their ears alone. Should she wait? she wondered. Or intrude? The decision was made for her when the latch rattled and the door swung open, and Brad's tall frame filled the archway. Tyler followed behind him, and she experienced a moment of irritation. If she had known Brad was only talking to her brother—

Nervousness flooded through her in that next instant when both men came to an abrupt halt when they saw her. Yet instead of the mocking smiles she expected to see, Tyler politely excused himself and hurried away. Brad simply stood there. A certain air of seriousness seemed to envelop the situation, and Shauna frowned, curious as to what had sent her brother off without a single insult thrown her way.

"Is something wrong?" she asked.

Brad raised a brow. "Should there be?"

She glanced in the direction Tyler had gone. "When my brother acts that way, yes." She settled her gaze on Brad again. "I don't suppose you'd tell me what's bothering him?"

Brad's wide shoulders lifted in a careless shrug as he came to stand near her. "You'd have to ask him, I'm afraid. If he wishes to tell you, he will. But we agreed not to speak of it with anyone." Resting a hand on the banister, he casually looked her up and down. "I never had the opportunity to tell you how beautiful you looked today. It's a shame the party had to be spoiled in such a way."

"It was just one of those things, I guess," she replied, stepping down off the last step. "I would have preferred it hadn't happened at all, for Mr. Clayton's sake, but it did. At least he was surrounded by friends at the time. It won't ease his loss—they were a very happy couple—but this way he didn't have to face the shock all by himself." She glanced toward the double doors at the end of the hall that led out onto the terrace. A team of servants was clearing away the remains of the party, which meant she would find no privacy there. "I'd like to talk something over with you. May we go for a walk?"

Before answering, Brad looked over his shoulder at the terrace, then extended a hand toward the front door. "Certainly," he nodded.

Bright sunshine greeted them outside on the steps. Ordinarily it would have pleased Shauna. She loved warm spring days and enjoyed a leisurely stroll bathed in their serenity. Today this was not the case. Leaving through the wrought iron gate, they turned down the sidewalk and traveled several yards before she drew up the courage to speak.

"I believe we've come to a crossroads, Brad, one that has to be resolved before we can go any further with this farce." Her voice was low and smooth and confident.

"And what crossroads is that?" he asked, smiling when her attention was away from him. He knew what she was after. He just wanted to see how she'd handle it.

"It's quite simple, and I'm sure you know what I'm talking about." She kept her eyes trained on the path they walked. "You're after Wrenhaven—which you'll have by marrying me—but you've openly admitted you don't intend to hold up your part of the bargain. I've given this matter a great deal of thought, and even though I risk my father's temper, I'll be left with no alternative than to tell him the truth, if you don't reconsider."

"The truth, Shauna?" he tested, taking her elbow to guide her in front of him as they passed by a couple walking toward them.

"Yes. I only offered this deal because I thought the two of us would have what we wanted." His closeness seemed to engulf her, and despite the cool breeze that played with her soft curls, she could feel a warmth beginning to grow in the pit of her stomach. "But if I'm the one to go without, then I'll confess my transgressions to Papa and take my chances with his decision."

"Even if it means marrying Nelson after all?" A

devilish twinkle lit up his eyes.

She drew in a quick, shuddering breath. "I pray not. I would not be any better off marrying him than you, should that be the case. But if that were to be his decision, then I would have to find some other means of escaping Nelson Thorndyke." They had come to the end of the block. Across the street and to the right stood a gazebo nestled among a group of trees. Without asking, she led him there and mounted the trio of steps. Inside, she turned to face him.

"I've never been one to beg. I resent having to do so now. But you've managed to place me in a very uncomfortable dilemma, and I feel that if we can come to some sort of terms, this union will please us both. But only *if* you'll give me your word that they do not include the matter of sharing bedchambers." A warm blush rose in her cheeks as she recalled the pleasure that experience had given her, and she wisely turned away that he might not see it in her eyes. "What happened between us was an accident. Neither of us planned it, and I'm sure if we could, we'd change it back. I'm not in love with you, as I'm certain you're not in love with me. It's a minor point, but one we can live with if we're each given what we truly want. In your case, it's Wrenhaven. In mine, it's being able to continue on with my life the way it was: free to come and go as I please, with no obligations or responsibilities to you. We'd have the same name, we'd live under the same roof, we'd appear to be husband and wife to all concerned, but that would be the extent of it." She looked at him again. "A simple enough compromise, don't you think?"

Brad had quietly listened to her explain every detail. He had heard both the anguish and the pleading in her voice. Some of what she said was true. And yes, it was an arrangement she could live with, but he wasn't so sure he could. Despite the quarrels, the harsh words, and her claim that that night meant nothing to her, he refused to believe she didn't feel something toward him. Maybe it was the look in her eye or the way she blushed whenever she saw him that made him doubt her. Whatever it was, he wasn't about to let it die before it had the chance to grow, just because of his pride. Maybe she didn't love him—like she said—not now, anyway. But given time, he planned to change that. Shauna Radborne was willing to marry him, and he wasn't going to do anything that might jeopardize that, not now, not after he had finally found the only woman he had ever known who so completely mystified him. She haunted his dreams, his every waking hour, and had somehow managed to capture his heart.

"Yes, Shauna," he answered softly. "A compromise."

Chapter Eight

The arrival of summer seemed as sudden as Shauna's change of mood toward Brad Remington. No one other than Moira noticed, however, and the young Irishwoman had been tempted several times to question her about it, but hadn't. Shauna wouldn't tell her, not if Moira got down on bended knee. The puzzling part wasn't that Shauna no longer appeared worried about the forthcoming nuptials, a date set and agreed upon by Pierce Radborne, Brad, and even Shauna herself, but that the young woman even seemed anxious for the day to arrive. There had been a small dinner party three weeks past to announce their engagement and the wedding day, and now that that time was soon to be upon them, the staff of the Radborne household was in frantic upheaval involving the preparations for that long-awaited ceremony, since the wedding ritual was to take place on the terrace.

Brad had been absent more often than not, and when asked, Shauna explained that he had moved into the manor on Wrenhaven to see to its refurbishing, leaving him little time for socializing. Moira wasn't surprised that his infrequent visits didn't upset her mistress. After all, that was what Shauna had wanted from the start—

her freedom. But what bothered Moira was Brad's willingness to go along with it. Or so it seemed. She had always prided herself on recognizing a man's character just by talking with him for a few minutes. She had decided that with Brad, Shauna had met someone who wouldn't give in to her demands. She still thought she was right about him, and just as soon as Shauna gave permission to start moving her things into the mansion, Moira planned to take the opportunity to speak with him again. She had to know his intentions if she were ever to feel comfortable with Shauna's decision to go through with the wedding.

"Moira," Shauna sang from the tub as she watched the pert young woman lay out her clothes on the bed, "you seem very distant. What are you thinking about?"

Concentrating on her task, Moira cautioned, "That it's improper for a young woman who's about to be married ta attend a masquerade ball without an escort."

"I'm not going to Sir Blakely's alone," Shauna laughed lightheartedly, squeezing soapy water from her sponge along the length of her outstretched arm. "My whole family is going."

Moira straightened with her hands on her hips. "I'm talkin' about Mr. Remington."

"What about him?" Shauna inquired lazily as she slid down into the warm depths of her bath water.

"He's the man ya are ta marry, not your whole family," Moira scowled. "It isn't proper for ya ta go to such a big party without him by your side. Especially with your weddin' bein' only the day after tomorrow. Ya'll start rumors, that's what ya'll do."

Shauna waved a hand dismissingly. "Let them talk. It will give them something to do. Besides, they'll have to get used to it sooner or later. Once we're married, they'll see us together even less than we are now."

"Oh, so that's it," Moira jeered, her dark head cocked to one side, her mouth puckered irritably. "He's agreed ta let ya have your way."

Shauna's puzzled green eyes looked askance at her maid. "Of course. It was part of the bargain. You know that." Sensing Moira might know something she didn't, Shauna sat up in the tub. "Why should that come as a surprise?"

Moira shrugged and turned to pick up a towel. "I just thought Mr. Remington would be different." She held out the piece of linen cloth and quickly wrapped Shauna in it as she left the tub.

"Different? How so?"

Moira ignored her to rub Shauna's back and arms dry with a second towel. "Doesn't matter," she mumbled.

"Yes, it does," Shauna snapped. "You're very seldom ever wrong about a person. If it surprises you to learn he's agreed to my conditions, I want to know about it."

"'Tis nothin' more than instinct, Miss Shauna," Moira admitted. "Instinct is far from the truth. Besides, what good will it do ya ta know me opinion when ya're gettin' married in two days?"

There was too much logic in that to ease Shauna's worries. It was a little late to change her mind. Her father wouldn't hear of it. She'd be Mrs. Brad Remington by noon on Sunday, whether she liked it or not. Shrugging off her fears *and* Moira's strange Irish premonitions, she squared her shoulders and walked to the bed to don her undergarments. She planned to enjoy Sir Blakely's party tonight, and nothing her maid could say or do would ruin that.

*   *   *

"Well, look at you!" Tyler exclaimed from the bottom of the stairs where he watched his sister's descent in obvious approval. "Brad's going to be sorry he missed this."

Beneath the black satin mask covering her nose, brow, and cheeks, its edges trimmed in ebony feathers and fanned out to give the appearance of an owl's hooded scowl, Shauna's face pinkened at her brother's compliment. "I take that to mean you won't be ashamed to be seen with me?" she teased, gracefully lifting the yards of black flowing silk to clear her step. Nearing the last tread, she held out her gloved hand to him. He eagerly and willingly accepted it.

"Never I," he chided, leaning closer to whisper, "but perhaps Mother will. You'll put her to shame no matter what she wears."

"Why, thank you, kind sir," she grinned with a deep curtsy. "Then perhaps it would be wise of me not to be in the same room with her this evening."

Tyler laughed. "The same house would be more like it, Sis," he admitted, holding his voice down and jerking his head toward the parlor. "She and Father are in there arguing over whether or not he should have invited Thorndyke to the wedding."

"Who's winning?" Shauna smiled.

"Well, Mother's doing most of the hollering, but you know who always has the final say."

"Papa," she replied at the precise moment Tyler supplied the information. "So that means Nelson is coming."

"Afraid so," Tyler crooned. "Does that upset you?"

Nothing about Nelson Thorndyke upset her anymore. He was no longer a threat. She shook her head.

"Yes, I suppose not," her brother sighed. "When a

woman's in love and about to get married, she's blind to everything around her."

His remark shocked her. "In love?" she queried with a laugh.

Tyler straightened his lanky frame and looked dubiously at her. "Yes, in love. Are you pretending you're not?"

Even though Shauna had yet to experience such an emotion, she was very sure what she felt for Brad wasn't love. "You've had more practice at it than I have. Why not tell me if I am."

"How can you not be in love?" he implored. "You're about to marry a man—a handsome one at that—who is someone neither Father nor Mother pushed on you. He comes from a respected family. He's young, healthy, a hard worker—" He stopped abruptly and frowned. "You did tell him about Sir Blakely's party tonight, didn't you?"

Shauna was suddenly very thankful she had donned her mask before coming downstairs. "Of course," she lied. "But you know Brad." She smiled and shrugged her bare shoulders, the puffy black sleeves bobbing upward. "He thinks working on the manor is more important than going to a stuffy ol' ball." She feigned a troubled sigh and moved away from her brother to check her appearance in the hall mirror. "I certainly hope this isn't an indication of what married life will be—him at home, me going to parties without him." She stole a secretive look at her brother through the silvered glass to see if she could tell whether or not he believed her.

"Oh, I doubt it," he quickly guaranteed her, totally duped by her worried facade. "He's only concerned with having your home ready in time for you to move in."

"I hope so," she sighed, forcing back a grin as she

tested one of the pearl-tipped hairpins to make sure it hadn't worked loose from her elegantly coiffured wig. "I truly hope so."

"What are you hoping for, Shauna?" her father's voice interrupted from the parlor doorway.

Turning to greet him, Shauna smiled warmly. "That tonight will be as much fun as it's promising to be."

As always, Sir Blakely's mansion was overflowing with an assortment of drinks, food, and guests by the time the Radborne carriage pulled up outside its front entrance. Music and laughter spilled from every window and doorway and the spacious side lawn was aglow with lanterns dotting the perimeter, the silhouette of strolling couples accented by a backdrop of golden light. Yet none of that really interested Shauna. All she cared about was fulfilling the required and expected formalities and venturing on to one of the rooms where she planned to remain the entire evening playing cards. Since the day Brad had first entered her life, she had been denied this pleasure, and tonight she intended to make up for it.

Obviously, word of Sir Blakely's masquerade ball had spread far and wide. Shauna had never seen so many people gathered in one place at the same time for as long as she could remember. The masks and elegant clothes made it difficult for her to recognize everyone, and after a while, she decided it didn't matter. After all, wasn't that the purpose of such a gathering? The disguises enabled all who felt so inclined to abandon proper behavior and thoroughly enjoy themselves as someone else. Shauna's mother lived for parties like this one, but only if her husband wasn't present. With Pierce in attendance, unless someone drew him into discussing business,

Roanna's evening would be long and boring. Shauna should have felt sorry for her mother, but she didn't. It was what the woman deserved.

"Need I ask where you're headed?" Tyler joked as he and Shauna stood in the hallway outside the ballroom, listening to the music and watching the steady stream of guests entering the large room with drinks in one hand, a plate of tasty delicacies in the other.

"If I'm to keep my identity a secret, I must go somewhere you aren't," she bantered with a smile.

Startled by her comment, he looked her up and down, then hurriedly inspected his own slender frame. "I hardly see where standing with me reveals your identity, Shauna," he argued.

"Well, look at us," she teased. "Even with the masks, it's not too difficult for someone to know we're related."

"How so?"

"Tyler," she moaned, taking his arm and leading him to the gold-framed mirror hanging over the black-lacquered buffet in the hall, her hand extended toward it. "We're nearly the same height. We both have on white wigs. The lower half of our faces show, specifically the finely boned features of our chins, and our mouths are the same. It's obvious we have similar slender builds, and the only difference between us, which really only adds to our likeness, is that you're dressed entirely in white, and I'm in black. It's almost as though we had planned it."

Tyler cocked his head from side to side as he studied his reflection, then hers. "I'm more handsome, however."

His gibe failed to provoke the response he expected. "Only with your mask on," she countered, holding back a giggle. "You'd scare everyone off, otherwise."

Tyler's mouth twisted. "Thank you, dear Shauna. You always know how to injure me deeply."

"Only when you ask for it," she returned, leaning in to kiss the corner of his mouth. "Now, be a good boy and go find someone else to torment." She glanced toward the closed game room door. "I intend to spend a quiet evening showing a few gentlemen how to really play cards."

"Without dancing with me first?" he objected.

Shauna's head jerked back around, her pale green eyes glowing from behind the dark mask. "You'd rather dance with me instead of Beth?" The smile disappeared. "She is coming, isn't she?"

Tyler shook his head. "Not this time. Her mother hasn't been feeling well, and she wanted to stay home with her."

"That's too bad, Tyler," Shauna sympathized, touching a gloved hand to his arm. "I would imagine the night will be a little dull without her."

Even as she spoke, her brother's attention was drawn away by the coquettish laughter of two young women watching him from close by. Glancing in that direction, Shauna quickly realized how wrong she had been. Tyler never allowed himself to get bored. She only hoped Beth would understand . . . if she ever found out. Tyler Radborne was a hopeless flirt.

Must have gotten it from Mother, she mused, remembering how artfully Roanna had deposited her husband into the capable hands of some of his associates—the longwinded kind—thus giving her a chance to slip away and do the sort of thing she enjoyed most—acting coy.

A smile parted Shauna's lips as she watched her brother casually walk toward the two giggling women. It was as if he'd forgotten all about guarding his younger sister. But Shauna didn't mind. He always criticized the way she played cards *and* how much she wagered. Tonight she was on her own, and she planned to win twice the amount she had brought with her.

Nodding politely at the manservant who opened the game room door for her, Shauna entered quietly and moved to stand near the huge fireplace where she would have a better view of the many tables positioned about the place. Each was full at the moment, but she knew that would change soon enough. It always did. Many sat down only to play a few rounds. Some stayed longer, usually until his spouse sent word of impending divorce should her mate not present himself by her side in the next minute. Others played until they had lost all of their money. In Shauna's case, she didn't see where she'd fall into any of those categories. In fact, *she* would walk away a winner.

Suddenly a glass of amber wine was held out in front of her, breaking her concentration and drawing her attention to the man who offered it.

"Ya looked thirsty, lass," he told her in a high-pitched, thick Irish brogue. "And like ya would enjoy a wee bit of company while ya wait."

Hesitant, Shauna took the proffered drink from his large hand and tried furtively to see past his deep scarlet mask for a hint to his identity, only to dismiss the effort when nothing about him seemed familiar. "Thank you," she murmured, dropping her gaze. After all, there was no reason why she should know him. Among all the men who came and went from the Radborne study, none of them had been Irish, and as far as she knew, Moira didn't have any relatives living in London. And she'd surely remember a man with a bright red beard who walked with a cane.

"You're not alone, are ya, lass?" he continued, his

dark eyes scanning the room and the various games of chance being played.

"No. I'm here with my family."

A deep chuckle sounded in her ear. "'Twasn't what I meant, but I suppose that will do." He took a sip of his wine. "Are ya any good at this?" he asked, nodding at one of the tables.

A sly smile parted her lips, and she stole a peek at him as he stood beside her watching the round of bets being wagered. "I enjoy it," she cunningly replied. "How about you?"

His broad shoulders, covered in dark red linen, lifted with his shrug. "Don't have much of a chance, meself. But I usually win a coin or two before the night is over." His attention changed direction suddenly and his eyes darkened beneath the frown his mask concealed. "Are ya sure you're not alone, lass?"

Puzzled by his insistent need to know, she glanced over at him in time to see him nod at something across the room. Following his silent bidding, she noticed a solidly built, older fellow staring back at her. His size and stature, as well as the flashy diamond ring he wore on the little finger of his left hand, instantly sent a nervous shudder through her. Until this very moment, she hadn't honestly thought Nelson Thorndyke's presence would bother her.

"He's starin' daggers at me, lass," her companion observed. "Could he be a jealous lover? Or your father, perhaps?"

"Neither," Shauna quickly replied, turning her back toward Nelson as she sipped her wine.

"Then he's taken a fancy to ya," he added. "Not unlike meself, I might add. Is he an admirer, someone I should be beggin' me leave because of? I don't want ta stand in the way of romance—"

"Believe me, you won't be," Shauna hurriedly assured him, taking a longer drink of her wine. Odd, until now she had always thought Tyler's overprotectiveness was unnecessary. Glancing covertly at Nelson to see that he hadn't moved, she turned back to study the assortment of alabaster figurines lining the mantel of the white marble fireplace, asking, "Why didn't you assume he was my husband?"

The Irishman laughed. "Many reasons. For one, a lass like yourself wouldn't be standin' here alone if she had a husband. A man would be a fool to abandon his beautiful wife to the likes of me . . . or that one. But more than that, ya strike me as an inventive young lass who would find her way out of marryin' a man old enough to be her father." He smiled over at her. "Am I wrong?"

His knack at having guessed the truth surprised her, but his flattery eased her tension. "Close. I'm to be married Sunday morning."

A wide hand flew to his chest. "Say it isn't so," he moaned, his dark eyes twinkling. "Just when I thought me luck had changed and I'd been blessed. . . ." The smile disappeared, and he hurriedly scoured the room full of men. "And where might he be? Surely he's close by?"

"He couldn't come," Shauna smiled. "And thank you for the kind words." She glanced briefly at Nelson. "And for keeping that one at bay. He *is* jealous, but I guarantee he's no lover of mine. Until I met Brad, Nelson had it in mind to marry me. My father was even considering it."

"Ah, but love ruled out," the Irishman concluded.

"Love?" she countered. "Nay. Merely a more suitable mate."

Shauna could barely see the stranger cock a brow

beneath his scarlet mask.

"Are ya sayin' ya don't love the man ya are to marry?" He shook his head and watched the round of cards being played at a nearby table. "You English have a strange way of choosing a spouse."

"And the Irish are different?" she laughed, relaxing in his company.

"Aye," he strongly promised her. "We don't look for a way ta increase our wealth. We marry for love."

His declaration reminded Shauna of Moira's confession, and she frowned. "Strange. That's not what my maid told me."

"A lass born and raised in England, no doubt."

"Moira Flanagan?" she chided. "Does that sound English?"

His wide shoulders bobbed in surrender. "Well, *most* of us marry for love."

"Have you?" she tested, secretively noting how his clothes fit him a little snugly around the middle and wondering if a thick patch of red hair was hidden beneath his periwig.

"Aye," he nodded, his attention still centered on the card game. "I found the lass I want ta marry."

"And you're here flirting with me." She looked past him toward the door, adding, "Or is she waiting outside for you?"

Strong white teeth showed with his smile. "She's waitin' in Dublin. I'm here on business."

Shauna fought hard not to laugh. "You call this business? Will she understand if you tell her you came to a masquerade ball without her and struck up a conversation with an unmarried woman?"

"I won't tell her I was here."

"Oh, I see." She chewed on her lower lip. "You're a scoundrel, sir."

The Irishman straightened his tall frame and faced her. "A scoundrel, is it? Simply because I took a moment out to chat with a beautiful woman? But what of yourself? In two days ya'll be saying 'I do' and you're here flirtin' with me." Devilment danced in his dark eyes.

The corners of her mouth twitched. "But *I'm* not marrying for love."

A slow smile spread over his face and he nodded in defeat. Turning back to watch the game, he took a drink of his wine, then boldly asked, "And what would it take for ya to fall in love, lass?"

The vision of Brad suddenly came to mind and spoiled her carefree mood. She hadn't ever honestly considered what she expected from a man, but maybe that was because she hadn't contemplated marriage to someone she loved. Brad certainly had a special way of reminding her that she was a woman, more so than any other suitor who had tried to win her hand. And he had somehow awakened hidden passions in her she never suspected were there. Frowning, she raised her glass to her lips. She doubted Nelson would ever have kindled such a fire in her. The image that thought conjured up made her upper lip curl in disdain. Yet what she and Brad had shared for those few special moments hadn't ended there. Every time she saw him, she felt warm all over. And when she was alone, she felt empty. Hardly a moment passed that she wasn't thinking of him. Her frown deepened. Perhaps it was only a physical thing. Her body had betrayed her once. It could be doing so now. Suddenly she sensed the Irishman's eyes on her, and she blinked and lifted her eyes.

"Does your silence mean ya don't know, lass?" he asked.

Shauna grinned and looked away. "I guess it means I don't really know what love is," she admitted.

"Or that you're scared of it," he proposed.

She stared down at the amber liquid she swirled in her glass. "Perhaps."

"Ya shouldn't be. It can be a glorious thing."

She laughed. "Are you speaking from experience?"

"Aye," he quickly confessed. "I thought I had been in love once before, but now I know differently. What I feel for the lass I'm goin' ta marry is much deeper than what I felt for . . . Brenna." The last came hesitantly.

"I hope so," she chuckled. "Seeing as how you practically forgot her name."

The Irishman cleared his throat and rubbed a finger along his lower lip. "Well, that was a long time ago."

"What happened to spoil it? Did she find out you'd go to parties without her?" Shauna teased.

"Something like that." He smiled and finished off his wine. "Care for another?" he asked, nodding at her glass.

"No. Thank you. If I drink too much, I won't have a clear head for the game, and I plan to win a little money tonight."

"Now *that* sounds like a challenge. May I join your table?"

Shauna presented him with a slight bob of her white curls. "I'd be honored."

A short time later found Shauna and her new friend engaged in a serious game of cards. Nelson had watched for a while, then left without even speaking to her, no doubt to inform her father where she was. The Irishman won the first two hands, Shauna, the next three, and all for low stakes. The other players jokingly asked if the two newcomers had set this up between them before joining the game, but as the night wore on and only they held the winning hands, the joking stopped. New players took the losers' places. The room began to thin out as some partygoers decided it was time they went home. Shauna and her friend continued to win. Somewhere around midnight, Tyler appeared with a beautiful woman on his arm, and Shauna quickly took note that she wasn't one of the first two her brother had approached. She excused herself from the game then, letting Tyler sit in for her while she had a glass of sherry and walked out the kinks in her back. The Irishman continued to win, and when her pile of coins started to dwindle, she politely thanked her brother for relieving her and sat down at the table again.

They played for another hour, until only Shauna and her friend were left. The room was practically empty, except for those who lounged near the fireplace smoking cigars and ignoring the last two players. The music, however, continued to float in, and Tyler, having grown restless watching, took his young woman back to the dance floor. As the mantel clock struck one-thirty, Shauna was dealt the best cards she had been given all night, but obviously, from the wager the Irishman made, he felt sure he could beat her. A frown knotted her brow as she glanced from the pile of coins in the middle of the table to the few she had left to bet, then at the hand she held, and her gambler's blood surged through her veins. Laying her cards face down on the table in front of her, she folded her arms along the edge and leaned in, deliberately allowing her bosom to rest on them as she stared over at her opponent.

"It would seem, kind sir, that I'm in a bit of trouble," she purred enticingly as she watched his eyes lower to feast on the treasure she had purposely offered him. The low décolletage of her gown barely covered the rose-hued peaks of her breasts, and if she leaned forward a little more they would threaten to spill from their restraints.

The Irishman visibly had difficulty drawing a breath to speak. "And what trouble is that, lass?" he asked, forcing himself to look at the soft green eyes staring back at him through the slits in her black mask.

"I haven't enough to match your wager."

He laid his cards down and leaned back in the chair. "Aye. 'Tis a bit of trouble."

"Would you take a promissory note?"

A lazy smile parted his lips. "Can't spend a piece of paper."

"I'm good for it. I assure you."

He chuckled and idly toyed with his cards. "No offense, lass, but I don't even know who ya are. Or what ya look like."

"My name is Shauna Radborne. My father is—"

"Pierce Radborne," he cut in.

"You know him?"

"Not personally."

"But you know who he is."

"Aye."

"And that his wealth far exceeds that of the guests here tonight—that he's probably richer than Sir Blakely?"

The Irishman nodded, but didn't appear to be convinced he would trust her.

Shauna touched her fingertips to the ivory cameo tied around her throat with a ribbon of black velvet, then the matching earrings. "I could give you these. They belonged to my grandmother. They're worth a substantial amount." When he started to decline the offer, she rushed on, "Only as a mark of my good intentions. I really don't want to part with them, but if I lose this hand, we can agree to meet tomorrow and I'll buy them back."

His dark eyes drifted from the offered jewelry to the pile of coins on the middle of the table. "I don't think they're enough, lass. Sentimental value far exceeds the real worth."

"Then you choose," she quickly suggested. She didn't want him to declare that the game was over. She could win this hand. She was sure of it. All she needed was—

"Your dowry," he replied, reaching into his waistcoat pocket for a tin of cheroots.

"My dowry?" The idea shocked her.

"Aye. A rich young lass like yourself isn't likely ta go to the altar without one." He looked away from her long enough to light his cigar.

"Well, yes, I have a dowry." Frowning, she glanced at the mounds of coins. "But it far surpasses the worth of your wager."

Grinning, he slid the rest of the coins stacked in front of him into the pile.

"Or that," she objected.

He took a puff on his cheroot and watched the smoke curl upward. "If the cost is too high, lass, then perhaps your cards aren't as good as ya think they are." He laid the cigar in the ashtray next to him and started to scoop in the money.

"No, wait!" she begged, reaching out to touch his hand. A second of hesitation made her bite her lip. She stared at him, the money, then at her down-turned cards.

They were the best she could ever remember being dealt. He couldn't beat her. She was just sure of it. Glancing over her shoulder toward the writing desk sitting in the far corner of the room, she gathered up her winning hand and stood. "I'll be right back. Don't move," she instructed, turning away. A moment later she came back to the table and tossed down a piece of parchment on top of the coins. "My dowry is the Wrenhaven estate. I've given the bearer of this note clear ownership." Smiling confidently, she sat down and nodded at his cards. "I call," she said, her heart thumping erratically in her chest as she watched him pick up the paper and read it.

"Are ya sure, lass?" he asked, his face an expression of doubt. "If ya lose, you'll have nothin' ta give your husband. He might not understand—"

"I won't lose," she firmly replied. "Now, either show your cards or I'll have to assume you were bluffing."

He stared at her a moment longer, his dark eyes having lost their devilish twinkle. "All right," he sighed. "But don't say I didn't give ya plenty of warnin'."

One by one he laid them down, slowly, precisely, almost reluctantly. By the time the last card showed, Shauna's head was spinning, tears burned in her throat, and panic knotted her stomach. Never in her wildest of imaginings would she have given second thought to the possibility of losing, yet in a matter of a few seconds, Wrenhaven had been gambled away. Both Moira and Tyler had tried repeatedly to warn her of how much trouble her favorite pastime might afford her someday, but she had never listened. It had always been her rule *never* to wager more than the amount she had with her. Tonight she had ignored that rule. She had been positive she could win. Her opponent had claimed he wasn't very

244

practiced in the sport, and during the course of the evening she had noticed that every time he had a winning hand he would play with the ring on his little finger. It wasn't much, but she had sat across the table from many a gambler in her time, and *every one* of them had some sort of tic that gave them away. Toying with his ring was the Irishman's. He hadn't done that with this round, leading her to believe she could bet the world and win. Yet, discovering that she had been wrong for once wasn't what tightened the muscles in her chest. She had lost Wrenhaven, Brad's Wrenhaven, her guarantee of a satisfactory marriage contract. Brad wouldn't marry her now. In a daze, she was drawn to look at the door at the end of the long, narrow room, the buzzing in her ears almost deafening, and through a haze she saw the tall, barrel-chested physique of Nelson Thorndyke, who stood there staring back at her. Gathering what composure she had left, she quickly averted her eyes, near tears and fighting back the desire to run screaming from the room. Once her father learned what she had done, he'd force her to marry Nelson as punishment. And rightfully so. She deserved to spend the rest of her life with the man for being so stupid, so careless and cocksure.

The chiming of the mantel clock brought her out of her stupor. She blinked, swallowed hard, and sucked in a deep, trembling breath. "I suppose you'll want to move in right away," she weakly concluded as she watched him collect his winnings and put them in a black cloth bag.

"Nay. I've business here in London ta take care of, then I must return home. I'm gettin' married soon." Sliding out of his chair, he stood and reached for his cane. He stared at her a moment until she finally had the courage to look at him. "I'm not a demon, Miss

245

Radborne. I don't gloat over someone's misfortune. I'll give ya time to explain to your fiance. It will be a month, maybe more, before I return."

"Thank you," she mumbled weakly, lowering her eyes.

"But don't take too long," he added after a brief moment of silence. He started to turn away and changed his mind. "Miss Radborne, might I offer a piece of advice?"

Green eyes glistening with tears looked up at him from behind black satin.

"If the man loves ya, and I'm sure he does—he'd be a fool *not* ta love ya—then tell him the truth—*before* ya marry him."

"But of course," she quickly assured him. "What would I gain by lying to him?"

Broad shoulders lifted in a lazy shrug. "A devious mind would see the benefit of it," he answered before a soft smile parted his lips. "But I think you're too smart ta fall into that trap. One lie always leads to another, and before ya know it, ya're in too deep ta get out."

His warning puzzled her. Why should he care what she did? Lying to Brad or telling him the truth wouldn't change what had happened. The Irishman had won Wrenhaven fairly. Even if she told Brad she had been tricked or cheated out of it, he still had her note. All he'd have to do was show it to Brad.

"Thank you for your concern, sir," she replied, coming to her feet, "but there's no need. It's my problem and I'll deal with it." The room had seemed to become rather stuffy in the past few minutes. Glancing to her right, she saw a set of french doors and decided a short walk in the cool night air would do her some good.

246

Without telling him good-bye or even looking at him again, she turned and walked away.

A strange look came over the Irishman's face as he watched the beautiful Shauna Radborne glide effortlessly across the floor and out through the double doors to the gardens beyond. He had never met anyone like her in his life, and he wished it could have been under different circumstances. Sensing he was being watched, he turned his head and found Nelson Thorndyke staring at him, his hatred pouring out through the slits in his mask. With a mocking smile, he bowed slightly to the man, then turned and exited the room.

Moonlight played among the shadows on the terrace, floating in and out like some mystical child playing tag. Soft breezes stirred the leaves and set the willows swaying to a lyrical tune of silent sounds. Crickets joined in the chorus. The sweet fragrance of flowers filled the air. Amidst the serenity, the figure of a woman appeared, slowly walking the flagstone path in quiet resolution and unaware of the symphony blaring all around her. She had come here to be alone and to think things out. Her mind was troubled. She had a decision to make, one that promised to change her life. The answer was simple. Tell the truth and let the rest come naturally. Yet, she hesitated, and she didn't honestly know why. She knew what the results would be, and that they would be far from pleasant. But either way, she would never be alone. Yet without the man of her choice that was truly what she'd be . . . alone. That revelation shocked her.

Suddenly, she felt a presence in the gardens where she walked. Turning sharply, she saw a dark figure step out of the shadows, and she gasped. Moonlight masked his identity, but bathed his broad-shouldered frame in a silver glow, and her heart beat a little faster in anticipation.

"How did you know I'd be here?" she whispered tremulously.

"I sensed it," he replied. "You have something to tell me."

She lowered her eyes and gripped the thick folds of her skirts in her hands. "Yes."

"And I will not like it," he guessed.

"Nay. You will not."

A heavy sigh escaped him and he turned his head to stare off into the distance. "Then lie to me," he whispered.

"But lying is a coward's way," she objected, tears glistening in her eyes. "And if I lie to you now, another will be told . . . and another. I will spin a tangled web of deceit from which I will not escape."

His dark eyes stared at her. "But have you not already done just that?" He moved closer and reached out a hand to stroke her cheek with the backs of his fingertips. "Have you not promised to marry me, to bear my name, to live your life with me as husband and wife while others think it's done out of love?"

"Yes," she murmured, her eyes closed as she savored his touch, the scent of him, his nearness. "But 'tis a lie only to them, not to you."

"Is it?" he challenged. "Then why do you hesitate to tell me the truth? Do you fear losing me?"

A single tear stole over the rim of her dark lashes and glided to her chin. "Yes," she whispered.

He lifted her face to look at him. "And why, do you suppose, is that? Could it be, my sweet, that you have fallen in love with me?"

"Nay. I love no man," she falsely denied. "Just as no man will love me. If I were a penniless old crone and you came to me on bended knee, I might believe. But I am not. You pretend to care because of what I offer in return."

"Then tell me the truth and hear my answer."

"Nay!" She jerked away from him and turned her back.

He followed, gently wrapping his arms around her trim shape and drawing her back against his chest, his face touching her cheek as he asked, "Why? Do you fear my wrath, that I will abandon you? Or perhaps that you will learn you are worth loving for yourself alone? Does that thought frighten you?"

"The thought that I will never know for certain frightens me."

"Trust your heart." He turned her in his arms. "Look into my eyes, hear my words, see deep into my soul. Listen to your instincts and know that I would follow you to the ends of the earth with no promise of love in return, just to be with you, to claim you as my own. I love you, Shauna Kathleen Radborne, as I have never loved another in my life." He lowered his head and warmly captured her lips.

At first she resisted, doubting his sincerity and knowing her own weakness. Then a need began to grow deep inside her, the need to feel loved no matter what the terms or conditions. Slipping her arms up around his neck, she kissed him hard, urgently, desperately. She pressed her body full length against his, surrendering to the heavenly feel of his hands roaming her spine, his mouth covering hers. Tears flowed freely down her cheeks. Her heart beat wildly. Her pulse quickened.

"I love you, Shauna Kathleen," he whispered against her lips as he bent slightly and swooped her up in his arms.

In the next instant he had lain her down on a soft cushion of tall grasses and had shed his clothes and hers. Moonlight graced the hard, rippling thews of his shoulders, neck, and chest, and masked his handsome face in a shadow. Lovingly, she caressed the sinewy strength of his arms, his ribs, the lean hips, pulling him down as she parted eager, willing thighs. Eyes half-closed, she raised her mouth to his, kissing him hungrily, greedily as she arched her back and welcomed the first thrust. His probing shaft found her, sending a shiver of exploding ecstasy throughout her trembling body. She moaned deliriously and parted his lips with her tongue to push inside, sharp teeth nibbling playfully.

He moved against her, sleek and hard, his mouth slipping to her throat, his hands gliding along the smooth, long length of her hip and thigh. Waves of passion washed over her, catching her in their swirling torrent. Her breath came in ragged heaves. Her pulse thundered in her ears. Her body burned with desire, and she was hot and cold, calm and fearful, hesitant and willing all at the same moment.

"I love you, Brad," she pledged huskily against his throat, her body moving in perfect harmony with his.

Then, of a sudden, he stopped. His face was still in shadows, she fought to see the expression there, a clue to his unexpected change of heart. A frown crimped her brow and a heaviness engulfed her when he lifted from her.

"Brad?" she weakly mumbled. "What's wrong? What

have I done?"

"Done?" he echoed, his tone cold and hard. "You've lied to me, that's what you've done. And now you'll pay the price." His tall form moved into the light, and a chilling horror seized her heart, for there bathed in silvery moonlight, his handsome face slowly, magically changed into the leering grin of Nelson Thorndyke.

"No-o-o-o!"

Shauna bolted upright in her bed, her body drenched with perspiration, her eyes wide and filled with tears. Her world was a jumble and several moments passed before the whirling fragments of her dream mixed with the comforting bits of reality. Breathless and drained of energy, she pushed back against the headboard of her bed, the sheets and coverlet crumpled over her lap. Pastel streaks of predawn spilled into her room through the open window and carrying with them the sweet fragrance of early morning. Soft breezes played with the lace curtains. She raked back the damp hair from her brow, her cool fingertips touching her fevered flesh while she fought to push aside her nightmare. Yet visions of Brad continued to haunt her.

Laying her head back against the wall behind her, she closed her eyes in an effort to calm her jittery nerves. Not only was it startling for her to be awakened from a dream gone horribly awry with the image of the one man who most threatened her sanity, but it was shocking, to say the least, for her to learn her imaginary world included Brad. She could easily blame her thoughts of him on the simple fact that she must face up to him within the next twenty-four hours, but to pretend she loved him? It was unthinkable! Her brother must have put that idea in her head.

251

Flipping off the covers, she touched bare feet to the floor and crossed to the washstand where she poured fresh water in the bowl and proceeded to splash the cool liquid over her face and neck. Standing erect, she allowed the silvery droplets to run down her throat and between her breasts as she let her head fall back, her eyes shut. A teasing breath of morning air chilled her as it floated all around her, billowing the skirt of her nightgown and stirring up the memories of her dream and what had led up to it. With a sigh, she picked up a towel, dotted her chin and neck with it, and crossed to the window to stare outside at the pale light of dawn staining the eastern sky.

After her disaster at the gaming table, she had gone out into the gardens in back of Sir Blakely's mansion to be alone and to think. The last time she had been a guest in his house she had set her sights on finding a suitable husband, one who would agree to her terms and solve her dilemma. She had found him. Or so she'd thought. Everything had gone smoothly at first, until Brad began to show a stubborn streak. He obviously resented being trapped, no matter what the payment. The more she had insisted, the more he'd fought her. He had even threatened to kill her, and even now she wondered if he had meant it and still would . . . especially after she told him that she had lost Wrenhaven in a game of cards. She cringed at how untterly stupid that sounded.

She had no idea how long she had strolled around the gardens, only that Nelson Thorndyke had suddenly appeared and sent her fleeing back inside. Just being in close proximity to the man made her realize how strong a chance there was now that he'd have every right to be wherever she was. Brad had no reason to marry her anymore. Nelson would have no competition. Her father would gladly consent to their union. That idea churned her stomach, and she turned away from the window.

Wandering back across the room, she absently reached out an arm and hooked her elbow around one of the tall posters on her bed. Pulling herself close, she pressed her cheek against its smooth graining. Tyler had noticed something was wrong with her the moment he bumped into her in the hallway. She had tried to blame her seemingly distracted state on being tired. Her brother wouldn't agree. He had said she was nervous about her wedding night, and that she was worried Brad would throw her out of his bed once he found out how inadequate she was. She wasn't sure how she had managed to present him with a reasonably convincing air of self-control, but she had. He was only teasing, as he always did, trying to get the better of her, to make her angry. Her response had been a reference to the improbability of Brad's kicking her out of bed before the temperature dropped in the place where Tyler would more than likely end up after a jealous husband shot him dead. He had laughed and yielded to the partial truth of her statement, that he would, indeed, burn in damnation for his sins. His mood had turned serious then, and for one of the few times in their young lives, Shauna knew he wasn't playing a game with her.

"If I didn't think you'd be happy with Brad," he had said, capturing her icy fingers in his hands, "I'd do everything in my power to prevent this wedding. You know that, don't you, Sis?"

The irony of his declaration had been that if he had known what was really going on, he probably would have told her father and the result would have been even more devastating than it already was.

253

"Yes, Tyler, I know that," she had replied. "I also know you're probably the best friend I have."

"I don't have to be," he told her. "I've known Brad now for nearly two months, and if you'd let him, *he* could be your best friend, besides being your husband."

Not after tonight, she had mused. Once I tell him about the new owner of Wrenhaven. . . .

"You do love him, don't you?" Tyler had gone on to ask, startling Shauna with his straightforwardness and trapping her into some kind of an answer.

She remembered having simply stared back at him for a moment in silence, not really sure what to say, then laughing nervously as she told him that not all marriages were based on love. He had seemed surprised, and for some strange reason he had apparently thought she had meant that Brad didn't love her.

"I know most marriages are arranged," he quickly added. "And I know a lot of them never develop into anything more, but with Brad it will be different, Shauna. You caught his eye the moment he saw you. Otherwise he wouldn't have asked Father's permission to court you. Now he wants to marry you, and it wasn't arranged." A devilish smile had curled his lips then. "And knowing you as well as I do, you'd have found a way out if you didn't want to marry him. You must feel something for him."

At the moment it's fear, she had thought. There's a real strong possibility he'll kill me when he finds out I gambled away Wrenhaven.

"Shauna," Tyler had interrupted, "if you're worried that Brad doesn't feel as deeply for you as you feel toward him, then do something about it. Use your charm and beauty on him. *Make* him fall in love with you."

The sweet song of the meadow pipit floated in through the window of Shauna's room, dissolving the vision of last night's conversation with her brother, and she slowly sank back down on her bed. Stretching out, she stared up at the ceiling in quiet contemplation. Her foolishness had finally gotten her into very serious trouble, and the only person to get her out of it now would be herself. Weighing all the options, she realized that going through with the marriage to Brad was the only sensible thing she could do. According to the Irishman, she had a month before he'd come to claim his land, and anything could happen before then. Why, he might even be killed in a duel or drop dead of apoplexy. God willing, he might even forget he owned Wrenhaven! A cunning smile curled her lips and she rolled over on her stomach, her chin cradled against her closed fists. Even if her luck failed her and the Irishman showed up at the front door one day, it would be too late to annul the marriage. Brad would have to divorce her. That would take time and money, and she truly doubted a man of his character and reputation would want it known he couldn't control his wife. A bright sparkle glowed in her green eyes. Why, Brad would probably be so angry with her that he'd *never* divorce her, just out of spite, and she'd have exactly what she had wanted all along . . . a marriage in name only.

The idea made her giggle. Feeling very sure of herself, she scampered under the covers, fluffed up her pillows, and happily fell back against them, her eyes closed and a contented sigh trailing from her lips. But only a moment passed before a frown marred her smooth brow and she was staring across the room at the early markings of dawn spilling in through her window, a pang of sadness stabbing at her heart.

Chapter Nine

A cloudless blue sky, warm sunshine, and soft breezes marked the day of Shauna's wedding. The Radborne household had been up and about since dawn in preparation for the big event. Bouquets of white daisies dotted with baby's breath and tied with white satin ribbons were artfully arranged around the terrace. Rows upon rows of wrought iron chairs, each tied with the same satin ribbon, neatly filled the gardens in perfect order. In the middle a path had been made and marked with a white linen cloth, on which the bride and her father would walk to a newly constructed lattice archway, its whitewashed woodwork filled with interwoven ribbons, daisies, and green ferns. Off to one side, a banquet table decorated in tiny white chrysanthemums, roses, and fragrant bridal wreath, displayed a vast assortment of food and drink, and in the center stood a multitiered cake, iced with white frosting and minute green trim. The ceremony and following celebration promised to be the biggest London had seen in years. The mood of all involved was light and cheery, yet upstairs in the bride's bedchamber tension ran high between maid and mistress.

"Ya haven't got time ta dally, Miss Shauna," Moira scowled as she stood beside the tub, a huge towel draped over her arms. "If ya're thinkin' ta delay the vows by loungin' in there, ya won't. All ya'll do is embarrass your father—"

"I'm not dallying," Shauna snapped, knowing full well that that was exactly her plan and that it was useless even to consider it. The wedding would take place this morning, no matter what she did to postpone it. "I'm just enjoying my bath, that's all. It's hard to guess when I'll be allowed such a luxury again."

Moira's brows came sharply together. "Ya're talkin' nonsense. Ya're marryin' a man, not a beast."

Shauna looked askance at her maid. "Are you sure?"

Moira's slim shoulders dropped. "Get out of the tub right now or I'll drag ya out. We've got a million things ta do and very little time. Ya might not be wantin' ta go through with this, but ya will, and I'm goin' ta see to it that you're the most beautiful bride ever."

"Maybe," Shauna replied with a vague smile as she rinsed off the suds from her arms. Bantering with Moira always seemed to make her forget her worries.

"Maybe what?" Moira demanded. "*Maybe* I'll drag ya out of that tub?"

"No," Shauna grinned, rising and stepping onto the braided rug. "Maybe I'll be the most beautiful bride."

"Ha!" Moira proclaimed as she wrapped her mistress in the towel and vigorously rubbed her dry. "I can't think of one who'd even come close."

"Oh, I don't know," Shauna playfully persisted. "I imagine there was a very beautiful bride some years ago."

The brisk movements stopped and Moira straightened with a frown.

"I'm talking about a young Irish girl who married the man of her dreams," Shauna finished. "You."

A bright red stain darkened Moira's cheeks. "No comparison," she flatly denied as she resumed her work.

"And why do you say that? Because you didn't have flowers and cakes and lots of guests? Because you didn't have a beautiful gown to wear? Because you and Keelan had to run off to get married?" Shauna challenged, tucking in the corner of the linen towel around her bosom while Moira went to the dresser for fresh undergarments. "I'm not talking about the ceremony. I'm talking about the bride. All the finery in the world wouldn't make a beautiful bride. The love shining in her eyes makes her beautiful."

Moira shrugged a shoulder, reluctantly yielding to the possibility. "If that makes a lass beautiful, then I guess I was." She sighed dreamily, a faint smile curling her mouth. "I did love him."

"And still do," Shauna guessed.

"Aye. And still do," Moira agreed, her dark eyes twinkling. "'Tis a shame ya won't be feelin' the same for Mr. Remington when ya walk down the aisle." Gathering up the white lace underthings, she crossed to the bed and laid them there, motioning for Shauna.

The conversation she had had with her brother came into her mind as Shauna donned a silk camisole. He was sure Shauna loved Brad, and he even implied that Brad loved her. She had to deny the former and she wasn't sure about the last. Brad had never said he did, and she knew he was only marrying her for Wrenhaven. Sitting down on the bed, she pulled on her white stockings and garters, remembering something else Tyler had told her.

"Use your beauty and charm," he had suggested.

"*Make* him fall in love with you."

Shauna wasn't sure it would work or that she wanted to try. Brad wasn't just any man. He was stubborn, headstrong, and not easily fooled. If she couldn't convince him that she loved him, he'd see right through her ploy. He'd know in an instant that she was up to something. Besides, until the Irishman sent word he was on his way to Wrenhaven, there really was no need. She'd wait. If it became necessary, then she'd consider it.

The excitement of the day and the reason for it really surfaced once Moira helped Shauna slip into her wedding gown. Six months ago she never would have dreamed she'd be doing something like this, and for a moment she considered sneaking out a side door and running away. Being married wasn't going to solve her problems. She knew that now . . . now that it was too late. She'd only be adding more.

"Ya look grand," Moira proclaimed with a smile as she stepped back to examine her work. "Mr. Remington will be pleased."

"Well, we certainly wouldn't want to disappoint him, now would we?" Shauna sneered, her fair brow wrinkled as she stared at her reflection in the full-length mirror. She would have preferred wearing rags to the ice-blue satin gown cut low over her bosom, its puffy gathered sleeves accenting the narrowness of her waist. Moira had outdone herself with Shauna's hair. Piled high on her head, soft ringlets cascaded down the back and sprigs of baby breath enhanced the golden highlights. Pearl earrings dotted her earlobes. A strand of similar gems adorned her throat and matched those sewn in at the waist of the gown and at the hem of her sleeves. Pale blue slippers peeked out from beneath the yards of flowing skirts, and in back a train of ruffled white satin spilled onto the floor and trailed a good foot or more behind her. It was, indeed, a magnificent wedding gown, and Shauna should have been proud to wear it. She wasn't. This whole affair was a hoax, and the only person fooled by it was the one who wanted nothing more for his daughter than her happiness.

"Are ya regretting your actions, Miss Shauna?" Moira's soft voice intruded.

Brought out of her melancholic blur of thoughts, Shauna smiled lamely and brushed at the tear that had mysteriously pooled in the corner of her eye. "Only that I've lied to Papa," she murmured sadly. "Had I been given a choice, I never would have deceived him so."

Suddenly, warm, comforting arms encircled her. Moira didn't speak, for no words were needed. Shauna knew that of all the people in her life, this maid, this devoted servant and longtime friend, loved her more than anyone else, including Tyler and her father.

"I've done a lot of foolish things in my life, Moira," she admitted with a sigh, "but never any as serious as this. Or as selfish. Brad wouldn't be marrying me if it weren't for Wrenhaven. I've forced him into it." She broke away from Moira and went to the window to stare down at the gathering of friends and relatives filling the gardens in expectation of the forthcoming ceremony. "It would serve me right to be left alone and penniless once he finds the woman he should have married. I won't blame him if he turns on me with hatred in his heart. 'Tis what I deserve. 'Tis what I've asked for."

"Nay, lass," Moira quickly argued. "Ya aren't givin' the man any credit. Or yourself. There's much ta love about ya, and in time he'll see it . . . if he hasn't already."

Shauna laughed softly and gave her friend a warm look. "Thank you for saying so, Moira, but our beginning was somewhat restrictive. I'm afraid there isn't much chance of his seeing me as anything more than a brainless twit who would do anything to have her own way. Hardly the makings for a lasting, loving relationship. And now—" She stopped abruptly when she realized she was about to tell Moira what had happened at Sir Blakely's two nights ago.

"And now what?" Moira hadn't missed the sudden change in Shauna's expression.

"And now we'd better get downstairs," she finished, averting her eyes and heading for the door.

"Shauna!" Moira seldom ignored the formal title used between maid and mistress, only when she was angry . . . or suspicious. "Ya were about ta say somethin'. What was it?" She hurriedly followed the young woman and slammed the door shut again after Shauna had opened it. "The hair on the back of me neck is standin' out and that can only mean one thing, Shauna Kathleen—trouble. What are ya tryin' ta hide?"

"Nothing," Shauna firmly argued. It wouldn't do any good to tell her. It wouldn't change what had happened.

Moira squinted one eye. "Then why has your face gone white all of a sudden? Look at me and say nothin' is wrong." When her mistress continued her silence and deliberately ignored her while she halfheartedly straightened the cuff on her sleeve, Moira's mind raced back over the events of the past few days, settling on yesterday more than any. She had assumed Shauna's desire to be alone in her room the entire day stemmed from her nervousness over the wedding. Now she wasn't so sure. "Ya've done somethin' stupid . . . again. Tell me what it

261

is, Shauna. I can't be helpin' ya if ya won't confide in me."

Shauna smiled weakly and reached for the doorknob, only to have Moira grab her hand. "There's nothing to tell."

"Nothin' ya *want* ta tell." Moira's brow crimped in an angry frown. "If I imagine the worst, I won't be too far wrong, I'm thinkin'. And what could be the worst." Slowly, the color drained from her face as she remembered her mistress's favorite hobby and thought of the connection it might have to her wedding. "Oh, me God, ya didn't." She whirled away, her hands pressed against her temples. "Say I'm wrong, lass. Tell me ya didn't gamble away your only hope for happiness?"

Moira's keen interpretation regarding the evening past at Sir Blakely's surprised and stunned Shauna. How had she ever managed to guess correctly without a single word or clue from her? What chilled her to the bone was the possibility that Moira also already knew what had happened between her and Brad in his room those many weeks ago. She mentally shook that off. Moira would have said something by now.

"I don't suppose I need ta ask if ya've told Mr. Remington?" Moira answered her own question. "Of course, ya haven't. 'Tis the real reason ya're scared ta go through with the weddin'. Ya fear for ya life once he finds out you're livin' on someone else's property. Did ya ever plan ta tell him?" She shook her head and faced Shauna. "Now that would be expectin' too much of ya. So what did ya have in mind? No, let me guess. Ya planned ta go ahead and become his bride, move into the mansion, and pretend nothin' was wrong. Me question is, what will ya say when the new owner comes ta claim his property?"

She batted her dark lashes, cocked her head coyly, and acted out a scene between her mistress and Brad. "I don't know what he's talkin' about, darlin'. I don't know this man. I never wagered Wrenhaven. I wouldn't be that *stupid!*" The last was directed at Shauna. "Who is he? What's the name of the man who will give your husband just cause ta throw ya out on the street? *And me!* He's sure ta think *I* had somethin' ta do with it."

Tears burned Shauna's throat. Moira had had many reasons to be angry with her in the past, and she had been. But none of those occasions even came close to the fury she saw gleaming in Moira's dark eyes at this moment. Biting a trembling lip, she swallowed hard and mumbled, "I don't know his name. I never asked him."

"Ya never—" Moira threw her hands in the air and spun away. "I don't believe it. Now, how do ya suppose I'll be able ta make the man a deal if I don't even know who ta ask?"

Shauna took a tentative step closer. "A deal? What sort of deal? What are you talking about?"

Moira glanced back over her shoulder at Shauna. "Well, I don't relish the thought of livin' in the streets, lass. I'm going ta see if the man's interested in selling Wrenhaven."

"Moira, I think you've been staying up too late at night," Shauna admonished. "Even if the man's willing to sell, where would we get the money?"

"Not we, lass. Me."

Shauna could hardly believe what she was hearing. "You? You don't have that kind of money. If you did, you wouldn't be working as a maid."

"Oh?" Moira challenged. "And why not? Has it ever occurred ta ya that I do what I do because I love it and for no other reason?" She faced her puzzled mistress. "When Keelan died, I inherited a nice sum, even though his father tried to block it. That along with me earnin's over the past fifteen years has added up ta quite a nice-sized amount. I was plannin' ta buy me a house one day when I was too old ta care for others, but as long as ya guarantee I'll always have a place ta live on Wrenhaven, I'm willin' ta loan ya the money ya need ta buy it back."

In all her days, Shauna had never been witness to someone's act of extreme unselfishness, nor had she imagined it would be directed at her. She was honored, but she wasn't deserving of it. "No," she growled through clenched teeth. "I won't let you do it. My . . . stupidity will not cost you every shilling you have." Fighting back tears of shame, she turned and opened the door. "I'll find some other way of dealing with it, and you'll not say another word about it . . . to me or to Brad. When the time is right, I'll tell him."

"And when will that be?" Moira replied hotly. "Before or after ya say 'I do'?" The cold, angry look she received in return for her warning failed to quiet her. "Mr. Remington is an exceptional man, Shauna Kathleen, but this time you've asked too much of him. Ya tricked him once and he knows it, agreed to it, but—"

"Enough, Moira," Shauna cautioned. "It's my problem, and I'll handle it." Glaring at her maid a moment longer, Shauna turned and left the room.

"Well, ol' boy, this is it," Tyler joked as he and Brad stood beside the set of double doors in the hallway awaiting the minister's instructions to step out onto the flagstone terrace and take their places beneath the flower-bedecked archway. "In a few more minutes you'll be legally unavailable to all the ladies in London." He straightened the lace cuff of his shirt and added, "The whole of England, actually. If that thought displeases you, now's the time to speak up. I'd be more than willing to tell Shauna that you've changed your mind."

A half-smile kinked Brad's mouth. "Why is it you're constantly warning me off marrying your sister, Tyler? Is there something more I should know about her, and this is your subtle way of getting me to ask?"

Tyler's blue eyes sparkled. "Quite the contrary. I think you know everything there is to know about her. I'm just not sure you're ready for the kind of life she'll give you."

"And what kind of life is that?" Brad asked, his attention directed away from Tyler as he casually studied the guests filling up the remaining seats in the gardens.

"Well, you're going to have to earn a lot of money just to keep her fashionably dressed."

Dark brown eyes, their depths twinkling with deviltment, glanced at him, the message Brad wished to convey quite evident and making Tyler laugh.

"It's a nice idea, Brad. But the two of you can't spend the rest of your lives in bed. Making love is grand, but you have to eat to keep up your strength, you know, and that takes money. But that's only the half of it. She likes to gamble."

An odd smile parted Brad's lips as he shifted his gaze back out to the dozens of guests milling about the place. "So I've heard."

"Then I think you should know that it's one thing she won't give up. I sincerely believe she'd sell everything she had just to be able to sit down at the gaming tables."

265

Tyler's expression turned serious. "It could be a problem for you."

"And I thank you for the warning," Brad smiled, laying a hand on Tyler's shoulder and squeezing. "But isn't that a part of the vows? For richer, for poorer, and all that." He wiggled his brows. "I also recall there being something about obeying."

"Ha ha!" Tyler exploded. "You'll have a tough time getting her to even remember having said it, let alone do it. That's what I meant when I said I'm not sure you're ready for the kind of life she'll give you. You'll spend your days earning money to pay for her faults, your evenings trying to track her down, and if you're lucky, you might wind up in bed together at night. But by then you'll be too tired to do anything important."

Laughter rumbled deep in Brad's chest. "I've never been too tired for that," he chuckled.

"And you've never been married to Shauna before," Tyler argued. "I don't mean to make her sound like some sort of witch, but she does have a way of casting a spell over a man. Look what happened to Nelson Thorndyke. Whenever he gets around her, he becomes a sniveling fool. I might not like him, but I have to admit he's got a good head for business, yet with Shauna, he acts like a three-year-old child." Frowning, he shook his head and mumbled to himself, "If my sister was smart, she would have married him."

"I beg your pardon?" Brad challenged with a grin. "I was under the impression that was the last thing you wanted for her."

Tyler's face paled and his eyes grew into wide, round circles. "It is . . . or was." He stammered and stuttered a moment. "I didn't really mean that the way it came out.

You're the best choice by far. You'll be able to control her. Nelson never would. But looking at it from Shauna's viewpoint, she should pick a husband she can wrap around her little finger. I doubt she'll ever be able to do that with you, but Nelson . . ."

"You may stop apologizing, Tyler," Brad chuckled. "I knew what you meant."

"You did?"

Clasping his wrists in front of him, Brad nodded. "And I assure you that you won't be disappointed in the way I handle my wife. She has a few lessons to learn, but once she has, she'll make a fine spouse. She'll be obedient, loving, caring, gracious and devoted."

"I think you're expecting too much," Tyler mumbled with a sigh.

Brad smiled broadly. "Well, it may take some time, but she'll come around."

"I hope I live long enough to see it," Tyler jeered. "Loving, caring, gracious, and devoted, maybe. But never obedient. She hasn't got it in her." His mood changed suddenly, and after looking over his shoulder toward the gardens, he took Brad's elbow and drew him further away from the door. "I've been meaning to ask you if you ever figured out who it was that killed Mrs. Clayton?"

The gaiety of the moment destroyed, Brad frowned and shook his head. "I wish I could say I had. Her death should be avenged, for Russel's sake, as well as the sake of her memory."

"Do you still think they were after you?"

"Not as much as I did at first, since there hasn't been any further attempt on my life," Brad confessed. "But it certainly doesn't make any sense for someone to murder her. There was nothing to gain by it."

"And what was to gain by having you killed?" Tyler pointed out. "I agree that Mrs. Clayton is an unlikely suspect in some major plot to rule the world, but you've hardly been in London long enough to win that kind of an enemy. And it can't be for your money. You don't have any. Besides, any inheritance would have gone to your brother." Tyler straightened sharply when a thought occurred to him. "Say, might there be some hidden family secret you don't know about, do you think? I mean, your father was a well-known and well-respected man in his time. And, according to *my* father, a wealthy one, too. Maybe someone is trying to get even for something done twenty years ago."

"I've thought about that," Brad admitted, "and it's the reason I've written to my brother. I was fairly young when our father died, and I never really paid much attention to his business affairs. Dane did, however. If that's a possibility, he'll be able to set me in the right direction."

"Did you also tell him you were getting married?" Tyler grinned.

The sparkle returned to Brad's dark eyes. "Yes. And I'd give just about anything to be there when he reads it. I hope he's sitting down when he does."

"It will be a bit of a shock, will it?" Tyler laughed.

"More than you can imagine," Brad remarked with a nod. "I've always been a little like you, my soon-to-be brother-in-law. I had an eye for the ladies and absolutely no conscience. Nothing in life mattered to me, except having a good time."

"And all of that is about to end," Tyler teased as he heard the string quartet subtly announce the beginning of the long-awaited ceremony. He grabbed Brad's arm and anxiously tugged him back toward the terrace. "And if you don't want to start this marriage out on the wrong foot, I suggest you don't embarrass the bride by being late."

Brad's first vision of Shauna nearly took his breath away. If he had any doubts about marrying her, they vanished the moment he saw her on her father's arm walking down the rose-petal-strewn path of white linen. Sunlight gleamed against her golden hair and warmed her ivory complexion, even though he was sure the ice-blue gown more fitted her mood at the moment. A slight blush colored her cheeks, and Brad wanted to believe it was a mark of her shyness. He knew better. Shauna Radborne had probably never been shy about anything in her life. And for that, he was thankful. They never would have met otherwise.

He noticed that her fingers were cold when he took her hand from her father and drew it across the bend in his arm. Was she frightened? he wondered, turning with her to face the minister. A soft smile played upon his lips. She had a right to be. He knew more about her than any other man alive, and she wasn't even aware of it . . . not now anyway. In time . . .

Shauna couldn't imagine how she had managed to walk this far without falling down. Her knees had started trembling the instant her father had met her at the bottom of the stairs in the back hallway. They were positively quaking now that she stood beside the man she was to marry. Secretively, she stole a glance at the handsome man at her side as he repeated the vows the minister instructed him to say. His voice was strong and sure, as if the words he spoke came from his heart. She cringed at the mockery of it. Would she be as convincing as Brad? She cast her eyes away from him, yet his presence seemed to stifle the very breath from her.

A chill darted through her when her attention unwittingly focused on the gold ring lying on the opened face of the Bible the minister held. That tiny piece of precious metal signified the pledge to live a lifetime with the man who slipped it on her finger. For an instant she considered putting an end to this charade. Then she thought of her father and how happy and proud he was at this moment, and she knew she couldn't do anything to destroy that for him.

The sense that the minister had turned his attention on her made Shauna start. Stiffening her spine, she gulped down the knot of panic that had suddenly cut off her breath and silently prayed the words would pass her lips when she opened her mouth to speak the vows. In hardly more than a whisper she pledged to love, honor, and obey, in sickness and in health. But when she added for richer or poorer until death did them part, she could feel herself getting lightheaded. Death would most certainly follow close on the heels of poorer. The band of cold metal slid over her knuckle, assisted by the warm fingers of the man who had willingly given her his name, and despite the cool temperature, the ring seemed to burn her flesh. Was it, perhaps, an omen? Had Satan made his presence known in that symbol of holy matrimony? She closed her eyes, barely hearing the minister's final words.

"By the power vested in me, I pronounce you man and wife. You may kiss the bride."

Whether it was the reverend's permission that brought Shauna around or the feel of Brad's strong arms encircling her as he turned her to him, Shauna abruptly came to her senses. This marked the end of all her scheming. She was wed. And all who had come to witness the union cheered and applauded as Brad lowered his head and gently kissed his wife. The touch of his warm lips against her own, the firm, unrelenting hand pressed against the small of her back, even the masculine scent of him filled Shauna with an overpowering augury that she had just made the biggest mistake of her life and that the days ahead promised constantly to remind her of that face. Nelson Thorndyke might not have been what she wanted in a husband, but there were unknown factors about Brad Remington that stirred her fear of him. Tyler might like him, and her father might have approved of the match, but that didn't mean Brad was pure and innocent. Somewhere deep inside him, evil lurked. She was sure of it. Drawing on every ounce of courage she had left, she discreetly brought an end to the kiss and stepped back, allowing her brother to wrap her in his arms and offer his congratulations. It was at that moment that her gaze unwittingly fell upon her maid. Moira stood just inside the entrance into the house. There was no smile on her face, no look of happiness, only disappointment, and Shauna quickly averted her eyes.

The next few minutes passed in a daze for Shauna. Scores of well-wishers shook Brad's hand, kissed her cheek, gave advice and offered their congratulations on what some called a match made in heaven. Shauna silently disagreed, but she managed to smile through it all and to carefully keep her gaze away from the spot where she had last seen Moira. She was having a difficult enough time pretending to enjoy herself without having to endure her maid's derisive scowl.

The five-tiered cake was cut and served. Champagne

filled everyone's glass. Music accompanied the laughter, and a good time seemed to be had by all. For appearance's sake, Shauna forced herself to stay at Brad's side, inwardly assuring herself that it would be the last time she had to make everyone think she cared an ounce for the man she called her husband.

Reverend Forbes appeared before them then, asking if the couple would accompany him to Mr. Radborne's study. There were documents to sign, and as much as he'd have liked to spend the afternoon in joyous celebration of their union, he had other duties to perform. Shauna hadn't realized just how much importance there really was in the ceremony until she took pen in hand and placed her name on the line beneath Brad's. After all, words were just words. But this . . . her head began to spin, and once she returned the quill to its well, she turned away from the desk and Reverend Forbes to slyly slink down in one of the wing chairs before the cold hearth. A moment later she heard the study door close and she lifted her eyes to find that she and Brad were alone. He sat with one hip on the corner of the desk, an arm laid casually over his thigh and his dark brown eyes staring at her, his glass of champagne dangling from his fingertips. Nervousness fluttered in her stomach, almost as if she had swallowed a hundred tiny butterflies, and she quickly took a sip of her drink.

"I doubt I've ever seen a more beautiful bride than I have this day," he murmured. "You'll honor the Remington name."

"Thank you," she said aloud, while inwardly she knew the mockery of such a statement. She was a liar, a cheat, and a fraud. How could she honor anyone's name? And she certainly didn't deserve his kindness. She took another drink and lamely asked, "Was Wrenhaven the way you remembered it?" Just the mention of the place made her grit her teeth, and she mentally cursed her recklessness at having mentioned the very source of her anxiety.

"And more," he replied. "I last looked upon it through the eyes of a carefree lad. I see it differently now. It shall be my home for the rest of my life . . . yours and mine." He cocked a brow and smiled softly at the way Shauna visibly whitened. "I think you'll like the place. Have you ever seen it?"

Shauna's golden curls glimmered with the slight shake of her head. "I'm not sure *Father* ever has." She frowned, staring into her goblet. "Nor do I understand why he hung on to it all these years. He should have sold it."

"I believe he intended to give it to his daughter as a wedding present."

Shauna's hand shook as she raised her glass to her lips. "And so he has," she mumbled into it.

"Yes," Brad agreed. "And I think once you're settled in, we should have a dinner party for your parents." He straightened mockingly when she turned startled eyes on him. "We must keep up appearances. We don't want your father thinking he's done wrong by you. Don't you agree?" He smiled broadly once she had nodded and looked away, a faint line showing between her brows. "Is something troubling you, Shauna?" he asked, setting aside his glass and rising. "You seem worried. Although I can't imagine why. You have a husband, and I have Wrenhaven. I must admit, however," he added, coming to stand beside her chair where he tenderly played with a gold ringlet of silken hair, "that I've done far better than you. I own my father's property once more, *and* I have a beautiful wife, as well. Granted there are restrictions concerning the latter, but perhaps someday that will change."

"Don't count on it," she grumbled, lifting her empty glass to her lips and whispering an oath when she discovered she had already swallowed the last drop of liquid courage. Distracted, she rose abruptly and went to the wine decanter sitting on her father's desk to pour herself another drink.

"Don't count on what, Shauna?" Brad continued, a vague smile wrinkling the corner of his mouth. "That given time I might change your feelings toward me? It's been known to happen. Not every marriage is based on love."

"Well, this one certainly wasn't," she snapped, finishing off the wine and pouring another. She whirled back a bit unsteadily to stare at him. "And why, for God's sake, would you even consider it? Just because you think I'm beautiful to look at doesn't mean there's beauty inside." She jabbed a finger at her chest. "Deep down here where it counts. I could be very ugly, for all you know." She smirked as if at someone else standing in the room with them and added, "Tyler thinks so." She raised her nose haughtily. "So does Moira." She squinted an eye and glared back at Brad. "And so would Papa if he knew what I'd done. The only one who would applaud me is Mother, and I don't care what she thinks." She raised the glass high and swallowed every drop. She settled her attention on Brad again, barely feeling the burning sensation scorch her throat and stomach. "Has she ever made a pass at you?"

Brad's brow furrowed. "Who? Your mother?"

"Uh huh," Shauna nodded as she absently pulled a lace handkerchief from her sleeve and dabbed at her neck with it. "If she hasn't, she will. She doesn't care if a man's married or not. Why should she? She doesn't care if *she's* married." She shook her head and set down her glass as she flipped the white hanky dismissingly. "And that's something I'll never understand. Why does she find it so important to flirt with every man she meets? Did you see her just now? Clinging on any man who gave her a second glance. It's disgusting! And that dress!" She gave her silky mane a toss. "Why, if it was cut any lower, she'd fall out of it. Hardly the proper behavior for the mother of the bride, now is it?"

Brad barely had time to digest Shauna's hostile words before they were interrupted by a knock on the door. He was about to call out and ask who it was when Shauna hurried across the room and grabbed the knob, swinging the door open wide. A stunned servant, a folded piece of parchment held in his hand, stood on the other side.

"A letter just arrived for you, Miss . . . er, Mrs. Remington," he nervously announced, holding out the mentioned item.

The title made Shauna giggle. "Thank you, Simmons," she nodded, plucking the sealed note from his fingers and pushing the door shut again before the man had the chance to reply. "I wonder who it's from," she murmured as she crossed to her father's desk and plopped down in the chair behind it. Tugging the wax seal loose, she opened the letter and glanced at the signature first. *Kelly O'Sullivan. I don't know anyone by that name,* she mused puzzledly. Then her eyes shifted to the message written above it, and the color began to drain from her face as bitter-cold reality cleared her head.

Congratulations, Mrs. Remington. I assume by now that you are Mrs. Remington. I trust you took my advice and told your husband the truth about Wrenhaven. If not, you'll have about four weeks to decide how to break the news to him, as I plan to be in London by the end of the month. I wish things could have been different. I mean, I wish you had had the winning hand that night instead of me, and that now you'd truly have something to celebrate. But who knows? Maybe some good will come out of this after all. Again, my congratulations on your marriage.

Sincerely,
Kelly O'Sullivan

"Shauna?"

The sound of her name on Brad's lips startled Shauna out of her trance. As gallantly as possible, she forced herself to smile as she refolded the letter and tucked it inside the sleeve of her gown. "What?" she asked.

"Are you all right? You look pale. It wasn't bad news, was it?"

"No, no," she quickly replied, awkwardly coming to her feet. "Just a friend I haven't seen in a while wishing us a long life together and explaining why he-er-she couldn't be here today." She rounded the desk and headed for the door. "I think it's time we got back to our guests. Don't you agree?"

A curious frown made its way across his brow and disappeared. "Perhaps so," he replied with a dip of his dark head. "We've been gone long enough already to set tongues wagging."

Shauna didn't understand his meaning. "How so?"

A wicked grin parted his lips as he leaned and reached

for the knob, whispering, "Why, some will think we've either sneaked out a side door to the nearest inn or ventured to your bedchambers to consummate the vows." Without giving her a chance to comment and certain they wouldn't be the kindest words he'd ever heard if he did, he took her elbow and guided her from the room.

The celebration lasted well into the early evening hours. Brad appeared to be thoroughly enjoying himself and quite willingly danced with any and all young maidens bold enough to ask him. Roanna took her turn several times, a point Shauna didn't miss, and drank a glass of champagne every time she saw them together. It wasn't that she was jealous. Heavens, no. She just didn't think it very proper for a woman her mother's age to be dancing so alluringly with her new son-in-law, while his bride of a few hours sat alone in the corner. If her head hadn't been swimming as fast as the couples on the dance floor, she would have marched right up to them and told her mother and husband exactly what she thought of them.

Night breezes brushed against her hot cheeks once Shauna had managed to pull herself upright and head further into the gardens away from the terrace and the embarrassing sight of Brad and her mother. Silver light marked the way and soon she found herself standing at the steps of the gazebo. Grasping the handrail for support, she steadied her balance and went inside where she leaned heavily against one of the decorative posts to stare up at the cloudless, black-velvet sky with its sprinkling of bright stars. For as long as she could remember, this was the place where she had come to sort out her problems. It was peaceful and quiet here and offered the chance to be alone. Yet as she stood there trying to focus her eyes and to stop her world from twirling on its tilted axle, she realized such a place no longer existed for her. Her problems were now insurmountable. She had dug herself a hole and fallen into it, and with a little help she'd soon pull the dirt in on top of her. Yes, that was exactly what she had done; she had buried herself alive.

Vaguely she sensed another's presence near the gazebo behind her, and she carefully turned in that direction, not really sure who she expected to see, but certainly not Nelson Thorndyke.

"Did I frighten you, Shauna? I'm sorry if I did," he apologized. "I saw you walk out this way alone and although I'd like to say I felt compelled to insure your safety, it isn't altogether true. I was hoping for this opportunity all day." He moved up the stairs and came to stand near her, not close but only a step away. "I've known you now for a good number of years. I've watched you grow from a young girl to a beautiful woman. I've seen your moods, felt your scorn, and even sampled your hatred, directed at me as well as others. And what I see between you and . . ." He paused as if the next words were painful for him. "Between you and your husband, is far from my definition of love. I'm not sure you even like him." He laughed almost bitterly. "I realize there's little hope of your even liking me, and some would call me a fool for not admitting defeat . . . especially now that you belong to someone else, but love knows no limits, Shauna." He turned away from her to stare out at the moonlit gardens. "I love you, Shauna. I have for a long time, and I always will. I just want you to know that if you ever need a friend—" He paused and smiled before continuing. "I'll settle for friendship. If you ever need a friend, someone to help you, to talk to, I'll always be here for you. I sense trouble ahead, and I want you to know I'll lay down my life to protect you." Brown eyes glistening with moisture, he glanced at her. "I'd do anything for you, Shauna." He raised a wide hand as if to touch her cheek, curled his fingers into a fist instead, and urned away, leaving the gazebo as quietly as he had come.

Shauna stared after him for a long while. It wasn't so much his confession that surprised her but the sincerity she had heard in his voice. She had always assumed that he, like all the others before him, had only expressed his desire for her out of greed. Obviously she had been wrong about Nelson Thorndyke, and she felt a little ashamed for condemning him without ever having given him a chance.

"It would seem I had better stay alert," a deep voice from the shadows announced, startling Shauna and nearly spilling her to the floor.

"Do you make a habit of spying on people?" she snapped, clutching the railing behind her as she watched Brad mount the stairs and lazily perch his hip on the banister, his face and dark eyes aglow with mischief in the silver light.

"Spying?" he questioned. "Is there a need for me to spy, Shauna? Was this a prearranged meeting between lovers, and as always the husband is the last to know?"

"Lovers?" she fumed, wondering at the warmth that had begun to creep up her neck and touch her face. "You're a simpleton to even say such a thing. You more than anyone know to what lengths I have gone to avoid that man. I married *you*, didn't I? That should convince everyone how much I detest him."

"Everyone except him," Brad grinned. "Perhaps you should listen to what he had to say, and take warning."

The nearness of her husband, the champagne, and her unexpected confrontation with Nelson made her head spin all the more. Weak, she moved to sit down on the bench near her. "What warning?"

"He's encouraged because he suspects you don't like me."

"I don't," she sneered, resting her brow against her fingertips.

"Then you should do something to correct that. Unless, of course, you *want* him to chase after your skirts."

"What I want is for *all* men, including you, to gather in a huge ship, sail out to the deepest part of the Atlantic, and pray for a savage storm to send you all to the bottom of the sea." She shot him an icy glare. "But I guess that wouldn't work. You've already managed to cheat fate in that respect once before."

"Yes, fortunately for you, I did," he countered.

Shauna sucked in a quick breath, ready to argue his claim, remembered how his situation had benefited hers, and grudgingly snapped her mouth shut again. "What are you doing out here?" she grumbled after a moment.

"I came looking for you. You just seemed to disappear all of a sudden, and I thought perhaps you might be sick."

"Sick?" She laughed sarcastically. "Only of watching you and my mother make complete idiots of yourselves. Has she asked you up to her room yet?"

The humor faded from his lips. "No, Shauna, she hasn't. Why do you think she would? I certainly haven't given her any incentive."

"You don't have to," she jeered. "You're a man,

280

aren't you?"

Sensing that the weight of the day's events, along with too much champagne, had made Shauna say things she ordinarily wouldn't, he chose not to reply. Instead, he left his place on the railing and came to gently take her elbow and draw her to her feet. "It's time we thanked our guests and started for Wrenhaven. It's a long drive, and I'm sure you're tired."

"Do you find her attractive, Brad?" Shauna blurted out, stumbling, then swaying into his arms, her hands pressed against his silk shirtfront. "More than me? If she asked, would you seduce her?"

"God, Shauna," Brad moaned. "What kind of a man do you think I am?" His tolerance of her antics was beginning to wear rather thin.

"Well, would you?" she pressed, failing to hear the anger tightening his words. "She's very beautiful. She might be older than you, but not enough to catch a man's eye. She's shapely, wealthy, and . . ." She giggled and raised on tiptoes to whisper against his lips. "And willing."

"She's also your mother," he growled, his rugged brow furrowed. "That alone is more than enough reason for me not to be interested."

"Oh?" Her fingers tightened around the lapels of his coat when her balance careened to the left suddenly. "Well, let's pretend she isn't. Would you then be so inclined?"

"Shauna . . ." he warned, his teeth locked.

"It's just pretend. Would you?"

"No."

Shauna tried unsuccessfully to square her shoulders. "Why not?"

281

"Because I'm married," he sharply replied.

Her features softened and a lopsided smile graced her lips. "O-o-h, that's very sweet. But let's say you're not. Let's pretend—"

"If you're looking for a list of reasons," he barked, tired of her game, "then I'll give them to you. First, she's your mother, as I've already stated. Secondly, I'm married. Third, she's the wife of a friend. Fourth, I don't like women who make the first move. But more important, I've grown rather choosy over the years. There was a time when none of that would have mattered. I would have seduced any woman willing. But no more. Maybe the vows we spoke didn't mean anything to you, but they did to me, and if I must, I'll live the life of a monk before I contradict the words I spoke at the altar." He glared at her a moment, then, "But *I'm* not what this is all about, am I? It's not me you're testing. You're searching for an answer to a question you've been asking yourself for some time now. Are you wondering why men are drawn to your mother and not you? Is that what really has you upset? Are you jealous, Shauna?"

"Jealous?" she shrieked, staggering back a step. "Of her? You think I'd like to have men drooling all over me? Well, I wouldn't. I don't."

"Then you should be glad she diverts them."

"Oh, yes," she sneered, swaying sideways and reaching out to grab his arm and steady her balance. "But what of Father? Do you think he's glad she sacrifices herself for me? Would you be, if you were in his place?"

"I'm sure your father is well aware of what's going on. He's not blind or deaf. If he didn't approve, he'd bring an end to it. But I think you're putting more into her actions than what is really there, Shauna," he scolded.

"Some women enjoy flirting, and that's as far as it goes. Have you ever seen your mother leave with a man? Have you ever heard any gossip about her being involved with someone? Don't be so quick to judge until you have all the facts. She may need the harmless attention of another man for the simple reason that she no longer receives any from her husband. I'm not blaming Pierce. He's a busy man, and sometimes a man in his position forgets about his family's needs."

Shauna wanted to believe he was right, but the image of a young child opening the door to her mother's bedchambers late at night and finding a stranger locked in the woman's arms prevented it. "And that makes it all right?"

"Shauna," he sighed, "I'm not trying to make excuses for her. I'm only trying to get you to look at both sides."

"Oh, I have," she rallied. "An unfaithful wife laughing behind her husband's back while he goes about his routine never suspecting a thing."

"Have you talked to her about it?"

Shauna laughed sarcastically. "Do you really think she'd be honest with me if I did? She's no fool. She's well aware of what would happen if Papa ever found out. She'd be poor again. And *that's* something Roanna Radborne will never be. Money is too important to her."

"Then what will you do about it?" he posed, gently wrapping an arm around her waist and guiding her from the gazebo.

"Do? Why nothing. *I'd* never deliberately hurt Papa."

"But you'll go on hurting yourself."

Shauna stumbled to a halt and turned to face him, teetering dangerously before Brad caught her arms just above the elbow. "I have no choice."

"Yes, you do. You can tell her what you feel, and if you're correct, she'll know someone's watching her. *If* living in a fine house and wearing expensive clothes mean so much to her, she'll change. But I suggest you give it a lot of thought before you do."

"Why?" she snapped, assuming Brad was feeling sorry for her mother.

"Because there's always the chance your mother and father have the same arrangement as you and I."

Her smooth brow furrowed, and she squinted her eyes as she leaned closer to stare. "What are you talking about?"

"Part of our agreement concerning this marriage was that I was free to have a mistress. To be unfaithful. Perhaps—"

"That's different," she snapped, jerking loose of his grasp and whirling away. Her vision blurred and she closed her eyes, only vaguely aware of the firm hand on her elbow.

"Is it? You've given me permission to be unfaithful. How do you know the same isn't true of their situation?"

"Because we don't love each other. They do." She raised shaky fingertips to her brow, mumbling, "At least Papa loves her."

"Ahhh," Brad replied, turning her in his arms and placing a knuckle under her chin to draw her gaze to his. "And therein lies the similarity," he smiled tenderly. "Perhaps your father knows about her indiscretions and looks the other way. He'll keep her as his wife no matter what the cost." His dark eyes lovingly roamed the fine features of her face and settled once again on her eyes. "As I will do with you."

Deep laughter echoed in her ears and she blinked once

she realized it came from her imagination. Kelly O'Sullivan had invaded her thoughts and made a mockery of Brad's confession. You won't once you learn Wrenhaven is no longer yours, she thought, the fog that had clouded her mind ebbing a degree. She glanced back toward the terrace. "We'd better get back. We shouldn't be rude to our guests."

Nodding his silent agreement, he took her hand and drew it through the bend in his arm, turning with her to walk down the stone pathway. A soft smile parted his lips when he felt her tremble, and he secretly stole a glance at her, certain he knew exactly what was going through her mind.

Chapter Ten

Quiet, still air, a road bathed in moonlight, the clip-clop of horses' hooves and the rattling of carriage wheels played accompaniment to the journey homeward. The romantic backdrop would have ordinarily set the stage and tempted young lovers, newly married, into sampling the pleasures to be had locked in each other's embrace. But not this couple, not this man and wife who rode inside the expensive landau in strained silence.

The distance to Wrenhaven took about two hours to cover. They had left the Radborne townhouse shortly before ten o'clock amid the shouts of joy and good wishes of all those who saw the newlyweds off. Shauna appeared at ease, until Brad had escorted her into the bridal carriage, and seeing that it was empty, asked where her maid was. Once Brad told her that Moira had been sent on ahead to prepare her mistress's quarters for the night, Shauna's seemingly relaxed state of mind turned dark. Sliding to the far side of the leather-cushioned seat, she cast her attention out the window and never looked at her husband again. Any reply she had to his questions or comments came short and crisp, and it didn't take Brad long to realize she feared what lay ahead. Since he felt she deserved to be nervous, even though he knew all he intended to do this night was show her to her room, he said very little that would comfort her. In fact, he purposely let her stew about it for three-fourths of the way home. Then, when he figured all he had to do to set her off was accidentally brush against her, he leaned forward and reached for the small brass trunk hidden under a blanket on the opposite seat.

"I thought you might enjoy a late-night snack of bread and cheese and a glass of sherry," he offered, holding up the bottle for her to see. He fought with the laughter burning his throat and added, "It might relax you."

The mere thought that he knew what plagued her sent a shiver down her spine. But rather than let him think he was right, she replied most calmly, "I'm quite relaxed, thank you. Just tired. It's been a long day." Her icy green eyes looked at him askance. "One I'll never forget."

"And well you shouldn't," he agreed, grinning roguishly as he popped the cork and nimbly poured the glasses full despite the rocking motion of the carriage. Handing her a glass, he raised his high and toasted, "To our long and happy life together."

Shauna's lip curled. "Long? Most assuredly, even if it is only a day or two. But never happy." She ignored his mocking frown of injured pride and drank nearly all of the sherry.

"Our time together won't have to be unhappy, Shauna. I'm more than willing to put our past differences behind us and start anew," he admitted as he reached inside the gold box and withdrew a platter of cut cheeses and slices of bread.

She finished off her drink and held out the glass for him to refill it. "It's too late for that," she frowned, knowing that even if she wanted to forget the past and start fresh, Brad would soon change his mind. The minute Kelly O'Sullivan knocked on the door and ordered Brad off Wrenhaven, Brad would turn on her like a caged lion suddenly set free.

"It's never too late, Shauna," he murmured as he poured the sherry into her glass.

She shook her head and closed her eyes, letting the warming effect of her drink dull her spirit. "Why, Brad? Why would you even be willing to try?"

Selecting a choice lump of cheese, he raised it to his mouth and casually replied, "I wish to have an heir, a son to bear my name that I will not be forgotten long after I'm dead." He popped the cheese in his mouth, then looked for a small slice of bread, ignoring her gasp.

"'Twas not what we agreed on," she raged.

"As well I know," he replied. "'Tis what I meant when I said I was willing to forget our past differences." He took a bite of the bread, chewed, and washed it down with a sip of sherry.

Shauna's nose raised loftily in the air before she turned to stare outside again. "Do all men look upon women as breeding mares? Do you take a wife only to have sons and give no thought to her desires, her needs, her fears?" She spoke the words aloud, but truly didn't mean for him to answer.

"Nay, Shauna," he sighed, leaning back against the seat, his arms folded over his chest and his glass held by the rim. "I, for one, do not. 'Tis the reason I took so long to marry. I was looking for the right woman. I wanted someone I could share my dreams with, my hopes, my sorrows, my life. I wanted a woman who would love me, despite my faults." He laughed and added before Shauna

288

could, "And yes, I have many. But with the help of a good woman, I would learn to correct those faults, and in return I'd love her back and we could grow old together watching our children scamper through the halls of Wrenhaven." He heaved a pensive sigh and continued as he stared off into space, "We'd stand side by side and weather the fiercest of storms. No one and nothing would come between us." He smiled crookedly and glanced over at her. "You know, for richer and poorer and all that."

Shauna's hand shook as she raised the glass to her lips. "And now, thanks to me, you'll never have that, will you?" she asked, feeling horribly guilty and very selfish.

His warm eyes raked over her. "Only if you truly want it that way," he softly corrected.

She couldn't bring herself to look at him. He'd know the truth the instant she did. There would never be a chance for them. The moment she'd sat down across the table from the Irishman, she had sealed her fate. Now it was only a matter of time.

The rest of their journey passed in silence. Brad reluctantly continued to refill her glass every time she demanded it, watching her grow more intoxicated with every turn of the carriage wheel and suspecting something new had pricked her conscience. Shauna, unaware that she alone had nearly finished off the sherry, slipped into a state of depression. She was feeling sorry for herself, for her father, and even for Brad. Moira had tried to warn her, but Shauna wouldn't listen. No one would get hurt by her scheme. Brad would have what he wanted and so would she. Now, because of her foolishness and greed, she had ruined everything. The only hope of salvaging anyone's happiness was for her to tell Brad the truth. Then, if he wished, he could divorce her. It wouldn't get Wrenhaven back, but at least he'd be free to marry a woman who loved him.

Love. The word seemed to ricochet around in her brain. What was love, really? She loved Tyler and her father. She loved Moira. She loved sunny days and snow falling quietly on the city streets. She loved roses, the smell of a spring rain, the sound of a waterfall. But did she have any idea what it felt like to love a man? Or to have him love her? Did she really wish to learn? Dizzy, she leaned her head back against the carriage wall, her eyes closed as she listened to the steady rhythm of the horses' hooves against the hard-packed earth. Maybe she was incapable of that kind of love. Maybe she wouldn't recognize it even if she was. Her thoughts turned to Brad and that night they had spent in each other's arms. She had *made* love, but had she felt it? Granted, he had set every inch of her aflame. He had stirred fires in her she didn't even know existed. But once they cooled, so had her feelings toward him. Or had they? Every time she saw him her heart beat faster and her pulse quickened. He made her blush and stumble over her words. She thought of him night and day. Was that love?

The carriage jerked to a stop. The door opened and she felt Brad's weight upon the step. Through a haze of silver light, his warm hand touched her and drew hers from the coach. Giddy from too much drink, she let him envelop her within the strong circle of his arms, and he carried her down a stone path to the front door of a mansion. Light spilled out from the wide archway and she buried her face in his neck, her arms clasped tighty around him. Someone spoke to her, but she didn't answer. She didn't want to break the spell she was under. The rock-hard muscles in his back and arms flexed with each step he took as he climbed a long circular staircase. At the top, she could hear someone scurry about to open a door, and the light from the hall sconces faded as he carried her into a darkened room. He laid her down on a soft cushion of feathers and she murmured her objection when he started to let go.

"Don't leave me, Brad," she breathed. "Stay with me a while. Teach me what love is."

The murmur of voices, the rustle of skirts, and the latch clicking shut vaguely penetrated Shauna's consciousness. Dreamily she sat up as gentle hands slid off her shoes, garters, and hose, then took the sprigs of baby's breath and the pins from her hair. Her long golden ringlets fell about her shoulders and she pulled them aside as she felt nimble fingers unhook the buttons up the back of her dress. She giggled impishly as the sleeves of her wedding gown glided down her arms. Leaning heavily against the strong, supporting arms that helped her stand, she awkwardly shimmied out of the dress and petticoats and playfully kicked them aside. The movement made her lose her balance and she fell into the aiding grasp that quickly caught her.

"Brad?" she questioned, fighting to focus her eyes on his handsome face as they stood in the stream of silver light coming in through the window. "Do you really think you could love me?"

"Yes, Shauna," he answered softly, smiling at the immodest way in which she wrapped her arms around his neck and pressed her body full against him.

"Do you think I could ever love you, Brad?" Bright, green eyes stared into his, all sign of mirth gone from their exquisite depths.

He kissed the tip of her nose and gently lifted a silken

strand of her hair from her brow. "I don't know. What do you think?"

"I think I could if you'd teach me."

"Teach you?" he chuckled. "I can't teach you to love me, Shauna. It must come from your heart."

"Then what is love, Brad? If it can't be taught, how will I learn to love you? How will I know if I do?"

"You'll feel it."

"Have you ever been in love?"

His dark brown eyes softened as he studied her face and smelled the sweet fragrance of her perfume. "I thought I had. But I know differently now."

"You do?"

"Uh huh."

"What do you know?" she dared, touching her nose to his.

A bright smile parted his lips. "I know you've had too much to drink."

Shauna straightened and leaned back with a frown. "What has that to do with love?"

"It makes you say and do things you'll regret in the morning."

"Like what? What might I say that I'd regret?"

He shrugged a shoulder. "You might tell me that you love me already and then have second thoughts about it when your mind is clear."

"Would that be so bad?"

"On the morrow, yes."

"But tonight?"

He smiled and struggled for the right explanation. How could he tell her that hearing those words would fill his heart with joy one minute, then all but kill him later when she recanted her declaration? She might have the strange illusion that men were strong and that was easy for them to protect their feelings, but that wasn't true. They could hide them a little better than women, but that was as far as it went. To hear his wife proclaim her love for him while caught up in the romance of a night such as this would only fill him with doubt. Was it truly spoken from the heart or merely a result of too much drink? He knew the answer to that one. At least in Shauna's case.

"Tonight, you should get undressed and slip into bed," he announced, reaching up to untwine her arms from around his neck.

A soft giggle and the feel of her warm body pressed closer to his disputed his suggestion, and Brad had trouble breathing.

"Only if you'll get undressed and slip into bed with me," she whispered against his lips.

A flash of white teeth showed with his smile. "A tempting offer, but one I must refuse."

"Why?" she grinned. "Are you afraid?"

"Afraid?" he echoed. "Of what?"

"That you'll like it."

Warm laughter rumbled in his chest. "Oh, I'm sure of that."

"Then you're afraid I won't."

His dark eyes sparkled. "It's a strong possibility."

"Then let's find out," she dared, her hands sliding to the buttons on his shirt.

"Shauna," he moaned, catching her wrists.

"Ohhhh, no," she argued, pulling free and resuming her task. "You've got to learn to get over your fear. You're not a bad sort, Brad Remington. A little brisk at times, but you'll overcome that with help." She popped the top four buttons free, changed direction, and untied

293

his ruffled ascot, then began working on the fastenings up the front of his waistcoat. "You're a very handsome man and you shouldn't be ashamed of it."

"Ashamed?" he laughed, gently trying to misdirect her hands.

"Yes. You should use that to your advantage. All you have to do is smile that charming smile of yours, whisper a few endearing words, stand a little too close so the lady can feel the warmth of you. Hypnotize her!"

"Is that what I've done to you?" he asked, devilment crackling his words.

Her round green eyes glanced up at him and her movements stopped. "I don't think so."

"Then why are you trying to strip off my clothes?"

Her fair brow wrinkled briefly with thought. "To find out if I love you."

"There are other ways to do that, Shauna. Better ways."

A wicked smile curled her mouth. "I don't think so," she said, throwing her arms around his neck again. "Do you?"

The sweet scent of her, her scantily clad breasts pressed against his chest, her willingness clouded Brad's reasoning. He wanted to say that he did, that just falling into bed with someone didn't prove a thing, especially when their actions were motivated by too much drink. More than that, however, he knew he'd be the object of her scorn in the morning once she realized what she'd done. She'd accuse him of taking advantage. It would ruin what might have been a beginning for them. More than anything he wanted her to fall in love with him, but it mustn't be based on what they did in bed. He already knew she was capable of stirring the fires in his soul, and unless she was lying to herself, she had to know what kind of effect he had on her. Drawing in a long, deep breath and closing his eyes, he took her arms from around his neck and set her from him.

"Another time, perhaps, but not now, Shauna," he firmly told her.

Her lower lip jutted out prettily. "Don't you want to make love to me?" The question came in a trembling whisper.

He sighed heavily, resignedly. "More than anything in my life, but—"

"Then why do you hesitate?" Slender hands swept downward, indicating her shapely form. "Do you find me undesirable?"

He shook his head, tearing his gaze away from those curvaceous limbs. "You're the most beautiful woman I've ever known. You're my wife. I have the right to lie with you. But I won't. Not now. Not this way."

A confused frown marred her brow. "Why?"

"Because this isn't really what you want."

"It isn't?" she questioned, swaying to her left.

"No." His reply was short and crisp. "Look at you. You can't even stand up."

She grabbed his hand and pulled him to the bed. "Then let's lie down."

His grip tightened around her fingers and held her steady. "Standing or lying in bed won't make a difference. How can you possibly know what you want when you're too drunk to—"

"Ohhh, I get it," she cut in. "We're married now, so you're no longer interested. Is that how it works?"

"What?"

"Well, you were more than willing that night I came to

see you at the . . . the . . ."

"The White Horse," he finished.

Shauna nodded. "Yes. The White Horse. You were willing then but now that we're married, you're not." She shrugged and plopped down on the bed. "I guess that's the way it is when your married. That's how it is with Mother."

"No, Shauna," Brad corrected, sitting down beside her and taking her hand. "First of all, you're only guessing about your Mother's situation. As for us, I intend to be faithful. There will never be another woman in my life now that I have you."

"Really?" She smiled brightly at him. "That's very nice of you to say." She bent her head and freed the knot in the strings of her camisole. "Then let's go to bed."

Her insistence and the innocence she displayed amused Brad. "You're not going to give up, are you?"

Her shiny curls glimmered in the soft light when she shook her head and continued with the lace ribbons.

"Then I'll make a deal with you," he offered, trapping her hands in his before she had gone too far and revealed those tempting breasts for him to feast his eyes upon. "You slip under the covers, lay your head on the pillow and close your eyes while I undress. If you're still willing by then—"

He chuckled at how fast and nimbly she yanked down the coverlet and sheet and scurried beneath them to do exactly as he bade. Her long golden hair fanned out across the wide pillowcase, and moonlight bathed her soft features, stirring Brad's desire to place a kiss upon her cheek, even though he knew what that would bring. Forcing himself to look away, he rose and quietly went to the window to stare outside at the quiet countryside. He would give her a few minutes to fall asleep, and then he'd sneak from her room. In the morning, if she was willing to talk, they'd discuss her feelings then . . . in the clear light of day.

A movement below in the gardens caught his eye, and he straightened sharply, straining in the silvery darkness to see what it was. Silence floated all around him, and he reluctantly, begrudgingly relaxed. Since coming to Wrenhaven some three weeks past, strange things had been happening, most of which disturbed his sleep. Though many of them could be explained, the odd noises he heard late at night, the rustling of leaves when no breeze stirred them, the snapping of twigs when everyone else was abed piqued more than just his curiosity. He had yet to see anyone, but instinct warned him they were out there . . . somewhere . . . sneaking around in the dark. The question was, who? And what brought them here? Barnes, a silver-haired gentleman Radborne had hired to look after the place all these years, told Brad that up until a few weeks ago there had never been any trouble on the place. He and his wife, Elice, and the groundskeeper, H.T. Rutherford, had lived on Wrenhaven since shortly after Mr. Radborne had purchased the property, and although Barnes had occasionally seen riders cutting across the land down near the bend in the river, no one had ever come to the house. In his opinion, it was nothing to worry about. Yet Brad was worried . . . or skeptical, perhaps. Since returning to London he had heard about the smuggling going on—and what better place to conduct such illegal business of this sort than on a piece of land where no one lived? He wanted to believe that was all it was, yet the memory of how Eimile Clayton died kept coming to mind. Closing his eyes, he drew in a deep breath and turned around. It was after midnight and he was tired.

"You're still dressed, Brad," a soft voice observed, and he jerked his eyes open to find Shauna standing before him. "Do you need help?"

He started to reply, but she cut him off with a shake of her head.

"I was always told brides were the ones who were nervous on their wedding nights. Now I'm not so sure." She moved closer and reached out to slide his jacket off his shoulders. It thumped on the floor, then cushioned the descent of his waistcoat and finally his shirt and ascot. "I won't hurt you," she whispered, bringing a smile to his lips, which quickly turned to a pleasurable grimace when her fingertips traced the deep ridge of muscle and bone above his lean, flat belly. His pulse quickened and it was difficult for him to remember why he had denied her. He sucked in a breath to explain and moaned instead when her warm, moist lips kissed the hollow in his throat and her open palms glided over his chest. But when her fingers dipped to the hook on his breeches, he caught her wrists.

"Shauna," he begged, inwardly cursing the strange power she had over him.

"Hush," she commanded. "You promised to love, honor, and obey, remember? Well, it's time you obeyed, honored my request, and proved your love."

His resolution slipping fast, especially once he saw her unfasten the lace strings of her camisole and pull the thin fabric apart to expose the deep valley between her breasts, he drew on his last ounce of mettle and gave his only condition. "I surrender, Shauna, but only if you swear to me that in the morning, when you've had time to think this through, you won't hate me for giving in."

"Hate you?" she grinned a bit crookedly. "I plan to learn how much I love you. Teach me, Brad. Teach me all I need to know." Alluringly, she draped her arms around his neck, caught her fingers in the thick mass of hair at his nape, and pulled his mouth to hers.

Brad felt as if every fiber of his being had been scorched with fire and set ablaze the instant their lips touched, and he no longer cared what drove her into his arms. Slanting his mouth across her parted lips, he kissed her savagely, fiercely, and with all the passion he had tried so hard to control. Clasping one arm around her slender waist, his other hand cradling her head, he crushed her to him, his body molded against hers. A burning desire raged through his veins, made his heart thunder in his chest and his pulse beat wildly. He breathed in the scent of her, tasted the sweetness of her mouth, and thrilled at the touch of her fevered flesh pressed against him. His mind reeled, fearing it had all been a game, and that once she came to her senses she would break the magic with a word, a look, a sign. Yet until it came, he would take what she offered willingly and without reservation.

A new warmth flooded Shauna, one not caused by her intake of drink but one of a headier brew. It began low in her belly and spread through every limb, every inch of her, and the sweet memories of another time locked in this man's arms exploded in full, raging color. She moaned as his mouth trailed kisses down her throat, his moist tongue dotting a wet path and burning her flesh where it touched. She called his name in a breathless whisper and frantically wriggled from the restricting boundaries of her chemise once his fingers unlaced the cords and slid the garment from her. She cried out in

299

blissful agony as his dark head lowered and his open mouth claimed the taut peak of her breast, while his hands roamed the length of her spine, the small of her back, her firm buttocks, then down the silky measure of her thighs. Dropping to his knees, his hands encircled her narrow waist and pulled her close. He sampled the sweet flesh of her bosom, across her ribs, her flat belly, then dipped lower, and Shauna gasped at the pleasurable intrusion. Mesmerized by quivering sensations of unexplainable rapture, she closed her eyes and let her head fall back, long golden strands of hair cascading earthward in a torrent of satiny waves, her knees weak, her body trembling.

Suddenly his lips met hers again, his hands cupping her face in a firm yet gentle grasp as he kissed her sweet mouth, her chin, her nose, while whispering her name over and over again in a delirious frenzy of wild rapture. In a desperate need to feel his hard body pressed to hers, she urgently wrapped her arms around him, pulling him close as she answered his kisses with fire and passion. Tongues clashed, hearts pounded, and flesh upon flesh yearned for a greater release. Bending, he caught her up in his strong arms and carried her to the bed, there to bend a knee upon the mattress and fall with her still wrapped in his embrace. He rolled her beneath him as he bruised her lips with hungry kisses. Her nails raked his broad, muscular back. Her lips clung to his as she felt him kick off his shoes, then unhook the fastening of his breeches. Their passion soared beyond limits, and in a tempered violence, they tore his clothes from him. Their naked bodies touched full length, and for the briefest of moments they lay still, his dark eyes staring into the sea-green depths of hers.

"Love me, Brad," she begged in a hoarse whisper choked with desire.

"I do," he breathed.

"Then show me how to love you. Show me the way," she urged, pulling him down.

Their bodies forged as one, they moved in blissful harmony, hands searching, exploring, lips hungry and eager. He parted her trembling thighs with his knee and lowered himself to her, his hardened manhood hitting its mark in a glorious union of wild abandonment. He moved deep and long and sure within her, hearing her delighted gasps of pleasure, her moans as joyful tears moistened her dark lashes and her body gleamed with perspiration. His own heart thundered in his ears, his blood surged through his veins, his passion ran high. He moved faster, harder, matched by her own need to be fulfilled. In divine rapture, they soared on the wings of ecstasy to a heavenly plateau where no mortal world existed, there to hover on the edge of delirium before a magnitude of tiny sparkling stars exploded all around them, blinding them and draining their strength. Sated and filled with contentment, they drifted earthward wrapped in each other's loving embrace.

A long while passed before Brad pushed himself up and rolled to Shauna's side, exhausted and spent, yet pleasurably so. Shauna nestled herself in the crook of his arm, her head lying on his chest, her eyes closed, and a smile on her lips. Brad had had every confidence in the world that sooner or later it would come to this, that in time Shauna would be his wife in every sense of the word, but he had never imagined it would be on their wedding night. Brushing away a damp tendril of her hair from her brow, he pressed a kiss there, basking in the feel of her

301

warm, naked body molded against his, and frowning as he wondered what the morning would bring. Would she remember everything that was said this night? Would she hate herself for what she had done, or worse yet, would she blame him? Would she hate him? A half-smile broke the serious line of his mouth and his dark eyes glowed. It wouldn't be the first time she declared her hatred or pointed an accusing finger. He had grown used to it. And even though she had spurned him, hadn't they found their way here? It could happen again . . . and again.

A soft breeze whispered into the room and caressed their naked flesh. Chilled, Brad gently stretched for the coverlet and pulled it up over them, grinning at his wife's contented sigh and her reluctance to let go of him. Perhaps he would have to endure her wrath on the morrow, but for now he'd enjoy the feel of her pressed against him, her love . . . whether it came from her heart or not. Closing his eyes, he drifted off to sleep.

Shauna came awake with a start, the visions in her dreams spilling over into reality, and she jerked upright in bed. The sudden movement, however, made her wince in pain, and she raised trembling fingertips to her temples, hoping to still the thunderous pounding in her head. Closing her eyes to block out the blinding glare of the morning sun, she silently cursed the day and the uproarious chatter of the birds outside the window, wishing both would go away and leave her alone to die in peace. She could remember drinking too much champagne—or was it sherry?—and when she tried to run her tongue over her lips, it felt as if she had swallowed a whole bale of cotton. Squinting one eye open, she carefully scrutinized the room for the washstand with its pitcher of water, only then realizing she hadn't any idea where she was. Lowering her hands, she straightened a mite to study her surroundings, slowly coming to the conclusion that wherever she was, she must be safe for the moment. Then bits and pieces of yesterday flashed to her mind: taking a bath, arguing with Moira, getting married. . . . That horrifying memory made her gasp, then shrink in renewed pain, and she slowly crumbled back down on the soft, feather mattress. *Now* she remembered. She had started drinking right after the ceremony, and as best as she could recall, she hadn't stopped until someone put her to bed. *Someone?*

Her eyes came open again as she fought to sort out the vague pieces of yesterday's events. It wouldn't do for Brad to have the advantage. Yet the harder she tried, the more her head thumped, and she gave up forcing herself to think about it for now. She'd get dressed, have something to eat, and go for a walk in the fresh air . . . alone . . . away from everyone, and especially her husband. The title made her cringe, and rather than lie there and suffer, she flipped off the covers and started to rise. But the instant her bare feet touched the floor, the sight of her naked limbs and torso made her moan in agony, and tears flooded her eyes. Moira would never see her to bed without a nightgown! It could only mean one thing!

A noise outside her room in the hall shot her out of bed in a flash. She'd endure the pain just as long as she could get dressed before someone came in. Spying a satin and lace nightshift draped over the chair, she hurriedly grabbed it and slid it down over her head just as a knock sounded on the door.

"Miss Shauna?" Moira's voice called out. "Are ya awake, lass?"

"Yes," she returned, then mumbled quietly as she carefully slipped back under the covers, "but I wish I wasn't. I wish this whole affair had been a nightmare." She settled herself down and bade her servant enter.

"Did ya sleep well, lass?" Moira's cheerfulness only aggravated her mistress's pain.

"Well enough," Shauna muttered, closing her eyes. "I assume this is Wrenhaven."

"Aye. And a grand place it is, Miss Shauna," Moira commented as she crossed to the window to open it. "It's twice the size of your father's townhouse, with acres of rollin' green grass and trees." Pausing, she dreamily closed her eyes and sucked in a deep breath. "And lots of fresh air. 'Twill put color in your cheeks, lass."

Not today, it won't, Shauna thought, touching cool fingertips to her fevered brow. I doubt anything could.

"I've taken the liberty of orderin' a bath for ya, lass," Moira continued, turning away from the window. "And once you're dressed, Mr. Remington would like ya ta join him for breakfast in the dinin' hall."

Her green eyes sprang open. "You've talked to him this morning?" Shauna nervously asked. She honestly didn't think he'd be the type to discuss his private affairs, but with Moira—well, she had a way of getting a person to say things they'd ordinarily want kept a secret. "What did you talk about?"

Moira raised a curious brow. "The weather, mostly. He introduced me to the staff and said he hoped I'd like it here. Then he showed me about the place. Why? Was he supposed ta tell me somethin'?"

304

"No," Shauna quickly replied. "I . . ." she gulped and cast her eyes away from her maid. "I just didn't expect him to be up this early."

"Early?" Moira laughed. "Most everyone else ate breakfast hours ago, lass. By the time ya've bathed and gone downstairs, they'll be thinkin' about eatin' again." She turned away and went to the armoire to select a gown for her mistress to wear.

Shauna glanced at the window, doubting it could be that late, and realized by the way the sunlight fell into the room that Moira had spoken the truth. "Why did you allow me to sleep so long? You're usually pounding on my door at first light."

"Your husband said ya needed your rest," Moira threw back over her shoulder. "And it was rather late by the time ya arrived here last night."

Shauna's brow wrinkled as the indistinct vision of her being carried from the landau came to her mind. She couldn't remember having seen or talked to her maid, but obviously Moira had been somewhere close by. What she did recall, however, were the strong arms holding her firmly in their grasp and that those same arms had lain her down. After that, everything was a blur.

"Moira," she asked hesitantly, "who put me to bed?"

"Why, your husband, of course. 'Tis what ya wanted."

Shauna's cheeks darkened instantly, and despite the incessant pounding in her temples, she struggled to sit up, the coverlet held beneath her chin. "It was?" she meekly questioned. "Did I actually say so? Did you hear me say it?"

"Aye," Moira responded, turning back to show her mistress the gown she had chosen. "Will this one do?"

Shauna numbly nodded her head while her mind raced

back over the evening past. She could see the landau and vaguely remembered that Brad had offered her sherry and something to eat, the latter of which she had refused. They had talked . . . about her mother, maybe, about love, and she recalled thinking she shoult tell Brad about Kelly O'Sullivan. Her face wrinkled worriedly. But had she? The rest of the conversation was unclear. The image of a long, beautiful staircase came to her, the flickering light from hall sconces, a darkened room, and Brad standing by the window looking out as though something annoyed him. Oh, God! She had told him!

A soft rap sounded against the bedroom door and Shauna hardly noticed the team of servants who entered carrying a tub and buckets of water. They disappeared almost as quickly as they had come, and she unwittingly allowed Moira to pull her from bed, strip away the nightgown, and help her into the sudsy bathwater. Its warmth eased away the ache in her bones but fell short of soothing her troubled mind. How had she told him? Gently, and with all sincerity? Had she made it easy on him or just blurted it out? And how had he taken the news? Had he been angry, as he had a right to be? Or had he gone to stare out the window in silence? She quickly examined her arms and legs and sat up to inspect various other parts of her body for bruises. Finding none, she sank back down in the water, relatively certain he hadn't beaten her for what she'd done, and unaware of the puzzled look she received from her maid. She honestly didn't know Brad that well, but she guessed him to be the sort who didn't become violent when he was upset. At least, not right away. Maybe he was saving it for later . . . when he could catch her off guard. She frowned nervously and picked up the sponge floating near her knee.

"Moira," she said as she halfheartedly washed her neck, "how did Mr. Remington seem to you?"

"Seem?" Moira repeated.

"Yes. Did he appear to be upset about something?"

Moira thought for a moment, then shook her head. "Distracted would be a better word. I had ta repeat everythin' I said ta him at first. Then he seemed ta dismiss whatever he was thinkin' about and brightened up. Why? Should he be?" She scowled suspiciously at her mistress. "Are ya tryin' ta tell me ya got him in bed and then told him ta enjoy his last night at Wrenhaven?"

Shocked by the woman's bluntness, Shauna gasped and jerked her head around to glare at her. But the buzzing in her ears and the unrelenting throbbing of blood in her temples made her cringe. Pressing her fingers against her brow, she closed her eyes and denied the statement. "I wouldn't be that cruel."

"No, of course, ya wouldn't," Moira agreed sarcastically. "Ya wouldn't dream of marryin' him without tellin' him what ya'd done first."

"Moira, please," Shauna gritted out between clenched teeth. "I'm really not in the mood for one of your lectures. I know what I did was—"

"Wrong?" Moira cut in.

Shauna managed to give her an icy glare. "I know what I did was selfish, but I'm sure Brad will understand once I explain why."

"Oh, of course, he will," Moira jeered. "The man's a saint. He'll cradle ya in his arms, stroke your hair, and say, 'That's all right, darlin'. I didn't really want ta live here anyway.'"

"Moira!" Shauna's pain took second place to her rage. "I've never treated you like a common servant, but if you don't hold your tongue, I'll order you out of this room."

"And then what?" Moira challenged, not at all affected by her mistress's threat. "You'll be all alone. You'll lose the one friend ya have."

"A friend wouldn't talk to me the way you do."

"That's what makes me a friend. I don't lie to ya." Laying the towel she had draped over her arm back down on the chair, Moira headed for the door. "Perhaps it's a lesson ya should learn." She twisted the knob and freed the latch. "If it isn't already too late."

The crack of the door slamming shut echoed painfully in Shauna's head and she hurriedly clamped her hands over her ears . . . as if it would do any good.

"Sometimes, Shauna Kathleen Radborne, ya make me so angry," Moira fumed aloud a she fled down the hall toward the staircase, unaware of the tall figure standing at the bottom of the steps watching her. "If I didn't love ya like a sister, I'd pack me bags and—" The rest went unsaid when she glanced up and saw Brad smiling at her. Wondering if he had heard, she nervously looked back toward Shauna's room, mentally calculated the distance between husband and wife, and knew there was a strong possibility. "I . . . I didn't see ya there, sir," she smiled weakly as she descended the stairs. "Have ya been there long?"

"Long enough, Moira," he grinned. "And her name is Shauna Remington now."

Moira's face reddened and she paused on the staircase a few steps from him. "Sir?"

"You said Shauna Kathleen Radborne. I was just reminding you that she's married now."

"Aye, sir," she mumbled, dropping her gaze. "Forgive me. It will take me a while ta get used to it."

"As I'm sure it will for all of us."

He held out a hand toward her, which Moira hesitated before taking. Such treatment of a servant was uncommon and something Moira had never expected. But then, this entire situation was anything but ordinary. She gave him a curious look and withdrew her hand once she stood on the floor next to him.

"You know, one of the problems with a house this size is that sound carries. My father always knew when I was being disrespectful simply because he could hear every word I said as I climbed the stairs to my room." He smiled brightly. "Which, as I recall, was quite often. He'd send me there as punishment for something I'd done." The smile came again as he turned his head to look up the long, winding staircase toward the rooms above them. "I'm hoping someday to catch my own son doing that." He laughed and looked at Moira again. "Not that I'm wishing for a rebellious little hell-raiser. I'm only hoping to have a son. Of course, if my father were alive, he'd say I deserved to have an offspring who behaved the way I did. And I probably do. For the boy's sake, I hope I can be as understanding as my father was."

Moira smiled lamely, sensing there was a point to this discussion.

"I was wondering if you might have a moment to talk, Moira," he asked, nodding toward the study. "There's something I'd like to tell you. But you'll have to promise me that it will be our secret. Shauna is never to know."

The suspicious, worried look in the woman's dark eyes disappeared, and a smile graced her lips. "I've got all the time in the world, Mr. Remington."

"I don't know how you manage, Tyler," Shauna

grumbled as she carefully pushed herself up from the tub and gingerly stepped to the floor. The slightest movement seemed to intensify the hammering in her head. "You can drink all night, stay up until dawn, and never seem to be bothered by it." Bending at the knees, her head held straight, she scooped up the towel and slowly wrapped it around her slender frame. "I will *never* touch another drop of champagne or wine or *sherry* as long as I live," she vowed. "Providing I last the day." Feeling a little queasy, she closed her eyes and fumbled for the chair, gently lowering herself onto the seat. "Damn you, Moira," she hissed. "Why do you have to show a stubborn streak when I need you most?" With the towel tucked loosely around her bosom, Shauna leaned forward to cradle her brow in her hands, her elbows propped on her knees as she contemplated suicide rather than to go on suffering this way. Willing herself not to get sick, she concentrated on quieting the pulsating rhythm in her temples, behind her eyes, and deep in each cheekbone, thus failing to hear the door to her room open in back of her.

"Try this," a deep voice instructed, and Shauna nearly fell off the chair, her red-rimmed eyes shooting upward to stare at the one who spoke. She shriveled in pain again.

"Sorry," Brad apologized. "I didn't mean to startle you. I thought you heard me come in."

"Well, I didn't . . . obviously," she snarled, lowering her head in her hands. A silence followed, one in which Shauna could feel her husband's mirth. "What do you want? To gloat?"

"I never gloat over someone's misery," he contradicted. "That's why I brought this."

A bloodshot green eye peeked through the fingers covering her face at the glass he held out to her. "What is it?"

"An old family remedy."

"In my case, poison," she sneered, hiding her eyes again.

Brad chuckled softly. "You could say that. At least, that's what Dane always told me. And I must admit it doesn't taste véry good." He gently took one of her hands and shoved the glass into it. "Sometimes the cure is worse than the ailment, but I guarantee you'll feel better if you drink it."

She stared apprehensively at the bright red liquid with its specks of black and green floating on top. "Only if it kills me. And right now I'd settle for that." She took a whiff of the concoction and wrinkled her nose. "It won't come right back up, will it?"

Brad shrugged a shoulder. "Never has before. But I guess there's always a first time."

She gave him a damning look. "Thank you. That's very comforting."

"Only telling you the truth. There's a chance. But I doubt it. You're not as sick as I've been on occasion."

"Don't bet on it," she argued, staring at the kaleidoscopic brew as if she expected to see something swimming in it.

Brad understood her reluctance, since he had felt much the same the first time Dane had ordered him to drink it. Placing a finger on the bottom of the glass, he guided it to her lips. "Drink."

Shauna could feel her stomach churn. She had no reason to trust him. She wouldn't blame him for jumping at the opportunity to get even. But right now *anything* was better than feeling the way she did. Pinching her nose with one hand when the obnoxious odor assailed her, she closed her eyes and poured in the mixture.

"All of it," he instructed when she started to lower the glass, an insistent finger raising the container even higher. "It won't do any good otherwise."

She would have liked to growl at him but didn't, knowing she'd drown if she tried. Like an obedient child, she swallowed every drop, then gasped for air. Her eyes widened, tears moistened her lashes, her face whitened all the more, and she was sure that at any second she'd spit fire as the liquid ran down her throat, burning all the way to her stomach. Yet once the scorching sensation began to ebb and she could drag air into her tortured lungs, the relief was almost immediate. The muscles in her stomach relaxed, the achiness in her joints disappeared, and for the first time that morning, the bright sunlight didn't hurt her eyes. Carefully, she rocked her head from side to side, testing her balance and wondering if the recovery was only temporary. To her astonishment, her thunderous world quieted and her vision cleared. It was almost like being reborn.

"Better?" Brad asked once he saw the smile lift her mouth.

"Much," she happily admitted. "I'm truly amazed. For a while there I thought I was going to die, and I was even praying I would. What was in that?"

"A little of everything," he grinned, taking the glass and setting it aside. "Would you like to get dressed now and have something to eat? Then I can introduce you to Wrenhaven."

Suddenly reminded of her scant attire, Shauna blushed profusely and hugged the linen towel to her bosom as she stood and hurried toward the armoire and, hopefully, a robe. "Yes," she mumbled, "I suppose I should eat something. If you'll give me a few minutes, I'll meet you downstairs." Finding a satin and lace wrapper styled in the same design as the nightgown she had worn for Moira's benefit, she quickly threw it across her shoulders, slid her arms into the sleeves, and dropped the towel to the floor as she pulled the sash tightly around her waist, her back to Brad all the while.

"I'm in no hurry," he said. "And since your maid is elsewhere right now, I thought I could help you dress."

Aghast, Shauna spun around, her eyes wide, her mouth agape.

Brad shrugged wide shoulders. "Well, I am your husband. There's nothing wrong with that. If I hadn't stopped to chat with one of the servants, I would have helped with your bath."

Shauna's cheeks darkened even more. "You most certainly would not have. I thought we had an agreement?"

Devilment sparkled in his brown eyes. "We do. But that was only in regard to sharing a bed." He glanced at the aforementioned item, then back at his wife. "And I'm beginning to wonder about that."

The satin robe did little to warm the chill that shot across her shoulders and up the back of her neck. "What do you mean?" she beckoned hesitantly.

"Well, after last night . . ." He let the sentence go unfinished.

"What about last night?" Visions of him carrying her to the bed and laying her down, then stripping away her clothes made her knees tremble. Had he taken advantage?

"You don't remember?" he asked, a mocking concern weighing down his words before he answered his own question with a shake of his head. "No, I don't suppose you do. You were pretty drunk."

Shauna took a tentative step forward. "Are you implying . . ." Her gaze darted from Brad to the bed and back again. "You're not trying to say we . . ."

Brad raised his dark eyebrows and sighed as if he regretted telling her the truth. "I'm afraid so. But it wasn't my idea."

"What?" she shrieked, not believing him for a minute.

"I tried to change your mind, but you were very insistent."

Shauna's brow furrowed angrily. "Oh, I'm sure you did. And I'm sure I was." She started toward him, her chin lowered, her eyes snapping fire. "I suppose you're going to tell me that I forced you, that I ripped off your clothes and threw you down. Or maybe I threatened you . . . with a knife or a pistol?"

Brad shook his head and stepped back as she approached. "No. It was nothing like that. What I meant was that I tried to warn you that you'd regret it in the morning and blame me." He smiled lopsidedly. "I guess I was right." He quickly retreated to his left when the wall behind him offered no escape. Shauna continued to advance.

"And why, pray tell, would I *want* to lie with you? Have you forgotten celibacy was *my* idea?"

"No. But you could have always changed your mind." The heel of his shoe caught the leg of the bed as he passed by and he stumbled in his effort to be free. He wasn't truly worried about her being strong enough to cause him any serious harm. He was simply enjoying his ability to goad her on. When she lunged for him . . .

"And you were right there more than willing to comply." She tossed her silky mane. "What excuse did I

314

give you? Tell me that. Tell me exactly what I said."

"You said you wanted me to teach you how to love me."

Shauna's mouth dropped open and she started to flatly deny his charges, when a vague recognition of their late-night conversation cut her short. They had discussed love, but as far as she was concerned it had had nothing to do with them. Confused, she ceased her pursuit of him to search her mind for the answers, for the bits of their dialogue where she had asked him to teach her about love. If she had, she couldn't remember doing so. What she did recall was questioning the different types of love, and that none of them included what she felt toward Brad.

"You asked if I thought I could ever love you," he continued, encouraged once he saw the puzzled look on her face. "You wanted to know if there was a chance you might feel the same. I told you there was, but that last night wasn't the right time to find out. You insisted. I hesitated. But when you promised not to blame me the next day, I gave in. Any man would have, Shauna," he murmured in all seriousness as he slowly came to stand near her. "You're a beautiful woman. You're alluring, soft, and at the time you were willing. That, added to the fact that you're my wife . . . well, I didn't—"

"You didn't think with your head or your heart," she sneered, suddenly doubting all of what he said. "You listened to your male needs, your desires, and cunningly shifted all blame on to me. You did last night, and now you're doing it again."

Brad jerked back when she thrust out a finger and jabbed it in his breastbone.

"You're nothing but a wily knave preying on

315

unsuspecting females."

Brad hardly thought that analysis was anywhere close to the truth. "I beg to differ, Shauna," he argued with a frown as he absently rubbed the tender spot on his chest. "I've never had to resort to trickery to get a woman in my bed." She started to snap back a comment, but he continued on with little time to draw a breath. "I tried to warn you, whether you care to believe me or not. But I honestly don't think that's what's really behind all this. I suspect you're hiding something from me, and luring me into your arms is your way of covering up. You're determined to start an argument with me because you're hoping I'll walk away and never speak to you again. What is it, Shauna? What are you hiding?"

The vision of red-bearded Kelly O'Sullivan flashed before her eyes, and she shrank back, her gaze dropping away from Brad. So she hadn't told him, after all. Her secret was safe . . . for the time being, anyway. "I can't see where you'd think I was hiding something just because I'm angry with you for not holding up your part of the bargain." She turned from him and started to walk back to the armoire, but he caught her arm in a firm but painless grip.

"Then look me squarely in the eye and say I haven't guessed correctly."

Shauna could feel a nervous veil of perspiration dampen her entire body. She had always been able to lie to Tyler and get away with it, but this man could hardly be compared to her brother. She swallowed the knot in her throat and lifted her eyes. "There are a lot of things about me I wish to keep to myself." She jerked her arm free. "And you've no right to ask me about them. Just as I've no right to ask you about your past."

316

"I have nothing to hide," he rallied. "My conscience is clear. Is yours?"

"No. It isn't," she sneered. "My deepest, darkest secret is that I detest men . . . you included."

Brad chuckled derisively. "That's hardly a secret, Shauna. Everyone who knows you is aware of your dislike. It's a shame there wasn't a witness last night. Then the whole world would know what a little liar you are."

Shauna sucked in an outraged breath, eager to argue the point, but she changed her mind. He was absolutely right, of course. Angrily she brushed past him and went to the dresser to open the top drawer. "If you'll excuse me, I'd like to get dressed now. I haven't eaten yet today, and unless you'd care to answer to my father, I suggest you don't allow me to starve to death."

"If I thought depriving you of food would bring you around, I'd lock you in this room. But you're skinny enough as it is. So I'll use other methods of taking that chip off your shoulder."

Shauna spun back. "Skinny?" She shot herself a quick once-over. "I'm not skinny." Knotted fists flew to her hips. "And what chip? I don't have a chip on my shoulder."

"Oh?" He raised a dark brow. "Then why are you always trying to prove something?"

"Like what?" she countered.

"That you're capable of living your life without a man to clutter things up."

She cocked her head arrogantly to one side. "You said it. I didn't."

"You're wrong there. You say it every time you look at a man . . . every time you look at me." He moved closer.

"But there are those rare occasions when you let your guard down and you're actually nice to be around. I say rare because I've only seen it happen twice."

Shauna's lip curled and she narrowed her eyes. "Let me guess. Those rare occasions wouldn't happen to have anything to do with the times we made love, would they?"

"They're the only times I can remember that we weren't arguing with each other . . . the way we're doing now." He was standing very near her, and his mood seemed to change. "I'm not your enemy, Shauna. I'm not out to strip away your identity."

"Only my clothes," she mocked, jerking the robe tighter around her as if to emphasize her point.

Irritated, he sighed heavily and looked away while he contemplated turning on his heel and stalking from the room. "I'm not really sure why I bother with you, Shauna."

"Then don't," she snapped, deciding that he was standing much too close. She started to go around him but he moved to block her path.

"At times I wish I could," he glared, his brown eyes dark. "But I'm stuck with you. You're my wife. We live under the same roof, and this house might be big, but it's not big enough for you to hide yourself in. We're bound to run into each other now and then. I'd like to live in peace, if not harmony. But more than that, I guess I feel sorry for you."

"Sorry?" she exploded.

"Yes, sorry," he repeated. "You're a very confused young woman. Your mind tells you to hate me but your body betrays you. You're afraid to trust me, afraid if you do, your heart will win."

318

"My, aren't we an arrogant lot?" she challenged. "Have you even considered the possibility that you're just not the right man for me? That when he does come along, I'll know it the instant I see him? Just because we're married doesn't mean I'll fall in love with you. The marriage document doesn't assure that."

A vague smile twitched one corner of his mouth. "It doesn't have to. I'm guaranteed of it every time I stand too close to you . . . like I am now. I can see it in your eyes. I make you uncomfortable."

"*That* is an understatement." She jumped back when he reached out as if to loop a bright yellow curl around his finger.

"Why do you suppose that is, Shauna? What about me makes you uncomfortable?" he continued, moving closer and trapping her against the dresser at her back. "It's certainly not fear. You showed no fear of me last night, though I must admit the amount of sherry you had could give false courage." His eyes moved from the silken strands lying against her bosom to her eyes, then dipped to her trembling mouth. "And there is some fear, I suppose, but not of me. You fear the overpowering sensation I arouse in you."

"Yes. You do arouse something in me. It's called immense disdain."

Her attempt to convince him failed. "I wish I could believe that," he whispered. "It would make things so much easier."

Shauna's body trembled when the warmth of his nearness penetrated the thin fabric of her robe and burned every inch of her. "Then why not pretend?" she asked, unaware that her gaze had lowered to his full, sensual mouth.

"I've never been very good at pretending," he admitted in a husky voice, his left hand rising slowly to cradle her delicate jaw. "I've always believed in honesty."

Shauna's head began to spin when he brushed his lips against hers. Her strong reserve was fading fast, and she wondered if he could hear how noisily her heart was pounding in her chest or sense the strange desire that curled through her veins and set her blood on fire. He was about to kiss her, and despite her denials, she craved the feel of his mouth pressed hotly to hers. In unwilling surrender she closed her eyes, tilted her head back, and waited in breathless anticipation.

"But if that's what you want," he murmured, his warm breath caressing her flesh, his other hand framing her face in his grasp, "then that is how it shall be. All you have to do is say otherwise. But not now. Take your time. We have the rest of our lives to decide how we want to live them." With that, he placed a brotherly kiss on her brow and turned away.

The hot flush in her cheeks turned from well-defined passion to unbridled rage. The rogue was mocking her! Her eyes flew open and she drew a breath between clenched teeth, ready to hurl the vilest of slurs against his heritage, only to stutter and fume as she watched the bedroom door close behind her husband.

Chapter Eleven

The rattle of carriage wheels against the cobblestone drive and the barking of dogs alerted the servants of Hampshire manor that a guest had arrived. They hurried out to perform their duties. The huge frame of Marcus Deerfield descended from within the expensive landau once the coach's door had been opened and the step dropped into place. Without a word of recognition or approval, Deerfield paused on the sidewalk to stretch and to survey the property belonging to his associate. A vague, evil smile curled his mouth as he thought that one day Hampshire would be his, as well. Once he had Pierce Radborne where he wanted him, he would eliminate Billingsly in much the same manner as he had Lucus's uncle. Turning his head while he doffed his white gloves, he stared up at a second-story window, behind which the servants of Hampshire had found their beloved master, Edgar Billingsly, hanging by the neck from the chandelier. The old man hadn't had to die. His stubbornness and his threat to inform the authorities about Deerfield's plan had killed him. Actually, Marcus regretted having had to send his men to murder Lord Billingsly. Edgar was well respected in Parliament, more so than his cowardly

321

nephew, and his power would have brought about the completion of Deerfield's scheme much sooner than by using Lucus. It had been a setback, one Marcus didn't appreciate, but everything had worked out all right in the end . . . or so far, at least. Marcus's gaze dropped to the front door, and his smile widened. Yes, Lucus would die the same way as his uncle, only this time Marcus would personally be the one to slip the noose around the milksop's neck.

"If you'll wait in the parlor, sir," the butler instructed once Deerfield stood in the foyer. "I'll tell Lord Billingsly you're here."

Marcus arrogantly glanced from the doorway of that room to the study's entryway on the opposite side of the wide hallway. "Tell him I'm in there. We have business to discuss . . . important business, and I don't wish to be kept waiting."

He cast the man a challenging look, then headed for the study, failing to see the hate-filled gleam in the butler's eyes. But then, Marcus didn't have to see it. He was well aware of the feelings most people had for him, and he didn't care. Being softhearted and weak had caused his father's death, and Marcus Deerfield had made an oath beside the man's grave that not only would he avenge Fulton Deerfield, but he'd never feel an ounce of remorse, and he would never allow his feelings to stand in the way. And that included the lovely Shauna. Thinking of her made him frown, and once he was alone in the study, he poured himself a glass of wine and sat down in the chair behind the desk, his dark eyes snapping. It had been foolish of him, of course, ever to have thought she might find something appealing about Nelson Thorndyke. It would have made things so much simpler if she had. Now he had Remington to contend with. Trying to poison him hadn't worked, and now that Shauna was married to him, Marcus couldn't touch him. If Remington died, Wrenhaven would belong to Shauna. He doubted Shauna loved her husband. The proud bitch loved no one but herself, and being a widow would work to her advantage. She'd have a place to live, money, and the right to remain single the rest of her life if she so chose. Tossing back his head, he swallowed the wine in one gulp, knowing that would be exactly what she'd think once she saw her husband buried. But Marcus had other plans.

A movement in the doorway pulled his attention to Lucus Billingsly standing there, his dull brown hair pulled back off his milky complexion with a satin ribbon, his clothes in disarray, as though he had hurriedly donned them, and his breath coming in ragged heaves. Glancing at the mantel clock, Marcus noted the time.

"You sleep with the innocence of a babe, Lucus," Deerfield mocked. "Have you no conscience?"

Clumsily straightening his silk ascot, Lucus grumbled, "I could say the same for you. I spent the evening past walking the floor, wondering where all of this will lead us. I only just now fell asleep. Or so it seemed." He stepped into the room and closed the door. "And must you be so rude to my servants? I'm having enough trouble with them without you making me look weak."

"You are weak, Lucus," Deerfield drily accused. "And as for my having a conscience . . . no, I don't. And you'd do well to remember that. One mistake, one little complaint on your part, and I'll find someone to take your place."

"And run all the risks," Billingsly jeered as he came to

the desk to pour himself a glass of wine. "Do you ever put yourself in jeopardy, Deerfield?"

"Why should I when there are plenty of your kind around?"

Billingsly's brow wrinkled. "My kind? What do you mean?"

Leaning forward, Marcus handed the man his wine glass to refill. "The kind too stupid to do anything more than what they're told. You're living proof of it." He snatched back the glass and settled in the chair again. "When I found you, you were begging in the streets. You lived in a filthy room above a pub and you hadn't a coin in your pocket."

"I beg your pardon," Lucus objected in a rare show of courage. "As I recall, I met you at Sir Windom's Men's Club."

"And how do you suppose you got there?"

"Got there?" Lucus gasped. "I was invited, of course."

"You were invited to join only after your luck changed."

"My luck?"

"Are you denying the fact that at one time you weren't worthy of sweeping up the place?" Marcus cocked a brow, waiting for Billingsly's response. "Yes, of course you are. Well, I know differently." Cupping his glass in both hands, he leaned forward to rest the goblet on the desktop. "You really don't think our meeting was accidental, do you? I planned it that way. Just as I made sure you'd find that purse full of gold coins in the alleyway in back of the pub. Just as I saw to it you won every game of cards you played until that night at Sir Windom's. I knew of your weakness for gambling and used it against you. I let you win a few rounds, then I took back every shilling I gave you."

The pain in Billingsly's chest took his breath away. He knew Marcus Deerfield was ruthless, but he had never imagined just how much. "Why did you bother? Why go to such an extreme?"

"Quite simple, ol' boy. I needed you to be in debt to me. Now, how would I have managed that if you had nothing to begin with?"

"And then you made sure I'd lose it all to you in front of witnesses. And not just anybody, but men of rank, men of authority, so that I couldn't claim I'd been cheated or tricked." Feeling faint, Lucus stumbled to a chair and sank into it. "God, the irony of it. I *had* been tricked and more than likely cheated, as well."

"Tricked, yes. But not cheated. You're a lousy card player, Billingsly. A twelve-year-old boy could do better." Enjoying Lucus's misery, Deerfield fell back in the chair and took a leisurely drink of his wine. "And, of course, it didn't stop there, did it, *friend?*" The last was issued sarcastically.

"Oh no. You're smarter than that," Billingsly whined. "You explained how I'd never have to pay you back. All I had to do was sign a paper agreeing to the murder of my Uncle Edgar and promising that once I had power in Parliament, I was to use it to help you."

A sneer curled Deerfield's lips. "I'm surprised you never figured it out." He casually raised the glass to his lips and took a swallow. "But then, I shouldn't be too surprised. You've never been too smart."

Lucus would have liked to argue the point, but he couldn't. If he'd been smart, he never would have signed that paper. He never would have gambled away his newfound wealth. He would have taken the money and opened the little bakery shop he had always dreamed of owning. And if he had the courage now, and a way to achieve such a goal, he'd ransack Deerfield's home for that damnable document he had so carelessly and foolishly signed. Then he'd show the bastard just how much power he really had in Parliament. He'd publicly accuse Deerfield of murdering his uncle and see him hanged for it. Unwittingly, he smiled.

"Planning something evil, Lucus?"

The question brought him around, and his pale complexion turned ashen. "What makes you think that?" he asked nervously, averting his gaze as he gulped down his wine.

"You always get that faraway look in your eyes whenever you're planning something, and since your life is fairly stable, except for your involvement with me, it makes sense to assume you'd like to change that part of it. And you will. But only after we've taken care of Radborne." Marcus smiled crookedly. "So put those thoughts aside for now, Lucus, dear boy, and try to concentrate on what I'm about to tell you."

Finishing off his drink, Billingsly rose and came to the desk to refill his glass. He never indulged in anything stronger than tea so early in the morning, but today was an exception. He needed it to calm his nerves and build up his courage. Just as soon as he was rid of Deerfield, he'd sit down and figure out a way of exposing the man without involving himself. His hand trembled as he lifted the decanter, wishing he could just pull a gun and shoot him . . . in the back, of course. He never liked watching the expressions on a man's face while he was dying.

"So tell me why you're here." His teeth rattled as he

spoke and he clamped them shut as he turned away to seek the safe distance sitting in the chair offered him.

Deerfield's dark eyes brightened with humor, as he watched Billingsly cower in his seat before answering. "Talbot has notified me that Remington's been asking a few questions."

Billingsly's head shot upward. "What kind of questions?"

"It seems he's noticed our men late at night."

"Well, what did you expect? I told you that you'd have to find some other way of smuggling in the goods than by using Remington's property."

"Not if we're careful," Deerfield declared, toying with the ring on his little finger.

"Don't be riduculous! You can't be too careful with Remington. In the few months he's been in London he's built up quite a reputation for being very astute. I've also heard he's making inquiries about hiring someone to build a factory right there on Wrenhaven."

A strange smile parted Deerfield's lips. "Really?" he questioned, his mind racing with ideas. "Has he had any luck?"

"Not so far. He can't find anyone willing to back him. He's well liked around here, but not enough to risk money on. Remember, the only wealth he has is tied up in Wrenhaven."

"So it is," Marcus crooned, a devious gleam shining in his eyes. "Then I guess it's time Nelson helped him out."

"What?" Billingsly's face wrinkled in confused surprise. "Whatever can you be thinking? If he gets help building that factory, Remington will be earning a decent profit in no time at all. Then how will you ever expect to gain ownership?"

327

"Oh, I think I know a way, thanks to you."

"Me?"

Marcus reached up to rub his chin. "I had wanted to do things differently, but since I can't get my hands on Shauna for a while, we'll go after her father first."

"How? What are you planning?"

"Remington needs money. Who, of all the aristocrats in London, would you say is the wealthiest?"

Billingsly thought for a moment then replied, "Radborne, I guess."

"Very good, Lucus," Deerfield sneered. "And since Remington is married to his daughter, don't you suppose Radborne would want to help?"

"Of course. But from what I've heard, Remington won't ask him. Pride, I suppose." Billingsly's lip curled. "Damn fool. Can't live on pride. If he was a good businessman, he'd make Radborne a deal."

"Exactly," Marcus added. "And Radborne wouldn't hesitate. So, we'll have to make sure he's unable to help."

"How?"

"That's what you're here to do. It's what I had planned from the start. You're to use your influence. Sir Blakely is having another party in a few days, and I want you to attend. You're to subtly talk with every man there and let them know Remington is a bad risk, that you have it on good authority that he fled his debts in the Colonies, and that he'd more than likely do the same thing here if his business fails."

"All right," Billingsly concurred. "But that doesn't take care of Radborne. He likes his new son-in-law, and you know how his mind works. He'll fix it so he'll still make a profit even if Remington fails . . . which I doubt will happen. The industrialists are gaining power every day."

"We don't want Remington to fail. That's not what we're really after."

"It's not?" Billingsly was confused.

In silence, Marcus stared at his cohort for a moment, wondering how anyone could be that stupid. "No, Lucus, it's not. We're after Wrenhaven, Shauna, and finally Radborne himself."

"But—"

"But what? But how will we succeed? One step at a time, that's how." Reaching into his pocket for his tin of cheroots, he lit one up and exhaled a puff of white smoke to watch it curl and drift toward the ceiling. "I'm sure you know how dangerously low the treasury is because of the war. It will be your suggestion in Parliament to tax those who can afford it . . . namely Pierce Radborne. I want you to see to it that all his assets are tied up so tight he can't afford to loan Remington a single shilling."

"And then what?"

With the cheroot clamped between his teeth, Marcus smiled. "Simple, ol' boy. Then Nelson Thorndyke will move in . . . hand extended in friendship and his purse stuffed with money. Remington will have no alternative but to accept Nelson as his partner."

Billingsly nervously pulled a lace handkerchief from his sleeve and dabbed at the perspiration dotting his brow and neck. "A . . . partner?"

Deerfield's eyes glowed. "Most assuredly. Nelson's money, Wrenhaven as collateral."

"But that doesn't make any sense, Marcus. How will Nelson's loaning him the money get you Wrenhaven? It won't take Remington long to pay back his debt."

"That's the beauty of it, Lucus, and where having someone on the inside will benefit us all."

Billingsly's pale brow wrinkled. "How?"

"After Remington signs an agreement with Nelson, Talbot will steal the document and bring it to you. You'll add the clause that in the event of Remington's death *before* the loan is repaid, the property will become Mr. Thorndyke's."

"My God, Marcus, if I was found out for having done such a thing, I'd be—"

"Hanged," Deerfield snarled. "Just as you'll be hanged if you don't. *I'll see to that!*" His huge fist slammed against the desktop, rattling everything sitting on it and bringing a whimper from the man who felt he had just been condemned to the fiery depths of hell.

Shauna's first week at Wrenhaven and as Brad's wife passed slowly for her, and each new day that dawned brought her closer to having to tell Brad the truth, a fact that made her edgy and quarrelsome. In the beginning she had spent most of her daylight hours in her room reading or sewing tapestries. When the confinement seemed only to add to her distress, she ventured outside to work in the flowerbed, something she had grown very fond of doing. She seldom saw her husband. He seemed totally involved in business matters concerning the estate and the factory he planned to build down near the river. He went to bed late at night in the room next to hers long after she had retired, and he rose early every morning. On occasion they dined together in the evening, and if it hadn't been for those few times, she might have thought he had deserted her.

Tyler came to visit nearly every day, but rather than spend the time with her, he chose to closet himself off in the study with Brad. At first, it angered her that her very own brother preferred her husband's company to hers, and she had tried to pretend indifference. But by the third meeting, and because even Moira acted strangely toward her, Shauna was beginning to feel deeply and hopelessly alone, despite the many servants roaming about the place. Out of boredom, she decided to take over the management of the household affairs, and when Brad suggested they invite her family for dinner sometime soon, she set about with a flourish planning the menu and selecting the wine. She realized she was doing exactly what she had claimed she never wanted to do—act like a wife—but in spite of it, she found it not only enjoyable but a way to pass the time and get her mind off Kelly O'Sullivan.

Mid-July, as always, consisted of long, hot days. The nights were intolerable. Unable to sleep for the third night in a row, Shauna rose from her bed and went out onto the balcony overlooking the spacious gardens she was so proud of for a cool breath of air. Moira had been right in her description of Wrenhaven. There were more trees surrounding the manor than in all of London—or so one was led to believe. Thick green grass offered a soft cushion on which to walk barefoot if she wanted, and the sweet perfume of the hundreds of flower blossoms afforded a tranquil serenity to Shauna's troubled mind.

Bathed in moonlight, Shauna stretched, tilted her head back, and closed her eyes, sweeping the heavy mass of hair off her neck as she sucked in a breath of the fragrant air and felt the soft summer breeze mold the silky fabric of her nightgown to her damp body. Crickets chirped from somewhere below her, and in the distance she could hear the occasional belch of a frog or hoot of an owl. Silvery light filtered down through the leafy overhang of oaks and beech trees, flooding the sculptured gardens in an ashen glow and bringing a soft smile to Shauna's lips as she drank in the quiet beauty of it all. It was so peaceful here that it was hard for her to imagine that she had at one time wondered if she would ever learn to like living in the country. City life was so fast paced that there never seemed to be enough hours in the day to accomplish all that she wanted. But here . . .

Turning, she leaned against the railing and watched the hypnotic sway of the tree branches in the gentle breeze, unaware of the dark figure standing on the balcony next to hers. Moments passed while she savored the mesmerizing quietude of her surroundings, but it wasn't long before her thoughts betrayed her and her mind wandered to the one person who had so completely shattered her life. She couldn't understand her feelings for the man who was now her husband. In the beginning she had thought her scheme would work, that Brad would want nothing more of her than the land she could give him, and that she would be content with only his name. Yet she had come to realize that *she* was the one who wasn't satisfied with the arrangement. There was something about him that excited her and lingered in her thoughts long after she was alone. There was a certain aura about him, a mystifying, enchanting magnetism that constantly drew her to him, both physically and mentally. She liked watching him while he worked, whether at his desk in the study with his head bowed over the papers he contemplated or outside at the stable, his jacket doffed, shirt sleeves rolled up, and sweat making the fabric cling to his well-muscled back. Her breath would catch in her throat whenever he'd glance up and smile at her or when he offered nothing more than his profile while he stared thoughtfully off into the distance, his mind elsewhere than on the one who stared at him. She enjoyed the sound of his laughter and the deep resonance of his voice when he spoke. She liked the way he walked, the way he smelled, the way he cursed when he thought no one would hear him. He was firm with those in his employ, yet he could laugh at his own mistakes when he wrongly accused them of something they hadn't done. He was kind, generous, caring, a hard worker, and very determined to succeed on his own. He was the sort of man any woman would be proud to claim as her husband. So why couldn't she?

"Because it wouldn't be fair," she murmured, pulling her long hair off her neck and twisting it into a thick cord. "I really don't deserve him . . . not after what I've done." She honestly would have liked falling in love with him, but she knew she mustn't let that happen. She'd only get hurt in the end, and rightfully so. He'd walk out on her the instant he learned she had gambled away Wrenhaven to a perfect stranger. And not so much for the fact that she hadn't lived up to her part of the deal, but rather because he'd chosen not to live with someone as selfish as she. A line formed between her softly arched brows and her mouth turned downward. If he loved her, he'd stay. But what was there to love about Shauna Kathleen? She had been spoiled her whole life and was used to and demanded things her own way. She was a snob. She wouldn't dream of doing any physical labor she thought beneath her. She was only out for things that pleased *her*, no matter who got hurt in the process. She was short-tempered and sharp-tongued, and she never tried to hide her true feelings. So what did that leave that would interest a man? That question stabbed at her heart.

Until now, all she could offer was wealth. She didn't even want to give a man heirs.

Suddenly, the vision of three laughing little boys running through the gardens filled her thoughts, and she smiled. Close in age, they had the dark hair and rugged features of their father, and her green eyes. They held wooden swords in their hands and fought a fierce battle with an invisible enemy, standing shoulder to shoulder as they defended their home. She could see them riding horses as young men, working alongside their father at the factory as adults, arguing with suppliers, getting married and starting families of their own. She could even imagine their children coming to visit their grandfather. A tear moistened her lashes, and when she blinked, it raced for her chin, for even though it was all make believe, Shauna herself wasn't truly a part of it. If Brad had three fine sons, *she* wouldn't be their mother.

Inexplicably, the beauty of the scenery around her turned ugly. Angry, she straightened and moved for the door, intending to go back inside, back into the darkness where no one or nothing could see her cry. Yet, when a strange gnawing played upon her consciousness, she was drawn to look to her right, and she stifled a gasp when she discovered Brad had been watching her from his balcony.

"I see you were unable to sleep as well," he murmured, his broad, bare chest gleaming with perspiration in the soft moonlight as he sat with one hip on the railing, his back pressed against the wall. "I don't know how anyone can in this heat." He turned his head to stare out across the gardens, his dark features bathed in the ashen glow. "I don't remember it being this hot as a child." He smiled softly. "But I guess children have a better tolerance for things they can't change."

"How . . . how long have you been sitting there?" she asked hesitantly, remembering the few words she had spoken aloud.

"Since before you came out." He produced a lighted cigar and took a puff, and Shauna wondered why she hadn't smelled its aroma before now. "So I wasn't spying, if that's what you're thinking. I usually sit out here for a while before going to bed. It helps me relax. But I'm not really sure it will tonight. It's almost unbearable inside. In fact, I'm tempted to bring out a pillow and blanket and sleep here." He pointed the cheroot at the floor of the small balcony, and then chuckled. "Imagine what the staff would think if I were found curled up out here. 'Damn Colonial. They're such barbarians,'" he mocked good-naturedly.

His lighthearted mood eased Shauna's nervousness and she came to sit on the railing of her balcony, a distance of twenty feet or more from his. "I've never know anyone who lived in America before you. Tell me what it's like."

"It's not a whole lot different from England . . . scenerywise, I mean." He continued to look out at the rolling hills covered with huge trees, pausing occasionally to draw on the cheroot. "I think you'd like it. Maybe we can sail there sometime and you can meet my brother, Dane, and his wife. They'd like you."

I doubt it, she thought, frowning.

"Boston is more like London than any other town I visited, I suppose, but I enjoyed Williamsburg, Virginia most. Maybe that's because I lived there the longest."

"If you liked it so much, why did you come back here?" she asked without rancor or sarcasm.

A broad shoulder lifted. "I guess I just never realized

335

how much I missed Wrenhaven until after Dane got married and I was left on my own. Strange thing about having an older brother always there to look out for you; you're never forced to think for yourself." A wide grin parted his lips as he turned his head to look at her. "Not true in your case."

Shauna could feel a blush warming her cheeks and she lowered her eyes. "Yes. I doubt anyone will ever be able to control me. I don't know anyone who'd be willing or foolish enough to want to try."

"Oh, I wouldn't agree with that," he contradicted. "That part of you is what makes you so appealing."

Shauna laughed. "And you, sir, are making up stories."

"Not at all," he objected. "Why do you suppose some men decide to give up a comfortable life to sail the seas? I'll tell you why. They enjoy—no, they *thrive* on adventure. The ocean is the most untamed resource in the world and probably always will be. It's a challenge. Just to cross her is a feat. To understand her takes patience and skill. To conquer her is the ultimate goal, one many have died trying to reach."

"Are you likening me to the ocean?" Shauna asked coquettishly.

"In some ways, you are. Your willfulness, determination, your stubborn streak are things to conquer."

"And what happens once that's achieved? If it ever is," she posed, truly flattered by the comparison. "Will the victor look for another challenge."

He leaned back against the wall again and inhaled a puff of smoke, his gaze drifting out across the gardens. "Some would, perhaps. But not me."

His confession made her heart flutter, and somewhere

deep inside her, hope sprang up. "'Tis noble," she replied, choosing her words carefully. "But suppose that once that happened and you discovered another side of me you didn't like, would you then be tempted to look for some other quest with which to fill your hours?"

He was quiet for a moment, then shook his head. "I know all there is to know about you."

She wished that was true, but knowing otherwise, she added, "Perhaps I hold a secret locked in my heart, and the key to open it is love and trust. What then?"

"Do you have such a secret, Shauna?"

He looked over at her, and she trembled. Averting her gaze, she realized that no other time would be more fitting than now to tell him the truth. She took a breath to speak and changed her mind, silently damning her cowardice and wondering at its cause. What was the worst he might do to her? Strike her? The bruises would heal. Call her names? They would fade from her memory in time. Say nothing at all? The pain registered in his eyes would tell her more than words. Cast her out? Of all the choices, the last brought tears to her eyes. 'Twas what she deserved more than his wrath, but it was something too frightening even to imagine. In the short time they had known each other, he had become a very vivid part of her life, so much so that living without him was something she refused to do. Blinking back her tears, she swallowed the knot in her throat and took a deep breath, willing herself to be strong. There was little doubt in her mind that that was exactly what would come of all this. Sooner or later she would have to deal with it. Cursing her selfishness, she decided to wait.

"Sometimes a person has a secret that they're not even aware they have," she replied instead, forcing herself to

337

look straight ahead rather than at Brad.

"There's only one secret I pray is hidden in your heart, Shauna." He waited until she had turned a surprised look his way before he rose, flicked the cheroot out over the banister, and added, "Only one." Pausing for a moment to return her stare, he nodded his dark head, bid her goodnight, and went inside, leaving Shauna there alone in the bright silvery light shining down on her.

The next morning found Shauna working in the flowerbed on the west side of the house where it was shady. Her talk with Brad the night before had left her both pleased and ashamed. He had admitted—though not in precise words—that despite all her faults, and if given the chance, he could love her. It thrilled her to know this, yet the realization that she had betrayed his trust played heavily on her conscience. It worsened when she heard the hoofbeats of an approaching horse and rider, and she glanced up to recognize the leather pouch slung over the visitor's shoulder by its strap. Glancing about to make sure no one else had heard his arrival, she quickly came to her feet, dusted off her hands, and rushed toward the man.

"'Mornin', Mrs. Remington," the letter-carrier smiled with a nod of his head as he politely removed his hat and stepped to the ground. "Been quite a hot spell we've been having."

"Yes, it has," she answered, mustering all the will she had not to lunge for the pouch and tear through its contents. She was almost sure of what she'd find.

"I have a couple of letters for you," he went on, bowing his head as he searched the leather bag for them.

"Actually one is for your husband."

With his attention away from her, Shauna nervously glanced toward the manor and the front door, praying she'd have the time to hide her letter in the deep pocket of her apron before anyone saw her.

"Came all the way from the Colonies, it did," he added, handing the sealed parchments to her. "Must be from his brother."

Shauna smiled lamely. "Yes. I suppose it is. Thank you." She forced herself to stand where she was, the letters clutched to her bosom, while she waited for him to don his tricorn and mount.

"Well, good day to you," he finished, touching the brim of his hat and turning the animal around.

"Good day," she replied, thankful her full skirts masked her quaking limbs. With her back to the house, she stole a glance at the letters she held, selected the one addressed to her, and slipped it in her apron pocket before turning around. She'd give Brad his letter, then hurry to the privacy of her room to read her own.

She found Brad working in the study with his diagrams and lists of supplies needed to build his factory, just as she had suspected she would. Pausing in the open doorway, she waited until he sensed her presence and looked up. The smile he gave her warmed her heart and tore at her guilt at the same instance. Lowering her eyes, she stepped into the room, the sealed parchment held out to him.

"This just came for you." She neared the wide desk and leaned to hand it over. "I was told it came from the Colonies. Your brother, perhaps?"

Brad quickly tore the wax seal and glanced at the signature. "You're absolutely correct," he beamed, his eyes expressing his delight. He missed the conversations he and his brother had and hadn't realized how much until seeing the letter penned in Dane's hand. Looking up at his wife, he nodded at the chair sitting in front of the desk. "I'll read it to you."

Anxious to escape to her room, she declined. "It's personal."

"Not enough not to share with you. We're married. Remember?"

I've thought of nothing else since the moment I said "I do." she silently admitted as she reluctantly sat down.

Dane wrote first about his wife, Brittany, and the joys of being parents to three rebellious boys, which made Brad laugh and reminded Shauna of her imaginary family. He said he hoped that someday his brother would experience the same nerve-racking tribulations of being a father, but added that he wouldn't change any of it if he were given the opportunity. He loved his wife and his sons, and the happy times far outweighed the troubled ones. He went on to report that the newly formed Congress of the United States was actively establishing itself and that the last of the British soldiers had gone home. He had been given recognition for his work with the Sons of Liberty, and he was hoping to take his family back to Boston to live. He asked if Brad had had any luck in fulfilling his dream of owning their father's property again, and Brad paused here to explain that when he'd left the Colonies neither he nor his brother were sure that whoever owned Wrenhaven would be willing to sell it. He also took a moment to tell her that he had already written to Dane and filled him in on everything that had happened in the past two months.

Not everything, Shauna thought somberly. And if my

letter says what I think it will, you'll have to write your brother another letter explaining how your dream was ruined by a very self-centered woman . . . your wife.

"He says that he and his family have discussed coming to England for a visit as soon as they're settled again and when he's sure they'll have a place to stay once they're here," Brad recited, a warm smile parting his lips. Looking up, he chuckled and added, "That's his way of telling me he still doubts I'll ever settle down."

Shauna returned his smile, though it never quite reached her eyes, and shifted uncomfortably in the chair, hoping she would be excused before much longer. The knot in her stomach was making her squeamish and she needed a breath of fresh air.

Brad went on to say that Brittany sent her love and her hope that England held all the answers to her favorite brother-in-law's problems. But that if it didn't, he was to know that he was always welcome in her home. He was quiet for a long moment after that, and Shauna quickly noticed that he had a faraway look in his eyes, as if he might be thinking of another time, another place. Yet no smile graced his lips while he sat there reminiscing, and Shauna wondered if his thoughts were sad or unpleasant. Could it be he was thinking of the young woman Tyler had told her about, the one Brad had loved and lost? Feeling as though she was intruding and had no right to be, she quietly came to her feet and left the room.

Alone in her bedchambers, Shauna locked the door behind her and fell back against it, her mind and her heart racing. She couldn't understand why she had suddenly felt jealous of a woman from Brad's past, but she had. Perhaps she envied the tender relationship they had obviously shared or worried that if she were to die,

Brad would never recall the moments *they'd* shared with anything more than animosity.

And what more could you expect? she silently asked herself. What have you ever done to warrant more? You've cursed him from the start, lied to him, cheated him out of a future, and despite all that you're still concerned with only *your* welfare.

Feeling sick inside, she closed her eyes and chewed on her lower lip. She really didn't want to be remembered that way. What she had started out to do had been done in all honesty and truth, and he had agreed. Her smooth brow crimped. Well, sort of. He had called it blackmail. She had called it a business dealing. He could have said no anytime he'd wanted. *And lose Wrenhaven,* her conscience screamed. Clamping her hands over her ears, she let out a throaty growl and stormed to the bed, there to practically throw herself down upon it. If he had said no, the property never would have been hers to wager at the gaming tables. And although she might have been married to Thorndyke right now if he had declined, he at least would have stood a chance of buying it from her father. So, in retrospect, this whole mess was of his own doing!

"Oh, it is not," she hissed, shoving off the bed and crossing to her open balcony doors.

The noonday sun beat mercilessly down on the countryside in a blinding glare, turning the dark green grass a paler shade and bleaching nearly all the color out of the flower blossoms. The air hung still and heavy, and even though it was uncomfortably hot in her room, she knew standing outside just now would probably make her swoon. Perspiration dotted her brow, and when a droplet trickled down her throat, she absently grabbed the corner of her apron and dabbed it against her neck. As she did so, the letter worked free of its hiding place and fluttered to the floor, bringing Shauna's attention to it almost immediately. Immobile, she stared down at the folded piece of paper, praying it was only a message from her father, yet certain it wasn't.

And if you allow it to lie there a hundred years, it won't change anything, she mused soberly. You might as well open it and see what Mr. O'Sullivan has to say.

Bending, she hesitantly pinched the corner of it between her thumb and first finger, as if the paper was too hot to touch, and slowly returned to her bed to sit down. Gulping the lump in her throat, she gritted her teeth and popped the wax seal.

Dear Mrs. Remington—I know I told you that it would be a month before I'd be returning to London to claim the property I won in our card game, but I was able to finish my business here in Dublin much sooner than I thought. This is to notify you that I should be arriving on Wrenhaven within the week or so. I can only hope you've settled everything with your husband before then. Sincerely—

Kelly O'Sullivan

Panic threatened, and Shauna's entire body began to tremble with such violence that the letter slipped from her fingers and floated to the floor. Dear God, what was she going to do? She couldn't just allow Mr. O'Sullivan to ride in unannounced, stroll right up to Brad and shake his hand, introduce himself, and then proclaim right out of the blue that *he* was the owner of Wrenhaven! Brad wouldn't believe the man, and he'd more than likely order him off the place. A fight was sure to ensue, and

343

someone would get hurt, *and it would all be her fault!* Her mind racing with various, confused ideas on how to solve her dilemma, she absently began to pace the floor, pausing when one solution seemed better than the rest. She'd shake that one off, knowing it wouldn't work, and begin her aimless trek all over again. Finally, in the midst of all her frantic considerations, the doorknob to her room rattled and Moira's voice called out in concern. Not up to hearing her maid's berating comments, Shauna steeled herself against the chaotic ramblings in her head and calmly went to the door to unlock it.

"Are ya feelin' poorly, lass?" Moira asked once her mistress had let her in. "Ya look a little pale."

"Too much heat," Shauna offered. "I was thinking about lying down for a while."

Moira cocked a dubious brow. "Are ya sure it's not because of your husband's guest rather than the heat?" she posed.

"Guest?" Shauna repeated, glancing out into the hall as if she expected to see the person. "What guest?" Visions of the redheaded Irishman flashed before her eyes. "Who is it?" she demanded nervously, her hand gripping the doorknob to steady her balance.

"Mr. Thorndyke," Moira frowned. "Who were ya expectin' it ta be?" She tilted her head to one side and sighed. "Ya don't have ta answer that. Ya were thinkin' it was the new owner of Wrenhaven. I can see it in your face. Ya haven't told your husband yet, have ya?"

"Moira, please," Shauna warned, her hands raised in front of her. "Don't lecture. You can't possibly make me feel any worse than I already do. And you can't tell me something I haven't already told myself."

"Does that mean you're goin' down ta tell ya husband

the truth just as soon as Mr. Thorndyke leaves?"

Shauna took a quick peek at her maid from out of the corner of her eye as she walked past the woman toward the balcony. "No," she mumbled.

"And why not? What are ya waiting for? To wake up? This isn't a dream, lass."

"I know that," Shauna admitted a bit sharply. "I'm just trying to figure out some way of never having to tell him."

Moira snorted derisively. "The only way I can see that happenin' is if Mr. Remington's dead."

"Moira!" Shauna shrieked. "Don't ever say that! If I don't come up with a solution *before* Mr. O'Sullivan arrives, there's a strong chance someone *will* get hurt."

Moira's eyes narrowed. "Mr. O'Sullivan, is it? Now, how would ya be knowin' his name? Ya told me ya never asked who he was."

Without realizing it, Shauna's gaze dropped to the floor and the letter lying there. She jerked her attention back up on her maid, praying Moira hadn't noticed. She had, however, and before Shauna could race to the spot, Moira hurried over to it, bent, and scooped up the letter, holding the parchment out of Shauna's reach when she made a grab for it.

"That's personal, Moira," she snapped. "You have no right to read my letters. Give it to me."

"When did he say he'd be arrivin'? Today? Tomorrow? Next week? How long do ya have, Shauna Kathleen? Should I start packin' your things?" She held her at bay with a hand clamped securely around Shauna's elbow.

"Next week," Shauna hissed, lunging for the letter again.

Moira easily held her off. "Next week. So you're gonna wait until the last possible minute. What are ya goin' ta do in the meanwhile? Seduce your husband? Make him fall in love with ya, so he'll forgive ya rather than throw ya out into the street? And me right along with ya!"

"I would if I thought it would work," Shauna snarled. "But not for the reason you're thinking."

Moira chuckled sarcastically. "And what other reason is there?"

Shauna stopped struggling and pulled loose of her maid's iron grip. Turning, she went back to stand in the open balcony doorway, her back to her maid as she stared out at the cloudless blue sky. "I'd like for him to think of me in the years to come as someone who regretted her actions and had tried to make up for them. I don't want him to hate me, even though he has every right. I was stupid and selfish and foolhardy, but I'd like him to realize that I did all that *before* I learned to . . ." She frowned when the right word seemed to lose itself in her thoughts. "Before I learned to care about him, about his feelings, before I learned there are other people who matter besides me. It might still sound a little selfish, but it's really my way of apologizing for all the hurt and anguish I'm sure to cause him."

The angry expression on Moira's face disappeared and tenderness replaced it. Moving quietly, she came to stand beside her mistress. "Was that so hard ta say, lass?" she asked comfortingly.

A trembling sigh shook Shauna. "Not really. It just took me a long time to pick the words."

"And they were beautiful words, they were." Reaching up, she gently pulled a long strand of golden hair off Shauna's shoulder. "Ya spoke the truth, lass. Ya said the words ya felt in your heart. Why not tell them ta your husband? Say them just the way ya told me. He'll forgive ya, lass. He'd have to."

Shauna smiled softly. "I'd like to think that, but I can't. Wrenhaven was his dream, and I've taken it away from him. No amount of apologies, promises, or words will ever change that. I'll tell him, if I must. But I'd prefer to spare him that. I'd like to talk with Mr. O'Sullivan first. Perhaps he'll understand once I explain, and we can strike a deal."

Moira's color seemed to pale a little. "Talk to him, lass?"

Her attention still focused on the azure sky, Shauna nodded.

"But ya can't," Moira quickly objected, without any thought, straightening and turning away once she realized how it must seem to her mistress. Stealing a glance at that one to find Shauna frowning back at her, she quickly amended. "I mean there's no way for ya to talk to him until it's too late. Ya don't know where ta find him, do ya? He'll just ride up ta our front door, and if you're not there ta greet him, well . . ." She shook her head. "No. Ya can't risk it. Ya must talk to your husband first." Flustered, Moira handed Shauna her letter and hurriedly moved to the door. "I think maybe it's best ya do as I suggested."

"And what's that?" Shauna asked, her brow furrowed in total confusion as she turned to watch her maid rush off.

Reaching for the doorknob, Moira swung the portal toward her as she prepared to leave the room. "Woo him, lass," she called over her shoulder. "Make him fall in love with ya."

The click of the latch made Shauna blink at the finality the sound implied. She had known Moira Flanagan for a long, long time, but she had never seen her act this way. She couldn't quite say what it was that seemed unnatural about Moira's actions, unless it was her haste in leaving or perhaps her failure to add one last biting comment . . . the way she always did. Shrugging it off, Shauna dropped her gaze and spotted the letter in her hand. Crossing to the bed, she sat down and held the parchment up before her eyes, realizing that what Moira had said about her not knowing where to reach Kelly O'Sullivan was true. He might still be in Dublin or already on his way here. Her gaze shifted to the door, and a slow, calculating smile curled her lips. She might not know where to find the Irishman, but she certainly knew where her husband was.

Chapter Twelve

By early evening, Shauna's curiosity about her husband's abrupt departure turned to worry. None of the staff seemed to know where he had gone or why or when and if he'd be returning home to Wrenhaven that night. All any of them knew was that he had left shortly after talking with Nelson Thorndyke, a conversation that had been held behind closed study doors. Shauna could only assume it had something to do with business, since nothing else had seemed of any importance to her husband over the past several days, and she was wishing she had decided sooner to become involved in his work. If she had, she might know what it was that had sent him off without a word to anyone. As it was, all she could do was wait.

Her talk with Moira earlier and the maid's suggestion that she set about making her husband fall in love with her gave Shauna a different idea. Her father had always told her that she had more common sense when it came to business dealings than a lot of his associates, and she decided to prove it to Brad. It wasn't so much that she thought Brad could use her help, but rather as a way to spend time with him, to get close, to force him to notice her in ways other than romantically. If he came to see her as a partner instead of just his wife, he'd learn to respect her, to count on her, maybe even fall back on her when he needed someone's opinion. It was a difficult feat to accomplish in such a short time, but her very existence depended on her success, and she was willing to give it a try. After all, what had she to lose?

She had left her bedchambers, then, with the intention of speaking to Brad under the pretense of merely wishing to know why Nelson had paid him a visit. The simple fact that Thorndyke was a neighbor, in her mind, wasn't enough. The man never had been known as a friendly sort, and a social call seemed highly unlikely. If she could get Brad to tell her why Nelson had shown up unexpectedly in the middle of the morning, it would open the way for her to talk about matters concerning Wrenhaven. However, once she had descended the staircase, crossed the wide foyer, and stepped through the open study doorway, she had been very surprised to find Barnes searching through the papers on her husband's desk. When confronted he seemed ill at ease, but he explained that he had given a list of kitchen supplies to Mr. Remington earlier and that he was only hoping to add two more items to it. He apologized for giving her the impression that he was snooping where he shouldn't be and went on to report that her husband had told him to look for the paper on his own, that Mr. Remington hadn't had the time right then to do it himself. The excuse sounded logical, and if it had been any other member of the staff, Shauna wouldn't have given the matter another thought. But it wasn't just anyone else. It was Barnes, an odd little man who made her horribly uncomfortable. Thinking to question Brad about it later, she asked the butler where her husband had gone in such a hurry, only to be told that Barnes didn't know. Dismissing him then, she waited until he had left her alone before crossing to Brad's desk and sitting down behind it.

She had spent the next two hours examining her husband's files, documents, bills, and projected expenses for purchasing materials to build a factory. Compared to the cost of the operation, plus the initial funds to erect the building, the profit from such a venture promised to be high enough to repay a loan within the first year. Until then, she realized, the purse strings for the people of Wrenhaven would have to be pulled tight, and Shauna vowed to start right away. With that thought came another, a way of cutting down on the money they'd need to run the estate. Stacking all the papers on the desk into a neat pile, she pushed them aside and reached for the quill and a piece of parchment on which to make notes. She'd start by making a list of all the people who worked there, their type of job, how they were paid, and if the work they did was necessary. If not . . . well, they'd have to be let go. She thought of Barnes and his wife, the butler and housekeeper, and she wondered if there was some way to do without them.

Leaning back in the chair, she ran the feather tip of her quill beneath her chin, creating a mental picture of Elice Barnes as a quiet, somewhat browbeaten woman in her early fifties. Shauna didn't dislike Mrs. Barnes—the woman was always pleasant to her whenever their paths crossed during the day—but if Shauna asked Mr. Barnes to leave, his wife would go with him. And it was he Shauna didn't like. He seemed to resent the invasion of Wrenhaven by its owners and staff, although he never voiced his disapproval. It came in the form of looks, his reluctance to do as told, and his repeated claim that the old way of doing something had worked, so why change it? Shauna had never mentioned it to Brad or even Moira, but now that she realized something had to be done about the finances, Barnes would be at the top of her list.

Having completed her paperwork, Shauna left the study to stroll in the gardens for a while and contemplate her decisions. Since she hadn't taken the time to talk to her husband about his plans for the factory, she had no way of knowing if he had approached her father about a loan. She couldn't imagine his asking anyone else, yet she wondered if his pride might have gotten in the way. Her father never would have asked a family member, but then Pierce Radborne had never been in Brad's situation. On the chance that that was exactly what Brad thought, she decided she'd talk it over with him at dinner and offer any encouragement he needed.

Deep in thought, Shauna hadn't realized how far she had walked away from the house until the path came to an end and a spacious lawn opening up in front of her on the other side of the gardens. A soft, dreamy smile parted her lips as she stood transfixed, imagining a yard full of guests milling about the place. Once Wrenhaven was financially sound, she and Brad would have lots of parties. They'd fill the house and lawn with hundreds of friends and business associates and all of London would come to know the Remingtons as very influential people. Her thoughts took a sudden, horrifying change of direction then when one of her imaginary guests turned to look at her and she recognized Kelly O'Sullivan, his limp, the red beard.

"Damn," she murmured, turning toward the stand of

oaks to her left. Unless she could make some sort of deal with him—a share of the factory's profit until she had bought back Wrenhaven from him—there was no need to plan parties or cut expenses. There really wasn't even a need to talk with Brad.

Angry, depressed, and frustrated, she wandered through the thick growth of trees until the faint sound of voices penetrated her musings. Coming to an abrupt halt, she turned her head to listen and to get a bearing on the direction from which they came. A moment or two passed before she decided the men were down near the river, since she could hear the lapping of water against the bank just ahead of her, and in hopeful yearning she started toward them, thinking one of the two was Brad. Dried leaves, broken tree branches, twigs, and thick shrubbery hampered her journey and announced her presence long before she called out to him, and it wasn't until she had climbed down the slope and stood all alone in the clearing at the edge of the river that she sensed whoever had been there didn't want her to find them. Frowning curiously, she studied her surroundings and the impressions in the soft earth, making note that while one pair of footprints had seemed to walk down the bank and into the swift, flowing current, the other headed in the direction of the manor. An uneasy feeling came over her then, though she couldn't explain its cause, except that her discovery raised a few questions, and she turned to retrace her steps, thinking to discuss it with Brad. There was always the chance he knew what was going on down here—after all this was close to the location where he intended to build his factory—and the men she'd heard talking could have been people he had hired to inspect the area. She wanted to accept that, but deep down inside she honestly doubted it. Otherwise, the men wouldn't have run off.

In her haste to be away she snagged the hem of her skirt on a prickly bush, and she stumbled and nearly fell once she pulled it free. Fear rode high and tickled the flesh up the back of her neck, and she shot a worried glance all around her when it seemed the woods had taken on a deathly quiet and invisible eyes were staring at her. A noise to her right startled her and she jerked around, certain she'd see a brutish giant with a huge ax held in his hands ready to strike. Instead she spotted the bobbing white tail of a rabbit as it fled the scene, and she nearly collapsed to her knees in relief. She was letting her imagination run wild, and if she didn't get ahold of herself, she'd be racing through the woods screaming like a madman. Sucking in a deep breath, she exhaled slowly while she watched the furry little creature make his escape, darting in and out of cover until he seemed to just disappear.

The same way the man had, she mused, taking a tentative step forward. Fighting off the instinct to be careful, she followed the path the animal had taken, and to her surprise she found a cave buried in the hillside and hidden among the trees and bushes. Judging from the size of the opening, she assumed it was large enough to hide a man, and she quickly altered her plans to go any further. She had no way of defending herself should someone be inside, and suddenly the reason for secrecy of any such person wasn't something she cared to learn just then. Backing away, her attention riveted on the dark aperture, she listened for any sounds coming from that direction and failed to watch where she was going until it was too late. Tripping over a log, the hard earth came up to meet her, and she winced in pain in her backside, managing somehow not to make a sound while she silently damned the men for luring her there in the first place. Gathering up her skirts, she started to push herself to her feet when she espied a shiny gold object half buried in the dead leaves near her. Brushing them aside, she lifted the pocket watch by its broken chain to stare in quiet bewilderment. Did it belong to one of the men? Would he miss it and come looking for it? Would he kill her if he found her with it? Not wishing to know, she scrambled to her feet and darted off back the way she had come.

Shauna had spent the rest of the afternoon in her room. She had bathed, changed her clothes, repaired the torn skirt of her discarded dress, and sat staring at the gold watch. She really couldn't explain any of what had happened there in the woods, and she knew only that it was something she had to tell Brad. But as the minutes turned to hours and the hours stretched into late afternoon and Brad still hadn't returned home, she began to imagine all sorts of insane things, the worst being that Brad had stumbled upon the men by the river just as she had done and they had killed him. That was a chilling and horrifying thought, one she didn't care to dwell on, and she hurriedly left the solitude of her room to go back to Brad's study to wait.

Barnes appeared in the doorway somewhere around six o'clock to announce that dinner was ready if she cared to eat. Realizing that she had skipped the noon meal and that she was indeed a little hungry, she told him to have the cook serve it in the dining room and that she would be along shortly. But rather than hurry from the study, she rose from behind the desk and went to the window to stare out at the waning sunlight and the road leading to

355

the front door of the manor. She couldn't imagine what had sent Brad off so mysteriously, and she was tempted to ask Barnes if he had overheard any of the conversation between her husband and Nelson Thorndyke. He would have been insulted, of course, that she would even think there was a chance that he had, and she would expect him to react that way even though they both knew that listening was his favorite pastime. She had caught him in the hallway outside Brad's study on two separate occasions, and both times he had claimed he was waiting for the appropriate moment to interrupt. She hadn't believed him, but she couldn't really prove otherwise. Yet, he was the only one of the entire staff who knew everything that was going on, and he wasn't shy about voicing his opinion on various matters. So why didn't he know where Brad had gone?

Struggling with the overpowering urge to cry, she turned away from the window, thinking it best she fill her mind with other thoughts, and she went to the door. She had just stepped into the foyer when she thought she heard the faint sound of horse's hooves outside on the drive. Whirling, she raced for the front door and swung it wide, her pale green eyes filled with hope as they strained in the fiery glow of the dying sunlight to focus on horse and rider. Silhouetted against an orange backdrop, he was unrecognizable, and she raised a hand to shade her eyes as she watched him rein his steed onto the circular cobblestone drive. Within moments she realized the man was not her husband. He was simply too lanky to be Brad.

"Good evening, Sis," Tyler grinned as he guided his animal to the hitching post and dismounted. "Do you always greet your visitors this way?"

"I thought you were Brad," she frowned, her disappointment clearly marked in her tone.

Failing to recognize her concern, he asked playfully, "You two have a fight?"

Shauna shot her brother a smoldering look. "No."

"Then why did you come flying out the door just now with a worried look on your face?" He smiled devilishly and ascended the pair of steps to stand beside her.

"Because I am worried," she replied, looking past him toward the road again. "He left this morning without a word to anyone."

Tyler shrugged it off. "I would imagine he went into town to talk with someone about the factory. He probably didn't say anything to anyone because he saw no need. He'll be back before nightfall."

Shauna glanced at the sky. "Then he'd better hurry."

Coming to realize her feelings, he wrapped an arm around her shoulders and gave her a squeeze. "Calm down, Sis. You of all people should know how businessmen behave. You lived with Father long enough."

"But Papa never went running off like that after talking to Nelson."

"Thorndyke?" Tyler straightened, his brow furrowed.

"Is there any other?"

"You mean Thorndyke was here talking to Brad? What about?"

Shauna's mouth puckered. "If I knew that, I'd probably know why Brad left in such a hurry, and I wouldn't be standing here trying to explain it to you."

Her gibe only strengthened his sympathy. "You really are worried." Taking her by the shoulder, he turned her to face him squarely. "But there's got to be more to it than that. You wouldn't be so upset if there wasn't. Tell me everything."

Shauna shrugged, realizing even before she said anything how silly and groundless her fears really were. "Promise not to laugh?"

"I'd never laugh at anyone who's afraid," he assured her. "And especially you. You're not only my sister but my best friend. Now tell me what has you so upset."

She smiled softly at his pledge, hooked her arm in his, and drew him to the settee to sit down. "I went for a walk this afternoon—beyond the gardens. It was quiet and there was just enough of a breeze to carry the sound of men's voices. I couldn't understand what was said and because I thought one of them might be Brad, I went looking for him. I wound up at the riverbank but all I found was footprints and a man's gold watch." She turned round, green eyes on her brother. "And a cave."

"A cave," Tyler repeated. "What was in it?"

"I don't know. I didn't have the courage to look. You see, I could hear the men talking the whole time I approached, and without thinking there was anything strange going on, I called out to Brad before I could see either of the men. I could be wrong, but I think they ran off when they heard me because they didn't want me to know who they were or question their reason for being there."

Tyler continued to frown as he contemplated her words. "Where did you find the watch?"

"On the ground near the cave, hidden under some leaves. The chain's broken and I figure whoever owns it doesn't know he lost it. But that's not all. There were two sets of footprints. One looked as if the owner walked right into the river. The other set—" She stopped to glance over her shoulder at the house and lowered her voice to a whisper. "The other headed this way."

"May I see the watch?" he asked after a moment of silence.

"Of course," she nodded, rising and taking her brother's hand. "It's in Brad's desk."

A moment later the two stood silently in the study while Tyler examined the timepiece. "It could belong to just about anybody," he sighed, disappointed. "There's no initials or inscription." He closed the lid and turned it over in his hand. "But whoever owns it is bound to be upset once he learns he's lost it. It looks to be a very fine watch." He handed it back to Shauna. "For the time being, I'd suggest you hide it someplace safe, until you can show it to Brad. What happened in the woods might all be quite innocent, but until you're sure, I wouldn't tell anyone else about it. Including Moira. She has a way of letting things slip." He smiled reassuringly at her, then frowned. "I understand your nervousness about this, but I don't see the connection to Brad."

Shauna's green eyes lowered sheepishly and a slight blush stained her cheeks. "Just my imagination probably, but when he disappeared so suddenly without a word, I started thinking that perhaps he'd stumbled onto the men the way I had and they—"

Tyler realized what she meant and he quickly wrapped his arms around her, pulling her close. "I'm pleased to hear you show concern for your husband, Shauna. But I don't think you have to worry about him. He's not an ordinary man, as I'm sure you've come to realize. He can take care of himself." He kissed the top of her head and leaned back to look in her face. "Chances are, something Nelson said made him angry and he's off somewhere thinking it over."

"Like what?"

Tyler laughed and shook his head. "I don't know, really. I'm just giving a possibility. You know how angry Thorndyke always makes me. If he said the sky was blue, I'd do anything to prove him wrong. I'm not saying Brad is that . . . well, for a lack of a better word, he's not that hardheaded. But Nelson could be the reason Brad left and at the same time have nothing to do with the men in the woods. I really believe they're two separate incidents and have nothing to do with each other." He waited a moment to allow Shauna to digest his observation, then asked, "Feel a little better now?"

A warm smile parted her lips. "Yes. Thanks to you."

"Good. Then do me a favor."

Knowing Tyler loved to tease her, Shauna cocked her head suspiciously. "Tell me what it is first."

"When Brad gets home, let him know I stopped by."

Shauna's brow wrinkled. "Aren't you going to wait for him? I was just about to have dinner. Can't you stay long enough to dine with me?"

"Sorry, Sis," he apologized, hooking an arm around her neck and guiding them toward the door. "I haven't the time. I promised Brad I'd go to Cambridge for him."

"Cambridge?" she echoed. "What's in Cambridge?"

"Not what. Who," he answered, pausing at the threshold. "There's a man there—a carpenter, who used to work for Brad's father years ago. Brad wants me to find him and ask if he'd be interested in building the factory for him." He shrugged and took Shauna with him into the foyer, unaware that their conversation was being overheard. "At least I think the man lives in Cambridge now. I'm not really sure. The last anyone heard of him, he and his family had moved there from London. Be sure and tell Brad, since he thought the man was still in London. I don't want him to wonder what happened to me when I don't show up tomorrow with an answer. All right?"

"Of course," Shauna agreed. "But I still wish you'd stay for dinner."

"What's this?" he laughed, pausing at the front door to look at her. "My little sister actually *wants* to spend time with me? Has married life changed you so? Has that rebellious nature of yours softened? Or could it be you're lonely?"

Shauna wrinkled up her face. "I'd have to be lonely to want to subject myself to you," she rallied, though the sparkle in her eyes belied the air of callousness she tried to convey.

"Then thank God you're lonely," he grinned, leaning to kiss the tip of her nose. "I'd be terribly hurt if you found no reason at all to want to see me." His mood turned serious. "We've had our disagreements and some awful arguments growing up, Sis. But I want you to know that I, at least, never once felt anything less than love and admiration for you. I'm pleased you married Brad. He'll make a fine husband, and once the factory's built and he's paid off his debts, the two of you will be able to enjoy the kind of life you deserve." Realizing how out of character that sounded for him, he smiled devilishly and added, "And I won't have to take care of you anymore." He laughed and sidestepped the knotted fist thrown at him as he quickly scooted through the open door and onto the marble slab out front. "Say hello to Moira," he called as he hurried down the stone path to his horse. Freeing the reins, he easily swung himself up into the saddle. "And tell Brad I'll be back as soon as I can." He paused a moment to stare at the beautiful young woman smiling back at him, his feelings for her radiating from his pale green eyes. Then with a nod of his head, he spun the steed around and raced off down the drive.

Shauna dined alone, strolled in the gardens for a time, sat behind her husband's desk in the study, then took a book from the shelf to read by the cold fireplace in the parlor. Daylight hours disappeared into darkness. The mantel clock struck eleven. She reread the pages a third time after her mind wandered and she couldn't concentrate. She remembered Tyler's assurance that Brad had only gone to London on business. She bid Moira goodnight and told her she'd retire later . . . after her husband returned. She drank a glass of wine when her eyelids drooped. The clock chimed twelve. She paced the floor. Moving out onto the terrace, she gazed up at the moonlit night. A rabbit dashed across the path in the gardens and made her smile. A soft breeze tugged at her skirts and stirred up the fragrance of flower blossoms. A movement to her left caught her eye, and the memory of that afternoon flared up to renew her fears. She went back inside where it was safe and sat down in a wing chair, her legs curled under her, her head resting on the upholstered back as she stared over at the mantel clock shadowed in a silvery light. She listened to its hypnotizing rhythm, her eyelids heavy. Without realizing it, she drifted off to sleep.

The white lace curtains billowed in the gentle wind. Platinum streams of light fell into the room. A figure crossed them, and the tall, dark silhouette of a man shaded the dreaming figure in the chair. A long while passed as he stared down at the sleeping form before he turned away. From somewhere in the room a bright yellow glow warmed the darkness and played heavily on Shauna's lids. With a start she came awake and sat upright in the chair, her worried, frightened gaze searching out the candle and the one who had lit it.

"Brad!" she exclaimed, springing to her feet and rushing toward him. "Oh, Brad." His deep laughter filled her ears and chased away her fears as she flung her arms around him and held him tight.

"Had I known what my reception would be, I wouldn't have taken so long to come home," he chuckled, enjoying the warmth of her slender body pressed against him. The pleasure was short-lived, however, when she stiffened suddenly and stepped back. His disappointment furrowed his brow and he pouted playfully at her.

"And had I known you were all right," she spat, her jaw set in a hard line, her eyes narrowed, "I would have met you with a broom in hand. How dare you run off without a word!"

"Run off?" he questioned, white teeth showing with his grin. "I merely had business to take care of in London. I must admit I hadn't planned to be gone this long, but I didn't think it would matter to you if I stayed away a week." His smile mocked her as he devoured the slim length of her. "Dare I hope you missed me as a wife misses her husband?" He stepped forward, intending to enfold her within his arms, and winced at the stinging slap she gave his hands.

"A husband who cares for his wife wouldn't behave in such a manner," she scolded. She stiffened her spine and placed her clenched fists on her narrow hips. "And what kind of business would demand your attention until the wee hours of morning?" She gave him a scalding look and added, "Perhaps a serving wench—one who filled more than just your mug with ale?"

"Careful, Shauna," he warned devilishly. "You're sounding more like a wife every minute." He rested back on his heels and crossed his arms over his chest, his head cocked to one side. "And might I remind you that it was *your* idea I find a woman willing to fulfill my needs?"

The image of him locked in another woman's embrace burned her pride and stained her cheeks a scarlet hue. She quickly turned away to hide her unexplainable injured feelings and to clear her head and think of a logical excuse. "A serving wench in a public tavern is hardly being what I'd call discreet," she snapped.

He had seen the pained look on her face and hoped it meant he had struck a jealous vein. He decided to test her. "It was an out-of-the-way pub, and nearly empty. I was very careful."

The muscles in her throat constricted with the threat of burning tears.

"Had I known you had changed your mind and were waiting up for me, I wouldn't have dallied."

"Dallied!" she exploded, turning on him. "Is *that* what you call it? Dallying?"

Mirth danced in the dark depth of his eyes and he lowered his gaze to mask the humor he felt. He had spent the entire day visiting suppliers and getting estimates. He had eaten a late supper—alone—then paid her father a visit. They had closeted themselves off in Radborne's study to share a glass of wine and discuss the financial difficulties Pierce was experiencing of late. It had been a matter most disturbing to him, and Brad hadn't wanted to leave until he was sure he had helped soothe Radborne's worries a little while trying to conceal his own. Brad had approached every businessman he could think of with his proposition to borrow the funds he needed to build his factory and had repeatedly gotten the same answer: sorry, but it's too much of a risk right now. Nelson Thorndyke was the only one willing to help, but his conditions weren't what Brad wanted. Out of desperation he had gone to speak with his father-in-law. He would have preferred their relationship remain as in-laws rather than business associates, but with the way things were going, and because he needed some method of supporting Wrenhaven, he had had to swallow his pride. Now, with the problems Pierce faced, Brad realized there might come a day very soon when he'd have to offer his help to him. He also realized this was something he'd keep from Shauna.

"Well, maybe dallying isn't the right word," he grinned, his voice low and his gaze warming considerably. "But whatever I call it, I still fail to understand your anger. And the reason you waited up for me. You never have before."

Shauna refused to tell him that she had been worried about him. Gulping down her misery, she turned away from him and went back to the chair to sit down. "Tyler was here this afternoon. He asked that I let you know he's on his way to Cambridge."

"Cambridge?" Brad repeated, the humor of the moment fading. He left his place by the hearth to sit in the chair next to his wife. "What's in Cambridge?"

"The carpenter you wanted to hire. Tyler said the man and his family moved there some years ago, and he's gone to look for him. He didn't want you to worry when he didn't show up here tomorrow the way he promised he would." She couldn't bring herself to look at him, afraid he'd read something into the expression on her face. But when she remembered Thorndyke's visit this morning, she lifted a frown his way. "What did Nelson want?"

Now it was Brad's turn to feel uncomfortable. Spotting the wine decanter on the table, he rose and went to it. "Nelson?" he asked, pouring the dark red liquid in a glass.

"Yes, Nelson. Moira told me he was in the study with you. The two of you haven't become friends, I hope."

"Well, he is a neighbor, Shauna. That's something we can't ignore."

"Why not? Just because our boundaries meet doesn't mean we have to be friends with him. I married you to get away from him. Remember?"

Smiling, Brad raised the glass to his lips and took a swallow. "Yes. I remember. You married me out of need and for no other reason." He cast a glance at her over his shoulder. "The way I married you out of need." Facing her, he leaned back against the table and folded his arms. "And since it was a mutual agreement, what I do in regard to Wrenhaven and who I choose as friends or partners is none of your concern. So don't lecture me, Shauna."

She wasn't sure if his biting words hurt her or merely surprised her. In either case, her chin dropped and she stiffened her body. "I'm not picking your friends or telling you how to run the estate. I'm simply trying to warn you."

"Of what? That Thorndyke shouldn't be trusted? I know that. I've been around for a while. But between the two of us—you and me—I've had a lot more experience dealing with crafty investors."

"Investors?" she repeated, coming to her feet and following Brad from the parlor. "You're not saying Thorndyke has offered to help? Oh Brad, don't let him get an edge. Papa never would."

"I'm not your father," he hissed, walking into the study ahead of her. Setting his wine glass on the desk, he lit the hurricane lamp and sat down in the leather chair. "But even your father wouldn't let personalities interfere with business," he added, reaching for the stack of papers piled neatly on one corner. Realizing he hadn't straightened out his desk before leaving for London, he frowned. "Was someone in here today?"

Remembering her reason for coming to the study earlier, Shauna squared her shoulders and raised her chin. "Yes. Me."

He glanced up at her. "Why? Were you bored and felt like cleaning? Or were you snooping?" He settled his attention on the papers he spread out in front of him.

"Snooping?" she shrieked indignantly. "If I'd been snooping I wouldn't have put the desk in order so you'd know I was here. I'd have left it the mess it was." She gritted her teeth and advanced, leaning on her hands braced against the edge of the desk. "And if you're so smart, why did you leave all of this sitting out where anyone could see it? Why didn't you lock it up in a drawer? You know how Barnes is." She jerked back up. "Or maybe you don't. Are you aware he spends most of his day outside this room eavesdropping?"

"To what? The shuffling of papers?" Brad asked, not at all interested.

"It doesn't matter what he hears, only that he's listening. It's none of his business what you do in here," she argued.

"The same as it's none of yours."

"Damn you," she barked. "If you can't see the difference, then damn you." She spun on her heel to make an angry exit.

"Shauna," he called, regretting his outburst. It had been a long, tiring, disappointing day, and he was taking it out on her. "I'm sorry. That was unfair of me. Please. Sit down and let's talk a while."

She paused at the doorway with her back to him, telling herself she really should keep on walking. Yet the need to be with him—although she couldn't understand it—refused to let her take another step. "About what?" she asked softly, her head bowed as she toyed with the ribbon on her dress.

"I don't know," he sighed as he leaned back in the chair. "Let's talk about your day. What did you do with your time?"

"You mean besides snooping through the things on your desk?"

A bright smile parted his lips. "I thought you said you weren't snooping."

"I wasn't," she reiterated, whirling back.

"So tell me what you were doing," he encouraged as he secretly admired her beauty bathed in lamplight. The yellow glow added highlights to her golden hair, caressed her silken skin, and enhanced the curve of her slender throat. He fought down the urge to go to her and catch her up in his arms.

"You really want to know?"

He nodded, his smile widening.

Excited now and anxious to tell him her plan on a way to cut expenses, she grinned and hurried over to the desk to sort through the pile of papers. "I made a list . . . of all of our people and their jobs and how they're paid."

Locating the document, she eagerly rounded the desk and handed it over for him to examine. "If we could eliminate a few jobs and have some reassigned, we could save a little money. It would only have to be a temporary kind of thing . . . until the loan for the factory is repaid."

Brad was impressed with her interest in Wrenhaven, but something on her list made him frown. "You're proposing we dismiss Barnes and his wife. I can understand doing without a butler, but who would do the housework?"

"Me!" she replied exuberantly.

His chin sagging and his surprise registered in his eyes, he asked, "You. You'd do the cleaning? Your *willing* to do such menial labor?"

"I wouldn't mind," she assured him. "It would only be until the loan was repaid and we could afford to hire the help."

He stared at her in awe for a moment, then glanced at the paper again. "You've also proposed Moira do the cooking."

"Yes, I have. She's a very good cook, and I'm sure she wouldn't object."

"You mean you haven't discussed it with her."

"I didn't think I should until I showed this to you and you agreed."

Smiling, he leaned back in the chair. "And who would help the mistress of the house bathe and dress and do her hair?"

"I can manage that on my own," she proudly announced. "I doubt we'd be having any parties for a while where I'd need her assistance, anyway." Turning, she leaned back against the desk. "So what do you think?"

He lifted dark brows as he studied the paper again. "I

369

think it's an excellent idea. I'm just not sure we'd have to go to that extreme just yet." He smiled up at her and opened the top drawer of his desk. "But I'll keep this for when we do." Slipping the paper inside, he straightened with a curious frown when he spotted a gold object already in the drawer. "What's this?" he asked, holding up the watch.

Shauna's eyes widened instantly, and a chill darted up her spine at the memory of how the watch had found its way to the desk drawer. "It's the real reason I waited up for you. I had forgotten it once I saw that you were safe."

A deep line formed in his suntanned brow. "Safe? From what?"

Remembering her brother's comments, she laughed unassumingly. "My imagination, more than likely. Anyway, that's what Tyler said."

"I'm not following," Brad remarked, his interest aroused. "Would you care to explain? Whose watch is this? And what is it doing in my desk drawer?"

"I don't know whose it is. I found it down near the river when I followed the sounds of men's voices, thinking you might be one of them."

"Tonight?"

"This afternoon." She could see the concern on Brad's face. "You weren't one of them, were you?"

His head shot up. "Are you saying you didn't see the men?"

"No, I didn't. They ran off before I got there."

Brad studied the watch again, snapping open the lid, closing it and turning the timepiece over in his hand several times. "Does anyone other than Tyler know about this?"

"No." She sensed trouble. "Why? Does it mean something?"

"I'd like to say no. But I'm not sure." He stuffed the watch in his pocket and stood. "I've got to ask something of you, Shauna, and you've got to give me your word that you'll do as I say. Do I have it?"

She nodded hesitantly.

"This must remain our secret. No one is to know about the watch or the men or that you're aware someone was trespassing down by the river. Not even Moira?"

"Tyler already suggested that. He said to just tell you. I haven't told anyone and I won't, if that's what you want."

"Good," he replied, turning to collect the papers on the desk. Opening a bottom drawer, he stacked them inside, slid the drawer shut again, and locked it. "And you're right about my leaving my work out where someone can see it." He tucked the key in the pocket of his waistcoat. "From now on, everything stays locked up." He glanced at the open door, hurriedly rounded the desk, and crossed the room to peek out into the hallway. Seeing that the foyer was empty, he stepped back and closed in their privacy. "I'll also be sure no one listens in on my conversations."

Shauna could feel her body tremble. "Why, Brad. What's wrong? Are we in some kind of danger?"

"I hope not, but we can't take any chances." Coming to her, he took her arm and guided her to a chair. He hadn't planned on telling her any of his suspicions, but now that she had unintentionally gotten involved, he had no other choice. "I've been hearing things late at night, noises coming from the woods. I've never been able to catch anyone, and Barnes assures me that it's only someone cutting through our property. It's possible, I suppose, but what has me curious is that it keeps reoccurring. Once, I can excuse. But continually. . . ."

He shook his head.

"So what or who do you think they are?"

"Couldn't be as simple as someone setting traps."

"Or?"

Brad shrugged and sat down in the chair next to hers. "Or something as dangerous as smugglers."

"Smugglers?" she breathed. "Dear God, Brad. What will you do if they are?"

"I'll have to catch them first. But even that won't be enough. The man behind it will never allow himself to be personally involved, and he's the one who has to be stopped. Otherwise he'll just move his operation somewhere else."

"Then let him," she quickly replied. "I'm sure you've already realized that you'll be suspect if the authorities hear about this. After all, it's happening on your property."

"If that's what's really going on."

Shauna straightened in her chair. "Well, what else could it be? And since when do you believe everything Barnes tells you? I'm not ashamed to admit I don't trust him. He's hardly what I'd call a faithful servant."

"Don't be too quick to judge, Shauna," Brad gently scolded. "He's had this place all to himself for a good number of years, and it's difficult for him to take orders all of a sudden. But to put your mind at ease, I'll tell you that I've already talked to your father about him. Pierce assures me that he's a good man, a little stubborn, but trustworthy. It's the reason your father hired Barnes and his wife to look after the place."

"Did you tell Father your suspicions?"

"No. He's got his own problems to deal with without worrying about mine."

"Then maybe you should just go to the constable yourself and tell him about this."

"Tell him what, Shauna? That I hear noises at night and that my wife found a watch by the riverbank? Hardly solid evidence of smugglers."

"Then what are we to do?"

"*You're* to stay away from the river. As for the men you heard there . . . well, I'll have to figure something out."

"You'll be careful, won't you? You won't go after them alone, will you? If you're right and they are smugglers, they won't hesitate to kill you."

Her flood of questions brought a warm, devilish smile to his lips, one Shauna didn't miss. Knowing what it meant and how her inquiries must have sounded, she blushed and quickly came to her feet.

"I'm simply thinking of myself, sir," she claimed. "If you were shot, I'd have to take care of you. If you were killed, the management of Wrenhaven would fall into my hands. Either possibility is not to my liking."

"I'm sure they aren't," he grinned, rising. "And in that respect, I promise not to allow anything to happen to me. After all, I know how much you're looking forward to spending the rest of your days with me." He stepped closer and took her elbow to guide her to the door. "You know, Shauna, if the roles were reversed, I'd be very happy to care for you if you were shot. I'd feed you, change the dressing, bathe your fevered brow." He shrugged and opened the door. "If you were killed, I'd even mourn your death and wait a respectable time before remarrying."

His admission shocked her, and she jerked her arm from his grasp. "A week at most, no doubt," she sneered, facing him. "And who would you choose this time? A brainless twit with huge breasts eager for your fondling? A moonstruck wench with rounded heels so that she'd be ready at your every beck and call? One to have your brats—a dozen or more, and willing to breed a second batch if it be your wont?" Tossing her silky mane, she headed for the stairs. "But of course. You wouldn't know how to handle a wife with common sense and the courage to speak up. Just as you don't know how to handle me."

A broad smile stretched his lips and laughter threatened as Brad watched the sway of her hips while she climbed the stairs. Think what you like, my love, he mused gaily. But one thing is for certain. I *do* know how to handle a little firebrand like you. His gaze shifted to her slender back and narrow waist. And time will prove me right. Within the week, sweet Shauna, you will throw yourself at my feet and beg my understanding. You will know who is the wiser and oft repeat it. He masked his glee when she paused midway up the staircase and turned to stare haughtily back down at him.

"Have you no reply, dear husband?" she challenged. "Has the truth struck you mute?"

"Nay," he sighed, moving to the bottom of the stairs. "I was merely considering which method to use."

Some of Shauna's arrogance faded. "Method?" she queried apprehensively, a trembling hand reaching for the banister to steady her quaking limbs as she watched him climb the steps toward her. "Method to use for what?"

"For handling a shrewish wife," he answered confidently, his stride strong and sure while his dark eyes neverleft hers.

Shauna stumbled when she tried to mount the stairs

backwards. "And what methods are there to choose from?" she questioned, turning sideways, one hand gripping the railing, the other holding a fistful of her skirts as she sought to stay ahead of him.

"My father taught his sons that a man's wife should be treated with respect, that a gentle touch brought greater, more pleasing results than a closed fist."

"*You'd beat me?*" she howled, tripping on a step. She winced at the impact of hard wood against her derrière when she sat down rather abruptly. But the pain vanished instantly once she realized she'd get no sympathy from the man coming after her. Struggling with her cumbersome skirts, she awkwardly came to her feet. "Your father was right, you know. Only a brute would strike a woman." She stumbled up a few steps when he continued to advance. "You're not a brute, Brad. I've always said that . . . well, maybe not out loud," she added when his smile contradicted her claim. He was gaining on her, and she decided to flee rather than banter words. Hiking up her hemline, she turned and raced up the last five steps. Her feet hardly seemed to touch the floor as she ran down the hall to her room, but her mistake came when she thoughtlessly glanced back over her shoulder to see how much distance she had between herself and her husband. He had already cleared the last step and was closing in on her, a discovery that made her shriek and lose her concentration on the direction she took until after she had pssed by the door to her room. Once she realized she had, she staggered to a stop and stared wide-eyed, first at the entrance into her room, then at her husband. It only took her a second to calculate the impossibility of running inside and closing the door before he was on her, and she reluctantly admitted defeat. With hands held up in front of her, she slowly backed away, unaware that the last remaining exit in the hall was to *his* bedchambers.

"Brad, I think we should talk about this before you do anything rash," she nervously stated. "I'm not the sort of woman who will bend under violence. It only infuriates me all the more. Ask Papa. He never punished me in the manner you're considering."

"Maybe he should have," Brad replied, the twinkle in his eye deepening. "Had you been taught self-denial at a young age, you probably wouldn't have trapped yourself in the predicament you're in right now." He continued to advance, backing her toward the end of the corridor. "You would have looked for a husband out of love. You would have been eager to bear his children. You would have demanded your right to stand at his side and share in his dreams, his trials, the good times and the bad. You would have cried when he hurt, laughed with his joy, shared his pain, his happiness, and never regretted marrying him for an instant." He paused a few steps before her. "What have you to look forward too, Shauna? With the way things are between us right now, is there even an ounce of happiness in your future? Or will you spend your life alone in a big house filled with servants, ignoring the man you call your husband? Will going to parties and balls be enough? And when the golden highlights in your hair turn silver and there are no grandchildren to warm your heart, what will you do then?" He cocked his head to one side. "Will you curse the day you married out of need instead of love? Will you curse me for letting it happen?"

As much as she hated to admit it, Shauna knew he was right. Her future looked very bleak. What he didn't know was that his future promised even less. Because of her, he would be stripped of his lands, his pride, his fortune. Tears burned her eyes and she lowered her gaze, shame drawing her sandy brows together and staining her cheeks a soft red.

"There were many times, while I was growing up, that I refused to listen to my father," he went on to say. "But his advice concerning women always proved correct. Even though the thorns of a rose will prick a finger, its fragile stem will break if sorely abused. I would, if I could, smell its sweet fragrance and gently cradle the tender blossom in my hand rather than hurl it to the ground and crush it beneath my heel. I think of you as that delicate flower, Shauna. Somewhere among the thorns is a passionate, vibrant bloom ready to be picked. My quest is to do so unharmed."

Stepping forward, he slowly raised a hand to stroke her cheek with the backs of his fingers, his eyes searching hers. When he saw no resistance shining in them, he moved his hand behind her head and drew her close. His lips tenderly brushed hers, while his other hand caught her waist and pulled her full against him. Tilting his head, he tasted the corner of her mouth, then captured her trembling lips in a gentle but searing kiss. His warm breath fell softly against her cheek. His muscular frame branded her slender body. His desire blended with hers and clouded her reasoning. He had sparked the flame of passion deep within her, and Shauna moaned, despite her will to fight the overpowering sensation he never failed to arouse. Weak, her fiery spirit dissolved into a blissful, willing need to feel his naked flesh against her own. Entwining her arms around his neck, she kissed him hard and long and hungrily. She chased away all thoughts of guilt and basked in the pleasure of his embrace, his silent vow that he wanted her in spite of her ravings, her tricks, and sharp tongue. Where others before him had fled with injured pride, this man came to her time and time again without a pledge of loyalty or love . . . or even of a future.

When he bent to catch her up in his strong arms, she clung to him as if fearing her life would end should she lessen her hold. The toe of his shoe nudged the door open on silent hinges, and he quickly bore her with him into the moonlit room. The balcony doors stood ajar and soft breezes played with the lace curtains adorning them, carrying with them the sweet melody of crickets and the fragrant smells of dewy grasses, pine and flower blossoms. Yet neither of them noticed, for their passion ran high and filled their thoughts with more delightful treasures.

Bathed in a platinum stream of light, he slid his arm from beneath her knees and gently set her down. Dark eyes filled with lust caressed the fine features of her face, her golden mane, and the slender length of her satiny neck before he lowered his head to sample the sweetness of her tender flesh. His lips brushed against a delicate ear and stirred up the fragrance of her hair, an intoxicating scent that reeled his already unsteady world. He had truly expected to meet her reluctance when first he touched her, and in blind hope he dared go further, wondering when he would awaken from this dream. The bonds of wedlock had given him a wife. Would those same invisible bonds entwine their hearts and souls as one? The answer was too painful to consider. For now he would take what she offered, and on the morrow he would bear her rage in silence.

Cool night air caressed her naked flesh once he had stripped away her clothes, yet anticipation burned every inch of her. Unashamed, she helped him disrobe, eager to feel his hard, sinewy body touching hers. Trembling fingers traced the steeled length of his shoulders and back, down his spine to his buttocks, and her breath caught in her throat when she pulled his hips against her and felt the evidence of his desire. Warm hands cupped her face and drew her mouth to his. His tongue parted her lips to probe inside, a sweet intrusion that tasted of wine and unleashed passion. He kissed her fiercely, desperately, and when his fingers caught the tender strands of her hair at her nape, she gasped in tortured pleasure at the subtle pain he inflicted when he pulled her head back to sample the smooth skin beneath her chin. Her body yearned for the feel of his hands exploring every curve, and he did not disappoint her. He touched her slender back, her hips, her thighs, trailing a burning path across her flat belly, her ribs, then on to cup her breast, his thumb stroking its peak. She moaned again when his mouth seared a molten path down her throat and captured the taut nipple, and without realizing it, she entwined her fingers in the thick dark mass of his hair, guiding, directing him. A delighted giggle escaped her when his tongue circled the rose-hued peak, then melted into a delicious murmur once he sucked greedily, playfully there. Wishing to taste the sweetness of his kiss again, she entrapped his face in her hands and drew his mouth to hers. A fire erupted within her then, and in a breathless whisper, she begged him to make love to her.

Eager to do her bidding, Brad swept her up in his arms, carried her to the bed and fell with her upon the feathery softness. Rolling her beneath him, he parted her thighs, then hesitated, bracing his weight against his elbows while he paused to look into her eyes. He would never know if what he saw in their exquisite green depths was truly what he longed to see or merely the imaginings of an aching heart, for he had neither the courage to ask nor the strength to hear her answer. This woman he called his wife, this minx, this trickster had wedged her way into his very soul, and if it was God's will for him never to hear her say the words, what they shared this night would last him a lifetime.

Shauna arched her hips to welcome his first thrust and marveled at the exploding rapture their union caused. He moved, sleek and long, his breathing ragged in her ear, his heart thundering against her naked breast. The sinewy strength of his body guided her, teased her, and drove her ever higher, each fiery sensation more glorious than the other. Her body ached with mounting desire and the need for blissful release, and she wondered deliriously if she could bear it a moment longer. Yet when it came and she trembled in sweet agony and heard his shuddering moan, she felt both contentedly happy and horribly sad at the same moment. Drifting earthward wrapped in his embrace, a seed of longing suddenly took root in her heart and began to grow; a puzzling kind of feeling that kinked the soft arch of her brows as she lay breathless in his arms. Something was missing, though she couldn't put a name to it. Was it shame? No. She had no reason to feel shame. They were man and wife. Guilt? Over what? He knew when he married her that theirs was not a marriage based on love.

Love. The word seemed to wrap itself around her as if it meant to choke the very breath from her. Was that what was missing? She closed her eyes and laid her head on

Brad's chest, hardly aware of the steady beating of his heart beneath her ear. This thing that knotted her insides wasn't the absence of love. Or was it? Could it be she longed to hear him say he loved her? But why? What would she gain by it? If he proclaimed his love, would it be enough? Would it bring her peace? And what would she say in return?

Biting her lower lip, Shauna opened her eyes to stare out across the room at the velvety black sky with its twinkling of stars and silvery moon, her mind filled with confusing thoughts and her heart lying heavy in her chest.

Chapter Thirteen

Shauna came fully awake when she felt someone ease his weight from the bed as if in an effort not to disturb her. Startled and unfamiliar with her surroundings, she grabbed the sheet draped over her naked form and raised up on one elbow, blinking away her dreams and struggling to focus her eyes. Nothing about the room or the bed in which she lay sparked any recognition in her brain, and for a moment she wondered if she might still be asleep. Then a movement near the balcony caught her attention and she gasped as she sat upright, hugging the thin fabric up beneath her chin, her eyes wide and straining to identify the man masked in the early shadows of predawn. Only a second passed before he sensed he had been discovered, and when he turned to look at her, Shauna collapsed back against her pillow.

"Brad," she breathed. "You frightened me."

Warm eyes smiled back at her. "I didn't mean to. I thought you were asleep or I would have said something."

Inching up, she adjusted the pillow behind her and leaned back against the headboard, comfortable in his presence despite her lack of dress. "Is something wrong?

Or do you always rise before the sun?"

His tall, dark figure moved across the faded light coming in off the balcony, and she noticed he had donned only his breeches. "Couldn't sleep. I guess I'm not used to sharing a bed."

Soft laughter trickled from her. "I find that hard to believe. Perhaps you mean you're not use to *sleeping* next to someone."

"Perhaps," he murmured, coming to stand near the end of the bed. "I see you have no trouble with it. You slept pretty soundly until now."

She knew he only teased, but rather than let him have the last word, she countered, "Because I don't have a guilty conscience. You're the first to lie beside me, and you're my husband. It's all quite proper."

"And will that change now that you've sampled what it's like?" he tested. "Proper or not?"

"Only if it bothers you," she mocked playfully. "I wouldn't want to be the cause of your roaming about in the middle of the night. You need your rest."

"If I lose sleep because of a golden-haired temptress in my bed, it will be well worth the sacrifice."

Shauna blushed at his compliment and nervously raked her fingers through her long strands of hair, oddly embarrassed and painfully aware of her appearance. "I must look dreadful, and I'm sure if the sun was high over the ridge, you'd change your mind."

"Nay. Never that," he grinned softly. "Even at your worst, you'd still be very beautiful."

"Then you, sir, are either fickle or blind," she rallied gaily.

"Fickle . . . perhaps. Blind?" He shook his head and leaned a shoulder against the tall bedpost, his arms folded

383

in front of him, his gaze devouring her lithe form shadowed provocatively in the subdued light. "I'm blind to all others now that I've found you."

"And will you say the same when I'm old and wrinkled?" she laughed. "Or will a young thing catch your eye and turn your affections away from me?"

"For better or worse, in sickness and in health, for richer or poorer."

The last spoiled the mood and stole the smile from her lips. How desperately she wanted to believe that. Glancing toward the balcony, she noticed how the start of pale pinks and muted yellows were already staining the gray sky in the east. Morning would be fast upon them, and although Shauna had enjoyed spending the night with her husband, she wasn't quite ready to tell the household . . . or Moira. Yanking the sheet free from the foot of the bed, she draped it around her and stepped to the floor.

"Moira will be up soon," she mumbled, gathering up her clothes, "and I don't want her to worry when she finds my bed empty."

"Moira won't come to your room for hours yet, Shauna. Stay with me a while," he asked softly. "It's so rare, these times we have together when we're not bantering words or fighting off blows. It seems we're either at each other's throat or making love." His mouth twitched with a half-smile. "I must say I prefer the latter, but perhaps if we work on the first, we'll find a peaceful solution."

With her underthings, petticoats, and dress clutched tightly against her bosom, Shauna stared quietly back at him. Why bother? she thought sadly. Once you've learned what I've done, you'll gladly share separate rooms. You might even think it best we never see each other again. She dropped her gaze and bent to pick up her shoes. And who would blame you? I deserve your scorn, your hatred. Pretending otherwise is unfair. I shouldn't lead you on this way. The truth will only hurt that much more. She turned for the door, pausing when she reached it to look back at him. I love you, Brad Remington, she silently admitted. I didn't know it until just now, but I do. Blinking back her tears, she made a quiet exit.

Shauna busied herself with work the rest of the day, purposely avoiding Brad. She waited to eat breakfast until after he had gone to the study, helped Mrs. Barnes strip the sheets from the beds and sort the laundry while he met with some men in the parlor concerning the factory, and hid herself in her bedchambers at noon when Brad went to the dining room to eat. In the afternoon she worked out back in the gardens with Mr. Rutherford, the groundskeeper. He was a quiet sort, but more than willing to teach her about maintaining sculptured shrubs, how to fertilize the flowerbeds, and recognize weeds from new growth among the vegetable plants. Exhausted from her full day, she had Moira bring her dinner tray to her room and afterward retired early.

The following morning started out in much the same way. She had slept late, dined alone, then collected a rake, hoe, pruning shears, and gloves to work on the rose bushes out front. She had artfully avoided a conversation with her maid when Moira tried to remind her that a certain unwelcome Irishman was due to arrive within a few days by telling her that she had everything under control and she shouldn't worry. She didn't, of course, but she wasn't about to admit different. Besides, there was still the chance Kelly O'Sullivan would meet with a fatal accident before reaching Wrenhaven.

The noonday heat had become almost insufferable, and, unable to eat, Shauna accepted a tall glass of cider from Libby, the cook, and went back outside to sit in the shade of a huge oak near the front of the manor. Settling herself down in the cool grass, she leaned back against the thick tree trunk and closed her eyes, fanning her face with the wide-brimmed bonnet she had taken from her head.

Brad viewed the scene from the window in his study where he stood smoking a cheroot and reluctantly awaiting Nelson Thorndyke's arrival. For the past week and a half he had tried every resource he could think of to borrow the money he needed for his factory and had been turned down every time. He knew it was only his frustrations making him think that way, but he had begun to wonder if the aristocrats of London resented having a Colonial living and working in their midst. He couldn't honestly blame them for their feelings, but he had no desire to go into partnership with anyone. And that was exactly what they were forcing him to do. And with, of all people, Nelson Thorndyke.

Shauna hadn't had to warn him about the man. What Pierce couldn't tell him about Nelson, Brad had found out on his own. Thorndyke had lived in the colonies before and during part of the war—just where and how he had earned a living, no one knew—but he had returned to London a very wealthy man, which led Brad to believe that however Thorndyke had acquired his wealth, it couldn't have been legal. The man claimed to have grown up in a small town south of London, though no one had ever heard of the Throndyke family until Nelson made an appearance. He told everyone it was because his father had died when he was a young boy and his mother had taken him to America to start a new life.

Even though Pierce had told Brad that Nelson was very shrewd when it came to business matters, something Brad could attest to, it wasn't enough to convince Brad that Nelson had always been honest in his dealings. And what bothered Brad more than anything was the fact that the man didn't have a single friend. Of all those with whom Brad had discussed Nelson Thorndyke, not a one would admit he liked him. Stranger still, they didn't respect or trust him, either.

"And here I am about to agree to become his partner," Brad mumbled as he chewed on the end of his cheroot. "If there was just some other way...." Angry and flustered, he turned away from the window and the vision of his lovely wife to sit down in the leather chair. Well, maybe Thorndyke wouldn't put up the money for the factory without being a full partner in the venture, but Brad wouldn't sign the agreement unless another clause was added: within the first year, Brad would have the right to buy Nelson out.

"I can't believe you would do something that stupid, Brad Remington!" Shauna raved when she confronted him later in the study, demanding to know why Thorndyke had paid him another visit. "You actually signed a paper agreeing to let him be your partner? How could you? Don't you know what kind of a man he is?"

"Yes. I do. He's the *only* man willing to take a chance on me, and he's got the money to back it up," Brad rallied, furiously shoving himself up from the chair. Storming across the room, he reached past his wife to slam the door shut. "And if I had known you intended to tell everyone within earshot just what you think of me and how I handle my affairs, I wouldn't have told you." His eyes snapping with rage, he leaned closer. "Forgive me for being *stupid,* but I thought you had a right to know. Unlike you, *I* don't keep secrets." He glared at her a second longer, then tore back across the room to throw himself in the chair again and angrily shuffle through his papers.

A mixture of thoughts raced through Shauna's head. What did he mean when he said he didn't keep secrets . . . implying that she did? Surely he didn't know about Kelly O'Sullivan. If he did, he'd say something. As for thinking she had a right to know what his plans were for Wrenhaven—well, she was flattered, even though she didn't agree. But what did it really matter, anyway? The property no longer belonged to Brad. Legally he couldn't do a thing. The Irishman was the only one who could decide the future of Wrenhaven. A chilling thought struck her, and she staggered to one of the chairs by the hearth. If Brad signed an agreement with Nelson Thorndyke guaranteeing him half of the profits from the factory in exchange for the money it took to build it on property that didn't belong to him . . . If Brad spent a single shilling of that money . . . She cringed at the thought of how much trouble her husband would be in. Nelson Thorndyke would never understand how it had happened, and he certainly wouldn't be very forgiving. He'd more than likely see Brad thrown in prison! She could feel the color draining from her face.

"How soon?" she asked weakly.

Brad shot her an angry frown. "For what?" he snarled.

"How soon before you start work? Before Nelson gives you the money?"

"Next week," was his simple reply, an answer that gave her hope. Mr. O'Sullivan was due to arrive before then. It was a gamble and a slim one at best, but maybe, just maybe, he would listen to her story and find it in his heart to help her . . . to help Brad. Perhaps Mr. O'Sullivan had enough money to fund the building of the factory and *he'd* be willing to become Brad's partner. After all, his letters and his lecture that night at Sir Blakely's showed he wasn't a callous man. Together they just might be able to come up with a plan that would benefit them both. Closing her eyes, Shauna whispered a breathless prayer that Kelly O'Sullivan would turn out to be her savior rather than her foe. Without another word, she rose and quietly left the study.

Dark, rolling clouds scurried across the black sky and hid the bright silver face of the moon. A sudden gust of wind rustled the treetops and carried in the sweet smell of rain. Moisture hung heavy in the air and distant flashes of light bounced from one ominous thunderhead to the next as if playing tag with some mystical partner.

Brad watched the activity from the balcony of his bedchambers in quiet solemnness. The heated words he had exchanged with his wife earlier still scorched his thoughts and wreaked havoc with his conscience. Shauna had a right to be worried and even angry with him for agreeing with Thorndyke's proposal. He hadn't liked doing it himself, but there hadn't been any other way. What he honestly regretted was his reaction to Shauna's concern. He shouldn't have shouted at her. Glancing over at the empty balcony next to his, he wondered if she might still be awake. He hadn't seen her after their confrontation in the study, and he could only assume she was still upset with him. Not that he could blame her. He understood her fears. If he didn't keep a close eye on Thorndyke, there was a chance the man would take advantage of him. Hadn't Pierce warned him in a roundabout way? Suddenly remembering that he hadn't tucked away the signed document in a safe place where no one would find it, he turned back and went into his room, hurrying across the darkened chamber to the door. Without breaking stride, he twisted the knob and swung the portal open, intending to step out into the hall. Instead he came to an abrupt halt when he found Shauna standing there, her fist raised as if she were about to knock on the oak panel.

"Shauna," he said, bewildered and very surprised by her presence. "Is something wrong?" He leaned to look past her, unaware of the effect his half-naked state of dress had on his wife. He had shed all of his clothes except his breeches before going to stand on the balcony and hadn't given his attire a second thought when he'd decided to go to the study. And the shock of seeing his beautiful spouse in the hallway just outside his room dismissed any chance there might have been for him to consider his lack of clothing.

"No. Nothing's wrong," she frowned, forcing her gaze away from the rippling bronze muscles in his chest. The soft light of the hall sconces played invitingly with the exquisite curves of his arms and highlighted the thick cords in his neck, a spot she suddenly found herself wanting to kiss. Drawing in a silent breath, she steeled her crumbling will to be strong and said, "I came to apologize."

"Apologize?" he echoed, truly surprised. "For what? For voicing your opinion? If anyone should apologize, it's me. I'm the one who lost his temper."

"Maybe," she murmured, her eyes still averted. "But you didn't have to tell me, and I should have realized that. I shouldn't have called you stupid."

A warm smile kinked his mouth. "I guarantee it isn't the first time I've been told I'm stupid. And you know the old saying: the truth hurts." His smile broadened when she laughed and looked up at him.

"I'd be angry too if someone reminded me of the dumb things I've done. You're right. The truth hurts." She shrugged and absently glanced down the hallway. "It's still no reason for me to have said what I did. I just don't like Nelson, and now it seems I might be stuck with him."

"Might be?" Brad questioned. "I don't understand."

Glancing nervously at him, she reconsidered telling him her idea, noticed the lightning flashing across the sky behind him through the open balcony doors, and asked if he'd be willing to talk in the fresh air for a moment. When he nodded, she stepped past him and went outside on the balcony, sensing his warm body following closely behind her. A long silence enveloped the couple standing side by side at the railing as they watched the silvery display of light among the black clouds and enjoyed the cooling breezes sweeping in across the rolling countryside.

"I must assume you've approached my father with your idea on the factory, otherwise you wouldn't have agreed to use Nelson's money."

"I would have preferred not having to do so, but yes, I

391

talked with your father about it," Brad replied, bending forward with his arms resting on the banister.

"And he turned you down?" Shauna couldn't believe it of her father, but she had to know.

"In a manner of speaking." He smiled sympathetically at her when she turned a frown his way. "Your father's experiencing some financial difficulties of his own right now, and he hasn't the capital to back such a venture at the moment."

"What kind of difficulties? I always thought . . . I mean, Papa never said anything to me about it. He used to always ask my advice whenever . . . well, not lately, of course." Her thoughts, like her comments, were running full force. "Did he say that specifically? Did he actually say he was having trouble?"

"I wasn't going to say anything about it to you, because I knew there wasn't anything you could do to help and I didn't want to upset you," he admitted, turning sideways to lean one elbow on the railing, the wrist caught in his other hand. "It might only be temporary, or it could become serious. I don't know, and neither does he. But he's being taxed quite heavily right now. Supposedly it's to build up the treasury because of the war. And there's dissension between England and France. I imagine they want enough money in the reserve should anything happen between the two countries."

"War?" Shauna breathed. "Do you mean there's a chance—"

"It doesn't look that way right now. But it pays to be prepared, and England isn't in the best shape. Those damn Colonials took their toll." He grinned devilishly, hoping to ease the tension he was sure she felt.

"Yes. Those damn Colonials," she chuckled. The

smile faded slowly from her lips as she allowed herself the pleasure of studying the handsome lines of his face—his rugged brow, deep brown eyes, high cheekbones, full, seductive mouth, the square jaw, and the small scar near his left eye. She frowned suddenly when she realized she had never asked him about it. Before she could catch herself, she raised a finger to trace the thin white line. "A jealous lover?"

"Hardly," he laughed. "A souvenir from the war."

"You were shot?" she gasped, feeling oddly fortunate that his foe's aim had been off.

"No. Cut." He ran the knuckle of his thumb across the scar, remembering the incident quite clearly. "Luckily I ducked just in time, or it would have been worse." He laughed at a thought and added, "You'd be married to Nelson right now, instead of having to deal with him as your husband's partner."

"Brad," Shauna warned, fighting down a grin.

Enjoying their playful mood, he leaned back against the railing and stared up at the dark sky. "I wonder if the two of you would be standing here talking right now the way we are." He nodded at his bedchambers. "Or in there doing something else."

"Brad!" she exploded, her face burning instantly. "I can assure you, I wouldn't have married him."

"Mmmm," he murmured. "But suppose your father had forced you. Do you think he'd have agreed to your terms the way I did?"

"Probably," she threw back. "And he'd have kept his part of the bargain for the same amount of time as you."

Brad cringed as if she had stabbed him in the heart. "Ouch. I guess I asked for that."

"Yes, you did."

He was quiet for a second or two, and Shauna could see the mischief working in his dark eyes.

"Do you suppose he'd be a good lover?"

Appalled by such a question and his audacity in asking, she stiffened, her mouth agape. Yet once she sensed he only teased and had hoped only to shock her, she decided to play along. "I'm sure he would have. Experience counts, you know."

Brad glanced over at her from out of the corner of his eye. "Not always. In the art of making love, innocence can be very alluring. It was in your case."

Shauna could feel her cheeks pinken, but she didn't want him to know he had embarrassed her or let him have the last word. "And now that I've lost my innocence, I'm no longer alluring. Is that what you're saying?"

The deviltry disappeared from his eyes. "Hardly. You're more alluring than the first time I saw you."

For some unknown reason his compliment made her nervous. Lowering her gaze, she turned back to study the horizon where the tall oaks swayed in the wind. "At Sir Blakely's party? There in the ballroom?"

"No. In the gardens."

Her brow wrinkled and she looked questioningly at him.

"Beth and I had gone there for some fresh air. We were a few yards from the terrace when you came out alone. Beth saw you first and remarked on your beauty, and never having been one to pass up the chance of looking at a beautiful woman, I had her point you out to me. That's when Tyler joined you, and it appeared the two of you were arguing."

Shauna could remember that moment most vividly. "That was you?" she breathed. "Beth was sitting down and—"

"I was standing next to her," he finished, his dark brows drawn together and a half-smile curling his lips. "I wasn't aware you had seen us."

"Oh, I saw you," she admitted. "And even though I didn't know who either of you was, I was jealous."

"Jealous?" he parroted. "Of what?"

Shauna lifted one delicate shoulder, finding it hard to explain what her feelings had been at that moment. "Of what I thought was young lovers stealing the chance to be alone. I guess I was wishing I had been Beth."

The expression on Brad's face showed his surprise, but he quickly masked it. "I'm sure if you were to ask, Beth would say you have more to offer a man . . . then as well as now."

"Nay." Shauna shook her head, and a torrent of long golden hair shimmered down her back. "I have material things; a fine house, rich gowns, jewels, and the like. But I never sought to steal a private moment with a man. 'Tis not that few ever offered, only that I never found a single one of them tempting enough." She closed her eyes, drew in a deep breath of fresh, sweet air, and tilted her head back. "I told my brother one time that I would not marry a man unless I knew he loved *me* and not the riches I could bring to the union. I was only playing with him at the time, but deep inside I knew I spoke the truth. So what did I do? I married you under those very same conditions I vowed would not enter into my decision." She laughed halfheartedly. "And it was I who did the asking. I was the one who offered wealth in exchange for my hand." She lifted pale green eyes to look at him. "Nay. Beth has far more to offer a man than I. She has honesty, innocence, and selflessness, all the attributes of a fine, adoring, loving wife."

Brad watched her a moment while she stared out at the

flashes of light searing the sky, noticing how the fragrant wind teased a stray tendril of her hair and molded her silk robe against her slender body. He had been with many women in his life, freely taking all they would give him without a moment's thought to consequence or that perhaps one of them had fallen in love with him. She had labeled him a scoundrel, a rogue, and until this very moment even though he had agreed with her—he hadn't honestly realized the meaning of the title. He had flirted shamelessly, wooed them into bed, then disappeared before the first light of morning, never once looking back or caring. Yes, he had been a scoundrel. But no more. Now he had Shauna, and she meant everything to him.

"There's nothing wrong with wanting to be loved for what you are inside," he answered tenderly. "And maybe we started off a little mixed up, but that doesn't mean you aren't capable of being a warm, adoring wife, or that some day we won't put our pasts behind us and live in trust and honesty." He smiled softly. "Maybe we'll even find room for love." Her green eyes glanced over at him, and his heart lurched in his chest when he saw the unshed tears shining in them.

"I wish I could believe that," she whispered, quickly brushing away the moisture that curled down her cheek. "I wish I could believe you'd forgive me for all the horrible things I've done to you."

"Horrible," he laughed comfortingly. "What have you done to me that's so horrible, Mrs. Remington?" He stepped back and gave himself a mocking once-over. "Do I look as though you've treated me horribly?"

Shauna blinked and averted her eyes. "What I've done doesn't show." Her guilt choked her and she swallowed hard. "I blackmailed you into a marriage you didn't want.

I set the conditions. I would have your name; you would have this land. But what good is having that which belonged to your father when there are no heirs? Again, I thought only of me. Separate bedchambers, I declared. 'Twas my way or nothing at all. Because of my selfishness, I've made you less than a man in the eyes of others, and you could do naught but stand back and accept it. I've mocked you, treated you shamelessly, and as the final blow, I—"

"Hush," Brad quickly interrupted, taking her by the shoulders and pulling her close. "That is how you see it. But let me tell you my side of it."

Shauna wanted to push away from him, her guilt and shame demanding she do so, but the warmth of his body, his sweet words, and the comfort she found enveloped within his embrace refused to give her the strength.

"Some may say I lost my mind to agree to such an arrangement," he began, his voice low, "and perhaps that's true. But not in the way most would think. Before I knew her name, I met a woman whose beauty and charm was so breathtaking that the mere sight of her changed the direction my life had taken. I didn't know it then as I do now, but that brief glimpse of her there in the gardens had decided my fate. I had traveled many places, seen glorious sights, met scores of people, but in that moment I knew how drastically it all paled in comparison. My world, though vast and full of adventure, narrowed to one singly enchanting vision: the woman I would make my wife. Had I been asked at the time, I would have denied the feelings, excusing them as mere curiosity." Gently, he placed his knuckle under chin and lifted her eyes to look at him. "I would have married you, Shauna, had there been no conditions at all. For you see, even if you had snubbed me and given me not a second look, I wouldn't have been discouraged. I would have chased you, seduced you, made you heavy with child had there been no other way, then claimed you as my own. You had become an intoxicating drink, a poison in my soul that affected all rationale. What you did or think you did made no difference then, as it makes no difference now. You were brought into my life for a purpose, and that was to be my wife." Smiling brightly at her, he added, "So banish those thoughts from your head, my love. I was not trapped by your games, but by your very existence."

Daring no words, for his confession as well as her turbulent emotions threatened her sanity, she bit down hard on her lower lip, tears glistening in her eyes. She had heard all this before from those who wished to share in her wealth, but none had ever spoken with such sincerity. Perhaps it was because she longed to believe him, that she needed to hear someone tell her, that despite all her faults and shortcomings, she was, after all, a good person. She didn't truly feel she measured up to all he had said—how could she? He didn't know the worst of it—yet his declaration touched her deeply, and she silently vowed she would change. She would be his wife in every sense of the word. Her pale green eyes, warming with her love, searched his handsome face for any sign of mockery, and finding none, she slid her arms up around his neck and pulled his mouth to hers.

Her willingness surprised Brad and gave him great pleasure at the same moment, since he hadn't imagined her response would be anything like this. He had meant the words he spoke, but she had no reason to believe him, for they were, after all, just words. She, no doubt, had heard them countless times before, from other suitors with no more in mind than merely to win her trust. Perhaps that was the difference. He wanted her trust, but more than anything else, he wanted her love. And if this was the beginning, he'd take full advantage. Slanting his mouth across hers, he parted her lips with his tongue to probe inside while one hand came up behind her head, the other pulling her hips against his. The instant their bodies touched and he could feel the warmth of her slender frame draped in silk, his passion erupted into a raging inferno and he lost the will to be patient. Bending slightly, he swept her up in his arms and carried her into his room.

Thunder exploded in the heavens all around them. The skies opened up to assault the earth with a torrent of rain and wind. Lightning seared the darkness. Yet the fury of the tempest went unnoticed by the couple locked in embrace. Passions soared. Desire burned rapidly through their veins. Eager fingers unhooked the fastenings of his breeches, the silk frogs of her gown, and slid the garment from them, to be kicked aside, forgotten. Ivory skin blended with bronze in the bright flashes of light. Golden hair contrasted with raven-black. Hands explored. Lips clung hungrily. Breathless moans were lost among the cracks of thunder. Two bodies, fused as one, touched full length and fell together upon a bed of feathery softness. Kisses trailed molten paths along satiny flesh, and hands roamed the many curves. Twisting and rolling in a fervor of rapture, they clawed and nibbled and sampled the sweetness of the moment. In the muted light of the raging storm, they came together in a burst of fiery splendor, mindless of the howling wind, the rain, the thunderous booms that shook the rafters and rattled the window-panes. And unaware, as well, that, below them, a dark figure stalked the unlit hallway and disappeared into the study unseen.

Tired and hungry after a day of one disappointment after another, Tyler shifted irritably in the saddle and jerked the collar of his jacket up higher around his neck to shield himself from the biting rain. With his tricorn positioned low on his brow, he concentrated on the faint yellow light coming from the windows of the inn up ahead on the road. It was nearing midnight, and had it not been another hour's ride to Wrenhaven, he would have continued on. But the cold rain had soaked through his clothes, and since he was already feeling chilled, he decided to wait out the storm while having something to eat. If need be, he'd spend the night, and visit Brad in the morning with his bad news.

It had taken him close to three days to track down the carpenter his brother-in-law wanted to hire, since the man didn't seem to stay in one place for very long. And when he finally thought he'd found him, a gray-haired woman met him at the door of the small house with a sad tale of how her husband had taken ill some weeks back and had died. Tyler knew Brad would not only be disappointed but saddened to hear of the man's death, since Theodore Keiffer had been better skilled with hammer and nails than anyone, but even more, because the man had been a friend of Aric Remington's. Tyler would have preferred telling Brad anything else rather than that the man was dead, for it seemed to both Tyler and Brad that nothing they attempted had gone favorably of late.

Drawing his horse in alongside another tied to the

hitching rail, Tyler dismounted and looped the reins securely to the post before dashing up the pair of steps and hurrying inside the inn. The commons was nearly empty save a dark-haired stranger sitting alone in a chair in the far corner, his concentration focused on the food he ate. Tyler paid him little heed as he stepped up to the bar to order a drink and something to eat, doffing his tricorn and shaking the water from it. Then, mug in hand, he turned to the hearth where a warm, crackling fire promised to chase away his chill and hopefully dry his clothes while he waited for the bowl of stew the innkeeper vowed to bring him.

A half-hour later found Tyler lounging sleepily in a chair, watching the dancing firelight and listening to the rain pelting the windowpanes. The storm hadn't lessened any, and he was seriously considering taking a room for the night when the front door of the inn was thrown open and a man entered hastily. Drowsy, Tyler glanced over at the newcomer and watched him approach the barkeep before settling back to study the orange flames again.

"I was to meet someone here," Tyler vaguely heard him say.

"Got several guests," the innkeeper replied. "What's his name?"

The stranger glanced nervously around the room, noting that the dark-haired man in the corner was paying more attention to his ale than to him and that all he could see of the second man sitting in the high-backed chair near the fireplace was his lower torso. He appeared to be asleep. He turned back and replied, his voice low, "Lord Billingsly."

The name meant little to the barkeep, even less to the

man drinking ale, but Tyler's attention piqued instantly. This wasn't the sort of place Lucus Billingsly frequented. It was too far from home, for one thing, and too rundown, for another. A snob like Billingsly would never allow himself to be seen in such a place, much less take a room here. Something peculiar was going on, and Tyler's curiosity begged him to find out what it was.

Forcing himself not to move, Tyler waited until the newcomer had been told where to find the lord and had started for the stairs before he sat up and stretched to peek over the back of his chair at him. Tyler's first glimpse of the man had been limited by the wide-brimmed hat he wore and his lack of interest. But now . . . now he saw him clearly, and although he didn't remember the man's name, Tyler knew he worked at Wrenhaven. In fact, his own father had hired him to look after the place. An eerie feeling crept over him as he watched the man mount the stairs. It wasn't so much the oddity of finding him here that bothered Tyler, but rather that the man had come out on a stormy night to meet secretly with Lord Billingsly. Waiting until he had disappeared up the flight of stairs and turned down the hall, Tyler came to his feet and approached the innkeeper.

"Excuse me, sir," Tyler apologized.

Setting aside the glass he was drying, the innkeeper leaned against the bar and said, "Yeah?"

"Did that man say he was looking for Lord Billingsly?"

"Aye, that he did." He picked up the glass again then squinted an eye at Tyler. "You gonna take a room, mister? Or try ta cheat me by sleeping in the chair? I'll charge ya just the same if ya spend the night by the fireplace or in a bed, so ya might as well be comfortable."

Tyler quickly dug through his pockets for the money

he needed. "Yes. I'll take a room." He slapped an added coin down on the bar. "The extra is for you not to say I was asking questions."

Glancing first at the silver and then at Tyler, the innkeeper scooped up the money and handed him a key. "Third door left. And I never saw ya."

"Thank you," Tyler nodded with a smile before turning for the stairs. He had just reached the landing at the top when he heard the front door of the inn open and a cold draft of wind followed him up the steps. But he paid it no mind, for his attention was riveted on the long, dimly lit hallway ahead of him. Thus he didn't notice the tall, burly figure of a man step in out of the rain, for if he had, he would have recognized Marcus Deerfield.

Whether it was the loud, earth-trembling boom or the brilliant flash of light that jolted Shauna out of a sound sleep, she came awake instantly, her slender body drenched in perspiration and her eyes filled with terror. Sitting straight up in bed, she gasped for air when it seemed an invisible hand had locked steely fingers around her throat and was squeezing the very life from her, and several minutes ticked away before she was able to breathe easily again.

Chapter Fourteen

"Good mornin', Miss Shauna," Moira chimed when she opened the bedroom door and found her mistress standing near a window looking out in quiet consideration. "Did ya sleep well?"

"Good morning, Moira," Shauna replied solemnly, her gaze centered on some object below her in the gardens.

Sensing something troubled the young woman, Moira quietly closed the door and came to stand next to her. "Would ya like ta talk about it?"

Brought out of her reverie by the question, Shauna blinked and forced a smile. "Talk about what, Moira?"

"About whatever it is that has ya so depressed. Ya can't fool me by pretendin' there's nothin' botherin' ya. I can see it in your face. Did you and Mister Brad have an argument?"

Shauna laughed at the absurdity of the statement. "I wish we had. It would be easier to resolve. All I'd have to do is apologize. But saying I'm sorry won't do it in this case, I'm afraid."

"Are ya talkin' about Mr. O'Sullivan?"

Shauna sighed heavily and nodded her head. "I had

planned to talk to Brad about it last night, until he said things that made me wish I was dead."

Moira's brow knit. "Now what could a wonderful man like your husband say ta make ya wish such a dreadful thing?"

Shauna closed her eyes and exhaled slowly. "That he'd never blamed me for all the awful things I did to him." Tortured by the memory of his unselfishness, Shauna turned away from the window and went to the french doors to open them and step out on the balcony. A soft, cooling breeze caressed her face as she stared up at the blue sky with its sprinkling of fluffy white clouds, and although there was a serenity in the brightness of the morning, it failed to soothe her worried thoughts. "Would you like to hear what else he told me?" she asked, sensing Moira at her elbow.

"Aye. If ya wish ta tell me," came the sympathetic response.

"Oh, yes. I'd like to tell you," Shauna admitted miserably. "Someone should have a good laugh over it. And I think you deserve to be that person. After all, you warned me often enough to tell Brad the truth." Fighting back the pain that stabbed at her heart, she leaned against her hands braced on the railing. "He told me he would have married me no matter what the conditions, that if I hadn't come to him with my proposition, he would have found some other way of making me his wife." She laughed almost sarcastically. "He said he'd even go to the extreme of getting me heavy with child to claim me as his own. He said he knew his life had changed the first moment he saw me. He could tell just by looking at me that he had found the woman he wanted to share his remaining days with. It's what he said last night." A sob

405

choked her and she angrily straightened her slim form and cleared her throat, not wanting to break down in a flood of tears. "It's what he said then, but will he still feel the same once he learns I cheated him out of Wrenhaven?"

"And why wouldn't he?" Moira snapped.

Shauna laughed derisively and faced her maid. "You're not serious, are you? You really think he'd forgive me for gambling away his future?"

"Aye!" Moira's own anger showed in her dark eyes, the frown, and the stiffening of her slender frame. "He said he knew ya were meant ta be his the first time he saw ya. Isn't that what ya told me?" She waited for Shauna's reluctant nod, then went on. "And did ya own Wrenhaven at the time?" She wouldn't let her mistress answer. "No. Ya didn't, and it made no difference. If ya don't own it now, how would it change his mind?" Squaring her shoulders, Moira grabbed Shauna by the arms and gave her a shake. "There's been enough lies. The time for playin' games is over! Ya are ta march down there to his study and tell him the truth. And if ya don't, I'll drag ya down there and *I'll* tell him! I've had enough of the two of ya tiptoein' around the issue. Ya're ta make peace so we can get on with what's important."

Moira's rage surprised Shauna but it also riled her temper. Yanking free of her hold, Shauna turned her back and went inside. "It's easy for you to stand there and tell me what I should and shouldn't do. You don't have to carry the guilt." Storming to the armoire, she flung the doors open and grabbed the first dress her hand touched. Tossing it on the bed, she headed for the dresser and her undergarments. "He'll be told the truth, but only when I decide it's time." Pulling off her nightgown, she quickly donned her things, then crossed back to the bed for her dress. "I've got to be free to pick the right moment and just how I'll tell him. I can't be rushed into it. Not by you or . . . or . . ."

"Mr. O'Sullivan?" Moira baited, her fists knotted on her hips.

Shauna gave the woman an icy glare, then reached for the dress and wriggled into it, deliberately choosing not to comment. Having fastened the buttons up the front, she crossed to the dressing table where she sat down long enough to brush back her hair and tie it in place with a satin ribbon.

"I still have work to do on the roses out front," she said as she went to the door and picked up her bonnet from the chair near it. "I'll be skipping breakfast, so you may inform the cook for me." Pulling open the door, she stepped out into the hall and paused to look back at her maid. "As for our discussion," she began, her chin held high until she saw the pained look in Moira's eyes. Sighing regretfully, she added, "I'll talk to him. Today. I'll tell him the truth, and you can spend the afternoon packing my bags." With a frown, she turned and headed for the stairs.

Shauna's heart thumped loudly in her chest as she descended the circular staircase and saw that the door to Brad's study stood open. She hadn't the courage nor the desire to talk to him right now, and if he was sitting at his desk, which he probably was, he'd certainly see her when she walked by, no matter how inconspicuous she tried to be. They had spent such a glorious night together—making love, laughing, watching the storm outside, reminiscing about their childhoods, until dawn had sent Shauna fleeing to her room—that she didn't want to ruin the sweet memories just yet by telling him that Wrenhaven belonged to someone else. Despite Moira's guarantee that it wouldn't affect his feelings toward her, Shauna sensed otherwise. She knew how angry and hurt she'd feel if *he* had lied to her.

As quietly as possible, she stepped off the last tread and started across the marble floor of the foyer toward the back of the manor where she had left her gardening tools, her eyes glued to the doorway. She hadn't realized she was holding her breath until she had a clear view of the interior of the room and discovered that Brad wasn't working there as Moira had implied. Heaving a breathless sigh of gratitude, she straightened and turned her attention on the path she took, only to jerk to a startled, abrupt halt when she came face to face with Mr. Barnes.

"Beg your pardon, madam," he said stiffly. "Didn't mean to frighten you, but you appeared to be concentrating on something important, and I didn't want to interrupt your train of thought."

It's more like you were hoping to find out what it was, she thought acidly. "And now you have my full consideration," she said aloud, as politely as she could manage. "Was there something you wished to tell me, or were you on your way to the study to look for another shopping list?"

Barnes's nose raised a notch, and she could see the contempt in his eyes. "Nay, madam. I was told by Mr. Remington that once you had arisen, I was to inform you that he had to go to London on business and that he'll be gone until nightfall."

Shauna felt oddly disappointed that Brad hadn't told her himself, and yet she was thankful he hadn't. She might have had to deal with her problem sooner than she had wanted to. Nodding her appreciation to the butler, she absently watched him turn on his heel and walk away while she fought with the loneliness her day would bring her without Brad. She had promised Moira that she'd talk with her husband about Mr. O'Sullivan sometime today, and she had already decided to spend the greater part of it in his company enjoying their last peaceful moments together. Now, because he had been called away on business, she was to be denied even that.

"Just punishment," she muttered, starting off after her tools again.

Had someone asked her two months ago if she'd ever consider getting down on her knees in front of a flowerbed and getting not only her skirts dirty but her hands and face as well, Shauna would have laughed at him. Yet as she knelt in the shade of the huge manor house and diligently pulled weeds, snipped off dead twigs and leaves, and considered which brightly colored blossoms she'd use for a bouquet, she felt both exhilarated and tremendously satisfied. It also helped to take her mind off her troubles. Totally absorbed in her work, she neither saw nor heard the rider approach until his shadow crossed the ground near her, and even then she paid it little heed, glancing briefly at the dark outline in the grass, then back at her roses.

"Good mornin', lass," the friendly voice beckoned in a thick Irish brogue. "Ya certainly can't be the lady of the manor, now can ya? I wouldn't imagine Shauna Remington on her knees in the dirt. But you English have always managed to surprise me."

The chilling sound of his words, his accent, the fact that he knew her name, and more important, that she had expected Kelly O'Sullivan to make his appearance anytime soon, froze Shauna to her spot. In a matter of seconds her world had crumbled down around her, and her only hope of surviving was that Barnes had been right in saying Brad wouldn't be home until much later. Drawing air into her tortured lungs when it seemed the weight of the universe lay heavily against her chest, she slowly turned her head to look at the one who held her fate in his hands.

With the sun at his back and a tricorn pulled low over his brow, Shauna couldn't make out his face, only that he had shaved off the beard and his cane was nowhere to be seen. Realizing she stared and that any second someone might walk outside to greet their visitor, Shauna awkwardly came to her feet.

"You're early."

Frowning, the Irishman cocked his head to one side and asked, "I am?"

Glancing toward the house when she suddenly remembered how nosey Barnes could be, she hurried over to her guest and whispered, "Yes. Your letter said this week sometime, but I didn't think it would be today. Have you told anyone you were coming here?"

"Only ta ask directions," he reluctantly replied. "Why? Does it make a difference?"

"It does if you told anyone your name. Did you say you were Kelly O'Sullivan?"

A broad smile parted his lips. "No, lass. I don't recall tellin' anyone me name was Kelly O'Sullivan."

"Good!" she said excitedly as she pulled off her gloves and dusted her skirt with them. "Then we have time to talk."

"Talk?" he questioned, obviously puzzled.

"Yes, before my husband comes home." She looked at

the front door again to make sure Barnes wasn't standing there, then motioned for O'Sullivan to dismount and follow her around to the side of the house where a tall oak offered shade and privacy. "Over here," she said, heading in that direction.

His warm brown eyes watched the gentle swish of cotton and the enticing sway of her narrow hips before the man easily swung out of the saddle and stepped to the ground. Carelessly tossing the reins over the nearby hitching rail, he took his tricorn from his head and followed the beautiful young woman's lead.

Upon reaching the shadow of the large tree, Shauna stopped and turned around to wait for Mr. O'Sullivan to join her. It was then, while his tall, broad-shouldered frame was bathed in sunlight, that she got her first honest look at the man who had won Wrenhaven away from her. He was incredibly handsome, with dark brown hair, a thin, straight nose, wide cheekbones, and a charming, somewhat devilish smile accented by deep dimples on either side of his mouth. His eyes sparkled with the same hint of mischief, and if Shauna hadn't known better, she would have sworn he wasn't the same Kelly O'Sullivan she had met at Sir Blakely's.

"You had a red beard," she said, without much thought.

O'Sullivan's hand touched his chin. "What?"

"At Sir Blakely's masquerade party. You had a red beard then. Now you have brown hair. How can that be?"

His mouth twitched in a half-smile. "'Tis the reason I shaved it off. I've never been fond of red hair." He cocked a brow curiously at her when she glanced away from him, then masked his puzzlement once she looked back again.

411

"And what about the cane? You walked with a limp."
She dropped her gaze to his black shoes. "I distinctly remember a cane."

"Sprained me ankle," he admitted. "But it's much better now." He shifted his weight to one side and wiggled his foot. "I took a nasty fall from me horse."

For a moment, Shauna pictured him as he had been that night. Although she had to admit that the white powdered periwig, the beard, and the scarlet mask had hidden most of his features, something about his appearance as he was today didn't quite match. Was he thinner, perhaps? Younger than she had imagined? She mentally shook it off, blaming her confussion that night on the wine she'd had to drink and the devastating results of her card game. That thought brought her back to the present.

"I apologize for all the questions, Mr. O'Sullivan—"

"Please," he interrupted. "Call me Kelly."

A nervous smile parted her lips, and she turned away from him. "After I tell you what I've done—or I should say, what I haven't done, you might not think me worthy of the honor."

"I sincerely doubt a beautiful lass such as you could do anythin' to offend me, Mrs. Remington," he quickly and cheerfully corrected. "And I'd be honored if ya would allow me ta call ya Shauna. It's such a fittin' name for a lovely woman like yourself."

"You may call me anything you like, and you probably will once I tell you what a coward I am." She lifted her green eyes to look at him. "Or better said, how selfish I've been."

"Selfish?" he repeated, his dark eyes reflecting his doubt and surprise.

She took a deep breath and blurted out, "I haven't told

Brad about our card game."

O'Sullivan's brows came together and he lowered his eyes as he moved past her toward the trunk of the tree. "Oh, I see," he murmured.

Before he could tell her how foolish that had been, Shauna swung around and approached him. "I just couldn't tell him that I'd lost Wrenhaven to you in a silly game of cards. This land belonged to his father, and he wanted it back."

O'Sullivan straightened, as if confused. "How did you come to have it?"

His question surprised her, and she laughed. "You must have had more to drink that night than I assumed you had. It was my dowry, and you forced me to use it as my wager."

O'Sullivan shifted uncomfortably. Scratching his temple, he smiled lamely and replied, "Aye. I did have a bit to drink that night, but that wasn't what I meant. Ya said Wrenhaven belonged to your husband's father, and he wanted it back. How was it the property suddenly became your dowry?"

"Oh," Shauna chuckled. "I guess that is a little confusing."

"A little," O'Sullivan agreed with a vague smile.

"After Brad's father died, he and his brother sold it to my father. My father gave it to me."

"So your husband married ya for your dowry."

Shauna took a breath to discredit the statement and realized how true it really was. "I guess you could say that," she answered quietly. "And that's what makes this all so horrible. I didn't love Brad when I married him, just as he didn't love me. But now—" She paused unable to say the words aloud. "Well, I'm afraid of what will happen to us when he learns you own Wrenhaven." Drawing on every ounce of courage she had, she raised her chin and looked him squarely in the eye. "I need to ask your help, your understanding, and your patience."

O'Sullivan lifted a brow. "'Tis a tall favor, lass. Are ya sure I'm able to do all that?"

Shauna shrugged hesitantly. "We won't know until I ask, I suppose."

"Then ask away, lass," he smiled. "I haven't got anywhere ta go right now."

"Good," she smiled weakly, "because this is a rather long story." She began by telling him about her dislike for Nelson Thorndyke, his connection to her father, the man's prior intention of marrying her and how, after all her efforts to be rid of him, Nelson had managed to worm his way into a partnership with Brad . . . on property her husband no longer owned. "So you see, Kelly, I was hoping you'd wait a while to claim Wrenhaven."

"And what good will that do ya? If your husband takes the man's money, he'll—"

"That's where you come in," she interrupted excitedly. "You're a rich man, aren't you. You wouldn't have been invited to Sir Blakely's otherwise. I'd like to introduce you to Brad as an old friend of the family we haven't seen in years, and you could pretend to show an interest in Brad's plans for a factory, so much so that you offer to back his operation, thus eliminating the need to use Nelson."

Kelly grew visibly troubled with the idea. "I don't know, lass," he began, his expression showing his reluctance.

Shauna was quick to cut in. "I realize it's a lot to ask, seeing as how Wrenhaven is yours and you should be the one deciding. I also realize I have a lot of nerve proposing such a plan, but there'd be something in it for you. Brad would be doing all the work and you'd have half the profit. He'd be sort of the manager, while you were free to sit back and not worry."

"For how long?"

Shauna's brow crimped. "I don't understand."

"How long would ya go on pretendin' your husband owned Wrenhaven? A month? A year? Until he died? It isn't fair to him, lass. Ya should own up to what ya've done *before* he's in serious trouble."

A chill tickled the hair on her arms. "You . . . you mean you won't help?"

"I'd love ta help, lass," he protested. "But I'm afraid I can't. I haven't the money it would take ta finance such an operation."

Shauna wanted to be angry with him. She wanted to blame him for all her troubles. She wanted to call him names, tell him he was a heartless cur who thought only of himself. Near tears, she turned away, knowing that Kelly O'Sullivan wasn't the source of her problems.

"I understand," she said solemnly. "I really do. And you're right, of course. I must tell Brad." A trembling sigh shook her, and she stiffened her spine courageously before facing him again. "May I ask one thing of you, then?"

The Irishman nodded, his dark eyes filled with sympathy.

"Would you allow me a day or two to figure out just how I'll tell him?" The hesitation that wrinkled his rugged brow spurred her on. "I'm not asking you to leave. You can stay here, of course. In fact," she smiled brightly, pleased with her idea, "we can excuse your presence to Brad by saying you're Moira's cousin."

An odd look distorted his face. "Moira's cousin."

"Moira Flanagan. She's my maid. You'll like her. She's Irish, too."

"Oh," he grinned halfheartedly. "I'm sure I will."

"Then you'll do it?"

O'Sullivan shrugged a wide shoulder, hesitant. "Well, I had planned ta stay a while. . . ." He shifted his attention to the manor. "But what about Moira? Miss Flanagan? Will she be willin' ta go along with—"

"Of course, she will!" Shauna pledged ardently. "Moira's my best friend. All I have to do is tell her."

He raised a dubious brow. "Ya mean she already knows about . . . about your problem?"

Shauna nodded. "Very much so. In truth, she feels the same way you do about it." Sighing, she reached out and took Kelly's arm to draw him toward the house, unaware that they were being watched. "She's told me time and time again how sorry I'm going to be if I don't tell Brad about this before it goes too far. She won't be pleased with this new little kink, I'm sure, but she'll go along with it simply because I asked." Noticing one of the stable hands walking toward the barn, she called out for him to see about their guest's horse, then pointed a directive hand toward the side door of the manor where she and Kelly could go inside.

"The last time we talked you said you were going home to Dublin to get married," she commented airily as she let go of his arm and stepped through the door he held open for her. "Am I to assume you've made some lucky lady very happy?" She missed the odd expression on his face as she continued on ahead of him toward the front hall.

"Ah . . . no, lass," he replied reluctantly. He was quiet a moment, as if searching for the right explanation. "By the time I returned, she had changed her mind." He smiled insipidly when Shauna stopped and turned around. "I guess I gave her too long ta think about marryin' a rogue like meself."

"A rogue?" Shauna argued. "You're hardly a rogue, Kelly O'Sullivan. You're one of the kindest, most understanding and generous men I've ever met." She thought of Brad and how he had those same qualities, and she smiled. "Your lady passed up a beautiful chance at a fine marriage, and I don't think it will take her long to realize that. I'm glad Brad didn't allow me to make the same mistake." She started off again, a loving smile gracing her lips. "You'll like Brad. The two of you have a lot in common." With her back to him, she missed the way he wrinkled up his face, as if what she had said was cause for discussion.

As they passed by the kitchen, Shauna stuck her head in the doorway and asked Lilly to fix a light lunch for her and her guest and to see it brought to the dining room in about a half-hour, adding that she wanted to show Mr. O'Sullivan to his room first. The cook replied that she'd be more than happy to and that she was glad to hear Miss Shauna was feeling like her old self again.

"Have ya been sick, lass?" Kelly asked as they made their way to the wide staircase in the foyer. He asked, but his concentration seemed more focused on his surroundings and who might suddenly appear through one of the doorways than on whether or not his companion had been ill.

"Not really sick, actually," she sighed, laying a trim hand on the banister as they started up the steps. "Just

417

too nervous to eat."

Kelly jerked to attention. "Nervous lass? About what?"

Soft laughter trickled from her. "About you." She cast him a playful smile over her shoulder. "I was worrying you'd show up before I had a chance to straighten things out between Brad and me."

Kelly smiled weakly. "And I did just that, didn't I?" he muttered.

"Well, it's not your fault," she quickly objected, stopping on the stairs before they had reached the landing. "I knew what I was getting myself into from the start. I was playing with fire, and I got burned." She frowned, her expression sad. "It's always easier to look back on the things a person's done and see the mistakes you made along the way rather than to see them coming. But I'd give *anything* to go back to the beginning and start over."

"And what would ya do differently, lass?" he asked in all sincerity.

Shauna thought about it for a minute. "Well, I never would have trapped Brad into marrying me, for one thing." She laughed at the statement and added, "Of course, there's a good possibility he wouldn't have given me a thought if we'd met under different circumstances . . . despite what he said." She smiled brightly at Kelly. "And I certainly wouldn't have sat down at the table across from you!"

"And then we never would have met," he replied, feigning injured pride. "Can't ya say one good thing came of all this?"

Shauna's smile disappeared as she studied the man's strong face, the dimples in his cheeks, and the sparkle in his dark brown eyes. "Yes. Something good did come of it all. You're a kind man, Kelly O'Sullivan. And I believe you're the first of your gender to have proven how wrong I've been about men."

"I beg your pardon?" he questioned, following her up the remainder of the steps when she turned away and headed down the hall.

"Until now I thought all men were cheats, liars and scoundrels." She missed the way he cringed. "Maybe it's because you're Irish."

"Maybe," he mumbled with a frown.

"Well, here we are," she beamed, stopping beside the second doorway in the hall. "I hope you'll be comfortable. I'll have Timmy bring up your things, and after you've rested and freshened up, we can have lunch."

"Thank ya, lass. Ya've been too kind."

"Me?" Shauna laughed. "Hospitable, yes. But you're the one who's been too kind. I'm sure God has a special place for you in heaven when you get there."

One corner of his mouth lifted in a weak smile. "I'm sure he does."

"Well," she sighed happily, "I'll leave you alone now and find Moira. It would be disastrous if Brad came home before I talked to her."

Kelly nodded, saying, "Yes. It certainly would."

"Shall we meet in the dining room in—say, fifteen minutes?"

"Aye, lass. In the dinin' room."

She started to turn, hesitated, then stepped closer and lightly kissed his cheek. "Thank you," she whispered, and before he could reply, she turned and fled down the hall.

The Irishman stood near the door of his room

watching the gentle swish of her skirts and sadly admiring the bounce in her step. He had made her happy, and he was really sorry he had. She'd hate him for it once she learned his secret.

Standing on the terrace in back of the manor watching her maid pick flowers and put them in a basket, Shauna steeled herself for the conversation they would have shortly. Moira had told her countless times to tell Brad the truth, and now that that time had come, she was about to ask Moira to be patient another day or two. Moira wouldn't like it, and she'd say so without reservation, but in the end, she'd do whatever Shauna asked of her simply because she loved her enough to let Shauna solve her own problems. Right or wrong, Moira knew it had to be Shauna's decision to make . . . and she had to make it on her own.

"Moira?" she questioned softly, approaching the woman as Moira knelt in the flowerbed.

"Aye, lass," she replied without looking up.

Hesitating a moment to run her tongue over her lips, for it seemed they had gone dry very suddenly, Shauna took a quick breath and went to the settee to sit down. "I have a favor to ask."

Moira's head came up, but she wouldn't look back at her mistress. "What kind of a favor?"

Shauna braced herself. "I need for you to pretend that Kelly O'Sullivan is your cousin."

"Whatever for?" Moira exclaimed, her dark brows drawn together as she turned her head and gave her mistress a surly glance.

Dropping her gaze, Shauna nervously fidgeted with

the gold band on her finger. "Because he's here."

The color instantly drained from Moira's face. "What?" she breathed, almost stumbling when she tried to rise. "Who's here?" She looked toward the house.

"Kelly O'Sullivan," Shauna frowned as she worked the ring up past the first knuckle, then jammed it back down. "He arrived a few minutes ago. Now I know you're not going to approve, but I asked Mr. O'Sullivan if he'd postpone saying anything to Brad until I had a chance to explain first. I intended to do it this morning but Brad had already left for London, and Barnes says he won't be home until this evening. I don't think it's fair to hit him with such news the second he walks into the house, so I plan to tell him in the morning . . . after breakfast. Until then I need a logical explanation for our house guest. And since he's Irish and you're Irish, I thought . . ."

"Where is he?" Moira demanded as she pulled off her gloves and tossed them in the basket of flowers.

"I gave him one of the guest bedrooms. He's probably been on a horse for some time, and I figured he'd like to rest up before lunch." Her curious frown met Moira's skeptical look. "Why? What's wrong?" She rose and hurried over to where her maid stood. "Moira, you seem . . . well . . . funny. What is it?"

"Did he *say* he was Mr. O'Sullivan?"

"Of course," Shauna declared. "Do you think I'd be stupid enough to just *assume* that's who he was, that I'd take for granted the first stranger to ride in was Kelly O'Sullivan? I told you, he's Irish."

Moira opened her mouth to say something, changed her mind, and started for the house. "In that case, lass, I better be speakin' to me cousin before Mister Brad comes home. We don't want ta be tellin' two different stories ta your husband. He'd know right off Mr. O'Sullivan wasn't who he pretended to be."

Shauna heard the underlying tones in Moira's voice but she couldn't even begin to imagine what they meant or what might be the cause. Realizing she never had been able to figure out what went through Moira's head when she was in one of her moods, Shauna shrugged it off and headed toward the kitchen, intent on serving Kelly O'Sullivan the finest meal he'd had in a long while.

Outside the closed bedroom door, Moira stood staring at it, her eyes narrowed and her mouth in a tight line. She wasn't sure what or who she expected to find once she knocked and the visitor presented himself, but she sure didn't plan on letting this impostor stay more than the time it took him to fall down the stairs on his way out. And he most assuredly would test the wooden treds with his rump, if he didn't move fast enough to suit her. Squaring her shoulders, she rapped loudly on the door.

"Just a minute," the voice on the other side said, and some of the fire in her eyes faded. She shook her head, telling herself it couldn't be . . . he was . . . but yet it sounded like . . . well, there was a chance. . . . The latch clicked and Moira lowered her chin.

The bright light flooding into the room behind him through the balcony doors placed the man in shadow, and Moira squinted her eyes, trying to make out his face, when of a sudden her wrist was seized and she was jerked into the room. The door swung shut behind her and her temper raged as she staggered to a halt and yanked loose of his grip. Whirling, her breath drawn and ready to hurl every vile, contemptible name she could lay on him, the words caught in her throat once she saw the dark, devil-may-care glint in the man's eyes and recognized the recklessly handsome face smiling back at her.

"Michael?" she breathed, as if doubting her own eyes.

"Aye. The very one," he grinned. When she didn't move or show even an ounce of joy over his presence, the mirth faded from his brown eyes and he cocked his head to one side. "Aren't ya goin' ta give your big brother a hug?" He took a step toward her, arms extended, and recoiled with a jerk when she raised a fist and clubbed his shoulder with it. "Is that any way ta say hello ta someone ya haven't seen in years?" He quickly backed away when she doubled up her fist again and growled at him.

"Suppose ya tell me how I should behave, *Mr. O'Sullivan*," she sneered, shadowing his every move. "But first, I think ya better explain why you're paradin' about as someone ya ain't."

Michael raised his hand and nodded at the door, silently warning her to keep her voice down. "If ya'll give me a minute to explain—"

"That's all I'll give ya . . . a minute. Then I'm goin' ta toss ya out of here on your ear. You're messin' in somethin' that's none of your business, and I'll not be takin' the blame for it, Michael McCord."

"Well, ya can't be blamin' me for the whole of it," he argued, his expression pained.

Moira cocked a dubious brow. "And who knows ya better than me? I've been witness ta many of your pranks, and I know ya *never* pass up the chance ta flirt with a beautiful young thing." She stood arms akimbo. "But I'll be tellin' ya somethin' ya better listen close to, big brother," she mocked. "Shauna is married, and you're not ta come between them. They're havin' enough trouble without your interferin'."

"'Twas not me intention," he vowed, a brown hand laid over his heart. "I came ta Wrenhaven ta visit me sister and wound up bein' mistaken for Kelly O'Sullivan." He shrugged. "Whoever that is."

"He's Shauna's conscience," Moira snapped. "And now ya've gone and ruined it all."

Puzzled, Michael frowned. "Ya mean she's . . ." He made a circling motion at his temple with one finger.

"No, she's not daft," Moira scolded. "But thanks to you, she's delayed tellin' her husband the truth."

"About her losin' his property to O'Sullivan in a card game," Michael finished.

Moira nodded and went to the door. Upon opening it, she glanced out into the hall and then motioned for him to follow her. "I can't risk anyone overhearin' us. Let's go out back in the gardens where I can explain everythin' ta ya."

Eager to understand the strange goings-on that apparently involved his sister, Michael raised a hand toward the exit. "After you, Mrs. Flanagan."

A puzzled frown wrinkled Shauna's smooth brow as she stood beside the windows in the dining room watching Kelly O'Sullivan and her maid in the gardens. They seemed to be arguing, though Shauna couldn't imagine why, unless Moira resented his willingness to play along with Shauna's scheme even for a minute longer. Suddenly nervous over the prospect that Moira might change Kelly's mind about waiting, Shauna turned back for the door, thinking she had better intervene. After all, Moira was just her maid, and if Shauna told her do something, then— She came to an abrupt halt when

424

she lifted her eyes and saw Barnes standing in the doorway.

"Beg your pardon, madam," he said in his usual stiff manner, "but you have a visitor."

Confused, she glanced back in the direction of the gardens and Mr. O'Sullivan, wondering if Barnes was trying to tell her something she already knew.

"Mr. Thorndyke, madam," Barnes continued when he sensed her bewilderment. "He's waiting in the parlor. Will he be joining you and your other guest in the dining room?"

I hope not, she mused anxiously, annoyed that he had chosen such an inconvenient moment as this to call on her. "Did he say what he wanted?"

Barnes's nose raised loftily. "No, madam. I'm only the butler."

Her shoulders drooped. "Yes, Barnes. I'm aware you're only the butler," she sighed, slightly miffed. "What I meant was, did he ask to see me or had he hoped to talk with Mr. Remington?"

"He asked to speak with your husband and when I informed him that Mr. Remington was away, he asked if he might speak with you in his stead."

"Very well," she frowned, wishing she didn't have to be alone with him. "Would you inform Moira and her . . . ah, cousin where I'll be, and that I'll join them in a few minutes?"

"Yes, madam," Barnes nodded before turning away.

Although Nelson Thorndyke didn't truly deserve any special kind of treatment in her mind, Shauna was glad she had taken the time to brush her hair and change out of her soiled dress after having knelt in the dirt earlier. She didn't want him to get the wrong impression, which he surely would once he saw that the mistress of the house had taken on the duties of the hired help. Giving her silky mane a toss and straightening her spine, she started off for the parlor.

"Good morning, Nelson," she smiled pleasantly once she had entered the room and he came to his feet. "I trust you're well." She fought hard not to cringe when he took her hand and placed a light kiss there.

"A little distressed, but otherwise fine," he admitted with a sigh.

"Distressed?" she mimicked, crossing to the buffet and pouring him a drink when he nodded his appreciation of her silent offer. "I would think you of all people would have little to distress you." She handed him the glass and sat down in a chair opposite him.

"It is not for myself I feel this way, I regret to say," he admitted, flipping out the tails of his coat and graciously sitting down again. "And I'd give my entire wealth not to have to be the bearer of such bad news." Frowning, he set aside his drink untouched, and settled his attention anywhere other than on his lovely companion.

Shauna grew uneasy at his silence. "Is Brad all right?" she blurted out suddenly, her face a picture of worry.

"He . . . he's fine," Nelson replied, surprised by the genuine concern he heard in her voice. He had never imagined the haughty Shauna Radborne would ever feel any kind of tenderness for someone outside her family, much less for the man she called her husband. He hadn't believed she truly loved Brad Remington when she married him, and until a moment ago he had doubted she ever would. The idea that he might have been wrong upset him. "I'm sorry if I gave you the impression that someone's hurt. As far as I know, your family is well. But I have heard some unsettling rumors, dangerous rumors where your father is concerned." He rose abruptly, unable to look at the worried expression on her face, and crossed to the windows looking out over the front lawn. "Damn, I wish your husband was here. I'd prefer telling him."

"Well, he isn't," Shauna reminded him, her annoyance cutting into her tone. Rising, she came toward him. "Brad may be my husband now, but that doesn't mean he's the one who should be advised first of problems concerning the Radborne family. In fact, he should be the last, since he's only an in-law. *I'm* the daughter. Now tell me what you came here to say, Nelson, and *I'll* decide whether or not Brad should learn of it."

"Shauna," Nelson pleaded, facing her. "I didn't mean it that way. I swear to you. I just meant I'd rather you hear it from your husband instead of me."

"Hear what?" she snapped, tired of bantering words with him.

The look on Nelson's face showed his torment, and before he went on, he gently but firmly took her elbow and escorted her back to her chair. "None of it has been proven. It's only rumors. But for a man in your father's position, the mere gossip could ruin him."

"What gossip?" she spat through clenched teeth.

Nelson sucked in a deep breath and exhaled in a rush. "It's been said . . . by some members of Parliament . . . that your father is suspected of being a French sympathizer."

"That's absurd!" Shauna exploded, jumping to her feet. "My father is probably more loyal to England than the king!"

"I know that. His friends know that. But there are claims that he's involved with smugglers and that he's turning over the profits to the French."

"It's a lie!" she replied hotly. "Why would he? And

why the French? It's certainly not for personal gain. Everyone knows he's one of the wealthiest men in London!"

"They also know who his stepfather was," Nelson grimly added.

"His . . . ?"

"Yes," Nelson finished. "Liggett Dupree, French ambassador to England, a man who made his wealth solely on the misfortunes of others—*Englishmen!*"

"But that happened years ago. . . ." Shauna argued, "when Papa was a little boy . . . before Grandmother married him. Papa had nothing to do with it."

"People have long memories, Shauna," Nelson added, his tone hard. "Especially those who were hurt by him. You might not be aware of it, but some of the men Dupree destroyed couldn't handle the disgrace. He actually *drove* them to suicide."

Shauna's knees went suddenly weak and she sank back down in the chair.

"Now, because of these vicious rumors, the resentment has been stirred up again. All anyone can see is a man who profited from his stepfather's cruelty at their expense, and they want revenge."

"But that's not fair," Shauna moaned, tears burning her eyes.

"Hatred works in strange ways, my dear."

"Hatred!" she snapped. "They have no reason to hate my father. He's innocent." Blinking back her sorrow, she jerked herself out of the chair and began to pace the floor. "Something has to be done. We've got to find out who started these rumors and discredit him. We've got to prove Papa has no connection to smugglers—" A chill darted up her spine and shot across her shoulders as she suddenly remembered the men she had stumbled across by the river and Brad's guess that they might be smugglers. Feeling sick inside, she turned for the door. "Please forgive my rudeness, Nelson," she apologized in hardly more than a whisper, "but I'd like to lie down for a while."

Nelson hurriedly came to his feet and followed her from the room. "I understand," he said softly. "And I wish I'd have had good news for you." Pausing near the front door, he gently touched her arm. "Let me know if there's anything I can do for you . . . or your father. Pierce is probably the only real friend I have, and I'd like to return some of his kindness."

Shauna doubted he really meant it, but rather than argue, she nodded politely and lingered long enough to watch him cross down the sidewalk to his horse tied at the rail. Mounting, he tipped his tricorn her way, then swung the animal around to trot off down the lane. A gleam of loathing darkened her eyes as she pushed the door shut to block out the sight of him. He'd be the *last* person she'd ask for help. Turning for the study, her head down, she failed to see the couple standing at the far end of the hall.

"Who was that with Shauna?" Michael asked, his brow furrowed.

"Nelson Thorndyke," Moira sneered as she stared at the closed door. "He's the reason Shauna's in this mess she's in. If ya ask me, the world would be a better place without him in it."

"I take that ta mean ya don't like him," Michael replied, grinning.

"Not many people do," Moira remarked, turning for the dining room, her brother following closely on her heels.

"And why is that?"

"Don't know exactly. He just has a way of rubbin' a

person the wrong way, I guess." She stopped suddenly and faced him. "Why ya askin', anyway?"

Michael shrugged it off. "He reminded me of someone."

"Someone *you* know?" she laughed. "Ya don't run in the same circles as Nelson Thorndyke, Michael, if ya know what I mean. He's got more money in his pocket than you had in your hands all last year. Where would you ever meet someone like him?" She straightened and raised a brow. "And speakin' of last year, where have ya been? I've had nary a letter from ya in the past five."

"And I might say the same for you," Michael challenged.

"Don't change the subject," she snapped. "I had no idea where ta send a letter, since ya insist on movin' around all the time. But me—I've never left London since the day Mr. Radborne hired me. What have ya been doin' that's so important ya couldn't take the time ta write to your own sister?" Her fists found their way to her hips. "And come ta think of it, why are ya here now? Ya always told me ya hated England. Are ya in some sort of trouble and think ta have me bail ya out?"

Michael shot a worried glance back toward the door. "I'll be in a lot more trouble if ya don't keep your voice down."

"Aha! I knew it!" she exclaimed, grabbing his arm and pulling him across the room for more privacy. "Out with it, Michael Patrick McCord. What have ya done this time?"

"It's a simple misunderstandin'," he vowed, hoping she wouldn't press it any further. He was wrong.

"A misunderstandin', ya say?" She squinted her eyes at him. "Ya cheated at cards and got caught. Or is there an enraged father out there somewhere lookin' for the man who got his young daughter with babe? I know how ya like ta gamble, but I'm thinkin' your taste for the lasses holds more interest for ya. Ya never could keep your breeches on for very long."

"Now don't go blamin' me, Moira," he objected. "I've had ta fight them off a time or two."

"Ah, sure ya have," she mocked. "Must have been the ugly ones. So what are ya plannin' ta do? Wait here until it's safe ta go home ta Dublin?"

"That might be sooner than I thought," he grumbled with a frown.

"What's the matter? Don't ya like bein' told what a rake ya are?"

"Not from me own sister, I don't," he grunted. "I thought ya would be happy ta see me." He shrugged and sighed heavily as he turned his back on her, a bright sparkle dancing in his eyes. "But if that's the way ya feel, I guess I'll be movin' on."

"Ya will not!" she exploded, grabbing his sleeve. "Ya let Shauna think ya were someone ya're not and by God ya'll see it through till the end. I'll not have her thinkin' I ran ya off. I'll be savin' that until after she knows the truth." Scowling angrily at him for a moment, she bit back any further comment she had and turned for the door, failing to notice how the playful twinkle in her brother's eye disappeared as quickly as she exited the room.

Michael hadn't honestly planned to get himself caught up in someone else's problems when he had enough of his own, but Shauna Remington had offered him the perfect disguise he needed. He'd masquerade as Kelly O'Sullivan until he was sure he had escaped the hangman's noose.

Chapter Fifteen

"I know it's none of me business, lass," Michael spoke up as he and Shauna sat alone on the terrace having tea in the late afternoon. "But ya haven't said a word since we sat down. If somethin' is troublin' ya, I'd like ta help . . . if I can."

Shauna tried to force a smile and failed. "I'm not sure there's anything anyone can do to help, I'm afraid. But your offer and your concern are most appreciated."

"Has it somethin' ta do with the man who paid ya a visit this mornin'?" he persisted.

"Not directly," she replied, heaving a long sigh. "He was merely the bearer of bad news."

When she fell quiet again and stared off into space with a worried, anxious frown marring her smooth brow, Michael took a sip of his tea and wrinkled up his nose. He hated tea and much preferred the taste of a cool mug of ale. But it wasn't Michael Patrick McCord sitting in the wrought iron chair next to his hostess; it was Kelly O'Sullivan, a man of good manners, and Michael had to play the part . . . even if it included drinking tea. Setting aside his cup and saucer, he lounged back and sucked in a deep breath of fresh air. "I don't mean ta tell ya how ta

432

think, lass, so forgive me if it sounds that way. But are ya sure ya can believe all your visitor claims?" He smiled and brushed a piece of lint from his breeches. "I've never been one to take much worth in the gossip a man spreads." His grin widened when he saw how his comment had brought a sparkle to her eyes.

"Funny you should put it that way. Nelson *was* repeating rumors he'd heard." She turned her head and stared up at the pale blue sky marked by the glowing ambers and reds of the dying sun. "Yet his stories rather explain Papa's financial problems."

"How so, lass?"

Returning her cup to the saucer sitting on the silver tray, she was thoughtfully quiet for a moment. "If I tell you this, you must promise me you won't tell another soul. Especially Moira. She sometimes blurts things out, and Brad said I wasn't to tell anyone."

"Ya have me word on it," he pledged.

Shifting in her chair, she faced him, one hand laid on the arm, the other in her lap. Sunlight reflected golden highlights in her hair and bathed her ivory skin in a warm glow, and Michael suddenly realized how very fortunate Brad Remington was. He also concluded that if the man didn't straighten out the problems he had with his wife, Michael would step in. He could see the love this woman had for her husband, It was something Brad shouldn't toy with for much longer. Forcing himself to listen to every word she spoke, he soon came to understand her concern.

"But ya're not thinkin' the men at the river—assumin' they are smugglers—work for your father, are ya?"

"Of course not," she assured him. "But you must see how it will look if what Nelson claims is true. If they are smugglers, and they're caught, everyone will be convinced Papa hired them. After all, this land belonged to him first. And now, because Brad and I live here, they'll think we're in on it, too."

Michael raised his brows. "I see what ya mean. And I understand your worry. I guess what should be done is ta set a trap ta catch these men and then turn them in ta prove your father's innocence."

"Yes. Brad thought so too. But he also said that that wouldn't be enough. We have to catch the man behind it, and Brad feels whoever he is, he won't be so easy to uncover."

"Aye, lass. He's right," Michael agreed. "The man in charge no doubt has hidden his tracks so well no one will be able ta follow them ta his doorstep. Unless . . ." He frowned, giving his idea some consideration.

"Unless what?" Shauna asked excitedly.

"Well," he shrugged, "there's a couple of ways a man could go about findin' out the truth. Ya can beat it out of a person, for one. But the more civilized method would be ta make a temptin' offer."

"Such as?"

"No man wants ta go to prison." He thought of himself at the top of *that* list. "So ya make the smugglers a deal. The name of their employer for their freedom. After all, they're just puppets. Most of the time men like that don't have the brains it takes ta run such a scheme, so turnin' them loose really poses no danger."

"I think that just might work," Shauna murmured, feeling a lot better now that she had talked it over with someone she trusted. "I really do. And I'll wager Brad will agree, as well."

"Oh, don't do that, Shauna," he warned, his brown

eyes glowing in the fading sunlight.

"Do what?" she asked, alarmed. "Tell Brad? But I must. I can't do this alone."

"I'm sure ya can't," he chuckled. "I mean ya shouldn't wager. It has a way of gettin' ya in trouble."

It took a moment for her to realize he was teasing her, but once she had, she laughed gaily. "That it does, Mr. O'Sullivan. And I swear to you, I've given up that little hobby."

Michael considered her declaration for a moment, as well as the lovely profile she presented to him when she turned her attention on the young maid who appeared then asking if her mistress and Mr. O'Sullivan would like more tea. He was quick to decline the offer and issued a silent word of thanks when Shauna suggested that perhaps he'd care for a glass of wine instead. The couple remained quiet until after Claramae returned with her tray and poured them each a glassful of the dark red liquid, a taste of which Michael gratefully savored with his eyes closed. It wasn't as good as ale, but it far outranked the tea he'd been drinking. Settling back in his chair, he stretched out his long legs and watched the flight of a huge bird soaring effortlessly about the treetops in the horizon.

"Have ya told your husband yet?" he asked after a while.

His question made her laugh. "How could I? He's been gone all day."

"I don't mean about the card game, lass," he replied, lifting his glass to his lips and taking a sip, his gaze still focused on the graceful journey of the bird. "Have ya told him that ya love him?"

Shauna could feel her cheeks pinken instantly. She'd

435

only spent a few hours with this man and he already knew things about her that even she had only come to realize lately. Embarrassed, she studied the wine glass she held. "What makes you think that I do? We've only been married a short time, and you know the conditions of that union."

"Aye. Ya said ya didn't love him when ya took the vows and that he didn't love you." He smiled softly at her. "And that's probably true. But not anymore. I can see the love ya feel for the man in your eyes and hear it in your words whenever ya speak of him. I have yet ta meet your husband, but unless the man's blind, he should know it, too. If not, ya shouldn't hold back. Tell him how ya feel. Ya might be surprised."

Shauna couldn't explain why, but talking about how she felt toward Brad made her uneasy. She laughed nervously, took a sip of her wine, and shifted uncomfortably in her chair.

"Are ya afraid if ya do that you'll find out he doesn't feel the same?"

Shauna hated to admit it, but that truly was the reason. "Yes," she whispered, taking another drink.

"And what happens if ya never take the chance? Ya will spend the rest of your life lovin' a man without touchin' him. Ya'll keep your separate bedrooms and die wonderin' what it would have been like." Sitting up, Michael turned in his chair to face her. "I've had me share of romance, lass, but I can honestly say I have yet ta meet the girl of me dreams. And I can truthfully say that if I was in your husband's shoes, I'd have tried most anythin' ta win your love. Perhaps that's what he's doin', but ya can't see it for the worry ya feel."

Shauna started to reply and changed her mind.

"Ah, Shauna, me love," he quickly responded, setting down his glass and reaching for her hand. "If ya're thinkin' he'll hate ya once he learns about Wrenhaven, let me guarantee ya, he won't. Love is not based on material things. If ya had no place ta live but out under the stars with a blanket of grass for your bed, your feelings will never change. As long as ya have each other—"

"But that's the catch," she interrupted. "I don't know that we do." Pulling free of his hand, she stood. "I'd like to think that. I really would."

"But since ya don't, ya won't risk it," he finished. "So ya'll keep silent about lovin' him, tell him ya lost Wrenhaven ta me, and let him walk out of your life never knowin' otherwise." Shaking his head, Michael came to his feet and crossed his arms over his chest. "Ya're thinkin' with your head, lass, and not your heart."

A half-smile lifted the corner of her mouth as she stared at him. "Are you sure you're not really related to Moira? You sound just like her when you talk like that."

For a second Michael thought he had said something that had given him away. Laughing, he scratched his chin and added, "We're all related to each other in some form if ya think about it long enough. And if Moira has been tellin' ya the same things as I've been sayin', then maybe ya ought to listen to us. Ya might find some truth in it."

A soft smile parted her lips. "Yes, I suppose there is some truth in it." She quickly raised a hand to silence him when he took a breath to add something. "But . . . I must decide when and just how I'll tell Brad. If I decide to admit I love him, it has to be under the right circumstances."

"I agree," Michael avowed. "So why not tonight?"

Shauna's shoulders sagged.

"Hear me out," he exclaimed. "There's no better time ta talk of love than on a moonlit night. The fragrance of your hair, your perfume, the tenderness of the moment will lend a magical aura, one no man alive could escape or resist."

"Trap him," Shauna observed.

"If ya must," Michael beamed. "But I'll tell ya this, lass," he added in all seriousness. "If ya wait another day, I'll step over our boundaries of friendship and tell him meself."

His threat didn't surprise her. "I believe you would." Reaching up, she gently touched his cheek, then turned and went into the house.

"Well, I'll be damned," came a female voice from the shadows.

Spinning around, his eyes searching the darkness, Michael heaved a sigh once he spotted his sister standing there. "Ya shouldn't be for sneakin' up on a man like that," he berated as he picked up his wine glass and finished off his drink in one swallow.

"Had it been anyone else, I'd agree," she grinned, stepping onto the terrace. "But with you it's the only way I'll learn just what kind of a man ya really are."

Michael's brow crimped. "What's that supposed ta mean?"

"It means, dear brother," she whispered as she wrapped an arm around him, "that in the last five minutes I've learned more about ya than I have in me whole lifetime." She jabbed his chest with the end of her finger. "I never thought until now that ya had a heart or a conscience. I see I was wrong."

"Now why would ya think that, Moira Flanagan?"

438

"Because of your behavior. If ya had found a lass as vulnerable as Shauna, ya would have taken advantage."

"That's not true," he denied adamantly. "I have never stepped between a man and a woman in love." A roguish smile kinked his mouth. "Not deliberately, anyway."

Laughing, Moira shook her head and gave her brother a playful slap. "You're the work of the devil, Michael Patrick McCord."

"Aye, that I am," he agreed.

Many thoughts plagued Shauna's mind as she idly paced the floor in Brad's study, the most important being her concern for her father. Although she didn't know what to do exactly, she realized she had to help disprove the accusations brought against her family, and it seemed the easiest way was to catch the smugglers working on Wrenhaven, as Kelly O'Sullivan had suggested. Remembering the gold watch, she went to the desk and sat down behind it to open the top drawer. Perhaps there was something about it that would give her a clue to who owned it. Holding it in her hand, she rose and went to the window where the light was better, turning it over, opening the lid, shaking it, and finally holding it up by the broken chain. But as before, it offered very little, except perhaps that, judging from the numerous scratches on the face and lid, whoever it belonged to had had it a long time. A keepsake, perchance? she wondered. In that case its owner would most certainly want it back, and that would mean the bloody cur would go looking for it. A devious smile lit up her face. And if the man thought he might have lost it down at the river, all Brad had to do was have someone hide among the rocks and trees to watch for him. But whom would he ask? Whom could he trust? Especially since one set of footprints had trailed off toward the manor.

Frowning, she crossed back to the desk and returned the watch to the drawer. That didn't necessarily mean they couldn't trust anyone working here . . . except for Moira, of course. And now, Kelly O'Sullivan. A new thought occurred to her, and she leaned back in the chair, her elbow resting on the arm and one finger tapping her chin. Perhaps Kelly would be willing to do it. It was too dangerous for Moira and since Kelly really owned the property, he'd want to put a stop to any illegal activity going on that might implicate him.

Kelly O'Sullivan, she thought with a smile. She had never met anyone like him before. His patience and understanding amazed her. Any other man who had won a valuable piece of property like Wrenhaven wouldn't have wasted a second claiming it. But not Kelly. He was not only willing to wait, he was sensitive to her plight. He had actually given her advice on how to solve it. With a shake of her head, she rose and went back to the window to look outside, wondering how much longer it would be before Brad came home. Suddenly, Kelly's suggestion that she woo Brad into a receptive mood brought an impish smile to her lips. Some might have considered it as not playing fair, but Shauna was desperate. She didn't want to lose the first man she had ever come to love. Whirling about, she raced across the study and out the door.

The first sight of Wrenhaven after a long trip always made Brad feel good. It looked even better tonight as he spurred his horse up the drive. He hadn't meant to stay away this long, and he wouldn't have if he hadn't run into his old friend Harrison Roxbury. Shamed into having dinner with him, since he hadn't found the time to visit with Harrison the way he had promised he would, Brad had stopped off with him at a quaint little inn shortly after sundown. The meal had been excellent, but Harrison's topic of conversation hadn't been even remotely pleasant. He had heard rumors concerning Brad's new father-in-law, and although Harrison didn't believe them for a minute, he felt Brad should know about the gossip being spread around London. It was absurd, of course, that anyone would think Pierce Radborne was involved with smugglers, and Harrison assured Brad that he had and would continue to challenge anyone who said otherwise. Brad had expressed his gratitude for Harrison's loyalty, certain the man was genuinely sincere, but at the same time he had elected not to mention the episode at the river and the watch Shauna had found. Something bode ill about the whole situation, and until he knew more, he wasn't going to talk about it to anyone. That included his wife, if he could manage not to let on that something was bothering him.

The thought of Shauna and how they had spent last night brought a smile to his lips as he drew his horse in and dismounted. Slipping the reins through the brass ring of the hitching post, he wondered if there might be a chance for an encore. But as he headed up the sidewalk toward the front door, he silently told himself not to count on it. It seemed the only time they made love was after they had argued. He opened the door and went inside, smiling crookedly as he considered which subject

441

would guarantee him heated words with his wife. After all, what better way was there to soothe over a bitter exchange than in bed? But once he had searched the study, parlor, dining room, and kitchen and discovered that Shauna hadn't waited up for him, he lost all hope of a pleasant interlude with her. Disappointed, he headed up the stairs to his bedchambers, pausing at the door to Shauna's room to listen for any sounds that might indicate she was still awake. The silence seemed to mock him, and sadly he continued on to his own room, swinging the door open, stepping inside, and shutting it behind him all in one fluid movement. Perhaps it was best he got some sleep, anyway. He had a long day ahead of him tomorrow.

Brad only peripherally noticed that the balcony doors stood open and that a soft breeze floated in on a ray of moonlight as he crossed to the armoire and opened the door. An unexpected yawn caught him off guard, and while he stretched the tired muscles in his back he kicked off his shoes and slid out of his jacket, which he hung in the wardrobe. Pulling his shirttail free, he unfastened the buttons and shook off the garment, tossing it on a nearby chair as he considered when and how he'd tell Shauna about the rumors concerning her father. She'd, no doubt, be enraged, as well she should be. He didn't like them any better than he imagined Pierce did, but getting angry wouldn't solve the problem. Sitting down on the edge of the bed, he pulled off his stockings and tossed them on the chair with his shirt as he stood up again to unhook the fastening on his breeches. He'd have to take care of the situation down at the river first, then figure out why someone had set out to ruin Pierce Radborne. Once he had those answers, he felt sure he could bring an end to this whole mess.

He was about to slide the breeches off his hips when a strange feeling assailed him, a sense that from somewhere in the darkness a pair of eyes watched his every move. Unnerved, he guardedly turned around, his attention keen as he quickly surveyed the room, every muscle in his tall frame rigid. In that same moment, he noticed a lump in his bed, one that was big enough to be a person hiding under the covers, and a slow, devilish smile curled his mouth as he contemplated who it might be. Glancing back over his shoulder at the armoire, he decided the little prankster deserved to have the joke played on her . . . and just in case he was wrong—which he sincerely doubted—he'd be able to defend himself. Stretching, he retrieved the pistol from the top shelf and cocked the hammer, a sound that stiffened the slender shape draped in the thick quilt.

"Whoever you are, I suggest you move very slowly," he warned, a wide grin tugging at his mouth. "I'd really hate to put a hole in a perfectly good matress. Not to mention the bloodstains. They're so hard to get out."

"Brad, it's me!" came the tiny, frightened voice from beneath the coverlet. "Don't shoot me. I only wanted to surprise you."

"Me who?" he mocked, releasing the hammer and putting the gun away once he recognized his wife's voice.

"Me who?" she echoed in a rage as she jerked the spread down past her head. "Who else were you expecting?"

Moonlight fell across the bed and spotlighted her in its ashen glow, a vision that nearly took his breath away. Gathering his composure, he replied, "Well, to be perfectly honest, Shauna, I didn't ever expect to find you in my bed." He squinted and leaned forward. "That is you, isn't it?"

In a huff, she tossed off the coverlet and sat up. "Of course, it's me," she snapped. "But I'm beginning to wish it wasn't."

"Why? You said you wanted to surprise me, and you did."

She gave him a damning look. "The results weren't exactly what I hoped for." She slid off the other side of the bed and yanked down the skirt of her nightgown. "Would you really have shot me?"

Brad shrugged a wide shoulder. "Would have been a little tricky, seeing as how it wasn't loaded."

Shauna's chin dropped. "*It wasn't loaded*— How *dare* you frighten me like that with an empty pistol!"

"Would you have preferred it wasn't?" he challenged, masking his humor as his gaze devoured the sultry length of her garbed in silk.

Shauna raised her nose in the air. "If it had been, you probably would have shot yourself in the toe, anyway. That is, of course, if you'd had the time to reach it. I could have been a robber searching your room for valuables, you know. You came barging in here without a candle lighting the way and proceeded to disrobe as if you hadn't a care in the world. And the only pistol you had wasn't loaded. A lot of good that would have done you."

The corner of his mouth twitched as he lowered his gaze and slowly rounded the end of the bed. "Then maybe I shouldn't sleep alone," he replied, his dark brown eyes raking suggestively over her. "Or was that your surprise?"

Shauna's face flushed hotly. "It might have been," she returned, her anger of a minute ago fading as she envisioned the two of them locked passionately in each other's arms.

"I missed you today," he said quietly as he took another step closer. "I missed the sight of you, the smell of your perfume, that quirky little smile."

"Quirky?" she laughed.

"Uh huh," he murmured, drawing close. "One side turns downward." He gently reached out to touch her lips with his fingertip. "Right here." He moved within an inch of her, deliberately holding back though his arms ached to embrace her. "And when you laugh, it's like music to my ears. I love to hear you laugh. I love to watch you . . . sitting in a chair reading . . . working in the flowerbed . . . having dinner across the table from me. There isn't much about you I don't love, Shauna." A soft smile parted his lips. "Even your anger. Did you know your eyes turn the color of emeralds when you glower at me? And your hair . . ." He paused to enfold the shiny locks in his hand. "It reminds me of the early morning sun." He chuckled, then added, "That's just what you are: a breath of fresh air. No matter your mood, you awaken in me all the yearnings I've tried so hard to control." The smile returned. "You're a vixen, Shauna Remington, a witch who's beguiled me. I never would have thought that could happen to me, but it has. And I'm thankful for it. If I were to die tomorrow, I could truly say I'd lived a satisfying life . . . and all because you were a part of it."

A tear pooled in the corner of Shauna's eye and her chin trembled as she fought to still her reeling emotions. No one had ever said such wonderful things to her, and although she believed he really meant them, she felt unworthy of such praise. Theirs had been a turbulent, deceitful beginning, and because of her own stupidity, she had allowed the lies to continue. But no more. Tonight—after she made love to him—she would tell him the truth.

"Brad." The name came out before she knew she had wanted to speak. "I wish things had started out differently for us. I wish we could have met at Sir Blakely's party merely as two strangers would meet, rather than the way we did. I wish I had never had a need to blackmail you into marrying me. I'm not sure you'd still feel the same toward me as you do now—" She laughed softly and confessed, "You might not have even noticed me if I hadn't been so insistent. But had something developed between us, it would have been honest feelings."

"You think what I'm feeling now isn't honest?" he asked, his voice low and a pained expression crimping his brow.

"That's not what I meant." She sighed and moved past him to the open balcony doors. "What you feel for me right not is probably your honest feelings, but in a way you were forced into them. You didn't marry me because you loved me. You married me because you had to."

A vague smile lifted his mouth and he quickly hid it. "That's not entirely true," he said, coming to stand behind her and share in the peacefulness of the scenery spread out before them. "I had a choice. I always did. You weren't holding a gun to my head."

"I might as well have been," she whispered miserably. Closing her eyes, she drank in the feeling of his nearness, the masculine scent of him, the excited tingle he always aroused in her. "Why did you marry me?" she dared to ask.

"It's rather hard to put into words, actually," he

admitted with a frown. "And at the time, if someone had asked, I don't think I could have answered."

"Can you now?" She turned slightly to look at him, her back resting against the door frame.

A flash of white teeth showed with his warm smile as he cocked his head and reached out his hand to toy with the lock of gold hair falling over her bosom. "There were many reasons, I suppose. I wanted Wrenhaven, that's true. But I could have found another way to have it, if I had wanted to look for it. So that leaves only you. I had come to the decision long before we met that it was time I settled down. I thought owning my own property would take care of that. Then I saw you at the party, and I realized how wrong I had been. A man can't possibly find peace and happiness unless he has someone to share it with. I liked your spunk, your charm and beauty, your courage and your wit. And I was totally captivated by your audacity in thinking you could force just anyone you chose into marrying you. I guess I saw you as a challenge to my own individuality." He nodded and added, "And I saw a future of never-ending conquests to be achieved. To put it simply, Shauna, I fell in love with that hardheaded, strong-willed, obstinate female who came to my room that night with her marriage proposal *and* her list of conditions."

Shauna couldn't believe her ears. "What?" she breathed.

A warm chuckle escaped him. "I'm saying that that young woman got more than she bargained for. She not only gained a husband, but one who ignored the warning signs. I love you, Shauna Kathleen Remington, and there's nothing you can ever do to change that."

His admission of unlimited love tore away the last remaining fibers of the protective shell in which she had

447

encased her heart. Tears streaming down her face, she threw her arms around his neck and kissed him hard and long and passionately. Blind to everything around her, and especially to the reasons she had become his wife, her ardor grew hot and demanding, and within seconds he returned the fervent embrace. His mouth moved hungrily over hers while his fingers caught the thin straps of her gown and slid them off her shoulders. The silky white fabric glided to the floor and was quickly joined by the breeches he shed. Bathed in the silvery light coming in off the balcony, their hands heatedly explored iron thews, soft flesh, thickly muscled ribs, smooth curves, while their kisses grew fevered. With his mouth still sampling hers, he caught the back of her head in his wide hand, encircled her tiny waist with his other arm, and slowly lowered his treasure to the floor, where moonlight graced the coming together of two lost souls.

A moan escaped Shauna's lips as he trailed hot kisses down her throat to capture a rose-hued peak of one breast, and while his thumb teased the taut nipple of the other, she moved provocatively against his hardened frame. Cool night breezes played along their naked flesh and stirred their passion, and when his hand slipped to her thigh she called out his name in a breathless, urgent whisper. Her long nails raked the sinewy breadth of his back, along his spine to his buttocks, and her mind whirled in blissful ecstasy.

Their open mouths met again, more hungrily than before, and their breathing became ragged, their hearts beating wildly. Locking her fingers in his thick black hair, she thrust her tongue between his lips and arched her body against him, groaning at the pleasure of her naked breasts touching the hardened expanse of his chest. Bending her knee, she pushed up and rolled him beneath her. Rising, her legs straddling him, she tossed her head and tickled his neck and shoulders with her long silken tresses. His dark brown eyes watched her, and the lust she saw burning in them urged her on. Tonight she would be the aggressor. She would show him all he had taught her.

Running her pink tongue over her lower lip in a most sensuous, suggestive manner, she heard him moan and felt his body tremble, and a smile turned the corners of her mouth upward. Tilting her head back, she raised both arms and lifted the heavy golden mane off her neck very slowly, deliberately allowing him full view of her slender naked body: the definition of her ribs, her flat belly, her rounded, firm breasts. Stretching, she purposely thrust out her bosom and raised up on her knees as she trailed a fingertip down the side of her face, along the contour of her creamy white neck, the deep valley between her breasts, across her stomach, over her hipbone, and down her thigh to her knee. It was more than Brad could tolerate as his eyes watched the descent of her tempting invitation, and though he truly wished to view more, his passion raged nearly out of control.

His hand shot upward, trapped her long, velvety hair in a firm grip, and pulled her down to meet his ardent kiss. His heart thundered in his ears. His flesh burned with desire. Pushing down on her knee, he forced her to lie full against him, and in that same surprising moment, he rolled and caught her beneath him.

His manhood, hot and hard, met no resistance once he parted her thighs and sought out its pleasure. Braced on his elbows, his mouth moving hungrily over hers, he sampled the gift she willingly gave him, slowly at first, until his lust consumed him. Then, in a fervor of wild abandonment, they soared together beyond their earthly restraints in search of a heavenly release.

A long while passed before Brad raised his head and rolled from her to lie exhausted at her side. Pushing up on one elbow, she smiled happily at him while she traced the hard-muscled ridges above his lean belly and basked in the glow of his love.

"You know, Shauna," he chuckled after a moment. "We're going to have to learn to curb this uncontrollable appetite we have for each other. It could get a little difficult trying to explain the bruises on my elbows and knees." He sat up and glanced back over his shoulder. "Perhaps next time we should start a little closer to the bed."

Giggling, Shauna raised up on her knees, grabbed his wrist, and pulled him with her as she stood. "Do I take that to mean you're complaining?" she teased, pressing her hands against his chest and pushing him backward toward the bed.

"Just about the location," he promised, a bright sparkle shining in his eyes. She made such a fetching sight with her thick golden hair falling wildly about her shoulders and the blush of their lovemaking still warm in her cheeks that for a second he considered sampling her treasures again. But Shauna had other ideas, and when he raised his arm to encircle her, she ducked beneath them and scooted out of reach. But not before she gave him a healthy shove to send him sprawling backward on the bed. Her light and airy laughter filled his ears, and once he was able to sit up, he moaned his disappointment to see that she was wiggling back into her nightgown again. "You're breaking my heart, Shauna," he groaned playfully. "I had thought this meant we could spend the night together. But there you are all covered up again. Must you leave me to my imaginings?"

Brushing her fingers through her hair, she shook out her mane and bent to retrieve his breeches from the floor. "Do you think you deserve a second try?"

"A second try?" he echoed. "You make it sound like you didn't enjoy it." He made a grab for her when she walked past the bed to drape his breeches over a chair and missed when she agilely whirled out of the way.

"And would your pride be wounded if I said I didn't?" she teased, opening the armoire and reaching for his robe. Tossing it to him, she added, "We have things to talk about . . . important things; so I suggest you put something on."

"How about the two of us covering up with the sheets? We can lie close together and talk . . ." he wiggled his dark brows, "if that's what you really want to do."

Shauna shook her head at him in much the same manner as a mother would her child. "You're worse than a stallion hot on the scent of his mare. Don't you ever tire?"

Her comparison made him laugh. "I certainly hope that isn't how you view this . . . as simple animal lust."

"Is there any other way to see it?" Devilment sparkled in her eyes.

"Well, I'd like to think so," he replied, a mocking frown drawing his dark brows together as if her words had injured him.

"Then I suggest that's exactly what you do about it . . . think." She plopped down in the chair next to the bed—a safe distance from groping hands—and smiled back at him. Her mirth didn't last long, however, when the painful memories of her conversation with Nelson Thorndyke surfaced. "We had a visit today from your partner."

Her statement lacked the rancor that usually accompanied any reference to the man, and Brad quickly realized the seriousness of what she wanted to say. Slipping on the robe, he pulled the sash tight and tossed his legs over the side of the bed. "What did he want, Shauna?"

A long sigh raised and lowered her shoulders. "He'd heard rumors in London about my father—that some members of Parliament think he's a French sympathizer—and they're basing their accusations on the simple fact that his stepfather was the French ambassador to England a *long* time ago. Nelson doesn't believe any of it, but after he explained how the others are thinking, I must confess that it frightens me."

"And what did he say?" Brad asked softly.

Unable to sit still any longer, Shauna left her chair and began to pace back and forth in front of him. "Liggett Dupree—Papa's stepfather—married my grandmother when Papa was a young boy. He had already acquired his wealth by then, so neither Papa nor Grandmother had anything to do with it. And the man died several years before my father and mother met. We're all very innocent of any wrongdoing on my step-grandfather's part."

"Wrongdoing? Such as?" He caught her hand and pulled her down beside him on the bed.

"Papa only talked of it once, and only then because I pressed him. Nelson filled in the rest today. Apparently, there were some powerful men in Parliament who feared at one time that France would take over the rule of England, and because these men thought only of themselves, they wanted to be assured of their continued place in the government. They thought that by winning my step-grandfather's friendship they would have that. Thus, they used their authority to force the weaker men out, and in turn gave their property and money to the ambassador. I have no way of knowing if my step-grandfather approved or not, only that he took whatever was offered him. According to Nelson, the repercussions were awful."

"How so?"

"The acts drove several victims to suicide. Their families were shamed and many were left on the streets to beg."

A frown knotted Brad's brow. "I can understand the resentment *then* and how it would be aimed at Dupree, but what has that to do with your father?"

Shauna clamped her teeth together to still her quivering chin. "Nelson said there are rumors going around about Papa being involved with smugglers. Nelson also said that because of it, memories have been stirred. Those who were affected by Papa's stepfather see Papa as the same sort of man to prey on the weak, and he'll repeat what his stepfather did. Brad?" A sob choked her and she grabbed his hand. "You and I know none of this is true, but I'm scared."

Covering her slender fingers with his larger ones, he drew her hand to his lips and tenderly kissed it. "I know. I would be, too, if someone attacked my family in such a covert method."

"But it's not just *my* family, Brad. It includes you and me."

"Why do you say that? Did Nelson indicate we were as suspect as your father?"

"No. But think about it. He said the rumors claimed Papa was mixed up in smuggling, and you suggested that perhaps the men at the river were smugglers."

"I have thought about it," he admitted solemnly. "In fact I had planned to tell you that the reason I was late coming home tonight was because I ran into an old friend. We had dinner together and he told me pretty much everything Nelson told you."

"Then it's true? I mean, people really are talking about Papa?"

Brad shrugged. "Seems that way."

"Oh, God," she moaned. "What can we do?"

A dark frown shadowed Brad's eyes as he contemplated his idea. "I guess the first thing is to put a stop to whatever's going on down at the river. If I'm right and they are smugglers, we'll have to find out who they're working for. At least that way your father's name can't be linked to *them*." He shook his head. "But that might not be very easy. Their kind isn't always willing to talk."

"So, you beat it out of them. Or . . ." She perked up, anxious to relay Kelly O'Sullivan's advice. "You offer them a deal."

Her enthusiasm and her surprising, unnatural suggestion to use violence made him laugh. "*Beat* it out of them?"

Shauna straightened. "Yes. It's one way, but Kelly says you'd have better luck giving them a choice: prison or the name of their employer."

Brad's brow wrinkled and his complexion paled a little, but in the muted light Shauna didn't notice. "Kelly?" he repeated. "Who's Kelly?"

Flinching, she silently cursed her carelessness. She had wanted to wait for a better time to tell him about their visitor than now. Forcing a weak laugh, she replied, "Kelly O'Sullivan. He's Moira's cousin."

"Moira's cousin?" he echoed.

Shauna wasn't sure if it was her imagination or just her nerves that made her hear the doubt in his voice. "Yes," she answered faintly. "He arrived this morning just shortly after you left. He's here to visit Moira for a spell."

Brad shot a glance back at the door. "He's here? In the house?"

His reaction confused her. "Well, what did you expect? That I'd have him sleep in the stable?"

"No, of course not," he murmured as he slowly came to his feet and rounded the end of the bed as if he planned to leave the room. He stopped suddenly and faced her. "Does Moira know he's here?"

Shauna's smooth brow puckered. "Now what kind of a question is that? Certainly, she knows. They spent most of the day together. I told you, he arrived this morning."

Brad seemed to be satisfied with that until another thought struck him, and he scowled at her. "You also said he had ideas about the smugglers. Does that mean you discussed it with him?"

"I know I promised not to tell anyone," she began in her own defense, "but Kelly could see how upset I was after Nelson left and that I needed to talk to someone."

"But you don't even know who he is." He shook his head to correct that statement. "I mean, you don't know enough about him to be sure you can trust him."

"I know enough!" she blurted out. She'd trust her life to Kelly O'Sullivan. But, of course, Brad didn't know that, or why she felt that way. Nor could she tell him . . . not just yet, anyway. "I. . . I mean he's Moira's cousin. What more do I need to know?" Nervous, she decided to put him on the defensive. "Are you trying to imply there's a reason I shouldn't? Do you know something about him that I don't?"

Brad grew visibly uneasy. He cleared his throat, rubbed the back of his neck, and couldn't seem to stand in one place any longer. Or bear to have his wife's questioning look directed his way. "No. No, I don't know anything about him." He turned away and muttered under his breath, "Is *that* ever putting it mildly."

"Then let's drop it, all right? It's too late to change the fact that I told him about our problem, anyway." She watched him very closely, and when he seemed to agree, she added, "And who knows, maybe he could actually be of some help. I think his last suggestion was pretty good."

"About offering a deal?" he asked halfheartedly as he went to stand in the doorway leading out onto the balcony. "Yes. It's something to be considered." With his arms folded over his chest, his feet braced apart, he stared out across the gardens, though he honestly wasn't looking at anything in particular. He had too much on his mind at the moment to be admiring the scenery.

"So?" she urged, bothered by his lengthy silence. "Have you any ideas about how we're going to catch these men? We mustn't wait too long. Papa needs all the help he can get and as soon as we can give it."

"Yes, I know. But I really don't think your father's in any immediate danger."

"You don't?" she asked hopefully. "Why? What makes you say that?"

"Well, so far they're only rumors. There's no proof to back up any of it. And I think once we've taken care of *our* little problem, I can set my mind on figuring out why someone wants to ruin Pierce Radborne."

Shauna's lovely face crimped in confusion. "I'm not following you."

"I could be wrong," he admitted as he faced her, all thoughts of their house guest having faded. "It's really just a feeling I have, a hunch."

"Go on," she begged coming to stand next to him.

"As we've said repeatedly, they're only rumors . . . or gossip. And what's the definition of gossip? The spreading of hearsay, untruths. If someone labeled you a gossip, it would make you angry, wouldn't it?" When she nodded, he asked why.

"Because a person who tells things that aren't so is usually a very callous, mean, and sometimes vendictive—" Now she understood. "Oh my God, Brad. Are you saying that whoever started these rumors had a wish to get even with Papa for something?"

"That, or they want him out of the way."

"Of what?"

Brad shook his head. "I don't know. It's something we'll have to ask the man once we find out who he is." His dark eyes softened as they drank in the beautiful vision of his wife standing before him. "And we will, Shauna. I promise you that. Your father will come to no harm as long as I'm here to do something about it."

"You really mean that, don't you?" she asked, suddenly aware of the way they were dressed, the moonlit night, and gentle breeze, of the room in which they stood with its wide, inviting bed, and the fact that they were married and all was proper.

"Yes. I really mean it. I admire your father and I know him for the honest man that he is. I also know he'd never do anything to shame his family. He loves you too much." His brown hand reached out to trace the delicate line of her cheek. "Nearly as much as I," he whispered.

A pang of sorrow stabbed at her heart and she lowered her gaze. "I wonder," she murmured, turning away to step out onto the balcony, "just how much that really is." The nearness of him when he came to stand behind her and gently stroke her arms sent a warm chill through her, and she closed her eyes and let her head fall back against his shoulder.

457

"More than life itself, Shauna, for, you see, you *are* my life. Without you, I would cease to be."

"But, surely, you would find another if I was taken from you . . . for whatever reason," she tested, pained by the secrets she kept. "If your love for me turned to hate and you cast me aside, you would find another."

Warm laughter rumbled in his chest. "There is no chance of that, sweet Shauna. I searched too long and hard for the woman of my dreams to let anything take her away from me." He turned her in his arms and lightly kissed her brow. "My only hope is that someday you will learn to love me."

Tears filled her eyes and spilled over the rim of her lashes to fall unheeded down her cheeks. "Oh, Brad," she wept, "I don't deserve someone like you."

"Hush," he murmured, brushing his lips against the corner of her mouth. "You deserve all I can give you, and more. 'Tis I who am undeserving."

"Nay!" she avowed, throwing her arms around his neck. "Never that. 'Twas I who played games, who tricked you, stole from you. You turned your cheek not once, but twice, and still you stand before me as if you have much to prove. You have done that . . . time and time again. You have bared your soul and given me your heart, and all without the promise of a future or a word in kind." She stretched up on tiptoes, her body pressed against his and whispered, "Well, you have it, my husband. I *do* love you, and God willing, it will be enough."

His warm, dark eyes smiled down into hers as he slipped his arms around her and pulled her close. "More than enough," he murmured, his open mouth lowering to capture hers.

Chapter Sixteen

Morning gathered in the eastern sky. Wisps of white clouds, stained in the pinks and yellows of the rising sun, floated effortlessly across the pale blue horizon, and song birds filled the air with their sweet chorus. Gentle breezes stirred the tall grasses and carried with them the promise of a beautiful day.

Shauna viewed the loveliness from the comfort of the wide bed, her nakedness draped in the thin sheet she had drawn carelessly over her bosom, her long, flowing mane of gold cushioned on a white pillow, and a soft smile curling the corners of her mouth. Beside her lay her sleeping husband, and while she listened to his steady, restful breathing, she recalled the blissful night they had spent locked in each other's arms, words of love and devotion trailing from their lips. Yet with the dawn came the harsh reality that within a few hours she must tell him the truth. Sadness darkened her pale green eyes and spoiled the serenity of the moment. Turning her head, she quietly studied the man who shared her bed. Thick black lashes lay against his suntanned face, and the thin white scar gleamed in contrast to his bronze complexion. A slight frown marred his brow, and for a second she

459

wondered if he sensed her thoughts even in his dreams. His broad shoulders, his thickly muscled chest with its crisp matting of dark hair and sinewy arms tempted her to run her fingertips over the strong definition of curves. But as she raised her hand, he stirred and rolled to his side, presenting her with a view of the wide expanse of his back, and she changed her mind.

"I love you, Brad Remington," she whispered. "Until the day I die, no matter what happens between us, I will always love you." Lifting the coverlet from her, she quietly stole from the bed to gather up her nightgown and slip it on. At the door, she paused to watch him again, tears streaming down her face. After today they would never again sample the sweetness they had experienced this night past, and she had only herself to blame. Biting her lower lip to still her sobs, she lifted the latch and hurried from the room.

"You're up early, lass," Michael smiled brightly, turning at the sound of someone coming out onto the terrace and seeing Shauna. His warm, appreciative gaze followed the slender length of her from the top of her golden head, down the shapely curves covered in pink-and-white-striped cotton, to the pink satin slippers on her feet and up again. "Ya look grand." He reached to pull out a chair at the wrought iron table beside him and said, "I was about ta have me breakfast. Would ya honor me with your presence?"

Shauna hesitated a moment, glancing back over her shoulder as if looking for someone. Seeing that they were alone—for the time being, anyway—she nodded and stepped forward to accept his offer. "Have you seen

Moira this morning?"

Michael shook his head as he sat down next to her to pour them both a cup of tea from the silver teapot Claramae had brought him. "Are ya lookin' for her for some particular reason?"

"No," Shauna quickly answered. "I'm not really looking for her at all." She smiled weakly and took the cup and saucer he handed her. "That's why I asked. I'd prefer not seeing her this morning. At least not until after I talk with Brad." She raised the cup to her lips and winced when the hot tea burned her tongue.

"Am I ta understand he's not come home yet?"

"No. He's here," she advised, setting the cup and saucer back down on the table. "He returned home late last night."

"Than ya haven't talked to him," Michael concluded, leaning back in his chair to study the curious look on her face.

A tiny shoulder jutted upward. "Yes and no. I talked to him, but not about you. I mean, I told him the story I'd made up about you, but not the truth. It . . ." She frowned and dropped her gaze to her lap. "It just wasn't the right time."

A playful, knowing smile lifted his mouth. "Was it right for somethin' else, lass?" He laughed wholeheartedly at the blush that instantly darkened her fair cheeks. "Am I ta assume ya took the opportunity ta tell him ya love him? Ya certainly wouldn't pass up a chance like that, now would ya?"

His good-natured jest eased some of her distress, and she smiled. "Yes, I told him that I loved him," she grinned, her face hot. "Does that make you happy?"

"Me?" he chuckled. "I'm thinkin' it made *him*

461

happy." He tilted his head, trying to see her face when Shauna lowered her chin and shadowed her eyes with her hand against her brow. "It did, didn't it?"

"I suppose," she replied, fighting her embarrassment and the strong urge to laugh. "Could we change the subject?"

"Sure," he beamed, delighted that things promised to be all right between Shauna and her husband. "What would ya like ta discuss?" He picked up his cup of tea, took a sip, cringed at the bland taste and set the cup back down. If he were dying of thirst, he'd have to think twice about drinking that horrible stuff. A shot of whiskey, a glass of wine, or a mug of ale were more to his liking, no matter what time of day it was. He even preferred water to tea. He shook off the lingering taste of it and settled his attention on his lovely companion, frowning once he saw her troubled expression. "What is it, lass?"

"I was wondering how you'd react if you were Brad and I told you I had gambled away your home and married you anyway." Her soft green eyes glanced up at him.

"Well," he began, uncomfortable with the question. He wanted to tell her that Brad couldn't possibly be even half as angry as she was going to be once she learned who Kelly O'Sullivan really was. "It's hard for me ta know what Brad will say, lass. We're two very different men."

"I don't think so," she quickly said. "You're both kind, sensitive, straightforward, understanding—"

"Whoa there, lass," he begged, raising his hand to silence her. "You're gettin' carried away. I can't be speakin' for your husband, but I know I'm not what I obviously seem to ya." He scowled and quickly jerked himself out of the chair to pace the flagstone terrace. "I have me faults, and there are those who would say they number in the hundreds."

"I've never seen any of them," Shauna vowed, surprised by his outburst.

He raised a finger in the air. "Ah . . . and 'tis because ya don't know me all that well."

"I know enough to know you're the first compassionate, understanding friend I've ever had. I consider Moira my friend, too, but she has never stood back and let me fall flat on my face without first berating me for my foolishness. And in this instance, she really doesn't understand my need to wait."

"Now don't be so hard on Moira," he replied. "She does what she thinks is right by ya. She loves ya like a sister. She told me so, and comin' from Moira that's quite a compliment." He turned away to pace again, missing the puzzled look on his companion's pretty face. "And an honor," he mumbled, more to himself than to Shauna. "She hasn't had too many chances ta say she loved anyone as kin."

A noise behind them cut short any further discussion of Moira and her feelings, as they both turned and found the very one about whom they spoke standing in the open doorway. The tight line of her mouth and the hard look in her dark eyes told them that she was upset about something, and they could only assume they had been overheard. But before any of them could speak their peace or apologize, Brad's tall frame appeared beside her.

"Have I interrupted something?" he asked once he noticed how uneasy everyone seemed to be, his gaze shifting from the woman at his side to the dark-haired stranger on the terrace and finally on his wife. Shauna quickly came to her feet and hurried toward him.

"Not at all, Brad," she assured him, thankful he had chosen this particular moment to come looking for her. She neither wanted to explain her comment to Kelly about Moira or to listen to that one's inevitable lecture on her mistress's inability to face reality. "We were just waiting for Claramae to serve breakfast," she replied, ignoring what she guessed would be a heated look from her maid.

Michael, however, wasn't as fortunate. With a shrug, he smiled lamely at his sister and turned to meet the man he had heard so much about and whom he had grown to envy in the past twenty-four hours.

"Brad," Shauna smiled, drawing her husband toward their guest, "I'd like you to meet Kelly O'Sullivan. Kelly, my husband, Brad."

While the two men exchanged a warm handshake, Shauna glanced covertly over at Moira and motioned with a toss of her blond head for Moira to leave the group alone. Shauna knew she had pushed her maid to the limit, and she feared the stubborn Irishwoman would ruin everything just by the look on her face. She was sure of it when Moira returned her gesture with a defiant shake of her head. Shauna tried again, scowling at her and jerking her head toward the door. Moira folded her arms in front of her and gave her mistress a challenging glare.

"So, Shauna says you're here visiting Moira," Brad was saying, and Shauna forced herself to turn her attention back to the men.

"Aye, that I am," Michael nodded. "And I must admit it's good to see me sister after all these years."

Shauna's heart flew to her throat, and her eyes widened in alarm. Cousin! She's your cousin! she wanted to scream. Oh God, now you've done it! Brad knows I was lying!

"Sister?" Brad questioned, glancing briefly at his wife. "I thought Shauna said Moira and you were cousins."

Michael straightened instantly, his tan complexion darkening a little. "She did?" He shifted his attention to her. Knowing it was too late to correct the error, he realized he'd have to do a lot of fast talking to get out of this one. "I . . . I'm sorry, lass, if I . . . well, I mean I must have misled ya. Moira's me sister."

Before Shauna could answer, her husband's strong arm came around her narrow waist and gave her a playful squeeze. "It's very possible she misunderstood, Mr. O'Sullivan. Shauna's had a lot on her mind lately." He smiled softly at her, then kissed her brow and offered an invitation for everyone, including Moira to sit at the table. Once they had, Brad turned his attention on the Irishwoman. "I would imagine you were quite surprised to see your brother, Moira."

"Surprised?" she answered coldly. "I guess ya could say I was surprised." She shifted her icy stare on Michael. "How long has it been since ya last came ta visit your sister, *Kelly?*"

"A few years," he answered, though the glare he gave the woman spoke a hundred words. He didn't like being caught in the middle any more than Moira liked having him there. But it didn't mean she should help it along. He truly liked Shauna Remington, and what he was doing was cruel. He knew that now. If only he had been honest with her at the start . . . if only he *could* be honest with her. . . .

"And how long are you planning to stay?" Brad asked, distracted for a moment when Claramae arrived with their breakfast. "You're welcome here for as long as you like." Picking up his knife, Brad began spreading jelly over his biscuit. "In fact, if you'd like to make it permanent, I could use the extra help building and running the factory I'm planning to erect here on Wrenhaven."

Both Shauna's and Moira's eyes fell on Michael in a flash. Shauna's had a look of pleading in them. Moira's held the threat of death. And Michael tried very hard to pretend he didn't notice either one.

"'Tis generous of ya ta offer," Michael answered as he concentrated on his plate of food. "But I haven't given much thought to me future." He stole a glance at Moira, then studied the slice of ham he was cutting. "And as Moira can tell ya, I don't stay in one place for very long." He stabbed the piece of meat with his fork, raised it to his mouth, looked first at Shauna, then Moira and added, "But since the idea is a temptin' one, I think I'll be takin' ya up on it."

"Ya will not!" Moira exclaimed, drawing the focus of everyone's eyes.

"And why not, little sister?" Michael challenged, his handsome face a picture of pure surprise, though his dark eyes held a hint of devilment only Moira recognized. "I'd be earnin' me keep. And judgin' from what ya've told me already, the Remingtons could use me help."

"About as much as they could use—"

"Moira!" Shauna admonished. "Don't be rude. Kelly's welcome here for as long as he'd like to stay."

The woman's tiny frame stiffened at the reprimand, and even though she took a breath to argue, she elected in the same instant not to say another word. She did, however, cast Michael another warning look, then asked to be excused, saying she had work to do and couldn't afford the time for idle chatter. Only Michael understood what she meant by idle chatter: that as long as Shauna didn't know the truth, Moira could argue all she wanted and it wouldn't do her a bit of good. Michael was Shauna's guest, not Moira's.

Brad's dark brown eyes settled their loving gaze on the beautiful woman he called his wife as Shauna apologized for her maid's outburst. She looked radiant this morning, and he could only hope it had something to do with how they had spent last night. He had waited a long time to hear her say that she loved him, and now that she had, he wondered if the trick he'd played on her would ruin it for him. His gaze shifted to the dark-haired man sitting across from him, and he was suddenly very glad Shauna was already married. This tall, good-looking Irishman might have posed a threat otherwise. Lifting his cup of tea and taking a drink, he smiled vaguely. And then again, maybe he wouldn't. Not if Shauna knew . . .

The rest of their breakfast passed uneventfully as the men talked about the factory Brad planned to build, the equipment needed to run it, and how many men Brad would have to hire to assure its success. The conversation turned then to the location of the building and how the river would be of great benefit in moving the finished product as well as bringing in supplies. At this point Brad openly admitted his concern about the discovery Shauna had made there and their discussion grew quite serious, ending with Michael's offer to help solve the mystery any way he could.

Shauna had sat by quietly listening to the men talk, and by the time Kelly pushed away from the table, stood, and held out his hand to Brad to confirm his pledge, Shauna recognized the possibility of a lasting friendship

467

developing between the two men. It was sad, however, that it would never come to be, and she fought hard not to let her sorrow show as she watched Kelly O'Sullivan walk back into the house.

"He's a nice man, Moira's brother," Brad remarked as he leaned back in his chair and studied the Irishman's strong gait. "I hope he'll stay here at Wrenhaven, despite his sister's objections. He's got a good sense for business, and he'll be a great help to me." A smile curled his mouth as he picked up his teacup again. "His devil-may-care attitude sort of reminds me of someone else I knew a few years ago."

"Oh?" Shauna replied nervously. The time had come to tell him the truth about Kelly O'Sullivan, but she was having a difficult moment saying it. "And who does he remind you of?"

Brad's deep brown eyes twinkled. "Me."

"You?" she echoed. "Why do you think that?"

Leaning in, his hands cradling his cup as he sat it back down in the saucer, he chuckled and replied. "I don't know exactly. Maybe it's because he seems to have no direction in his life . . . or that it doesn't seem to bother him. Even if Moira changes her mind and begs him to stay, I don't think he will for too long. He's got a restless spirit."

"Is that what you had?"

He smiled warmly at her and reached over to enfold her tiny hand in his. "Until I met you."

His compliment brought a blush to her cheeks. "And what had meeting me to do with it?"

"Everything," he answered, raising the palm of her hand to his lips. "I had the notion I was ready to settle down, but I wasn't positive until I saw you." The happiness in his eyes disappeared suddenly, and a troubled expression darkened them. Letting go of her hand, he came to his feet and turned away from her to walk several steps toward the gardens.

Seeing the instant change in him, Shauna quickly rose and followed him. "What's wrong?" she asked, standing at his elbow her hand touching his arm.

An awful silence hung between them, one Shauna could neither understand nor cared to figure out. Perhaps it was only her conscience, but she sensed he was about to say something that would severely alter their lives.

"I think it's time we were honest with each other," he answered quietly, his gaze locked on the ever-brightening eastern horizon, and Shauna's heart thumped heavily in her chest. "I know who Kelly O'Sullivan is . . . or I should say, who he isn't. He isn't the man you were led to believe he is. *This* Kelly O'Sullivan is actually Michael McCord, and he really *is* Moira's brother."

At first what he had said didn't register with Shauna. Of course, Kelly was Moira's brother. The three of them had agreed on that. She blinked, frowning. Well, not really. He was supposed to be her cousin—that was what she had told Brad—but Kelly had forgotten. He'd gotten mixed up and said she was his sister. But once Kelly explained, Brad had believed she had merely misunderstood him. She glanced toward the house. Michael McCord? Kelly O'Sullivan was really Michael McCord? Then where was the real Kelly O'Sullivan? Why had Michael McCord pretended to be him? Why had Moira played along with it? Her head began to spin, and the buzzing in her ears grew so loud she couldn't hear Brad calling out her name. Moira knew about Kelly O'Sullivan—so why would she allow her brother to assume his identity? What was the need? In a fog, she turned toward the back entrance to the house. It certainly explained why Moira was so nervous around Kelly—she shook her head—Michael. She had been afraid he would say something to give it away. As she walked, her temper began to simmer. By the time she reached the door, it was raging. They had played her for a fool, and she wanted to know why!

"Shauna, wait!" Brad called, hurrying to catch up with her as her slender figure, tight with fury, disappeared into the house. "I can explain. Please, Shauna, it's not their fault." He broke into a run once he realized she wasn't listening and nearly collided with Barnes coming onto the terrace when the man's untimely appearance placed him in Brad's path.

"Oh, excuse me, sir," Barnes apologized. "I'm afraid I wasn't looking where I was going."

"It's quite all right," Brad hastily replied, stepping to his left to go around, only to have Barnes move in the same direction. Surprised to find the way blocked, he jerked to his right. But Barnes, thinking to get out of the way, shadowed Brad's move, and they accidently bumped shoulders. Impatient, Brad stepped back and straightened his frame. "Are you dancing with me for some special reason, or might I be excused?"

Flustered, Barnes tugged on the hem of his jacket. "I . . . I came looking for you to inform you that you have a visitor, sir. He's waiting in your study."

Brad didn't have the time to entertain guests. He had to find Shauna and explain. "Who is it?" he frowned.

"The sheriff, sir. He says it's important and that he'd like to speak with you alone."

Dealing with his wife's bruised feelings suddenly didn't seem as important as it had a second ago. An urgent meeting with John Lundstrom could only mean something dreadful had happened —and more likely it had to do with Pierce Radborne. "Thank you, Barnes," Brad replied with a heavy sigh as he turned and brushed past the man. He'd talk with Lundstrom and let Moira contend with Shauna's rage for now.

Told she would find her maid upstairs, Shauna thanked Claramae and headed that direction, her skirts held high and her eyes snapping fire. At the landing of the circular staircase, she hesitated a moment, trying to decide just where Moira was, when she heard the muffled sounds of angry voices coming from Kelly's room.

"Kelly," she growled between clenched teeth as she lowered her chin and stormed the hall.

"You're a damn fool, Michael Patrick McCord!" she heard Moira howl through the thick wooden barrier, and she paused outside the door long enough to square her shoulders and gather her most demeaning assortment of words to throw at the siblings.

"*I'm* a fool?" he retaliated. "I walked in in the middle of this whole crazy mess. Ya can't be blamin' me for what her husband's done."

Some of Shauna's rage ebbed at the mention of Brad, and she let go of the knob she was about to turn.

"Oh, so now ya think it's *his* fault," Moira's shrill voice accused.

"And who else would ya blame? He dressed up in a red beard, a wig, and a mask and presents himself to his wife as Kelly O'Sullivan. He lets the poor lass go on thinkin'

471

she's gambled away his home, and for what reason, may I ask? Ta punish her? Ta teach her a lesson? *He's* the damn fool, if ya ask me."

"Well, no one's askin' ya!" Moira shouted back. "But just so ya know he isn't the heartless ingrate ya think he is, I'll tell ya why. He fell in love with Shauna practically the same day he met her, but he knew it would take a lot of work on his part ta make her fall in love with him. She was spoiled and had a strong hatred of all men."

"And he thinks this will change it?" Michael bellowed. "He'll be damn lucky if she doesn't take a pistol and blow his fool head off. Couldn't he see how much she loved him? Did he have ta play a trick?"

"It wasn't a trick!" Moira argued. "It was an accident."

"Ha!"

"Michael McCord, if ya don't shut your mouth and listen, I'm goin' ta lay me fist to your ear." A silence followed, during which Shauna drew a trembling breath and blinked back her tears as she leaned heavily against the door. "When he found out Shauna hadn't told him about the party at Sir Blakely's, he figured she was up ta somethin'. No one could blame him, since she had, in a way, blackmailed him into marryin' her. She was capable of most anythin'. So he decided ta find out for himself. That's why he dressed the way he did. And he never introduced himself as Kelly O'Sullivan. It was just a name he picked ta sign his letters, one he hoped would force her ta admit the truth."

If Michael wished to further argue the point, Shauna didn't stay around long enough to listen. The pain she felt tearing at her heart, the humiliation, and her inability to understand any of it sent her racing back down the stairs. She had to get away. She had to have time to think. She had to decide whether any of the sweet words Brad had whispered every time they made love were true or not. She had to sort out the truth from the fantasy.

"May I close this?" John Lundstrom asked, nodding at the door while Brad rounded his desk to sit down in the chair. "I don't think you want anyone hearing what I have to say."

"Of course," Brad agreed, certain the man meant Shauna. He waited until after the latch clicked quietly shut, then motioned for the sheriff to sit down. Leaning forward against the edge of the desk, he cupped his hands and silently prepared himself for the worst, though once Lundstrom began speaking, Brad quickly realized he hadn't come to Wrenhaven to discuss Pierce Radborne.

"Some will probably say I'm taking the coward's way out of this, and I probably am. But I thought you'd be better at handling the tragic news I have. I know how much Tyler meant to his parents and sister."

The hair on the back of Brad's neck stood out. "You're speaking in the past tense, sheriff."

Lundstrom's fluffy white brows dipped downward. "Yes, Mr. Remington, I am. Tyler Radborne's body was found late yesterday afternoon floating in the River Ouse about two and a half leagues north of Cambridge."

"Bloody hell," Brad groaned, heaving himself from the chair to stand at the window. He was quiet for a long moment, trying to get a grip on his sorrow. "How'd it happen?"

"We're not really sure. He could have drowned. But . . ."

"But what?" Brad demanded as he spun back around.

473

"But I don't think so. There were bruises on his neck and a lump above his right eye. He'd been dead for several hours, so his horse could have run off if Tyler had been thrown. It would justify the knot, but the marks on his throat make me doubt it was an accident."

"Murder," Brad whispered, even though he knew that was what Lundstrom meant.

"Yes, sir. That's what I'm afraid of. And it's why I wanted to talk to you first. I thought maybe you'd know why Tyler was so far from home."

Brad's stomach knotted and he sank back down in the chair. "He went there a couple of days ago looking for a carpenter I wanted to hire to build my factory."

"What's the carpenter's name?"

"Edmondson. Zack Edmondson. But if you're thinking he had anything to do with it, I can assure you he didn't."

"Why's that, Mr. Remington?"

"Because the man was a good family friend years ago."

"People change."

"Yes, they do. But once you meet Zack you'll know why I'm sure he had nothing to do with Tyler's death."

Lundstrom could see how much it pained Brad to talk about his brother-in-law, but it was his duty to ask questions. "Then would you mind saving me the trip?"

Spotting the wine decanter on the corner of his desk. Brad reached out and caught the bottle by the neck. "Would you care for a drink, sheriff?" When Lundstrom shook his head, Brad poured a stout measure into one glass and took a long swallow. "Zack is a very little man, not much taller than five feet, and thin. And by now he's probably sixty years old. He's no match for someone Tyler's size and age. Besides, he'd have no reason. You'd

474

be chasing daydreams if you went after him."

"Then who should I be chasing? Any ideas?"

Brad wanted to say that the sheriff should start looking right here on Wrenhaven, that somehow this whole bizarre situation *had* to be tied in with what was happening to Pierce. But he didn't. He couldn't. It was something he'd have to find out on his own. "No. No ideas. What about you? Have you talked with anyone yet who might have seen Tyler the day he was killed?"

"Not yet. But someone had to have seen something. Or heard it." Lundstrom pushed his tired frame from the chair. "It's really not my job, seeing as how it happened in another town, but I'm heading for Cambridge. I liked Tyler and I respect his father. Pierce did me a favor one time, and I'd like to pay him back. Can I assume you'll talk to Pierce and his wife? And that you'll tell them how sorry I am and that I'll do everything possible to find Tyler's killer? He didn't deserve to die like that." He shook his head. "No one does. Except the bastard who killed him."

"Yes, sheriff, I'll talk to them," Brad replied solemnly as he stood and rounded the desk to shake Lundstrom's hand and walk with him from the room. "Keep me informed of any progress. And if you need something, be sure to let me know."

"I will," the sheriff nodded. When they had reached the front door, he stopped and glanced back down the foyer as if he was looking for someone. "Please convey my sympathy to your wife. I know they were close." Once Brad assured him that he would, Lundstrom opened the door and mumbled with a shake of his head, "It will be a pleasure watching the bloody cur hang."

Brad stood silently in the doorway until long after the

sheriff had mounted and had ridden off down the lane. Telling Shauna that her brother was dead was the hardest thing he had ever been asked to do. Yet knowing of no way out of it, he truly wished he could just pretend Sheriff Lundstrom had never paid him a visit. With shoulders sagging, Brad slowly closed the door and turned for the stairs.

Blinded by tears of rage, frustration, and hurt, Shauna had fled the house and raced out into the gardens, unmindful of the direction she had taken, only that no matter how far she walked, it wouldn't be far enough. When she came to the clearing, she veered off to her left and sought the cover of trees. The last thing she wanted right now was to have Brad or Moira find her. She needed to be alone with her grief. She had to have time to make sense of what she had learned.

The way grew treacherous when the dense foliage, prickly bushes, and decayed tree branches hampered her step. She stumbled several times, falling painfully to her knees and snagging the skirt of her pink-and-white-striped dress. Yanking it free, she ignored the sound of rending cloth and continued on until her strength had waned and sheer exhaustion brought her to a staggering halt at the base of a huge oak. Sliding down along its trunk, she collapsed onto the ground in tears.

Her rage wanted to claim that Brad had planned this all along . . . from the moment she had approached him with her offer. She had insulted him, angered him, forced him into something he wanted no part of, and he had decided right then to get even. Hadn't he admitted to her one time that he wanted to teach her a lesson? She had thought he'd meant it in regard to her showing up at his door unchaperoned. Now she wasn't so sure. What he had truly meant was that he wanted to prove to her that he wasn't the kind of man she could mold to fit her needs. A sob shook her and she hugged her arms to her. Had what she'd proposed been that awful that he had had to seek revenge to such an extreme? Was it a part of his plan to make her fall in love with him, then laugh in her face? And why involve Moira?

Her agony weighed heavily against her chest, and she struggled just to breathe. *Moira.* Moira had been her friend and companion for a very long time. What had Brad done to turn the woman against her? Had he poisoned her mind with untruths? Had he promised her money for her silence? Her help? Or merely convinced her that he loved his wife? Pulling up her knees, she wrapped her arms around them and buried her face in her skirts, weeping forlornly when it seemed everyone had deserted her. Brad had even won her brother's friendship. Tyler never came to visit *her.* He came to see Brad. Roanna liked Brad too. That had been painfully obvious. And if she asked her father. . . .

"Oh, Papa," she whispered. "Have I lost you, too?"

The snapping of a twig behind her instantly brought her to full awareness. Her head came up, ears alert and her eyes wide as she listened for a clue to the intruder's whereabouts. The rustling of leaves to her left and in back of her made her cringe. The noise was much too close, and it was in that same instant, while she was tyring to decide if it was Brad or Moira, that she realized she had aimlessly ventured toward the river. Her heart thundering in her ears, she slowly shifted to her knees and turned around, her body pressed against the tree trunk to steady her balance and to mask her presence as she ever so slowly peeked out to see who had stumbled across her place of refuge.

"Mr. Rutherford," she breathed, too low to be heard. What was the groundskeeper doing out here? His job only included caring for the lawns surrounding the manor and the gardens in back. He had no reason to be this far from the house, unless Brad had sent him to look for her. Her chin trembled and she clamped her teeth together. But of course. Brad wouldn't come himself. He'd have someone else do it for him. She didn't really matter to him anymore. He had what he wanted. He had Wrenhaven. Fresh tears burned her eyes, and she stifled the sob that threatened to give her away. Ducking back behind the tree, she laid her brow against the rough bark. fighting for control, struggling to turn her heartache into hatred. Moira had been absolutely right when she told Michael that her mistress's feelings toward men were anything but complimentary. She detested them, abhorred their arrogance, their conceit, and how they thought all women too unimportant for anything more worthwhile than bearing their children.

"And you're no different, Brad Remington," she hissed beneath her breath as she slowly sank down again. "You used me, played me for a fool, stole my heart *and* my only friend. Well, that has come to an end. No more. You'll not abuse me any longer." Angrily, she wiped away her tears and stiffened her spine. They might be husband and wife, but from this point on it would be the way she had wanted it from the start: in name only. He'd have his precious Wrenhaven, but that was all he'd have. She'd give him nothing else! There would never be an heir. The name of Remington would die with him, and

478

she'd spend the rest of her days congratulating herself. He'd be the one to lose.

The sounds of Rutherford moving away intruded upon her thoughts, and she smiled. The fool had practically stepped on her and he still didn't know she was anywhere close by. It just proved how stupid men really were. Leaning to her left, she peeked out from around the tree at him, grinning sarcastically. Her glee was short-lived, however, once she saw the way he continually stopped to examine the ground, as if he was looking for something small enough to hide beneath the dusting of dried leaves. Footprints, perhaps? Her gaze shifted to the area around her where she had walked, quickly realizing that the thick undergrowth, the moss and the blanket of foliage prevented a person from leaving much of a trail. She frowned back at Rutherford. Besides, he was only a gardener. He didn't know anything about tracking people. So what was he looking for? A cold eerieness tickled its icy fingers down her spine. Could he, perchance, be looking for his watch?

Suddenly fearing for her life, Shauna jerked back behind the tree, her heart pounding so loudly in her temples that she could barely hear Rutherford's departure as he moved closer to the riverbank a few hundred feet further on. She could be wrong about him, she silently told herself. Maybe the watch had nothing to do with the men she had heard that day. Maybe Rutherford had lost the watch while he was fishing one afternoon. It could all be very innocent. She could have let her imagination get away from her. She swallowed the knot in her throat and took a deep breath, trying to calm her nerves and force herself to think logically. Yes, she could have been wrong, but why hadn't Brad said as much after she had told him her story? Because he agreed with the possibility, that's why! But H.T. Rutherford? She would have guessed Barnes was the culprit, not nice Mr. Rutherford.

"I still think it's Barnes," she said softly. "And I'll prove it." She pushed herself up and turned around in time to see the man's stocky figure step behind a group of trees and out of sight. "I'll follow him and see what he's up to."

Shauna knew she'd have to pick her way very carefully. Just because Rutherford had moved a good distance ahead of her didn't mean he couldn't hear her if she stepped on a dried twig or her skirts rustled the leaves lying on the ground. With slow deliberation, she started out, the hem of her dress gathered in her arms as she gingerly placed the toe of her slipper on a rock or log or bed of moss to muffle her progress. Inch by inch, foot by foot, she followed, her gaze shifting from the path she took to the flash of dark blue clothing she spotted periodically through the dense stand of trees. What seemed to be an eternity passed before the woods began to thin out and she could see Rutherford searching the riverbank in the very spot where she had found the watch.

It doesn't mean a thing, she angrily told herself as she selected a large, thick bush to hide behind. He still could have been fishing.

That favorable thought, however, quickly vanished when she heard the faint clip-clop of a horse's hooves from somewhere up ahead. Rutherford had heard them, too, for he paused in his task to look up. From the relaxed manner in which he stood, Shauna guessed he wasn't surprised by the visitor, and in fact he seemed to have been expecting the newcomer. He raised a hand in a halfhearted gesture of greeting.

"You still looking for that damn watch, Talbot?" the man accused as he reined his mount in beside his companion. "Why bother? Before long you'll have enough money to buy a hundred of them."

"I know that," Rutherford snapped, resuming his search. "And if you had any brains, you'd know why I have to find it."

"Then suppose you tell my why," the other man sneered. "Brains or no brains, I don't see the importance."

Talbot's shoulders slumped as he faced his cohort. "Because you idiot, what happens to me if someone else finds it? Someone who wouldn't appreciate what I'm doing . . . like Remington. What if he figured out who owned it and linked me to Deerfield's little scheme? I'd be thrown in prison and sentenced to hang." He studied the ground again. "And I'm sure Lord Billingsly wouldn't do anything to stop it. I'm not as important as his high-class friends. I wouldn't doubt it a bit if the little milksop tried to fix it so I'd be accused of working with Radborne, the same way he fixed it to look like Radborne's a smuggler working for the French." Thinking he had spotted the elusive watch, Talbot dropped to his knees and dug through the pile of leaves, only to come up empty handed . . . again. "Damn. I thought I'd found it," he hissed, tossing away the copper fishing lure.

"You know, Talbot," his friend observed as he swung down from the saddle, "I've been thinking about that myself."

"About what?" Rutherford snarled, his attention

riveted on the next likely place.

"About you and me and what happens to us once this thing's over. Deerfield don't owe us nothing. Once he has everything he wants, he'll probably get rid of us." He drew an imaginary gun and pointed the muzzle at his temple, mimicking the sound of gunfire. "The same way he got rid of old man Radborne's boy."

Neither man noticed the way the slender figure hidden in the scrubbery a short distance from them turned rock hard at the announcement. Nor how her face drained of color and a terrified look widened her eyes. They even failed to hear the small cry of anguish that escaped from her lips before she endured her torment in silence. Shauna felt as if the very life had been knocked out of her. Surely they couldn't be talking about Tyler! He was in Cambridge looking for a carpenter friend of Brad's. Tyler wasn't dead! No one had killed him! Near hysteria, she fell to her knees and clamped her hands over her ears. *He's alive! Tyler's alive and well. This whole thing is a nightmare! A hideous, satanic dream!*

"He won't stand a chance if we keep one step ahead of him," Talbot went on to say.

"What do you mean?"

"I mean, dear friend, I've already guaranteed myself a long life where that man's concerned. I've written down everything that's happened in the past five years, everything I've done because he ordered me to do it, and I've hidden it away. A diary, of sorts. All I have to do is tell him about it."

"Where?" his companion asked excitedly. "Where have you hidden it?"

Talbot straightened and faced the man. "You think I'd tell you? How do I know you wouldn't sell me out? Then we'd both be dead." He squinted his eyes and poked a finger at his accomplice. "And if you're smart, you'll write it all down, too. Everything! Including how he had me steal Remington's partnership agreement with Thorndyke so ol' Billingsly could change it, leaving the property to Thorndyke should Remington meet with a fatal accident." He laughed viciously. "Better said: *when* he meets with an accident."

"I suppose he's gonna have me do it," the other sneered. "As if one man could. That Remington's got quite a reputation, and I don't mind telling you, I don't even like being on his property. Every time I am, I get this strange feeling he's watching me." Shivering, he hugged his arms and scanned around him, as if half expecting Brad to appear suddenly.

What he did see, however, captured the man's full attention, for at that same moment, Shauna decided it was time she went back home. Her mistake was her desire to do so immediately, caused by the pain that blinded her to the dangers of being seen by the men. Too numb to think rationally, she clutched her heavy skirts in both hands, sprang to her feet, and bolted off, running as hard and as fast as she could.

"Talbot!" his companion shouted when he spotted the fleeing woman, certan she had heard every word.

Jerking upright with a start, a puzzled frown on his brow, Rutherford was nearly knocked off his feet when his cohort went charging by him. "What the hell . . . ?"

"It's the Remington woman!" he shouted back. "She heard us! We've got to catch her!"

That feat proved more difficult than he had first imagined. Shauna had a good headstart on them, and the thick underbrush obstructed their chase. Yet their superior strength and speed soon cut the distance in half, and when their victim failed to duck beneath the low-hanging tree branch in her path, they were able to capture her as she was knocked to the ground by a blow to the head.

A big hand quickly clamped itself over Shauna's mouth, preventing her from screaming at the top of her lungs. Her arms and legs were seized, and although she fought with all her might, she was lifted and carried back toward the riverbank.

"What the hell we gonna do now?" her first assailant demanded. "We can't kill a woman!"

"Shut up!" Rutherford growled. "We can't let her go, either."

"So what do we do? Tie her up and leave her here?"

Talbot's hold on her tightened when Shauna found a sudden burst of energy. "Yes, tie her up. But Deerfield can decide what he wants done." He jerked his head at the man's horse. "Have you got anything on him we can use to bind her?"

The other shook his head.

"Then tear the bottom off her petticoats. We'll use that," Rutherford ordered. "And stuff a piece of it in her mouth. We're too close to the house to risk someone hearing her scream."

A few moments later, Shauna suffered the indignity of being tossed painfully to the ground, her ankles tied tightly together, her wrists bound behind her back, and her mouth gagged. Tears blurred her vision of the men, but in her mind she saw them very clearly. These messengers of Satan had killed her brother and planned to murder her husband. If God willed it, she would escape them somehow and see that they paid for their heinous crimes; these two as well as Billingsly, and whoever Deerfield was. *She* would loop the hangman's noose around their necks and pull the lever. Struggling to push herself up on one hip, she silently damned the pair and watched Rutherford's friend gather up the horse's reins and prepare to mount.

"If Deerfield's not home, then go to Lord Billingsly's," Talbot instructed. "But don't come back until you've found one or the other. I'll wait here with the girl."

His cohort glanced nervously in the direction of the manor, suddenly realizing the gamble that would be. "You can't just sit here and wait. What if she's missed and someone comes looking for her?"

A frown contorted Talbot's face as he gave the comment consideration. "Yes. I guess you're right."

"How about hiding her in the cave?"

Talbot's attention turned on the dark opening practically hidden in the thick growth of trees and shrubs. "Yes. We'll hide her in the cave." He waved a hand. "Help me get her up."

Together the two men roughly tossed Shauna's wriggling form over Talbot's shoulders, and while he carried her to the small cavity buried in the hillside, his companion mounted and rode off.

"You shouldn't have followed me, Mrs. Remington," Talbot frowned as he awkwardly lowered himself on one knee and sat her down inside the dark, damp cave. "You should have minded your own business." He stared at her angry face a moment, certain of the thoughts going through her head. "But I guess it really wouldn't have done much good, anyway. Deerfield's out to have everything your father owns. I don't know why exactly, except that I've seen the hatred in his eyes whenever he talks of him." Sinking down on one hip beside her, his knee bent and his arm draped over it, he stared out toward the riverbank at the bright sunlight glistening in the water. "You weren't supposed to marry Remington, you know. It forced Deerfield to change his plans when you did, and I must say he didn't like that at all." His brows slanted downward. "And your brother wasn't supposed to be there at the inn. If I'd noticed him, I would have left without talking to Billingsly." His dark eyes filled with remorse, looked at his captive. "Whether you'll believe me or not, Mrs. Remington, I tried to stop Deerfield from killing him. He would have killed me for interfering if he hadn't still needed me. I agreed to the smuggling, but never to killing anyone." Realizing how repugnant that sounded, he snorted and turned his head away. "And here I sit with you waiting for Deerfield to decide what should be done with you. Damn if I ain't just like him . . . putting money and power ahead of everything else." Closing his eyes, he exhaled a tired sigh, wondering just when and how he had turned into the kind of man worthy of dancing on the gibbet.

"She'll come back, Mr. Remington," Moira promised him. "Once she's had time ta think things through. She's suffered a shock learnin' how we all deceived her, but I'm sure she'll forgive us just as soon as she's figured out why."

"God, I hope you're right, Moira," Brad sighed as he stood staring absently out the window in the study.

"And what if she's not?" Michael posed as he leaned against the door frame, his arms folded over his chest and a disgusted look on his face. "Will ya try another trick ta win her love? The love ya already had."

"Michael!" Moira exploded. "Shut your mouth. This isn't any of your business. And you're just as guilty as the two of us . . . pretendin' ta be someone ya ain't."

"I had me reasons," he argued. "But had I known who

486

this O'Sullivan was and what he'd done ta her, I would never have let her make the mistake."

"Ah, sure ya wouldn't have," Moira sneered. "Ya've never taken responsibility for your actions in all the years I've know ya, Michael McCord. Why would ya start now?"

Jerking away from the door, Michael stepped into the room. "And how long as it been since ya've seen me last? How do ya know I haven't changed?"

Moira straightened her slim figure. "Then prove it ta me. Tell me what brought ya dancin' back into me life after all these years. Tell me ya aren't in trouble . . . again. Tell me ya aren't tryin' ta swindle some poor fool out of his money."

"Enough!" the commanding voice at the window shouted. "There's no sense in fighting among ourselves. It won't change what happened." Turning, Brad looked at the siblings. "Let's put our energy into assuring Shauna that everything we did was done because we care about her. Yes, she's angry right now. Who could blame her? But I must agree with Moira," he added, his dark gaze falling on Michael. "Shauna will come home once she's thought this through, and then we can beg her forgiveness. *I* can beg her forgiveness." His wide shoulders dropped and he moved to sit back down in the chair. "Bloody hell! Why couldn't I have waited just a few more minutes? If only I had known. . . ." The sentence trailed off as Brad leaned forward in the chair and rested his brow against the heels of his hands, his elbows propped on the desk.

A curious, worried frown wrinkled Moira's face. Glancing briefly at her brother, she stepped closer to the desk. "Known what?" she asked softly, sensing something else was bothering Brad. But before he could answer, the sound of horse's hooves outside on the drive interrupted, and Moira hurried to the window to peek out at their visitor. "Nelson Thorndyke," she hissed. "He's the *last* person we need to see right now." She turned and rushed toward the door. "I'll get rid of him," she vowed, reaching for the doorknob to pull it shut on her way out.

"No, wait, Moira," Brad intervened. "Nelson has a right to know. It will be all over London by nightfall anyway. I'd rather he hear it from me."

Moira's cheeks darkened as she held her anger at bay. "I guarantee ya no one in *this* house will be repeatin' the personal problems of—"

Brad quickly raised a hand to cut her off. "I didn't mean that, Moira. There's something else. Ask Barnes to show Nelson in and then come back and sit down. Michael—" His gaze shifted to him. "You, too. You're a part of this family now. Lord knows you've had a front seat to all our secrets, so there's no need to exclude you now."

The knock on the front door prevented Moira from asking him to explain, even though she knew he wouldn't until he was ready, until Nelson Thorndyke was present as Brad requested. Nodding her head slightly, she turned and stepped into the hall. A moment later she returned and hurriedly took her place in one of the wing chairs by the fireplace. Michael elected to stand behind her, thus leaving the last chair for their guest. However, once Nelson Thorndyke's huge frame shadowed the doorway, Michael grew quite uneasy, something his sister noticed but wouldn't question in the company of others.

"Nelson," Brad nodded, "I believe you know Shauna's maid, Moira."

"Yes." Nelson smiled at her, though Moira refused him the courtesy of even looking at him.

"And the man behind her is her brother, Michael McCord. Michael, Nelson Thorndyke, my business partner and an associate of Shauna's father."

Reluctantly, Michael stepped forward to shake the man's hand, his gaze lingering on him long after Nelson had turned away to sit down. He had caught a glimpse of the man yesterday when he'd paid Shauna a visit and had thought then that he seemed familiar. Now he was sure his first instinct had been correct. What he didn't know was how tightly Brad Remington was tied in with him.

"I've asked Moira and her brother to sit in on this, Nelson, because what I have to say concerns us all," Brad began, a heaviness in his voice that no one missed. "Sheriff Lundstrom was here a little while ago."

"Sheriff Lundstrom?" Nelson repeated, frowning.

Moira asked what he had wanted, and Michael's tall frame grew rigid, his gaze subtly glancing at the only exit from the room.

Unable to answer right away, Brad left his chair behind the desk and slowly crossed to the window. He had no idea how Nelson would react to the news, nor did he honestly think it would matter all that much to him, since Tyler and he had never tried to hide their dislike for each other. But Moira was another matter. She had been a part of the Radborne family for years, and she would take the news of Tyler's death quite hard.

"A couple of days ago, Shauna told me that Tyler stopped by on his way to Cambridge while I was away on business. I had asked him to look up a carpenter friend of mine with the offer of a job, a man by the name of Zack Edmondson. Apparently Zack and his family had moved from London to Cambridge, and Tyler wanted to let me know that he was going there to look for him. At this point we have no idea what happened—if Tyler found

489

Zack and talked to him or if Tyler had learned Zack lived further north of town—we simply don't know why Tyler was so far from home." He paused a moment to draw in a long, quivering breath. "Sheriff Lundstrom's not even sure if it was an accident."

"Mr. Remington?" Moira's tiny voice implored, grief choking her words. "What are you sayin'?"

Turning to face her, his dark eyes sad and a deep frown pulling his brows together, Brad took a deep breath. "Tyler's dead, Moira. His body was found floating in the River Ouse north of Cambridge."

"Oh, me God!" Moira moaned, collapsing in a flood of tears.

"I don't believe it," Nelson murmured with a shake of his head. "How? Did he drown? You said the sheriff wasn't sure if it was an accident. What did you mean?"

"He had a lump on his head, which means he could have fallen from his horse," Brad quietly explained as he watched Michael kneel beside his sister and gently pull her into his arms. "But the marks on his throat indicate that Tyler might have been in a struggle."

"Bruises?" Nelson asked.

Brad nodded.

"But that doesn't really prove anything, does it? I mean, he could have been in a fight with someone that same night and later been thrown from his horse."

"It's very possible," Brad agreed, moving to the desk to pour Moira a glass of wine, which he then handed to Michael. "And we won't know anything until the sheriff has time to investigate."

"Tragic," Nelson sighed. "Simply tragic. Do Pierce and Roanna know?"

Brad shook his head. "Lundstrom asked if I'd be the

490

one to break it to them."

"What about Shauna? How's she taking it?"

Brad had no desire to share his personal problems concerning his wife with Nelson Thorndyke, and before he answered, he shifted his gaze to the siblings, surprised to see Michael glaring at the man. "She's . . . well, Shauna's a very strong woman. She'll deal with it in time," he replied ambiguously.

"Yes, I'm sure she will." Nelson sighed and pushed himself up from the chair. "I suppose she told you about my visit yesterday."

"Yes, she did."

Nelson shook his head. "It seems the Radbornes are having more than their share of problems."

Not wishing to upset Moira further, Brad rounded the desk and gently suggested to Michael that perhaps his sister should lie down for a while. Agreeing, Michael helped her to her feet, took the wine glass from her, and handed it to Brad before he led her from the room, his arms wrapped securely around her trembling form. Then, once he and Nelson were alone, Brad asked the man to sit down again, telling him that they had something important to discuss, a matter that concerned their partnership, Wrenhaven, and most of all, Pierce Radborne.

Hidden within the shadows of the tall oak trees surrounding the manor, a man stood secretly watching Nelson Thorndyke leave the house, climb into his carriage, and drive off, before he swung up into the saddle and reined his steed around to follow at a safe distance.

Chapter Seventeen

Alone in his study, Brad sat quietly in the chair behind his desk, his brow furrowed, his chin resting on his clenched fist, and his eyes staring blankly off into space. Moira had assured him that once Shauna came to grips with her anger and frustration over the trick they'd played on her, she would come back to the house . . . but only when she was ready. He wanted to believe that—in fact, he had told Michael that he did—but with each minute that passed, and because of the uneasy gnawing in his stomach that had it tied in knots, he was beginning to worry that Moira was wrong. He had so much to tell Shauna, some of it good, some bad, that he didn't know where to begin. Nelson claimed that there couldn't possibly be any smuggling going on down at the river or he'd have known about it, since he owned the land on both sides of Wrenhaven. Wagons carrying the goods would have had to cut through his land, and sooner or later someone in his employ would have seen them. Yet he had no logical explanation for the men Shauna had overheard, who had run away rather than face her. And now there was the possibility that Tyler had been murdered. *Why?* Had he stumbled across something

492

someone wanted kept secret? Did it concern the Radborne family?

Angry, Brad jerked himself out of the chair and went to the window. He just couldn't shake the feeling that all of this was tied together somehow: the men at the river, the rumors about Pierce, his financial problems, and Tyler's death. Yet he couldn't seem to fit the pieces together. Remembering the watch, he turned back to the desk and opened the top drawer. If only he knew to whom it belonged, it just might provide the link he needed. Lifting it up by the broken chain, he stared intently at it as he slowly lowered himself back down in the chair. Why couldn't the man have engraved his initials in it? *Anything* that would have given Brad a clue?

A movement at the door broke Brad's concentration and he quickly caught the watch in his clenched fist before looking in that direction, frowning curiously when he saw Barnes standing at the threshold.

"I beg your pardon, sir," the butler apologized. "I didn't mean to intrude." His gaze shifted to the hand that held the watch, a gesture Brad noticed immediately.

"Something wrong, Barnes?"

Barnes stiffened instantly. "No, sir. I was just wondering if you and Mrs. Remington would be having lunch on the terrace today." Obviously nervous about something, Barnes glanced over his shoulder, then stepped further into the room. "Might I have a word with you, sir?"

Brad cocked a brow. "About what, Barnes?"

The man hurried closer. "The watch you're holding."

"What about it?"

Barnes licked his lips and took a short breath. "May I see it? I might know who lost it."

493

Brad didn't move. "How do you know it isn't mine?"

The man shifted uneasily. "I . . . I overheard you telling Mr. Thorndyke about it. And if it's the watch I think it is, your wife could be in danger."

Brad bolted to his feet, his dark eyes snapping with rage. "What kind of danger?" he growled, reaching across the desk to seize the butler's ruffled shirtfront in his steel grip. "If you know something, Barnes, you better talk fast."

"P-Please, sir," Barnes begged, his blue eyes bulging. "I-I have to see the watch to be sure."

Giving him a rough shove as he let go, Brad dropped the piece of gold jewelry by the length of its chain and held it up before the man's eyes where he was sure to have a good look at it. "Well?" Brad demanded.

"Y-Yes, sir. I-I knew I was right."

"*Whose is it?*"

"Mr. Rutherford's, sir. The groundskeeper. H-He'd asked me if I'd seen it. He . . . he seemed very nervous about losing it, and when I asked him why it made a difference, he claimed it was his great-grandfather's. But I'd seen it before and I knew that was a lie. It wasn't that old. Then I heard you tell Mr. Thorndyke about Mrs. Remington finding a watch down by the river and that you feared smugglers were involved, and well . . . well, it sorta made sense to me."

A thousand different thoughts raced through Brad's head all at one time, none of which brought him any closer to understanding. "What are you trying to say?"

"He likes to gamble, sir. He always has, and lately I've been hearing how he's been losing . . . big. More than he earns working here. I think he's your smuggler, sir, and if I'm right your wife may have walked right into the middle of it." Before Brad could ask him to explain, Barnes rushed on. "I saw him heading toward the woods just after Mrs. Remington ran off a while ago. And neither of them have come back!" The last was nearly shouted at the top of his lungs, since Brad had already raced from the room. He had to find Shauna before Rutherford did.

Shauna had known the instant Rutherford and his friend spotted her that her very life depended on how clearheaded she remained. She had heard too much for them just simply to let her go, even if she promised not to say a word. They were responsible for Tyler's death, those two and the one they called Deerfield, and they'd have to be absolute fools to think she'd keep that secret, that and the knowledge she had that they planned to kill Brad, as well. Tears burned her eyes at the thought of her husband, and she struggled not to let them overpower her. She *must* stay calm. She had to recognize her chance to escape. Sucking in a deep breath, she gulped down her fear and settled her attention on the man crouched at the mouth of the small cave. As long as he continued to pay her no heed, she could openly work at the cloth binding her wrists.

Shauna guessed that nearly an hour had passed since her flight from the house. Surely someone had missed her by now. Someone had to be worried about her. Please God, her mind called out, send someone to look for me. Panic knotting her stomach, for she knew Rutherford's cohorts would be returning very soon, she struggled with her restraints, wincing at the pain she inflicted upon herself when the cloth dug into her flesh. If only they hadn't bound her ankles, she could push herself up on her feet and charge the man, whose back was to her. She could knock him down, maybe even kick him in the head, and then run with all her might. But they hadn't given her even that small advantage, and she forced herself to concentrate on the cloth ropes around her wrists.

Suddenly, Rutherford's stocky frame stiffened. He'd heard something. Shauna knew that by the way he cocked an ear to listen, and she quit her task to do the same, praying that whoever it was, he wasn't the man H.T. Rutherford expected. The sound of horse's hooves penetrated the chilling silence surrounding her, and Shauna's hopes plummeted. Talbot's friend had left on horseback, and the manor wasn't so far away that anyone from the house sent to find her would bother with a mount. Eyes wide with fear, her gaze shifted from the man hunched down at the opening of the cave to the bright sunlight outside, waiting for the shadow of horse and rider to cross it. A second later it came, and tears burned her eyes. Her worst fears had become reality, confirmed by Rutherford's eagerness to leave his hiding place.

"I'm sorry, sir. We didn't want this to happen, but it couldn't be helped," she heard Talbot explain as he stepped out of her line of vision. "I didn't know she had followed me." He laughed nervously, and Shauna recognized the sound of fear in his voice. "What's that for, sir?" The crunching of dried leaves beneath his feet as he staggered back a step or two seemed to ricochet off the walls of the tiny cave. "Please, sir. I-I didn't mean for it to—Oh God, *no!*"

The explosion of gunfire resounded throughout the woods, scattering birds from their lofty perches, penetrating the stillness and nearly tumbling Brad to his knees when he heard it. Stumbling to a halt, his face the expression of pain, anguish, and fury, he stood frozen in horror, fearing he had come too late. Then another roaring crack pierced the gloom, jerking Brad's tall frame upright, eyes alert, his shoulders rigid, and his mouth drawn in a tight line, nostrils flared. Sanity returned, willing his feet to move, and he bolted off in the direction of the gunfire, jumping debris in his path, dodging low-hanging tree branches, shoving others aside as he raced onward. His heart thundered in his ears, the air he sucked into his tortured lungs burned, but still he charged full gait. Where the trees thinned out and a steep embankment ahead threatened to slow him down, Brad merely fell to one hip, legs extended in front of him, one hand used for balance, and slid the leaf-covered distance to the bottom. Coming up on his feet, he never broke stride until he reached the riverbank and spotted the dark shape of a man lying motionless on the ground.

Caution warned him to advance slowly, and while his eyes scanned the shrubs and trees off to one side for any movement, he pulled the pistol he had wisely thought to carry, and guardedly approached. Hooking the toe of his shoe under the man's shoulder, Brad gently rolled him over, wincing at the sight of Rutherford's blood-splattered face and the huge hole in his head. Obviously, someone else had gotten here before him. But who? And where was Shauna? Crouching, he aimed his pistol at the trees and moved on. There had been two shots. Could it mean . . . ? He mentally shook off that idea, refusing even to consider the possibility his wife was dead. Then he heard someone moan up ahead, and he jerked his attention in that direction, sensing more than knowing it wasn't Shauna. Warily, he moved closer, his eyes and ears alert for any sign that it might be a trap. The groaning increased, and at the same moment Brad spotted a second man, practically hidden behind a huge rock, trying to push himself up to his feet.

"Michael?" he exclaimed, rushing forward to break the Irishman's fall when his legs wouldn't hold him. "What the hell are you doing here?" He set aside his pistol and quickly helped lower him back to the ground, frowning angrily once he saw how badly he was wounded.

"I-I followed him," Michael gasped, his dark eyes closed and his face contorted in pain.

"Who?" Brad asked as he ripped apart Michael's shirtfront to examine the vicious hole in his chest. A couple of inches lower and there would have been no need. "Who did this?"

Michael struggled to draw a breath and speak. "Thorndyke."

Brad stiffened. "Thorndyke? *Nelson* Thorndyke?"

"Aye," he moaned, pushing aside Brad's hands and trying to rise.

"Damn it, man, lie still. You're in no shape to be moving around," Brad harshly ordered. Tearing off a strip of Michael's bloodstained shirt, he quickly pressed it against the wound and instructed Michael to hold it there while he tore another piece and proceeded to bind it around the man's chest. "It will help for now, but that bullet's got to come out. You're to promise me you won't move while I go back to the house—"

"No!" Michael shouted, grabbing Brad's arm when he started to rise. "Ya don't understand. He's got Shauna."

Every muscle in Brad's body turned to granite. "What?" he seethed.

"He killed that one over there and took her. I-I tried to

stop him, but he—"

Brad's head shot upward and he glared out across the landscape toward the boundary dividing the two estates. "He . . . he killed Tyler, too. I . . . I was there. . . ." Grimacing in agony, Michael closed his eyes. "I-I'll explain . . . later. Go . . . get her! Take me horse."

Rage filled Brad, twisting his insides into a knot, tightening the muscle in his jaw, flaring his nostrils. Through clenched teeth, he ordered Michael to stay put, then bolted to his feet, his dark eyes searching the woods for Michael's horse. Spying the animal tethered to a tree not far away, Brad picked up his gun and raced toward it, yanking the reins loose and swinging himself up into the saddle. The steed let out a loud whinny, reared up on its hind legs, then galloped off under the urgent command of its rider.

Vicious laughter filled Shauna's ears as she glared hatefully back at the man who had carried her into the deserted warehouse and unceremoniously dumped her to the floor. No one had to tell her that this man, the one her father trusted, the one Pierce Radborne had thought worthy of marrying his daughter, was the man Talbot had called Deerfield. His reasons for wanting to ruin her father and to destroy the Radborne family were unclear to her, but whatever they were, they had to be the workings of a very sick mind.

"This really changes nothing," Marcus sneered. "I'll still have what I want. It'll just come about in another way." He laughed again at the fury he saw darkening her pale green eyes, then turned to close the door and drop the bar into place. "I've worked too hard and too long to just give up because Pierce's little girl got in the way."

Pausing long enough to peer out the window and make sure no one had seen them, he faced her again. "In fact, this is even better than the way I had it planned."

Grinning evilly at her, he approached, seized her arm in a painful grip, and hauled her to her feet. He had seen fit to untie her ankles, but the cloth ropes around her wrists and the gag remained. Giving her a shove, he directed her toward the back of the empty building and the room where Talbot's partner stayed. Once inside, he brutally pushed her toward the small cot and forced her to sit down.

"Just imagine how frantic your father will be when he learns the smugglers have taken off with his daughter," he jeered, his dark eyes glowing a demonic red. "He won't know where to look or who to look for. And all the while you'll be right here . . . with me."

His large hand tried to stroke her golden hair, but Shauna jerked away from his touch.

"You shouldn't have married Remington, Shauna. Now he has to die, too." He shook his head and strolled toward the table in the middle of the room, there to sit down in a chair and stretch his long legs out in front of him. "It's a shame, really. I must admit I liked the man. But I need Wrenhaven, and because of you, he's preventing me from having it." His eyes raked her slender form, undressing her, desiring her, but his desire to torment her with words was far greater than his wish to degrade her at the moment. He pulled a cheroot from his pocket and lit it, casually watching the puff of white smoke curl above his head. "I suppose you'd like to know why," he finally stated, his gaze falling on her again. "Or have you figured it out already?" He laughed at the demeaning look she gave him. "No? Then I'll tell you. I think you deserve to know."

Rising, he aimlessly trekked back and forth across the room. "Remember the discussion we had about your father's stepfather, Liggett Dupree, and how the man swindled the honest men of London out of everything they owned? My father was one of those men. His name was Sir Edward Deerfield. I was just a little boy at the time, but I remember it quite clearly. I also remember waking up in the middle of the night to my mother's screams and the horrible sight of my father hanging from a rope. He'd killed himself because he couldn't face the shame of what had happened to him. I vowed right then to get even with Dupree, but the bastard died before I could. So . . . I decided on the next best thing. I'd destroy his stepson." He stopped and smiled malevolently at her. "Your father." Raising the cigar to his lips, he took a puff on it and began his pacing again.

"I wanted to do to your father what Dupree did to mine. I wanted him to feel the pain I felt. So I started with his wife. I seduced her, thinking I could blackmail her into giving me the money I needed to pull this whole thing off."

Shauna could feel the bile rise in her throat at the callous way he referred to her mother, but she managed to control her desire to be sick. He'd only laugh at her.

"And you know what she did? She told me to go to hell, that she'd already admitted her unfaithfulness to her husband. I guess it was because of a little blond-haired girl who had walked in on us that night." He laughed uproariously at the small whimper he heard escape his captive. "Yes, Shauna," he sneered. "That was me you saw." Coming to the bed, he propped his foot on the edge and leaned in. "And your father, being the kind man he is, forgave us both!"

Anger replaced his odd sense of humor and he flung

501

himself away from her to walk back to the table and sit down. He was quiet for a long while, his brow furrowed, the muscle in his cheek flexing as he gnashed his teeth. "He never knew the identity of his wife's lover. Roanna never told him, and I left for the Colonies to steal the money I needed. But now—once this is over—I'm going to tell him. I'm going to let him know *I* killed his son, raped his daughter, fixed it so he was thrown in prison for treason, stole his land, *and* seduced his wife right in his very own bed!"

Terror crimped every muscle in Shauna's body, and she frantically struggled with the restraints around her wrists. This was no average man she was dealing with. He was insane, and once he was through with her, he'd kill her. She knew that. And she knew she had to get away. She had to warn her father. She had to save Brad. The thought of her husband brought stinging tears to her eyes. In the midst of this lunacy she had come to realize the truth about him, that everything she had heard Moira tell her brother about Brad was true. He *did* love her. And *she* loved *him*, with all her heart. Choking back her grief, she glared over at Deerfield, silently vowing that somehow, some way, she would escape this madman. *She would not let Brad die!*

The sound of racing hoofbeats against the hard earth bolted Marcus out of his chair. Yanking the pistol from his waistband, he stormed to the window and jerked the dingy curtain aside, howling a violent curse once he recognized the man closing the distance to the warehouse. In a rage, he spun around and descended upon his captive, viciously seizing her arm and dragging her to her feet.

"Let him come," Marcus snarled as he shifted his hold on her and cruelly trapped the long strands of her golden hair in his fist, using her body to shield his own. "He'll have to kill you to get at me."

A thunderous crash resounded throughout the warehouse and spun Marcus and his prisoner around. Shauna knew Brad hadn't let the barred door stop him. Marcus knew it, too. She could feel his body tense with the realization that he had finally met a man who wasn't afraid of him, a man who had come for his wife, a man who would tear him apart piece by piece with nothing more than his bare hands.

The silence that followed grated on Marcus's nerves. He had expected his adversary to storm the room where he stood waiting for him. Instead, a deathly quiet surrounded him, and he suddenly realized that using the man's wife to hide behind offered little, if any, protection. Nothing and no one would stop Brad Remington.

"Step out where I can see you, Remington!" Marcus bellowed, his eyes glued to the doorway of the small room, beyond which lay the black interior of the warehouse and the single shaft of light coming in through the broken front doors. "I'll kill her if you don't."

There was a rustling noise from somewhere close by, and Marcus shifted the muzzle of his gun from Shauna's throat to her temple.

"I mean it! I've got nothing to lose. She'll die!"

"And so will you," came the chilling reply.

The words seemed to come at him from all directions, and Marcus suddenly feared Brad Remington wasn't alone. He tightened his grip on Shauna's hair and shouted, "Step out where I can see you!"

A second passed before Brad's tall figure moved into the stream of glaring white sunshine, his body rigid, his dark eyes shadowed by a fierce frown, and a gun held firmly in his hand at his side, the muzzle pointed earthward. "Let her go, you bastard," he growled. "This is between you and me."

"Not until you drop the gun," Marcus shouted back.

Brad hesitated a moment, obviously doubting the wisdom of disarming himself, before he slowly raised his hand and tossed the weapon aside.

"You fool," Marcus hissed as he quickly brought the pistol around and took aim.

Realizing the ploy, Shauna ignored the pain Marcus inflicted on her and lunged her body sideways just as he fired. The lead ball missed its mark, and while Marcus brutally hurled Shauna to the floor, Brad charged him like a raging bull. A broad shoulder as hard as steel rammed into Marcus's midsection, knocking him off his feet and catapulting him backward across the room. They slammed into the wall behind them, lost their balance, and tumbled to the floor, a mass of bulging muscles, flinging fists, and growls not unlike two grizzly bears. Rolling, Brad dragged Marcus to his feet and smashed his knuckles against the man's jaw, reeling him back on his heels. Stunned but far from finished, Deerfield shook off the blow and landed one of his own to Brad's stomach, dropping him to his knees. Grabbing a fistful of his hair, Marcus raised Brad's head and struck the heel of his hand to Brad's temple, throwing him to the floor. Seizing the opportunity to finish the attack, Marcus kicked out with all the force of his body behind it and caught Brad in the rib cage with his foot. Blinding pain shot through every inch of him, and in a daze, Brad saw his foe racing for the door. A half-crazed, bellowing snarl exploded from his lips as he pushed himself up and chased after the man.

In the semidarkness of the warehouse, Marcus took too long searching for the loaded gun his opponent had tossed aside. Before he could brace himself for another round, strong arms caught him from behind in a steely vise that not only lifted him off the floor but crushed the very breath from him. Excruciating pain and the sound of cracking ribs filled his brain, teetering him on the brink of unconsciousness just as he was hurled halfway across the room to slam against the floor, landing on his shoulder. Numbness instantly shot down his arm, leaving it limp and useless, and while he struggled to draw air into his lungs, his eyes darted from one dark shadow to the next, insanity glowing like red-hot coals in their ebony depths.

Tears burned Shauna's eyes as she desperately worked the straps binding her hands. An eerie quiet had befallen over the place, and fearing Brad's death was the cause, she ignored the rasping of her flesh where it was rubbed raw in her attempts to break her bonds. Suddenly she felt the knot slip, and she pulled harder, twisting and turning her hands in an effort to stretch the loose-weave linen enough to free one hand. Her arms and shoulders aching, the delicate bones in her wrists bruised and her fingers numb, she gave one final tug, winning her long-awaited freedom.

Marcus sensed more than saw Brad move in on him. Weak, he struggled to rise and stumbled back a step, trying to clear his head and gather his strength. This would be a battle to the end, and there would be only one victor. Lowering his head, his eyes snapping fire once they focused on the man who meant to kill him, Marcus attacked, thinking to bury his shoulder in Brad's chest. But Brad expected as much and deftly stepped to one side, slamming his fists in the middle of Marcus's back as he raced on by and sending him crashing to the floor again. This time, however, he was not left alone to stagger to his feet. A huge hand seized his shirt collar, hauled him upward, and dealt him a paralyzing blow, that reeled him backward against the wall.

A howl of pain, blinding-white, numbing pain filled the lofty heights of the warehouse, jerking Brad to his senses, and he shivered as he stared at the writhing body of Marcus Deerfield hanging from the baling hook, its sharp, steel-pointed tip having pierced his flesh and severed his spine.

Suddenly, warm arms encircled him, and the haze that clouded his mind lifted.

"Shauna," he breathed, drawing her close and brushing his lips against her temple. "Oh, Shauna. I so feared I had lost you."

"And I, you," she wept, hugging him tightly, her head laid against his chest as she listened to the strong, steady beating of his heart.

"Say you forgive me," he begged. "Say you understand, for I swear I *shall* die if you don't."

Leaning back, she lifted her eyes to look at him, tears streaming down her face. "I do forgive you. And I understand. Truly I do."

A warm smile parted his lips and he cupped her delicate face in his hands, lowering his mouth to kiss her tenderly, passionately . . . and with love.

"Moira, will ya stop fussin' over me!" Michael howled when his sister tried a second time to tuck the blanket over his legs as the two sat enjoying the bright sunshine on the terrace. A week had passed since the incident at the river, and this was the first day he had been allowed out of bed. But only if he promised not to move around overmuch and to keep warm. As always, he rebelled against being told what to do . . . especially by his sister.

"I'm not fussin' over ya," she retaliated. "I'm just seein' that ya do what the doctor tells ya ta do."

His dark eyes narrowed. "Ya're fussin'," he repeated.

Laughter from the doorway behind them interrupted their bickering, and they both seemed to blush when they turned to find Brad and Shauna stepping out onto the terrace, his arms draped over her shoulders, hers around his waist, and bright smiles lighting up their eyes.

"Can't you two ever get along?" Brad teased, pulling out a chair beside Michael at the table and guiding his wife into it.

"Aye," Moira proclaimed. "We get along fine when hundreds of miles separate us."

"And as soon as I'm able, I'll be seein' that we never fight again," Michael rallied, squinting up his eyes at her.

"You can't mean that, Michael," Shauna moaned. "Brad and I want you to stay. Now that this whole mess is cleared up, there's a lot of work to do building Brad's factory, and he told me he could really use your help."

"I'd really like ta take ya up on that, lass," Michael confessed softly, reaching to pat the tiny hand resting on his arm, "but I've never been one ta stay in one place for very long."

Shauna turned to her husband. "You talk to him. Make him stay."

Frowning, as if giving some thought to an idea he had, Brad scratched his chin and said, "Well, once he's able to travel, I could shoot him again."

"Brad!" Shauna shrieked, while the siblings smiled at each other. "That's not funny. Michael was nearly killed."

"I know," he grinned. "And I'm sure he realizes I didn't mean it. If it hadn't been for him, I might never have found you. Deerfield had a long headstart on me, and to be quite honest, I don't think I ever would have suspected that Nelson Thorndyke wasn't who he pretended to be."

The group grew quiet for a moment, each reliving the horrors Marcus Deerfield had caused the Radborne family, as well as the fresh memory of Tyler's funeral only a few days past. For Michael, it was something he'd always look back on with regret.

He had been there that night in the inn drinking a mug of ale while he waited out the storm, and he had noticed the young blond-haired man the moment he stepped inside. He hadn't known Tyler Radborne, but after meeting his family, and especially his sister, Michael was sure he would have liked him.

It appeared that Tyler had come to the inn for the same reason Michael had, as the young man merely ordered something to drink and then sat down by the warm fire. Michael didn't pay much attention to him after that—he had been too busy with his own problems to honestly care if someone else was in as much trouble as he. There had been a young lass in Dublin Michael had grown quite fond of, the daughter of a very wealthy landowner, someone above Michael's station. He had been warned by her father to stay away from her, but since he had never been one to do anything anyone told him, he had ignored the threat. Then one morning the father had been found shot to death in his bedroom, and Michael had been blamed. Knowing that money and power would hang an innocent man, Michael ran.

He was on his way to visit Moira for a few days before sailing to America, thinking that perhaps an ocean would separate him from his problems. But trouble seemed to follow him wherever he went. It had been there in the inn . . . waiting.

He hadn't bothered to look up when Talbot entered, but he had heard him ask for Lord Billingsly's room and he remembered thinking how odd it was for an aristocrat to seek lodgings in such a place. He also heard Tyler question the barkeep, pay for a room, and start up the stairs. Michael had already decided to spend the night, too, since the storm hadn't let up, and he was about to approach the innkeeper himself when Deerfield opened the front door and went upstairs without looking at anyone. Michael didn't recognize him, but he was thinking there was too much activity going on to assure his safety. Any one of those men could have been someone sent to find him.

At the time Michael hadn't been aware that he had been given a room next door to Billingsly's. But later he heard the muffled, angry voices through the thin wall. He tried to ignore the violent words and had even considered asking for a different room when a loud thump jarred him out of the bed. He hadn't been sure, but it had sounded like a body being thrown to the floor. He was wishing now that he had interfered, that he had had the courage to ignore his own situation and go investigate. As it was, he did nothing until after he heard the men leave the room and head down the hall toward the back stairway. Curiosity drove him to look out the window, and he caught a glimpse of them carrying an unconscious body draped over their shoulders as they disappeared behind the stable out back. Realizing it was too late for him to do anything, and knowing that he would have been outnumbered, he had gone back to bed, getting little if any sleep the rest of the night.

The following morning he had gone to Wrenhaven, forcing himself not to think about what he had witnessed.

He certainly didn't want to risk his own life for someone he didn't even know. Then Nelson Thorndyke paid Shauna a visit, and he realized he was in the middle of it whether he liked it or not. He hadn't said anything to anyone, including his sister, thinking that perhaps he'd find some other way of letting the authorities know that this man had been involved in the murder of another. He had no idea what he planned to do that morning when he followed Thorndyke from the house. But it hadn't taken him long to figure out that something had to be done and that the responsibility had fallen into his hands. Keeping a safe distance between them, Michael reined his horse off the road when Thorndyke met up with a man along the way. They talked for a few minutes, and Michael saw the man gesture toward the river, as if giving Thorndyke directions. Then, while the man's back was turned, Thorndyke reached over, seized his companion's pistol, and shot him. It was in that moment that Michael fully realized the extent to which this man would go.

He trailed Thorndyke to the river's edge and stood by helplessly as he watched him shoot a second man in cold blood. But it was when he dragged Shauna from the cave and roughly lifted her onto his horse's back that Michael knew he had to step in. Thorndyke had other ideas, and the instant he saw Michael, he pulled a second gun without bothering to listen to Michael's proposal, that if he'd allow Shauna to go free, Michael wouldn't kill him. He cringed even now at the pain he had felt the moment that lead ball tore apart his flesh.

"Michael?"

Blinking away his memories, he looked up to find Shauna watching him.

"You're not blaming yourself again for something you had no control over, are you?"

510

A half-smile crimped his mouth. "Ya keep tellin' me that, lass, but I can't help thinkin' I should have done somethin' sooner. Had I—"

"Hush," Shauna gently demanded, reaching to cover his hand with hers. "No one blames you. Marcus Deerfield was an evil man, a cold, calculating monster. We're just thankful that he didn't kill you, as well." She smiled up at her husband who stood close by and added, "But if you really feel you owe us, then agree to stay here at Wrenhaven."

"I can't, lass," he frowned. "I've got ta be movin' on."

"Not anymore," a voice from behind them announced, and they turned to find Pierce and Roanna Radborne standing in the doorway.

Confused, Michael glanced over at Brad. He had confessed his reason for being in the inn that night to this man on the condition that he never reveal it to anyone. Now it seemed he had broken that promise. "What is he talkin' about, Brad?" he asked.

Gathering Shauna in his arms, Brad smiled back at Michael and said, "Because of you, Pierce Radborne won't have to go to prison. The rumors about him have ceased, due to your naming Billingsly as a part in this whole sordid affair, and Pierce asked me what he could do to repay you. So I told him."

Stepping forward, Pierce withdrew a paper from his jacket and handed it to Michael. "That's a letter from the sheriff in Dublin, clearing you of the murder of one Kevin O'Rourke. It seems he had an argument with an associate of his, and the man hired someone to kill him. You're free, Michael, free to go anywhere you want." He smiled and winked at his son-in-law. "Or stay here, if you wish."

A long silence passed while Michael stared at the

document he held, his head bowed and tears glistening in his eyes. He blinked them away before anyone noticed. "I'll stay on one condition," he proposed. "And that's if ya'll name your first son after me."

"Michael!" Moira exploded, appalled that he would make such a demand.

But Shauna didn't agree. "It's a wonderful idea, Michael, and one Brad and I had already decided on. Michael Patrick Remington." She squeezed her husband and added, "Has a nice ring to it, don't you agree?"

"Almost as nice as Roanna Remington," Brad replied, turning with Shauna still held tightly in his arms to look at the woman who stood mouth agape.

"I hope you'll agree, Mama," Shauna said, her eyes filled with love. "And I hope you'll forgive me for ever doubting your feelings for Papa. I had a lot of growing up to do, and in an odd way, I have Marcus Deerfield to thank for that. He made me see you as you really are."

Tears filled Roanna's eyes and spilled down her face. "Of course, I forgive you," she wept. "If there's really any need." Holding out her arms to her daughter, she quickly encircled Shauna's slender form.

"You know, Brad," Pierce whispered as he gave his son-in-law a nudge, "the worst is yet to come. You're going to have your hands full keeping that little filly in line. You realize that, don't you?"

A bright, loving smile parted Brad's lips and his dark eyes warmed at the sight of his wife. "Oh, I realize that, sir. But I look forward to the challenge." His gaze raked over Shauna's luscious curves as she turned to walk back to him. "I look forward to it," he murmured.

PLAYING WITH FIRE

I know exactly what's going through your mind right now, Brad," Shauna declared haughtily. "You'd like to kiss me. You'd like to wrap your strong arms around me and pull me against your bare chest. You'd like to entwine your fingers in my hair, feel its texture, smell my perfume. You'd like to brush your warm lips along my throat and nibble on my earlobe. You'd like to drive me wild with passion."

She stood only inches from him now, positive that she had guessed correctly, that she was stirring his blood, his desire, and that out of pride, he couldn't—*wouldn't* yield to his own needs.

With a seductive smile curling her lips, she lifted her soft green eyes to gaze into his. "You'd like to strip my clothes from me and carry me to that bed. But what you'd *really* like is for me to do all those things to you!"

Reckless, Shauna raised one hand and lightly traced the steely ripples of flesh over his ribs where his shirt fell open. "It would be a true victory for you if that were the case, wouldn't it, Brad? Tell me the truth."

"Should I start here?" she teased, lightly kissing his chin. "Or here?" Her lips moved to his throat. "Why don't you tell me to stop, Brad? Tell me I'm wrong."

Suddenly and shockingly, his arms encircled her, crushing her to his massive, naked chest and taking her breath away.

"You're not," he replied huskily, his mouth swooping down to capture hers. . . .